D1629850

A Very Murdering Battle

By Edward Marston

A Very Murdering Battle

EDWARD MARSTON

First published in Great Britain in 2011 by
Allison & Busby Limited
13 Charlotte Mews
London W1T 4EJ
www.allisonandbusby.com

A CIP catalogue record for this book is available from
the British Library.

10 9 8 7 6 5 4 3 2 1

ISBN 978-0-7490-0976-2

Typeset in 12/16 pt Adobe Garamond Pro by
Allison & Busby Ltd.

Paper used in this publication is from sustainably managed sources.
All of the wood used is procured from legal sources and is fully traceable.
The producing mill uses schemes such as ISO 14001
to monitor environmental impact.

Printed and bound by
CPI Group (UK) Ltd, Croydon, CR0 4YY

To Judith
with love and thanks
for the way that she fought every battle
in the War of the Spanish Succession beside me.

CHAPTER ONE

January, 1709

France was in the grip of the coldest winter for a century. Rivers froze, animals died in vast numbers and the seed corn for the next harvest perished in the ground. An almost perpetual frost blanketed the country. Icy fingers closed around the throat of Paris and tried to throttle it, choking off its commerce, squeezing the breath out of its administration and killing off at random the old, the infirm, the sick, the poor and anyone unable to find adequate protection against the relentless chill. It was the worst possible time to visit the French capital but Daniel Rawson had no choice in the matter. While his regiment was shivering in its winter quarters, he'd been dispatched into enemy territory on important business. It was not an enticing prospect. What made the visit bearable was the fact that he was able to stay with an old friend in a house that offered him a warm welcome and a roaring fire.

Ronan Flynn tossed another log onto the blaze, then appraised him.

'What, in the bowels of Christ, has got into you, man?' he asked. 'Only a lunatic would come to Paris in this weather. It will freeze your balls off.'

'It's the same wherever I've been,' said Daniel, 'and I hear that England fares just as badly. The Thames is solid ice and they hold a frost fair on it.'

'Then at least they get some pleasure out of the winter. There's none of that for us, Dan. The last harvest failed and we're facing a famine. Think what that means for me. I'm a baker now, remember.'

Daniel nodded. 'How could I ever forget?'

Flynn was a tall, rangy, raw-boned Irishman in his forties with long, grey hair that curled at the edges and which hung so low over his forehead that he was always brushing it back. He and Daniel had once fought together in the Allied army but his most recent military service had been in one of the Irish regiments in the pay of the French. The change of sides had not affected their friendship because the bond between them was too strong. After a rescue on the battlefield, the Irishman owed Daniel his life and would always be indebted to him. For his part, Daniel admired the ebullient Flynn both as man and soldier. Also, in view of what happened during his last stay at the house, he had reason to be eternally grateful to his old comrade.

'Bakers need flour,' said Flynn, worriedly, 'and there's little to be had. The Treasury tried to buy corn from the Beys of North Africa but they were stopped from shipping it to France by squadrons of British and Dutch warships.'

'You can't expect me to apologise for that, Ronan. War is war.'

'And bread riots are bread riots.'

'I'm sure you'll survive somehow.' Seeing the anxiety in his friend's eyes, Daniel quickly changed the subject. 'It's wonderful to see you and your family looking so well. Charlotte is as beautiful as ever and I can't believe the change in Louise. She was a babe in arms when I last saw her. How old is she now – three?'

Flynn brightened immediately. 'She's almost four, Dan, but she gives herself such airs and graces that you'd take her for a young lady, so you would. Louise can be a little devil sometimes and I love her for it. The girl has got such spirit.'

'She inherited that from her father.'

'Yes, she has Charlotte's looks and my mettle. Thank goodness it's not the other way round,' Flynn went on with a laugh, 'because I'm an ugly bugger and my dear wife – God bless her – is placid as they come. That's why I married her. After all this time, mind you, I still don't know why she married *me*.' He laughed again then narrowed one eye as he looked at Daniel. 'But talking of beautiful women, what happened to that darling creature you brought here the last time you stayed under our roof? She had the face of an angel. What was her name – Emilia?'

'Amalia,' said Daniel, fondly. 'Amalia Janssen.'

'I can tell from your voice that she set your blood racing. What man could resist her? You shouldn't have let her slip through your fingers, Dan.'

'I didn't.'

Flynn's interest quickened. 'You're still in touch with her?'

'I always will be, Ronan.'

Daniel gave him a brief account of the way that his friendship with Amalia Janssen had matured into something far more significant and satisfying. He'd first met her when he'd been sent in disguise to Paris to track down her father, Emanuel, a celebrated tapestry maker employed at Versailles by Louis XIV. Unknown to his patron, Janssen had also been working as a spy on behalf of the Allied army and, when exposed, he was promptly imprisoned in the Bastille. It fell to Daniel to rescue him from captivity, then spirit Janssen, his daughter, his assistant and his servant all the way back to Amsterdam. Such a feat would have been impossible without the help and advice of Flynn, who sheltered the fugitives until they were ready to sneak out of the city by means of cunning stratagems devised by Daniel.

Flynn was a good listener, sipping wine and tossing in the odd question to keep the narrative flowing. He was delighted to hear that his friend had finally found someone with whom he was ready to share his life.

'You've changed, Dan,' he teased. 'When we bore arms together, you had an eye for the ladies and took your pleasures where you found them. The handsome Captain Rawson broke lots of female hearts in his time.' He smothered Daniel's interjection with a raised palm. 'Yes, I know, I was just as bad – far worse, if truth be told. I had more than my fair share of conquests and I shudder at the thought of what I once was.' He looked upwards. 'May the Lord forgive me my sins!' he said with feeling. 'I was a different man then. It was before I met Charlotte and realised what it was like to love someone with every fibre of my body. When Louise came along, my life felt complete for the first time.'

'I'm very happy for you, Ronan – and full of envy.'

'Does that mean you'll follow my example and give up soldiering?'

'Oh, no,' said Daniel, seriously, 'I'd never do that.'

'You could if you had real sympathy for your wife. See it from her side. Marriage to an army officer is a species of hell. You never know from one day to the next if your husband is still alive. The constant anxiety will wear any woman down.'

'This war will be over one day.'

Flynn raised an eyebrow. 'How many years have you been saying that?'

'Peace talks are taking place at this very moment.'

'I'll wager anything you like that they'll come to nothing. You know that as well as I do. Be honest, Dan – can you *really* sniff peace in the air?'

Before Daniel could reply, Charlotte came down the stairs and emitted a sigh of relief. Wearing a plain dress that showed off her shapely figure, she had a shawl around her shoulders. She didn't seem to have aged at all since the last time Daniel saw her and looked more like Flynn's daughter than his wife.

'I finally got her off to sleep,' she said.

'That was Dan's fault,' argued Flynn, lapsing into the French he habitually used in conversation at home. 'That doll he brought for Louise got her so excited that I thought she'd be up all night.'

'It was a lovely gift. Thank you, Daniel.'

'No thanks are needed,' said Daniel. 'It's such a pleasure to see her again.'

'Don't leave it so long next time.'

Charlotte sat beside them and warmed her hands at the
fire. Fluent in French, Daniel chatted happily with her,
struck yet again by the fact that such an attractive young
woman had somehow met and married a wild Irishman
with a chequered past who was all of eighteen years older.
It was an unlikely union but man and wife were supremely
contented with each other. When Daniel asked how dire
the situation was in Paris, she became more animated,
gesticulating with both hands and bemoaning the
economies they'd been compelled to make.

'It's been a real ordeal,' she said.

'We're better off than many, my love,' Flynn reassured
her.

'That's no comfort to me, Ronan.'

'It ought to be.'

'I wonder how much longer we can go on like this.'

'There's bound to be a change in the weather soon,' said
Daniel, more in hope than with any certainty. 'Everything
will be back to normal then.'

'I've prayed for that to happen a hundred times or more,'
she said, sadly, 'but God doesn't listen to me. Madame
Vaquier thinks that this terrible winter is his way of
punishing us.'

'For what?' asked Flynn with mild outrage. 'Why punish
me when I lead such a blameless life? I'm the next best thing
to a saint.'

Charlotte giggled. 'I wouldn't say that, Ronan. Saints
don't use some of the rude words that you do. But,' she
went on, turning to Daniel, 'we mustn't bore our guest by
complaining about our woes. What brings you to Paris this
time, Daniel?'

It was a question that Flynn had the sense not to ask, knowing that his friend would, in all probability, be there to gather intelligence and not wishing for any further detail. He preferred to offer unconditional hospitality.

'Well?' pressed Charlotte with an enquiring smile.

Daniel weighed his words. He was about to speak when he saw movement out of the corner of his eye. He flicked his gaze to the staircase where Louise, the bright-eyed child with her mother's arresting loveliness, was sitting on a step in her nightdress. She was hugging the gift that Daniel had brought for her and was clearly entranced with her new doll. The girl unwittingly provided him with his cue.

'I came all this way to give Louise a present from Holland,' he said, beaming at her. 'Can you think of a better reason?'

Encrusted with frost, the palace of Versailles looked rather forlorn, its magnificence dimmed, its celebrated gardens turned to a white wilderness, its countless fountains no more than slabs of ice and its statuary deformed and diminished by the bitter weather. A veritable army of servants was deployed to keep the fires blazing in the rooms and the bedchambers but the long, wide corridors were avenues of gnawing cold. Huddled into a corner, the courier pulled his cloak around him and wished that he could slip off to the kitchens where there was sure to be a reviving warmth and even the possibility of a hot drink. Orders were orders, however, and he was forced to obey them. He was a dark-haired man of medium height and middle years. A regular visitor to Versailles, he was usually glad to leave it. Not on this occasion. When he glanced through the window and saw snow beginning to fall, he quailed inwardly. It would be a testing ride to Paris and one that he would rather not make, but his inclination carried no weight. The work was too well paid to ignore and too important to postpone. He was committed.

Everything was done by numbers. He was not allowed to move until the various clocks began to strike eleven times. Only when their echo had died away could he leave his post and take the second passageway to the left. Just beyond the third door on the right was a small oak chest. Inside it was the package for him. The courier never knew who put it there or who would take it from him in Paris. He was merely an intercessory. Even the signals used were in the form of numbers, allowing him to deliver the package to the right person in the right place at the right time. Conversation was unnecessary. What was in his secret cargo, he had no real notion. It was not his place to speculate. Discretion was absolute. That had been impressed upon him from the start.

It seemed to be getting even colder. Cupping his hands together, he blew into them to give his palms fleeting warmth then tucked them under his armpits. Time hung heavy. The wait became increasingly tedious. His fear of being discovered and challenged grew more intense. Then, at long last, he heard the clocks begin their choral tribute on the hour. One, two, three, four – he stamped his feet in time to the melodic chimes. Five, six, seven, eight – here was action at last. Nine, ten, eleven – he heard the crucial number fade into silence then he was off. Marching along the corridor, he turned left at the appropriate place then counted three doors on the right. Stopping beside the oak chest, he looked up and down to make sure that nobody was watching. It was the work of a second to lift the lid of the chest, snatch the package, hide it in a pocket and replace the lid.

When he stepped out of the building, he discovered that the snow had enlisted the help of an accomplice – a knifing wind that made the flakes swirl and that stabbed at his face. Pulling his hat down over his forehead, he hurried to the stables. His horse was even less willing to go out in a snowstorm and bucked mutinously. Once in the saddle, he mastered it with a fierce tug on the reins and a sharp dig with both heels. It emerged resentfully from the stables and trotted off into the wind. So intent was he on his mission that the courier didn't notice the two men concealed in the shadows. As he went past, they stepped out to watch. The younger of them was impatient.

'Let's go, Armand,' he urged.

'There's no hurry,' said Armand, lazily. 'We know where he's heading and his horse will leave plenty of hoof prints in this snow. We only need to get closer when we near Paris.'

'Do we kill him or take him alive?'

'We kill him, Yves. He's only a messenger and can tell us nothing. The man we're after is the one awaiting the delivery. He's the real catch.'

By the time that Daniel reached the little shop, the snow had stopped falling. It was, however, still more than cold enough to justify his thick cloak, wide-brimmed hat and gloves. He rode with a blanket over his horse so that it had some insulation against the elements. Paris was fairly empty at that time of the evening and nobody saw him turn into the side street where the premises were located. Since the shop was closed, he banged on the door and the

owner was instantly roused. The door opened to reveal
the diminutive figure of Claude Futrelle, the apothecary,
white-haired and with a wispy, white beard. As he studied
his visitor through bloodshot eyes, his voice was flat and
his face motionless.

'The shop is closed, monsieur,' he pointed out.

'I didn't come for medicine,' said Daniel.

'Then I can't help you.'

'I was told that you could, Monsieur Futrelle.'

'You were misinformed.'

'I think not.'

'Be off with you.'

'Your suspicion is understandable.'

'Farewell, monsieur.' When the apothecary tried to close
the door, Daniel grabbed it with a firm hand and held it
ajar. 'Leave go,' said Futrelle, angrily.

'Not until we've discussed the symptoms.'

'You said that you didn't want medicine.'

'I'm not talking about *my* condition,' said Daniel, 'but
that of France itself. It's eaten away with a disease that no
apothecary can cure. Don't you agree?'

Futrelle looked at him anew with a mixture of curiosity
tempered by caution. He asked a few apparently irrelevant
questions and Daniel gave him the correct answers. They
were talking in code. Once the old man was satisfied with
his visitor's credentials, he told Daniel to tether his horse
in the stable at the side of the property. The two men then
adjourned to a room at the back of the shop and sat either
side of a table. A crackling fire helped Daniel to thaw out.
Since there was still a vestigial suspicion in the apothecary's
eyes, Daniel produced a letter from inside his coat and

handed it over. Reading it by the light of the candle, Futrelle gave a nod. Daniel was accepted.

'You are welcome, monsieur,' he said.

'Let us remove all trace of this,' said Daniel, taking the letter from him and holding it over the candle until it was ignited. 'We don't want anyone else knowing who sent me.' He tossed it into the fire and it was soon consumed. 'There – it's as if it never existed.'

'One can't be too careful.'

'Pierre Lefeaux taught me that.'

Futrelle was startled. 'Pierre died years ago.'

'I know,' said Daniel. 'I found him hanging from the rafters beside his wife. He obviously hadn't been careful enough.'

'Someone betrayed him. He was a brave man.'

'I'm glad to see that you are equally brave.'

'Not me, monsieur,' said Futrelle with a self-deprecating laugh. 'Brave men don't tremble as much as I do, nor fear for their lives every time a stranger comes into the shop. Because I'm terrified of meeting Pierre's fate, I trust nobody.'

Daniel warmed to the old man. He was one of the go-betweens employed by the Allied army, people with a strong enough grudge against France to help its enemies by acting as repository for intelligence gathered by agents in the city. Futrelle had no idea what was in the various missives that he stored before passing them on at regular intervals. He just hoped that he was helping a cause in which he passionately believed and accepted – albeit nervously – the consequent risks.

'I have nothing for you at the moment,' he explained,

'but, as it happens, I expect a delivery this very day. Your arrival is timely.'

'It's no accident,' said Daniel. 'I was warned to be here on the thirteenth of the month because that's the date when word is sent from Versailles. I just hope that it gets through. This weather would deter most couriers.'

'He'll be here, monsieur, I assure you.'

'Will he come to the shop?'

'That's far too dangerous. The exchange is some distance away.'

'Do you always take the delivery?'

'No,' replied Futrelle, 'I have a number of agents and we take it in turns to be there on the thirteenth of the month. January is always my turn.'

'I'll go in your place.'

The apothecary smiled gratefully. 'Then you are doubly welcome, monsieur. I'd hate to go out on a night like this. I have potions to cure almost anything but being chilled to the marrow is a condition I cannot relieve. And I am of an age when I feel the cold more keenly.' He lowered his voice. 'He'll need to be paid first.'

'I have plenty of money with me.'

'You obviously came prepared.'

'Prepared and eager,' said Daniel. 'Teach me the code.'

Once on his way, the courier had found his journey less onerous than he had feared. The snowstorm eased and the wind became less capricious. It was still not a pleasant ride but at least he no longer had doubts about reaching his destination. Paris was some ten miles distant from Versailles, so he had ample time to get there. He stopped at a wayside inn to take refreshment and to rest his horse. With hot food and a glass of brandy inside him, he felt able to face the next stage of the journey. It never occurred to him that he was being trailed by two men. No sooner had the courier ridden off than the pair stepped out of the inn and made for the stables. Mounting their horses, they gave pursuit, staying close enough to keep him within sight and far enough behind him to avoid arousing suspicion.

When he reached Paris, the courier had hours to spare and decided to make the most of them. After picking his way through the deserted streets, he turned into a courtyard, dismounted, tethered his horse to a post then rang the doorbell of a house. Recognised by the servant who opened the door, he was admitted at once. The two men arrived in time to witness his disappearance.

'Do we follow him in?' asked Yves, impulsively.

'There's no need,' said Armand.

'But he'll be making his delivery.'

'He won't be handing over any correspondence here. He's making a visit of a very different kind. This place is a brothel.'

'How do you know?'

Armand grinned. 'How do you *think* I know?'

Yves was indignant. 'Do we have to stay freezing out here while he's between the thighs of some greasy harlot?'

'Show some compassion,' said his friend, tolerantly. 'Let him enjoy it. Before the night's out, he'll be dead.'

Even the meeting place had a number. *Les Trois Anges* was an inn in one of the rougher parts of the city but there was nothing angelic about it. Cluttered, low-ceilinged and dirty, the bar was gloomy and malodorous. The fire did little to dispel the abiding chill. Needing to make the exchange at precisely eight o'clock, Daniel arrived ten minutes early and bought himself a drink. The weather had robbed the inn of most of its habitués, so he had a choice of tables. He took one near the door, then casually put six coins on the table before arranging them in a triangle. It was all the identification needed. He sipped his wine and waited, checking, as usual, for any other exits from the building. In the event of an emergency, it was always wise to have an alternative means of leaving a place. The precaution had saved his life on more than one occasion. He looked up as the door swung open but it was not the courier he was expecting. The big, slovenly man who stumbled in was too early and hardly a person to be trusted with so important a task. His torn clothing, massive hands and fearsome gaze suggested someone used to manual labour. He would never have been allowed near Versailles.

Hunched over his table, Daniel used his arms to shield the telltale money. It was when a distant clock began to boom that he sat up and exposed the triangle of coins. The courier was punctual. He came in with a quiet smile on his face, walking past Daniel and appearing not to notice the signal on the table. He ordered a glass of brandy and stood at the bar as he sipped it, trading banter with the landlord. When he'd finished his drink, he bade farewell and headed for the door. Daniel was ready for him. Passing the table, the courier slipped the package into his hand and received a small purse in exchange. He let himself out. Daniel, meanwhile, had secreted the package in a pocket inside his cloak. It was all over in seconds. Nobody in the bar noticed anything untoward but the eyes at the window were more observant. They saw what they had come to see and acted accordingly.

Daniel lingered for a few minutes before downing his wine in one last gulp. Then he swept up the coins, thanked the landlord for his hospitality and went out. Intending to reclaim his horse, he was surprised to be confronted by two men who blocked his way. One of them held a pistol on him while the other extended a hand.

'I'll thank you for that package, monsieur,' said Armand.

Daniel was unperturbed. 'You are mistaken, my friend. I have no package.'

'It was given to you by the courier.'

'What courier? There's clearly a misunderstanding here. I received nothing from anybody. I was merely enjoying a drink. If you doubt me, ask the landlord.'

'We followed him from Versailles,' explained Armand, 'and the trail ended here – with you. As for the courier, the trail ended altogether for him.'

The two men moved apart so that Daniel could see the figure sprawled on the ground behind them. Enough light was spilling through the windows of the inn for Daniel to see that the courier's throat had been cut from ear to ear and that he was lying in a pool of blood. His visit to *Les Trois Anges* had cost him his life.

Yves raised the pistol and aimed it at Daniel's head.

'We'll ask you one last time, monsieur,' he said, menacingly. 'Hand over that package while you're still alive to do so.'

CHAPTER TWO

Daniel needed no convincing. If they could kill the courier with such casual brutality, they'd have no compunction about sending Daniel after him. He therefore came to an instant decision. Since he couldn't bluff his way out of the situation, a show of compliance was required. With a shrug of defeat, he reached inside his cloak.

'You have the advantage of me, messieurs,' he said, resignedly.

'Hand it over,' insisted Yves.

'I will, I promise.'

But it was not the package that he brought out. What emerged from his cloak was a dagger that flashed upwards and pierced the wrist of the hand holding the pistol. As Yves let out a cry of pain, the weapon jerked skywards and discharged its bullet harmlessly into the air. Daniel pushed him hard in the chest and he tottered back, tripping over the corpse and falling to the ground. Yves was more concerned with stemming the flow of blood from the wound than anything else but Armand wanted revenge. His hand went to his sword. Before the man could draw, however, Daniel kicked him in the groin, making him double up in agony, and shoved him on top of his friend. While the two of them struggled to get to their feet, they rid themselves of a stream of expletives. Daniel didn't hear them because he'd already run off to his horse and mounted it at speed. Not knowing where he was going, he galloped off into the night.

Armand and Yves were soon in pursuit. Cursing their folly and mastering their pain, they delivered a valedictory kick at the dead courier before staggering across to their horses. Though Daniel had a good start, there was an immediate problem. As he clattered over the cobbles, his horse's hooves echoed along the empty streets and gave a clear indication of his route. All that the two enraged men had to do was to follow the sound. There was a secondary consideration. Daniel was riding blind while they, he reasoned, probably knew the city well. They'd be aware of any short cuts and might be able to intercept him. Since he couldn't outrun them, he was faced with a choice. He could either hide somewhere or turn and fight. The obvious refuge was Claude Futrelle's shop but Daniel was unsure of finding it in time and, in any case, wanted to lead his pursuers away from the apothecary. It would be unfair to put Futrelle in jeopardy. Apart from anything else, the old man would certainly break under torture and endanger the lives of other agents. The complex network of spies simply had to be protected.

Daniel reined in his horse and listened. The sound of

furious hooves could be heard in the distance. They were after him and wouldn't give up until they caught him. The decision was made for Daniel. He had somehow to dispose of them before they killed him and recovered the documents he was carrying. Kicking his mount into action again, he rode on until he came to what appeared to be a commercial district. Warehouses loomed up on both sides of the road, then he passed a timber yard. When he came to a turning on the left, he took it, only to discover after fifty yards or so that he was in a cul-de-sac. Instead of being dismayed, Daniel was pleased. Here was a possible chance of turning the tables on his enemies. He rode back to the corner, dismounted and lurked in the shadows. Armed with a dagger and a pistol – and with long experience of escaping from such predicaments – he felt that the advantage had now tilted in his favour. He'd not only chosen the ground for combat, he had the element of surprise.

As the two riders approached, Daniel could hear them slowing their horses so that they could search for their quarry. He waited until they got closer then put his plan into action. Slapping his horse on the rump, he sent it galloping down the cul-de-sac. Armand and Yves responded at once, drawing their swords and spurring their mounts on. Pistol in hand, Daniel was ready for them. When they came hurtling around the corner, he let them get within yards of him before stepping out and firing his weapon at the nearest rider. The bullet hit Yves in the middle of the forehead, blowing his brains out and knocking him from the saddle. As it bounced on the ground, Daniel leapt forward to snatch up the dead man's discarded sword. Armand was shocked at the loss of his friend and infuriated that they'd ridden into a trap. Yanking on the reins, he pulled his horse in a semicircle then jumped to the ground. He could only see Daniel in silhouette but it was enough to set the blood pulsing through his veins. Sword in hand, he stalked his prey.

'Who are you?' he demanded.

'Why not come and find out?' invited Daniel, coolly.

'Yves was my friend. You'll pay for his death.'

'Take care that you don't pay for the courier's death. I'm not an unsuspecting man leaving an inn and there are no longer two of you against one. We fight on equal terms, monsieur, and that means you will certainly lose.'

Armand brimmed with confidence. 'There's no hope of that happening.'

'We shall see.'

They were now close enough to size each other up, circling warily as they did so. Daniel knew that his adversary would strike first because the man was fuming with rage and bent on retribution. Armand didn't keep him waiting. Leaping forward, he tried a first murderous lunge but Daniel parried it easily. Their blades clashed again and sparks flew into the air. Daniel was testing him out, letting him attack so that he could gauge the man's strength and skill. Evidently, Armand was a competent swordsman but he had nothing of Daniel's dexterity, still less his nimble footwork. Each time he launched himself at his opponent, he was expertly repelled because he was up against a British army officer who had regular sword practice. Aware that he couldn't prevail, Armand became more desperate, slashing away wildly with his blade and issuing dire threats as he did so. Daniel remained calm and chose his moment to bring the duel to a sudden end. Unfortunately, the frosted cobblestones came to Armand's aid.

As Daniel poised himself for a final thrust, his foot slipped and he was thrown off balance. Armand seized his opportunity at once, putting all his remaining power into a vicious attack that drove Daniel back until his shoulders met a wall.

Laughing in triumph, Armand went down on one knee to deliver what he felt would be the decisive thrust but Daniel was no longer there. Moving agilely sideways, he let his opponent's sword meet solid stone and jar his arm. Armand's moment had gone. A slash across the back of his hand forced him to drop his weapon, then Daniel thrust his blade into the man's heart. With a gurgle of horror, Armand slumped to the ground and twitched violently for several seconds before expiring. The commotion had aroused nightwatchmen in warehouses nearby and loud voices were raised as they came to investigate. First on the scene was a man with a lantern held up to illumine Daniel's face. Others soon converged on him. There was no time to search for his horse at the other end of the street. Tossing the bloodstained sword aside, Daniel pushed his way past the newcomers and melted quickly into the darkness, sustained by the thought that he'd saved the vital package and done something to avenge the murder of the hapless courier.

Army life had accustomed Ronan Flynn to having his sleep rudely disturbed. He was used to being roused in the early hours of the morning to make a hasty departure from camp. Rising well before dawn, therefore, was no effort for him and he'd settled into a comfortable routine. He awoke in the dark, got out of bed and groped for the clothes he'd left on the chair. Once dressed, he gave his wife a token kiss on the forehead, then tiptoed out and crept down the stairs. When he'd lit a candle, he made himself a light breakfast and reflected on the changes in his life. The visit of Daniel Rawson had left him with mixed emotions. Flynn was glad that his soldiering days were over and that he was now happily married to a gorgeous young woman in his adopted country. He had a new occupation and a new set of responsibilities. At the same time, however, he felt that something was missing. The sense of adventure embodied in Daniel had a heady appeal and he was reminded of the thrill of courting danger at every turn. While he had no wish to return to the army, he'd begun to feel regrets that had been dormant for years. Work as a baker was safe, undemanding and profitable. Yet it was also mundane and repetitive. It lacked the excitement and the camaraderie he'd found when in uniform.

Shaking his head, he tried to dismiss such thoughts. He knew who to blame. 'Damn you, Dan Rawson!' he said to himself. 'Why the devil did you have to come to Paris and stir up memories I've tried so hard to forget?' He addressed his mind to what lay ahead. When he got to the bakery, the ovens would already be lit by his assistant and Flynn would be able to start making loaf after loaf. It was a staple food that people needed every day. Providing it gave him satisfaction and, after all this time, he still savoured the tempting aroma of fresh bread. The bakery was owned by his father-in-law, Emile Rousset, but he'd been happy to let Flynn gradually take charge. It was a far cry from the menial jobs he'd done as a boy in his native Ireland. Having mastered his new trade, he applied himself to it and soon built his reputation. He was liked and respected by his customers for his excellent bread and for his cheery disposition. It was something of which Flynn could be justly proud.

Breakfast over, he put on his ratteen coat and reached for his hat. With an old cloak around his shoulders, he was ready to step out of the house into another wintry day. He carried the lighted candle, cupping a hand around the flame to prevent it from being blown out. In the stable, he set the candle up on a shelf and went to work in its flickering circle of light. After harnessing the horse, he had difficulty persuading it to go between the shafts of the cart and had to swear volubly in French at the animal. It was only then that he realised he was not alone in the stable. Something seemed to be moving under the pile of sacks on the back of the cart. Holding the candle in one hand, he used the other to grab a sickle that was hanging on a wall.

'Come out of there,' he ordered, standing over the cart.

As the sacks were peeled off one by one, Flynn watched with his weapon held high and ready to strike. Angry that someone had dared to trespass on his property, he resolved to punish the interloper. When the final sack was moved aside, however, a familiar face came into view. Daniel gave him an apologetic smile.

'Good morning, Ronan,' he said. 'I hope you don't mind me bedding down here for the night. I had a spot of bother.'

The Duke of Marlborough divided opinion. While everyone agreed that he was a supreme strategist on the field of battle, there were those who criticised him for what they perceived as his characteristic meanness. Compared to other generals in the Allied army, he maintained rather modest quarters and was quicker to accept an invitation to dine elsewhere than to offer hospitality himself. His friends argued that he was always in such demand as a dinner companion that he had to share himself around, but his many detractors discerned guile and parsimony. The protracted siege of Lille had extended the campaign season well beyond its usual limit and it was not until the subsequent fall of Ghent in the first week of January 1709 that hostilities were finally suspended. His coalition army was at last able to retire into winter quarters and try to keep up its spirits in the atrocious weather conditions. Unable to sail back to England, Marlborough contrived to get himself invited to stay in The Hague at the commodious home of an obliging Dutch general. When they saw him and his entourage take over half the entire house at no expense, critics said it was one more example of his stinginess, while others countered that he could hardly refuse such a generous offer and – rather than offend his host – had therefore accepted out of sheer politeness. At all events, it meant that the captain-general of the Allied army spent January in the Dutch capital, enjoying a warmth and comfort denied to the vast majority of his men.

Marlborough was not, however, idle. His day started early and he crammed a great deal into it – writing dozens of letters, planning the next campaign season, meeting with senior members of the Dutch army, wooing his other allies and maintaining a busy social life. Adam Cardonnel, his loyal and conscientious secretary, was usually at his side to assist, advise, console or congratulate. In the course of the long and arduous war, they'd been through so much together that they'd been drawn close. Their interdependence was complete. They were seated at a table littered with reports, maps and accumulated correspondence. Finishing a letter, Marlborough read it through before signing his name with a flourish. He pushed the missive aside with a long sigh.

'It was a waste of time writing that,' he said. 'It can't be sent in this weather.'

Cardonnel looked up from the document he was reading. 'Is it another appeal to Her Majesty?'

'Yes, Adam, and it's doomed to failure.'

'Not necessarily.'

'It is. The chances of my dear wife being clasped to the royal bosom again are extremely faint. She pestered Her Majesty to the point where she became intolerable. I'd never dare to say this to her, of course,' he admitted, 'but Sarah is largely to blame. She seems to forget that the Queen is recently widowed and still mourning her husband. Limited as the poor fellow undoubtedly was, she doted on Prince George. It's a time for tact and sensitivity, qualities with which my wife, alas, is not overly endowed. Had she not continued to browbeat the Queen, the rift in the lute wouldn't have widened beyond repair.'

'Her Majesty may yet relent.'

Marlborough shook his head. 'Too many of our enemies have the royal ear. My own position at home is fragile and my wife's antics hardly improve it. You see my dilemma, Adam?' he asked, face clouding with concern. 'If I'm deprived of the support of Her Majesty, how can I retain my position as the leader of the Grand Alliance?'

'It's surely not in any danger,' said Cardonnel, earnestly. 'One only has to look at your achievements in last year's campaign. Oudenarde was a triumph that rocked the

French to their foundations and it will take them an age to recover from the battle. You then took the prized citadel of Lille before bringing Ghent to its knees. It was one victory after another.'

'Then why do I feel so insecure?'

'Only you can answer that, Your Grace.'

Marlborough sighed again. He remained a handsome, distinguished and imposing man but, as he neared the age of sixty, there were clear signs of ageing. His face was more lined, his eyes had lost their sparkle and his back no longer had its ramrod straightness. Seen in repose, he seemed utterly to lack the energy and determination for which he was famed.

'If only Sidney Godolphin were not so unwell,' he resumed, ruefully, 'I'd have more hope. He could continue to solicit support for us. As it is, his position as Lord Treasurer is in question. Lose him and we lose our best ally.'

'I still say that you should have no qualms,' encouraged Cardonnel. 'Your very name strikes terror into the hearts of the French. It would be madness to relieve you of your duties.'

Marlborough fell silent. Overworked and under strain, troubled by migraines, frustrated at being confined to the Continent and sensing the impending loss of his authority, he was in a dark mood. As he turned over the possibilities in his mind, one soon assumed prominence. It allowed him to sound more positive.

'Perhaps I should petition Her Majesty,' he said, thinking it through.

'You've just done that very thing, Your Grace.'

'I talk not of my wife, Adam. This would be on my

own account. What if I were to request that I be appointed captain-general for life?'

'It's no more than you deserve.'

'Indeed, it is not. Hampered by the problems of leading a coalition army, I've nevertheless delivered three resounding victories on the battlefield and driven the French out of city after city. Such success should be recognised.'

Cardonnel grinned. 'You don't have to persuade me of that.'

'Can I persuade Her Majesty, I wonder?'

'There's certainly no harm in trying, Your Grace.'

Marlborough lapsed into silence again, dogged by anxieties about the wisdom of making such a suggestion to Queen Anne. When he won his remarkable victory at Blenheim, he'd been feted at home and granted a sumptuous new palace as his reward. Things were very different now. Over four years had passed and the Queen had become increasingly impatient with a war that was draining the nation's coffers and liberally spilling the blood of its soldiers. Given the situation, she might not be susceptible to an approach from Marlborough. It might be better to bide his time.

He turned to another cause of vexation. Covert peace negotiations were taking place and, to his chagrin, Marlborough was not directly involved in them. The thought that major decisions might be made over which he had no control was unnerving.

'What have we heard from the States General?' he asked.

'Very little,' replied Cardonnel. 'These are early days.'

Marlborough clicked his tongue. 'Dutch politicians move even slower than those parliamentary snails back in London.'

'It will take months before negotiations either founder or come to fruition.'

'If only we knew what that old fox, King Louis, is really thinking.'

'Well,' said the other, 'if he has any sense, he'll be guided by an incontrovertible fact – namely, that the Duke of Marlborough is invincible.'

'I don't feel invincible at the moment, Adam,' confessed Marlborough, wearily. 'I feel tired and uneasy. I feel as if everything is slipping away from me and I'm powerless to stop it from doing so.' He slapped the table with a peevish hand. 'I want to know exactly what's going on.'

'Then you'll have to wait until word comes from Paris,' said Cardonnel.

'*If* it comes,' corrected Marlborough.

'Have no fears on that score, Your Grace. We sent the ideal man.'

'Remind me who it is.'

'It's someone well versed in the art of working behind enemy lines.' Cardonnel smiled reassuringly. 'Captain Rawson won't let us down.'

It was not the first time that Daniel had been to the bakery and he knew how to make himself useful, responding quickly to orders from Flynn and putting the previous night's escapade temporarily out of his mind. He had learnt how to get the loaves out of the oven without burning his hands and, like his friend, he relished the odour of freshly baked bread. As a reward for his services, he was allowed to taste it. All that he'd told Flynn was that he'd got involved in an argument with two men and had lost his horse in the process. There'd been a long trudge across Paris in the dark and he'd arrived back at the house too late to rouse them from their slumber. Accordingly, he made a bed of straw on the cart and covered himself with a pile of sacks. It was only at the end of the working day that Flynn was able to press for details. They sat side by side on the cart as it rattled homewards.

'What *really* happened last night?' asked Flynn.

'I told you, Ronan – two men picked a fight with me.'

'Now why should they do that?'

'For some reason,' said Daniel, 'they didn't like the look of me.'

Flynn turned to him. 'I'm not sure that I like the look of you at the moment. You need a shave and your face is covered in flour. Louise will be scared stiff when she sees you.'

'Your daughter takes after you, Ronan. Nothing frightens her.'

'Coming back to these two men, who exactly were they?'

Daniel shrugged. 'I have no idea.'

It wasn't true. Since the men had followed the courier all the way from Versailles, Daniel knew that they had to be government agents of some sort. As a result, the report of their deaths would be taken very seriously. A hunt would be launched for their killer, based on the description of Daniel given by the nightwatchman who'd held the lantern to his face. Anyone trying to leave the city would come under intense scrutiny. Daniel didn't want to take the risk of trying to bluff his way past sentries. Yet it was vital that the package was taken to The Hague as swiftly as possible and handed over to Marlborough. It contained information from the very heart of the French government.

'Do you know what I think, Dan Rawson?' asked Flynn.

'What?'

'I think you're a dirty, rotten, two-faced, lying bastard.'

Daniel grinned. 'I take that as a compliment.'

'Why on earth I bother with you, I really don't know.'

'Yet you gave me such a cordial welcome.'

'That was a mistake. You're always bad news. Charlotte keeps asking me what you're doing here – and don't try to palm me off with that nonsense about bringing a doll for Louise. I'm not stupid enough to believe that.'

'How much do you *want* to know?'

Flynn pondered. 'Nothing,' he said at length. 'It's safer that way.'

'I'd never put you or your family in any danger,' said Daniel.

'You'd answer to me if you did.' The Irishman flicked the reins to get more speed out of the horse. 'What happens next?'

'I need your help to get out of Paris.'

'What's to stop you going out the same way you came in? I assume that you have a forged passport of some kind.'

'It might not do the trick a second time,' admitted Daniel.

Flynn shot him a glance. 'In other words, they're looking for you.'

'Let's just say that I need an alternative means of departure.'

'And why should I help to provide it?'

'You're under no obligation to do so, Ronan.'

'You're damn right I'm not,' said Flynn, moodily. 'There might have been a time when we were birds of a feather but that's no longer the case. I mean, taking all things into consideration, we've nothing at all in common.'

'I wouldn't say that.'

'Look at the facts, man. You're a soldier and I'm a civilian. You're a Protestant and I'm a Catholic. You're English and I'm Irish.'

'I'm half Dutch,' Daniel reminded him.

'Dutch or English – what does it matter? Both nations are fighting to defeat France and I've chosen to live out the rest of my life here. By rights, we should be mortal enemies. In fact, I don't know why I'm wasting my breath talking to you.'

'It's because we're two of a kind,' argued Daniel.

'Not anymore.'

'At heart, we're both adventurers, men who like to take chances.'

'You can't take chances when you have a wife and child, Dan.'

'Perhaps not,' said Daniel, 'but you can *yearn* to do it. You can still have that urge deep inside you even if you've learnt to control it. I simply don't believe that the Ronan Flynn I once knew has disappeared entirely.'

'Well, I have. I've been reborn as a decent, law-abiding, God-fearing human being who doesn't want any trouble.'

'Does that mean you refuse to help me?'

'Give me one good reason why I should,' challenged Flynn.

Their eyes locked and Daniel could see that his friend was serious. It was an awkward moment. Without assistance from his friend, Daniel would find it difficult to slip out of the city unseen. He was relying on Flynn to provide unquestioning help.

'Go on,' pressed the Irishman, 'give me one.'

'Very well,' said Daniel with a disarming smile. 'I offer you one very good reason. It's the only way you'll get rid of me.'

Flynn burst out laughing. 'You crafty devil – you've got an answer for everything, you silver-tongued son of a bitch. As a patriotic French citizen, I ought to turn you over to the police right now and have done with you.'

'But you're not going to do that, are you?'

'No,' said Flynn, putting a companionable arm around his shoulders, 'I'm just dying to see the back of you. For that reason, I'm going to get you out of Paris even if I have to throw you over the city wall with my bare hands.'

Daniel chuckled. 'I had something a little easier in mind.'

CHAPTER THREE

Amsterdam had not escaped the protracted cold spell. Its streets were frostbitten, its canals frozen and ice floated in its harbour. Holland was a maritime nation that relied on the free movement of its merchant fleet. At the moment, however, its ports were more or less paralysed. Fortunately, a prudent Dutch government had built up large reserves of corn, so the general suffering was not as great as in some countries. Yet it was still a testing time for the inhabitants of Amsterdam. The combination of glacial weather and a shortage of certain foodstuffs lowered the morale of the beleaguered city. Most people chose to stay indoors beside a fire and moan about their lot. What set the Janssen household apart from the majority was the fact that it reverberated to the sound of laughter and applause.

'It's magnificent, Father,' said Amalia, clapping her hands.

'More to the point,' observed Emanuel Janssen, 'it's finally finished. I've spent so much time on the Battle of Ramillies, I feel as if I fought in it.'

'It's a masterpiece.'

'Thank you, Amalia.'

'What do you think, Beatrix?'

'It's wonderful,' said the plump servant, staring open-mouthed at the tapestry. 'I hate the thought of battles but this one is different.'

The other servants agreed with nods and muttered approbation. What they were looking at in the extensive workshop at the rear of the house was the completed tapestry commissioned by the Duke of Marlborough and due to hang in Blenheim Palace. Now that its separate elements had been sewn expertly together, it covered one entire wall and spilt over onto the two adjacent ones. It was held in place by Janssen, Kees Dopff and the other assistants who'd toiled at their looms to produce the vivid pictorial record of an Allied victory against the French. Amalia was especially thrilled with the result because Daniel Rawson, who'd taken an active part on the battlefield at Ramillies, had been deputed to advise her father about details of the encounter. It was thus a joint effort by the two people she loved most.

There was, however, a potential drawback.

'Does this mean that we have to go to England in person to deliver it?' asked Amalia, warily. 'I sincerely hope that we don't.'

'Transport arrangements haven't yet been made,' said her father, 'and there's no chance of the tapestry leaving Amsterdam until the weather improves. Whatever happens,

Amalia, I promise you that you'll be spared the journey.'

'That's a relief.'

'I can't say that I'm looking forward to it. On the other hand, I can't resist the pleasure of seeing my work hanging at Blenheim Palace. It's a signal honour. However – under the circumstances – it's perhaps better if I go on my own.'

Amalia was grateful. As the men began to fold up the tapestry with great care, she turned away and thought about her ill-fated visit to England the previous year. What could have been an exhilarating event in her life had been marred by the Duchess of Marlborough's curt manner towards them and by the attentions of their host who had stalked Amalia relentlessly. Determined to seduce her, he'd tried to persuade her that Daniel had been killed in action and, to make sure her beloved was no longer an obstacle, dispatched an assassin to kill him. Though Daniel survived and was able to come to her rescue, Amalia's view of England had been fatally jaundiced. The country held too many painful memories to lure her back.

It was the same for Beatrix Udderzook who'd accompanied her to England.

'I wouldn't go there again for all the money in the world,' she said, stoutly. 'The only thing I enjoyed seeing was St Paul's Cathedral.'

'Yes, that was truly amazing,' conceded Amalia.

'I didn't like their food and I didn't like the way they treated us.'

'Then let's put it out of our mind, shall we?'

'We have everything we need right here in Amsterdam.'

'You're quite right, Beatrix.'

The servant's eyes twinkled. 'I usually am.'

Beatrix waddled off to continue her work, leaving Amalia standing beside her father, a round-shouldered man with a silver mane and beard. There was an air of fatigue about him as he looked down at the tapestry, now neatly folded up.

'It may be the last of its kind,' he said, sorrowfully.

'What do you mean, Father?'

'I'm not sure that I could attempt anything on that scale again, Amalia. My eyes are not what they were and a day at the loom leaves me more and more tired. In future, I'll have to take on commissions for smaller tapestries.'

'You should let Kees and the others do most of the work.'

'If I did that,' he complained, 'then, strictly speaking, it wouldn't be a genuine Emanuel Janssen tapestry.' He injected a note of pride into his voice. 'People have come to appreciate my distinctive touch. Anything that leaves this workshop must have that. I'll continue for as long as I can but at a slower pace.'

'I think that's very wise.'

'It's a necessity, Amalia.'

'I know.' She was struck by a thought. 'What a pity it would be if you were offered the chance of making another tapestry for Blenheim Palace and had to turn the offer down.'

'Oh, I doubt that His Grace would approach me again.'

'He will when he sees the miracles you've worked with the Battle of Ramillies. He might ask you to do the same for Oudenarde.' Amalia's face glowed. 'That would be such a treat for me.'

'Why is that?'

'Why else?' she replied. 'You'd need to speak to someone

who fought in the battle and that means Daniel would be appointed as your advisor again. I'd get to see much more of him.'

Janssen smiled. 'I don't weave tapestries solely for your benefit, Amalia.'

'Well, you ought to,' she teased.

'Besides, I suspect that Captain Rawson has far more important things to do than describing to me what happened at a battle last year. He'll be too busy thinking about fighting against the French *this* year.' He turned to her. 'Do you happen to know where he is at the moment?'

Amalia shook her head. 'No, Father,' she said, sadly, 'I'm afraid that I don't. The army has gone into winter quarters but the war continues in other ways. Daniel could be anywhere.'

Ronan Flynn's working day started much earlier than that of most Parisians but it finished sooner as a result. There was still a glimmer of light in the sky when he left the bakery with Daniel and drove back home. Having stayed another night with his friend, Daniel had worked hard baking bread in gratitude for the help that the Irishman was about to give him. There were limits to what he could ask Flynn to do and, at all costs, he had to keep his intentions hidden from Charlotte. She was a patriotic Frenchwoman and would not knowingly assist an enemy soldier. As far as she was concerned, he was simply an old comrade of her husband's and, as such, would always be welcome. Also, she was very fond of Daniel because he'd been so kind and obliging during his previous stay with them. When she agreed to go on a visit to a relative that evening, therefore, Charlotte had no idea that she'd be simultaneously aiding the escape of a British spy.

'What's it like out there, Ronan?' she asked.

'You won't notice the cold if you wrap up warmly enough,' said her husband. 'It will do you and Louise good to get out of the house for a while. You've been cooped up here far too long.'

'Is Daniel coming with us?'

'We'll take him as far as the city gate, my love. Delightful as your aunt is, I don't think that Dan would want to meet her. It's a family occasion. He'd only feel in the way.'

'What happened to his horse?'

'It went lame,' Flynn told her. 'He had to part with it. Dan will buy another.'

'Louise will miss him. He played with her for hours.'

'Yes, he'll make a splendid father, if ever he has the sense to get married.'

Her interest quickened. 'You told me that he and Amalia are very close.'

'It's true – Dan Rawson is more or less spoken for.'

'I hope he brings her with him on his next visit.'

'That may not be possible for a while,' said Flynn, tactfully. He heard a door open. 'That sounds like him now. Are you ready?'

Lifting up her daughter, Charlotte wrapped a cloak around both of them and nodded. Daniel put his head into the room. He'd been out in the stable, loading something onto the back of the cart. It was time to leave. As they set off into the twilight, Charlotte and Louise sat beside Flynn. Daniel, meanwhile, was seated in the back of the cart beside a large bundle tied up in an old tarpaulin. Hidden beneath the bundle was a coil of rope. All that he'd asked his friend to do was to take him to one of the city gates. From that point on, Daniel would be left to his own devices. The cart rumbled on through the gathering gloom. It seemed to be colder than ever. When they passed an inn, someone opened a door to go in and they had a tantalising glimpse of a cheering blaze in the fireplace, but it soon vanished.

If it were not for the fact that Charlotte's aunt was fairly decrepit, they wouldn't have considered turning out at that time of day in such hostile weather but they tried to visit her at least once a week and to take a supply of bread with them. For the sake of the old lady, they were prepared to make the effort. In Flynn's mind, the main advantage of the outing was that it would rid them of Daniel. Pleased to see him at first, he was uneasy at the thought that his guest had probably killed two men and made himself a fugitive. The thought was unsettling. Flynn would only be happy when Daniel had quit Paris altogether.

It was a tiresome drive but the city gate eventually came into sight, rising out of the darkness. There were four sentries on duty and they were questioning anyone who wanted to leave. Coals glowed in a brazier and they tried to stay close to it. When the cart reached the gate, Charlotte looked over her shoulder to bid farewell to Daniel but he'd already disappeared and so had the bundle inside the tarpaulin.

'Where has he gone, Ronan?' she asked in bewilderment.

'Forget him, Charlotte. Think about your aunt instead.'

'I didn't hear him get off the cart.'

'Dan Rawson moves in mysterious ways,' said Flynn,

wryly. 'The important thing is that he's no longer our problem.'

She was puzzled. 'But he wasn't a problem before, was he?'

Flynn watched the cart ahead of them being let through the gates. 'It's our turn next,' he warned. 'Let me do the talking.'

Though they couldn't see Daniel, he was keeping a close eye on them from his hiding place nearby. Having slipped quietly off the back of the cart, he'd taken the rope and the bundle with him. He was now standing at a corner that gave him a clear view of the gates. Careful not to implicate his friends, he waited until they'd been allowed out of the city before he went to work. Untying the tarpaulin, he let its contents spill onto the ground in a position where they could in time be seen from the gates. Straw, twigs and the accumulated debris from Flynn's stable formed a combustible pile. Daniel could pick out the sentries by the glow of their brazier and by the flaming torches either side of the gates. At the moment, however, he was invisible to them. He needed several attempts with his tinderbox before he at last ignited his little bonfire. When the twigs began to crackle, he picked up the rope and padded off into the darkness.

Having created a diversion, he crouched in readiness in the shadow of the city wall. At first the sentries paid no heed but, when the fire really took hold and blazed into life, they couldn't ignore it. Two of them strolled towards the fire while their colleagues watched them. With four pairs of eyes staring in one direction, Daniel had his opportunity. He didn't waste it. Having already tied a loop in the rope, he tossed it up at the battlements. Working in the dark, he found it difficult to judge the distance at first but he persisted and experience was his helpmate. Since he'd grown up on a farm, Daniel was used to catching recalcitrant livestock with a rope and he'd not lost his skill. As he tossed it up once more, he felt the rope lodge around solid stone and tighten as it did so. Confident that it was secure, he began to shin up the rope towards the top of the high wall.

Meanwhile, the two soldiers who'd gone to investigate the fire saw that it posed no danger to the nearby houses. Turning round to walk back, they were just in time to see a figure mount the city wall. Silhouetted against the sky, Daniel presented a fleeting target. Both men took aim with their weapons and fired but their musket balls simply explored thin air. Daniel had already jumped out of harm's way. Now outside the city wall, he still had to contend with danger. Alerted by the shooting, the two sentries still on duty opened the gate and went in pursuit of the fugitive. When they heard someone running at full pelt down a nearby street, they went in the same direction. Though they couldn't actually see him, they could track his movements by the clatter of his footsteps.

By the same token, Daniel was able to gauge the speed of the chase. He was fit enough to outrun the men but feared that mounted soldiers might eventually join in the hunt. In that event, he was bound to be cornered. His safety lay in getting rid of those in pursuit and that entailed separating them. After haring through a maze of streets, therefore, he stopped to listen to the running feet behind him. They'd picked up his scent and were closing in on him. Daniel stooped down until he found a loose stone then he stepped into a doorway and flattened his back against the door. Aware that their quarry had come to a halt somewhere, the soldiers slowed down to walking pace, using their bayonets to prod into any dark corners. When they turned into the street where Daniel was hiding, he took out his dagger and braced himself. Footsteps got nearer and nearer. He could soon hear the men panting for breath.

Just before they reached him, he tossed the stone down the street and it rolled noisily for several yards. Fooled by the trick, one of the soldiers broke into a run and went past the doorway. As the man's companion drew level with him, Daniel stepped out to clap a hand over his mouth while sinking the dagger into his heart. His victim sagged to the ground and let go of his musket. After sheathing his dagger, Daniel snatched up the weapon and used it to fend off the other soldier as he came hurtling at him. Bayonets clashed in the darkness. When he realised that his friend had been killed, the Frenchman went berserk, firing his musket and sending the ball inches past Daniel's ear before it ricocheted off a wall. Because the man was yelling obscenities at him, Daniel could hear how short of breath he was. There was no time for delay. The shot would soon bring inquisitive faces and act as a guide to any other soldiers who'd joined the search. A swift dispatch of his adversary was vital.

Daniel was no stranger to a musket. During his time in the ranks, he'd learnt to handle it with speed and precision. When the soldier made another lunge at him, therefore, Daniel parried the bayonet then used his own to thrust it deep into the man's stomach. All the fight was instantly drained out of his opponent and he slumped to the ground in a heap, groaning piteously. Doors and windows were opening. Curious heads popped out. Daniel didn't pause to answer any questions. Dropping the musket on the ground, he took to his heels again and zigzagged through the streets of suburban Paris until he felt he was completely safe. It was only when he slowed to a walk that he realised how cold it was. The temperature appeared to have plunged dramatically since he'd left Flynn's house. Warmed by his headlong flight and by the exertion of the duel with the soldier, he now felt the wind whipping at his face like a cat-o'-nine-tails. The first flakes of snow began to fall.

A shock awaited him. Pulling his cloak around him, he went in search of an inn where he could stay before acquiring a horse the next day. Eventually, he came to a short stretch of open country. When he reached a copse, he plunged into the trees for safety, looking over his shoulder as he walked along. It was a bad mistake. The next moment, he collided with something large and unyielding, forcing him to bounce backwards and blink in astonishment. He looked up and saw that he was confronted by a mounted soldier. In spite of all the effort he'd made to escape, Daniel had been caught. His initial impulse was to turn tail and flee but there was something odd about the man. He made no attempt to arrest or attack Daniel. In fact, he didn't move an inch and neither did his horse. Both remained motionless. When Daniel reached out to touch the animal's frosted muzzle, there was no response. He was overwhelmed with relief. Daniel hadn't been caught, after all.

Soldier and horse were two more casualties of a winter that had already claimed untold victims. They had, literally, frozen to death and were now no more than ghostly statues

among the trees. In all probability, they'd been there for
days before being discovered. If he stayed indefinitely,
Daniel feared that he was likely to join them as a grotesque
winter sculpture. He needed shelter. Brushing past the two
corpses, he hurried on as he sought a warm place to lay his
head for the night.

Amalia Janssen had never been short of admirers. Her
striking beauty and her shapely figure aroused a great
deal of interest and a number of suitors came forward.
She would not simply make an ideal wife for the man
fortunate enough to marry her, she was given additional
lustre by her father's renown. Emanuel Janssen was
famous throughout Europe for his tapestries. Such was
his pre-eminence that his skills had been sought by no
less a person than Louis XIV, King of France. To have
Janssen as a father-in-law was a distinct bonus. Amalia,
however, was deaf to all entreaties. When gifts arrived at
the house for her, she always made sure that they were
returned with a polite rejection. Blandishments of all
kinds were showered upon her but in vain. She'd already
made her choice and it was a sacred commitment. In her
opinion, every potential husband faded into nothingness
beside Daniel Rawson. He'd saved her life, won her heart
and enriched her horizons in every way.

Since they spent so much time apart, they kept in touch
by correspondence. During the campaign season, Daniel's
letters were few and far between, saying nothing about his
whereabouts or about the conduct of the war. Though they
tended to be short and written in haste, they were always
couched in love. For that reason, Amalia had kept every

letter and – whenever she had time on her hands – she read them in sequence, watching their friendship evolve over the years into something that was indissoluble. Seated in the parlour of her home, she was enjoying the correspondence yet again when Beatrix knocked and came into the room. She was a chubby woman approaching forty, with plain features and a lack of charm that had kept any serious male interest at bay. Putting her own disappointments aside, she took a sincere delight in Amalia's good fortune and had a deep admiration for Daniel Rawson. She was as much a friend as a servant and Amalia always confided in her.

Beatrix observed the piles of letters tied up with blue ribbon.

'There's no need to ask what you're reading,' she said with a chortle.

Amalia smiled. 'Daniel's letters bring me such joy.'

'And so they should. I just wish that there were more of them.'

'It's difficult to write when he's on the move, Beatrix, and he's very careful not to give away too much information in case they fall into the wrong hands.' Amalia grimaced. 'I can't bear the thought of that happening. These letters were meant for my eyes alone.'

'You've read bits of them out to me,' recalled Beatrix.

'I don't look upon you as a stranger. Besides, you were there when Daniel first came into my life. You've witnessed everything that's happened between us.'

The servant beamed. 'It's been a privilege to do so, Miss Amalia.' Her face darkened. 'Anyway, I didn't come to disturb you. I simply came to tell you that I think I saw that man again.'

'You *think* you saw him or you *did* see him?'

'I'm fairly sure that it was him.'

'And I'm equally sure that you're mistaken,' said Amalia, easily. 'I look out of the window just as much as you and I've never seen this phantom gentleman.'

'He's not a phantom,' protested Beatrix. 'He's as real as you or me.'

'And what was he doing?'

'Looking at the house, that's all.'

'Can you describe him?'

'Well,' said Beatrix, uncertainly, 'not really. He's never there long enough.'

'I fancy that you're imagining the whole thing.'

'I'm not, I swear it!'

'Then why has nobody else in the house spotted this man?'

Beatrix shrugged. 'I don't know.'

'How many sightings have there been?'

'I'd say it was three or four – all in the last few days.'

'Well,' said Amalia, 'I'm sure you believe that you saw this man but I find it hard to conceive that anyone would be foolhardy enough to stand in the road when it's freezing out there. What possible reason could anyone have for doing it?'

'Who knows, Miss Amalia? I just find it so upsetting.'

Amalia put a consoling hand on her arm. For all her apparent solidity, Beatrix was a nervous woman who was upset too readily. There'd been occasions before when her lively imagination had conjured up threats that never really existed, leaving her needlessly perplexed. As a result of those experiences, Amalia always took the servant's dire warnings with a degree of scepticism. They rarely had any real substance. In this case, there was a crucial factor to take into account. Like Amalia and her father, Beatrix had hardly been able to leave the house for weeks on end. Being trapped indoors for so long could be playing on her mind. The few people who passed the house did tend to glance at it. Amalia concluded that Beatrix had read far too much into someone's casual interest. The fact that the servant couldn't even describe the man properly suggested that there could have been more than one person showing an interest in the house, and that they'd blended together in Beatrix's imagination into a single entity. At all events, Amalia saw no cause for alarm.

'Stop fretting,' she said. 'There's nobody out there, Beatrix. When we lived in Paris and our house was being watched, we were all very much aware of it. But I don't have that sense of being under surveillance here. You're worrying when you don't need to. Besides, you're perfectly safe in here. Including father, we have four men in the house. Doesn't that reassure you?' Amalia gave her an affectionate pat. 'Your problem is that you spend too much time looking out of the window. There's nobody out there, I promise you. If there had been a man watching the house, one of us would have seen him as well. Yet we didn't, did we?'

Beatrix shook her head and accepted defeat. She must have been mistaken. Amalia had convinced her. Nobody was keeping the house under observation. Why on earth should they? She could sleep soundly again.

* * *

The man waited until night before he crept up to the rear of the house. Moving stealthily to the workshop, he rubbed frost from a window so that he could peer in. All that he could make out in the gloom was the shape of the various looms. Even in the punitive cold, he managed a quiet smile.

CHAPTER FOUR

Daniel Rawson didn't even know the name of the place. When he stumbled upon the inn, it was pitch-dark and the sign swinging creakily above the door was covered in snow. It was an old building with irregular walls, beams that had subsided in the course of time and oak settles polished to a high sheen by the impress of a century of backsides. There was a smell of damp and several indications of decay. All of the doors let in a draught. The flagstones on the floor undulated dangerously. Yet none of it bothered Daniel. Because he'd found shelter from the snowstorm outside, he was ready to forgive the inn its many shortcomings.

When he held his hands to the fire, he began slowly to thaw out. A glass of brandy helped the process and encouraged him to remove his hat and take off his wet cloak. Since the place was fairly empty, the landlord was glad of his custom. He was a big, bearded man of middle years with a gloomy outlook on life.

'This weather will be the death of me,' he moaned.

'It's done none of us any favours,' said Daniel. 'All France is suffering.'

'Nobody's stayed here for almost a month.'

'Well, you'll have a guest tonight, my friend. I need a room.'

'You can take your pick, monsieur.' He moved towards a door. 'I'll call the lad to stable your horse.'

'I have no horse,' said Daniel, stopping the landlord in his tracks. 'That's to say, I *did* have one but the poor creature slipped on the ice and broke a leg. I had to put him out of his misery.' It was a plausible lie and the other man accepted it. 'Can you tell me where I might buy another mount tomorrow?'

'There's only one place I know and that's a mile or more back in the direction of the city. It will be a long trudge on foot, especially if this snow keeps falling.' Self-interest brought a faint smile to his lips. 'You might have to stay here longer than you thought.'

That was the last thing Daniel intended to do. He was still on the very outskirts of Paris and wanted to get away as soon as possible. Having left two dead soldiers behind him, he knew that there'd be a thorough search for him. In one sense, the snowstorm was a boon because it would slow down any pursuit. At the same time, unfortunately, it would also hamper his escape. He felt able to take the risk of staying one night at the inn but lingering there any longer would be to court danger. It was some time since he'd last eaten, so he ordered himself a meal and sat at the table nearest the fire. Edible rather than appetising, the food was served by a dark-haired woman in her twenties with a swarthy complexion and a glint in her eye. After sizing him up, she gave Daniel a sly grin. As she leant over to put the platter in front of him, she let her breast brush gently against his shoulder. He ignored the signal.

The landlord was curious. 'Were you going towards Paris or away from it?'

'I had business in the city.'

'I wondered why you had no luggage with you.'

'I'm travelling light,' said Daniel, 'because I expected to be back home this evening – and I would've been had my horse not fallen.'

'What type of business might you be in, monsieur?'

'It's one that takes me to a lot of inns like this. I'm a wine merchant, though I dread to think what I'll have to sell. The last harvest failed and the frost has split the vines. There'll be precious little profit for me this year.'

It was a disguise that Daniel had often used in the past. His forged papers were in the name of Marcel Daron and he knew enough about wine to hold his own in a discussion with the landlord of an inn. They talked about prices and compared their individual preferences. All the time, however, Daniel was conscious of being watched by someone. Though he couldn't see her, he suspected that it was the serving wench. Deciding to go to bed early, Daniel was shown upstairs by the landlord. There was a rough-hewn quality about the accommodation. Luxury was not on offer. Given the choice of five rooms, he chose the one above the bar because some of the heat from the fire came up through the cracks in the ceiling and the gaps in the floorboards. Left alone with a candle, he went to the window, opened the shutters and looked out at the yard. Snow was still falling and a gust of wind blew it in on him. He quickly locked the shutters again.

When Daniel tested the mattress, he found it hard and lumpy but there were thick woollen blankets to keep out the cold and his cloak could act as an auxiliary layer. The creak of the floorboards outside warned him that someone was coming and his hand went by reflex to the pistol holstered under his coat. There was a tap on the door then it opened to reveal the serving wench. Because she was holding up a candle, he was able to take a closer look at her. While her hair was greasy, the woman was not unattractive. She had a pleasant face, a well-formed body and a crude charm. One hand rested on her hip as she grinned boldly.

'Do you have everything you want, monsieur?' she enquired.

'I think so,' replied Daniel.

'It's going to be a cold night.'

'Yes, I'm afraid that it will be.'

'Would you like an extra blanket, sir?'

'No, thank you. I can manage with the ones I already have.'

'There are other ways to keep warm,' she said, lifting a provocative eyebrow. 'Would you care for some company?'

'It's a tempting offer,' he said, politely, 'but, as it happens, I'm very tired. I'll be asleep as soon as my head hits the pillow.' She was crestfallen at the rejection. 'It's no reflection on you, mademoiselle. Under other circumstances . . .'

Anxious to dispel a misunderstanding, she stepped into the room.

'I hope you don't mistake me. I expected no reward.'

'I never thought that you did.'

'Please don't think ill of me.'

'I'd never do that,' said Daniel with an appeasing smile. 'It just happens that I am very tired.'

'Then I'll leave you alone,' she said, backing away and pointing a finger down the passageway. 'But if you do change your mind, my room is at the end.'

'I'll bear that in mind.'

As soon as she'd gone, Daniel propped a chair against the door so that it couldn't be opened. While he didn't have the slightest inclination to go to *her* room, he sensed that she might come to him again in the night and try to slip under the blankets. It was best to obviate that possibility. In former days, when he was a roving young soldier, he would have shown more interest but that life was behind him now. He already had a woman to warm his bed for him. Thoughts of Amalia Janssen were a blanket in themselves and they gave him infinite satisfaction. His precaution was wise. Not long after midnight, he heard footsteps padding along outside, then someone tried the door. When it refused to budge, more pressure was applied but the chair held firm. The disappointed serving wench eventually went back to her room.

Conditioned by years of practice, Daniel slept lightly. It was well before dawn when he heard riders approaching in the distance. Out of bed at once, he lit the candle then crossed to the shutters and unhooked the latch. Listening carefully, he picked out the sound of three horsemen and knew that they were heading for the inn. When they got closer, he eased one shutter ajar so that he could peer down into the yard. Three men arrived, reining in their horses and dismounting before tethering them. They marched purposefully towards the main door and one of them banged on it with the butt of his pistol. In the stillness of the night, the noise was ear-splitting. Daniel moved swiftly. Folding up two of the blankets, he stuffed them under the remaining one to give the impression that someone was sleeping in the bed.

He opened the shutters and saw that, if he tried to flee through the window, he'd have to negotiate the slippery roof of the storeroom below. That would be tricky in the dark. Yet if he left by means of the room at the end of the passageway, he'd be able to drop straight down to the ground with no intervening obstruction. Hat on and cloak over his arm, he moved the chair from the door and went out, closing the door behind him. Still with the candle in one hand, he walked to the room at the end of the passageway and used his toe to tap on the door. Then he let himself in and shut the door behind him. Roused from her sleep, the woman sat up in fright until she realised who her visitor was. Her face was split by a welcoming grin and she extended both arms in welcome. Her desires would be fulfilled. The handsome guest had come to her, after all. To her chagrin, however, he only stayed a matter of seconds. Opening the shutters, he tossed his cloak out, raised his hat to her then clambered through the window. She heard a thud as he landed in the yard. Her promise of pleasure had disappeared, leaving her torn between dismay, annoyance and a sense of betrayal.

Grumbling at every step, the landlord came downstairs and wished someone would stop beating a tattoo on his front door. He pulled back the bolts and opened the door wide. About to berate the unwanted caller, he changed his mind when his candle illumined three uniforms. He'd been hauled out of his bed by angry soldiers.

'What do you want?' he asked.

'We're looking for someone,' said one of the soldiers, pushing him aside so that he could enter. 'We're hunting a killer.'

'Well, you won't find him here. This is a respectable inn.'

'How many guests do you have here?'

'There's just the one at the moment.'

'Is it a man or a woman?'

'It's a man,' replied the landlord, 'but he's no killer.'

'When did he arrive?'

'He came on foot earlier this evening. He's a wine merchant whose horse broke a leg and had to be destroyed.'

The soldier looked upwards. 'Where is he?'

'He's probably sitting up in bed, wondering what all the noise is.'

'Take us to him,' ordered the soldier.

'You can't just barge in here,' protested the landlord.

'We can do as we wish,' said the man, grabbing him by the elbow and hustling him towards the staircase. The other soldiers followed. 'And if we find that you're harbouring a fugitive, we'll arrest you as well.'

'But I've done nothing wrong, I swear it.'

'Get upstairs.'

'Yes, yes,' said the landlord, obediently, 'but you're making a terrible mistake, I assure you. I've worked in this trade all my life. I know how to weigh up a customer at a glance. This gentleman is not the one you seek. I give you my word.'

Bundled upstairs, he was pushed along the passageway until he indicated a door. The soldier then shoved him aside and nodded to his companions. One of them snatched the candle from the landlord while the other opened the door. Both of them charged in and stood over the bed, using their drawn swords to prod at the blankets. When there was no response, one of them threw back the top blanket to show that there was nobody in the bed.

'Where the hell is he?' bellowed the man with the candle.

The explanation came in the form of departing hooves. They raced to the window and flung open the shutters. Down in the yard, a cloaked figure was riding off on one of their horses and towing the other two behind him. After yelling in vain at him, the three soldiers vented their fury on the landlord.

Daniel, meanwhile, made good his escape by courtesy of the French army.

Something was missing in the workshop. Emanuel Janssen had any number of commissions and enquiries from potential customers were coming in all the time. Both he and his three assistants were kept busy at their respective looms but they no longer laboured with the same controlled excitement. What was lacking was the sense of enormous pride they got from working on the tapestry for no less a customer than the Duke of Marlborough, the heroic captain-general of the Allied forces who'd trounced the mighty French army time and again as he protected Dutch territory and interests. On his return from England, Janssen had been able to describe the breathtaking scale and magnificence of Blenheim Palace. Marvelling at what they heard, his assistants were thrilled that a tapestry to which they'd contributed in greater or lesser degree would hang in a place of honour at Marlborough's home. It made them come to work each day with a spring in their step.

It was different now. They were merely producing tapestries for wealthy Dutch merchants or rich politicians, few of whom had any real taste. Instead of having a whole battlefield on which to leave their artistic mark, they were confined to smaller scales and more mundane subjects. Nicholaes Geel, the youngest of the assistants, complained bitterly about the poverty of their customers' imaginations. Even Aelbert Pienaar, the oldest and most tolerant of Janssen's employees, regretted that he couldn't work on something more inspiring. Kees Dopff was unable to speak his mind because he'd been born dumb but he overcame his handicap by developing a series of eloquent hand gestures and facial expressions. Like his companions, he was profoundly disappointed now that work on the Battle of Ramillies was finally over. Dopff was a small, thin, reserved man in his early thirties with billowing red hair that defied the attentions of comb and brush. He was the most naturally gifted of the assistants and, living at the house, was more or less a member of the Janssen family.

When Amalia came into the workshop, the looms were all working noisily away but she sensed a lack of enthusiasm in the staff. Pienaar gave her a warm smile and Dopff provided a nod of welcome. Geel, however, broke off to give her a cheerful wave. He was a tall, slim, sinewy young man similar in age to Amalia and he watched her with an adoration he found difficult to hide. Always friendly towards him, she offered him no encouragement whatsoever and

Geel accepted that he could never hope to compete with someone like Daniel Rawson. But that didn't stop him from feeling a surge of pleasure every time she came anywhere near him. Janssen strode across to his daughter, noting that she was dressed to go out.

'It will be freezing out there,' he warned.

'I can't stay imprisoned here for ever,' she said, 'so I'm going for a walk with Beatrix. We need a few things from the market.'

'How many of the stalls will be there today?'

'Oh, I think most people will brave the weather. They have a living to make, after all.' She looked at the tapestry folded up in the corner. 'I daresay that you're all missing Ramillies.'

'We are,' replied Pienaar, nostalgically.

Dopff nodded in agreement and gave a hopeless shrug.

'It's the best thing I've ever been privileged to work on,' said Geel, seizing the opportunity to talk to Amalia. 'Your father is a genius.'

'That's what I keep telling him, Nick,' she said.

'It's wonderful to work with a master of his trade.'

'An increasingly *tired* master of his trade,' corrected Janssen, massaging an ache at the back of his neck. 'But it's reassuring to know that I have the respect of my employees.'

'It's not respect,' said Geel, gaze still on Amalia, 'it's veneration.'

Geel and Dopff had both been apprenticed to Janssen and honed their skills under his expert tutelage. Pienaar, by contrast, approaching forty but looking a decade older, had only joined Janssen four years earlier but had quickly settled in. Of medium height and carrying too much weight, he was utterly reliable and very industrious. Until the death of his wife the previous winter, he'd been a talkative man. Pienaar now preferred to be alone with his thoughts and rarely started a conversation. The ebullient Geel had more than enough to say for all three assistants.

Janseen drew Amalia aside for a private word with her.

'Take care,' he said. 'The pavements are slippery.'

She was amused. 'Perhaps I should get a pair of skates.'

'They're far too dangerous.'

'People are skating on the canals all the time.'

'Well, my daughter isn't about to join them. Apart from anything else, it's an unladylike activity. You'd lose all dignity on a pair of skates.'

'But I'd have such *fun*, Father.' About to leave, she remembered something. 'By the way, have you seen anyone looking at the house?'

'Yes,' he replied. 'I've seen dozens of people. In my own small way, I'm quite famous. People are bound to stare at my house as they pass by.'

'You haven't seen one particular man, then?'

'I'd have said so if I had.' His brow crinkled. 'What's going on, Amalia? You asked me this question before. What's your concern?'

'Oh, it's nothing,' said Amalia, briskly. 'The man is not actually there. I *knew* that Beatrix was inventing the whole thing. She needs to get out in the fresh air to clear her mind. That's the best way to dispel her anxieties.'

For all his boldness on the battlefield, the Duke of Marlborough was a cautious man when it came to contemplating the future. He believed in covering all

options. Aware that peace negotiations were going on
between Grand Pensionary Heinsius of Holland and
Colbert de Torcy, the French foreign minister, Marlborough
wished that he could have some influence upon them.
Since he was excluded from the discussions, he worried
lest decisions were made to his personal disadvantage. He
therefore sent a stream of letters to his nephew, the Duke of
Berwick, Marshal of France. Any correspondence between
such sworn enemies might be viewed with astonishment
by most observers but Marlborough saw nothing wrong or
remotely treacherous in it. As the illegitimate son of Arabella
Churchill, Marlborough's sister, Berwick was a kinsman.
His father had been the Duke of York, brother to Charles II
and, later, King James II. Berwick therefore had a strongly
Jacobite lineage and chose to fight for Catholic France while
nurturing the distant hope that he'd one day see a Stuart
monarch restored to the English throne.

Since secrecy was essential, Marlborough always signed
himself with the monogram 'oo'. Two years earlier, the
captain-general had been offered a *douceur* of two million
gold livres for his good offices in arranging a peace
acceptable to France. Unable to achieve that, he'd now
written to Berwick to tell him that he hoped the offer
would still be honoured, knowing that his nephew would
be certain to pass on the hint to Versailles. At the time
when he was planning his strategy for the next campaign,
therefore, Marlborough was allowing for the possibility that
the current peace negotiations would come to fruition. In
that eventuality, he sought – and felt that he deserved –
the handsome reward once dangled enticingly before him
by the French. What would shock and sadden the other

commanders in the Allied army didn't trouble Adam Cardonnel in the least. He understood and approved of the way that Marlborough's mind worked. The war could not last for ever. Having given such sterling service for so many fraught years, the captain-general ought to reap a substantial benefit out of the peace.

After signing another missive to his nephew, Marlborough looked up as the door opened and his secretary came in. There was no need to conceal the letter.

'Well?' asked Marlborough. 'Has winter frozen the negotiations?'

'No, Your Grace,' replied Cardonnel. 'My information is that tentative discussions continue through the agency of an interlocutor, Herman von Petkum.'

'But we've no idea of their eventual outcome?'

'It's far too early to make predictions.'

'What is Louis offering?'

'We'd all like to know that, Your Grace.'

'And what has the old devil said about *me*?' wondered Marlborough, adjusting his periwig. 'I hope that old age hasn't dulled his memory. From the start, I've always been wholeheartedly for peace. He should remember that.'

'Nobody can review this war without thinking of you,' said Cardonnel with a sincerity shorn of any whisper of flattery. 'Your pre-eminence has acquired the status of a legend.'

'Even legends require remuneration for their services.'

'I'm sure it will be forthcoming, Your Grace.'

Cardonnel sat on the opposite side of the table and reached for some documents. The two men were soon absorbed in their reading. When there was a knock on the door, they glanced up as a man in the uniform of a British lieutenant stepped into the room with one hand on the arm of a dishevelled individual with a ragged beard and a torn cloak. Since the visitor held his head down, it was impossible to make out his features clearly.

'He claims that he has an important message for you, Your Grace,' said the lieutenant, sceptically. 'We searched him and relieved him of a dagger and a pistol. Yet we found no dispatches on his person.'

'That's because you didn't search me properly,' said Daniel, raising his head. 'My name is Captain Rawson of the 24th Foot and I'll thank you for the return of my weapons, Lieutenant. His Grace will vouch for me.'

Marlborough peered at him. 'Is that really *you*, Daniel?'

'I'd never have guessed,' said Cardonnel with a laugh.

The lieutenant was perplexed. 'You know this man?'

'Captain Rawson is a member of my personal staff,' said Marlborough, 'and I vouch for him without hesitation. Have his weapons ready for return.'

He snapped his fingers to dismiss the man and the lieutenant went out. Daniel immediately sat on a chair and eased off a boot. Concealed inside was the package he'd received from the courier in Paris. It was much reduced in size.

'I memorised what I could,' he explained, handing the package over and replacing his boot, 'so that I had less to carry. I destroyed what I no longer needed. If you give me pen and paper, I'll retrieve the information from my memory.'

'You've been away so long,' said Cardonnel, 'that we were starting to give up hope. It's such a relief to see you back here unharmed.'

'What happened?' asked Marlborough. 'Did you encounter problems?'

'None that I was unable to surmount,' replied Daniel, getting to his feet, 'though my visit to Paris was not without its setbacks.'

He gave them a brief account of his adventures, mentioning the death of the courier but saying nothing about his stay with Ronan Flynn and his family. They were highly diverted by the tale of how he'd escaped from the inn after depriving three French soldiers of their horses. On the long journey back to The Hague, there'd been many other obstacles to negotiate but Daniel made light of them. He'd completed his assignment and that was all that mattered.

Opening the package, Marlborough glanced through its contents.

'By all, this is wonderful!' he exclaimed with a chortle of delight. 'I have Louis's own words in my hand. This one paragraph sweeps away weeks of rumour and speculation. At last we know what he has in mind.'

'That could only have come from someone very close to the King,' noted Daniel. 'Evidently, you have agents in high places.'

'We have one particular source and that person is wholly reliable. Everything of importance that occurs at Versailles comes to his ears and – in time – is passed on to us. I regret that these documents cost the courier his life but he can easily be replaced. Thank you, Daniel,' he went on. 'What you've brought us is invaluable.' He indicated a chair. 'But do sit down,' he suggested. 'Adam will furnish you with writing materials and you can unpack that clever mind of yours. Like all good agents, you have an excellent memory.'

Daniel sat at the table. 'The mind is one place that can't be searched.'

Cardonnel passed him a pen, an inkwell and a blank sheet of paper. Daniel immediately began to write down the information he'd taken such pains to memorise. As he did so, Marlborough leafed through the rest of the letters, passing them on to Cardonnel after he'd read them. Daniel worked quickly and steadily, filling the page before reaching for another. When he read what had so far been written, Marlborough was astonished by the detail committed to memory. Page followed page until Daniel sat back and put his pen aside.

'Now you have everything that came out of Versailles that day,' he said, 'give or take a few grammatical irregularities.'

'This information is priceless,' said Marlborough, reading the final page. 'You're to be congratulated – congratulated and rewarded. I insist that you dine with us this evening.' His gaze fell on Daniel's beard and tattered cloak. 'When you've smartened yourself up a little, that is.'

'It's a kind invitation, Your Grace, and I accept it with thanks.'

'Your endeavours deserve more than a good meal, Daniel. You've earned a long rest. Take time off to enjoy the splendours of The Hague. It's a fine city. But no,' he added as he recalled Amalia Janssen, 'you're far more interested in the splendours of Amsterdam, aren't you?'

'That's where I most wish to be,' admitted Daniel.

'Then you must leave first thing tomorrow. I had word from Emanuel Janssen that my tapestry of the Battle of Ramillies is now complete. You can cast a discerning eye over it on my behalf. I can't wait to see it for myself.'

*   *   *

At the end of the working day, Nicholaes Geel was the last to leave. Janssen was the first to go, followed by Dopff. Pienaar remained long enough to ignite his pipe then he waved a farewell to his young colleague and waddled out. Left alone in the gloom, Geel picked up one of the candles and went across to the tapestry folded up on the floor. He carefully peeled back a corner of it to expose a tiny area of the battlefield. It was his own handiwork and he was immensely proud of it. Sitting down beside it, he caressed the tapestry as if he were stroking a favourite cat. Geel purred softly.

CHAPTER FIVE

Winter had relented somewhat in Amsterdam. The howling wind had gone, the frost was less harsh and there was a noticeable rise in temperature. It wasn't enough to thaw the ice in the harbour but at least it tempted more people onto the streets. Amalia and Beatrix were two of them. As they strolled along together, the servant had a basket over her arm so that she could carry anything that was bought. Sunlight filtered through the clouds and dappled the buildings. Birds were singing. Amsterdam was an attractive city, clean, well ordered and served by a network of canals. What had once been a sleepy fishing village was now the most thriving port in Europe, even if the vessels in its harbour were temporarily ice-bound. Amalia was intensely proud of the place where she'd been born and brought up. London might be larger and Paris more ostentatious but, in her opinion – and she'd visited both capitals – neither could rival her beloved Amsterdam.

'It's milder today,' she remarked.

'Then why do I feel so cold?' grumbled Beatrix with a shiver.

'You should have worn more clothing.'

'If I do that, I start to perspire.'

Amalia laughed. 'There's no pleasing you, is there?'

'I always hate winter. It's lowering.'

'Then you must make more effort to keep your spirits up, Beatrix. That's what I do and I know it's what Father does. We never let things wear us down.'

'Well, I'm different,' said the other, sourly.

They walked on and Amalia exchanged greetings with a neighbour who came towards them. Before crossing the narrow street, they paused to let some carts and coaches rumble past. Traffic was heavier than it had been for some time. It was as if the city had at last come out of hibernation. Something approximating normality was being restored. While Amalia was relishing the walk, she was conscious that Beatrix was morose and preoccupied. Fond of her servant, Amalia tried to bring her out of her reverie by engaging her in conversation.

'I told you that he was a phantom,' she said.

'Who are you talking about, Miss Amalia?'

'That man you thought you saw.'

Beatrix bridled. 'I *did* see him. I'd swear that on the Holy Bible.'

'You *believed* you saw him, Beatrix, and I don't criticise you for that. Our imaginations can play tricks on us sometimes. But I've made a point of looking out of the window every day and I haven't seen anyone keeping watch on us.'

'He's still there,' said Beatrix, grimly.

'You've actually seen him recently?'

'No, but I feel his presence.'

'Then perhaps you can explain why my father has never managed to catch sight of him. His bedchamber gives him a clear view of the street. Yet when I asked him if he'd seen this man of yours, Father said that he hadn't spotted anyone.'

'Then he should open his eyes,' muttered the other woman. Adopting an apologetic tone, she raised her voice. 'I don't mean to be disrespectful to either of you but you should be more . . .' her face puckered, '. . . more . . . oh, what's the word?'

'Vigilant?'

'Yes, that's it – more vigilant like me.'

'I think you're too suggestible.'

Though not understanding what Amalia meant, Beatrix was nevertheless offended. She sniffed loudly and lapsed into a hurt silence. Amalia had to pacify her before their conversation could resume. It was agreed that they'd talk about more neutral subjects. Argument was pointless. As far as the man was concerned, Beatrix was adamant that he'd been keeping watch on the house and it had unsettled her. The fact that nobody else had seen him was irrelevant. The servant trusted her own eyesight. It had never let her down before.

It was good to find more of a throng back in the market. Stalls had increased in number and something of the old bustle had returned. Amalia made some purchases from a bread stall and they went straight into the basket. Beatrix cheered up as she recognised familiar faces but it was when they began to look in shop windows that she became more animated. As they studied some fashionable dresses on display in one shop, Beatrice jabbed a finger at the glass.

'That would suit you,' she said with approval.

Amelia was unsure. 'Do you think so?'

'Blue is your colour and that style is ideal for you. I'd love to see you wearing a dress like that, Miss Amalia. It might have been made for you.'

No other servant was allowed to make such personal remarks to Amalia but Beatrix was different. The adversity they'd experienced during their ill-fated stay in Paris had bonded them together. Beatrix felt able to discuss almost anything with Amalia, who, in turn, didn't object when the servant occasionally took on an almost maternal role as she was doing right now. After scrutinising all the dresses in the window, they returned to the one favoured by the servant. She nudged Amalia.

'Persuade your father to buy it for you,' she advised.

'Oh, I don't know about that.'

'I'm sure that he would if you wanted it enough.'

'That may be,' said Amalia, 'but when would I ever wear it? That's a dress for a special occasion and there are none of those on the horizon.'

'Then your memory is very short,' chided Beatrix. 'One of these days, Captain Rawson might call on you. If that's not a special occasion, what is?'

Amalia gave a wan smile. A visit from Daniel would indeed be a special event but she felt that it was unlikely to happen. It was February now and she'd not heard from him for almost a month. The only explanation was that Daniel had been sent off on a secret assignment about which he couldn't tell her beforehand. All that she could do was to wait patiently and pray that he came to no harm. She looked at the blue dress once more. Beatrix was right. It would suit Amalia perfectly and she envisaged wearing it at a ball with Daniel at her side in his dress uniform. They'd make a striking couple. The image vanished instantly from her mind. It was wrong to build up her hopes, she told herself. Disappointment was inevitable. Amalia had to school herself to be realistic. Since she was in love with a soldier, she simply had to accept the consequences.

Daniel was probably hundreds of miles away.

It was almost impossible to startle Henry Welbeck. Having spent most of his youth and all of his adult life in the British army, he'd seen sights that would make most people vomit and he'd survived endless perils on the battlefield. A veteran sergeant in the 24th Regiment of Foot, he was a dour, cynical, teak-hard man with a well-earned reputation for maintaining discipline among his men. Welbeck loathed being stuck in winter quarters when there was little to do but eat, drink, smoke his pipe, play cards, keep his men under control and argue with his fellow sergeants. He was in the middle of a heated debate with Sergeant Curry when the apparition came into view. It was one of those rare moments when Welbeck was genuinely startled.

'Lord a bloody mercy!' he exclaimed. 'It's a ghost.'

'Hello, Henry,' said Daniel, clapping him on the shoulder. 'How are you?'

'I was fine until you came back from the dead to give me a scare.'

'I'm as alive as you are.'

'Yes,' argued Welbeck, 'but, to all intents and purposes, you're dead to me when winter comes. While I have to spend months of despair with the ranks, you sneak off with the other officers to wallow in luxury.'

Daniel grinned. Being chased by soldiers through the streets of Paris was not his idea of luxury but he wasn't about to say so in a tavern. Too many people were within earshot. Welbeck was sharing a table with Leo Curry, the only sergeant in the British ranks who was actually uglier than him. Curry and Welbeck enjoyed a combative relationship that usually stopped just short of blows. Yet they'd willingly slipped away together from the camp to a nearby tavern. Unlike them, Daniel wasn't in uniform but Curry recognised him and immediately became deferential.

'I can see that you two would rather be alone, Captain Rawson,' he said, rising to his feet. 'We'll continue our discussion another time, Henry.'

Welbeck glared at him. 'There's nothing to discuss, you pig-headed idiot.'

'I'm right and you're wrong.'

'Stop talking through that hole in your arse.'

'I'll be back,' warned Curry, raising a bunched fist.

As the sergeant walked away, Daniel took his seat. Though he was on his way north to Amsterdam, he'd made a slight detour to one of the camps where British soldiers were spending the winter months. Welbeck was his best friend and had been since they'd served in the ranks together. Over the years they'd weathered many crises, most recently when the pair of them bluffed their way into the besieged city of Lille in order to rescue an imprisoned woman. The three of them had eventually got out alive only to be shelled by their own artillery.

'What are you doing here, Dan?' demanded Welbeck.

'Don't sound so inhospitable.'

'You don't belong in a camp like ours.'

'I belong wherever my regiment happens to be,' said Daniel, loyally, 'and I wish I could spend more time with it. As it is, I was needed elsewhere.'

'Staying with Corporal John in The Hague, I daresay.'

'His Grace had other work for me. It took me to Paris where it's even colder than here. One way and another it was a hazardous visit. Believe me, I'd have been far safer here, listening to you and Sergeant Curry trading insults.'

'It's all in fun, really,' admitted Welbeck. 'Leo and I are two of a kind.'

'Yes, you're both as ugly as sin.'

They shared a laugh and exchanged a warm handshake. Now that he'd got over his amazement, Welbeck was very pleased to see Daniel, the only officer for whom he had any real respect. He broke off to buy his visitor a drink and to refill his own tankard. Back at the table, he appraised his friend.

'I hope you behaved yourself in Paris,' he said, meaningfully.

'Strictly speaking,' Daniel told him, 'I was there to *misbehave* and certain people took exception to that. I had to fight my way out.' He looked around before lowering his voice. 'I'll give you more detail when we're somewhere more private.'

'I'll remind you of that, Dan.'

Welbeck lifted his glass to acknowledge his friend before

taking a long sip. He was a stocky man with rounded shoulders and a barrel chest but it was his face that held the attention. Red, rugged and hopelessly misshapen, it was given a sinister aspect by the long, livid scar down one cheek. Daniel knew that Welbeck's body carried many more scars but the deepest wound had been inflicted on the man's soul. Continual exposure to war and its multiple horrors had robbed him of any belief in God and given him in exchange a kind of rabid atheism. Much as he loathed army life, he was quick to realise that it was the only thing at which he excelled, so he was destined to follow the drum in perpetuity. It made him a defiant pessimist. What Welbeck could never understand was how Daniel seemed to thrive on the very things that were anathema to the sergeant. Daniel had been through the same searing experiences, yet his soul remained unscarred and he was able to take pleasure from all he did in the name of the British army.

Welbeck spoke in a whisper. 'What are the chances of peace?'

'Your guess is as good as mine.'

'You're close to Corporal John. You must have heard something.'

'Talks are going on, Henry, but nothing has been decided.'

'What does your instinct tell you?'

'There'll be a lot more fighting to come,' said Daniel.

'And then?'

'And then – eventually – one day, years hence from now, we'll have peace.'

'What will you do when that happens?'

'I'll buy you a drink to celebrate.'

'I'm serious, Dan,' said Welbeck, fixing him with a stare. 'When this war finally ends, we're not needed any more. Our occupation is gone.'

'There'll always be a need for good soldiers.'

Daniel sat up with a start when he heard what he'd just said. Without thinking of the implications, he'd blithely committed himself for ever to a military life. Fighting was in his blood. He wasn't at all sure that Amalia would understand that and his mind went back to Ronan Flynn. The Irishman had turned his back on the army in order to embrace family life. Daniel wanted both – a wife and family in addition to continued service in a red coat. Welbeck saw the consternation in his friend's eyes and guessed its origin.

'You're thinking of *her*, aren't you?'

'I'm always thinking of Amalia,' confessed Daniel.

'Women and war don't mix, Dan. You know that.'

'His Grace is married and so are most of his senior officers.'

'But where are their wives?' asked Welbeck. 'They're pining away at home, wondering if they're still married or if their husbands are lying dead somewhere.'

Flynn had said something similar to Daniel but it still jolted him.

'I had the sense to stay single,' said Welbeck.

'Your turn will come, Henry,' teased Daniel.

'Hell will freeze over before I look at a woman.'

'You looked at Rachel Rees.'

'She wasn't a woman – she was a witch.'

'That's unkind. Rachel was a remarkable lady. How many other women would venture into an enemy stronghold in the way she did? It showed bravery.'

'I'd call it stupidity.'

'Then you showed the same stupidity in helping to rescue her.'

Welbeck was rancorous. 'That was my biggest mistake. We should have left her where she was. The best place for a woman like that is behind bars where she could be fed on raw meat.'

Rachel Rees was an ebullient Welsh camp follower who'd buried two husbands but was not averse to marrying a third soldier. It was Rachel who'd entered Lille with Daniel then been arrested as she tried to leave. Welbeck had been recruited to help liberate her, thereby earning her heartfelt gratitude. Embarrassed by Rachel's gushing affection for him, Welbeck had been relieved to hear that she'd decided to return home to Brecon. At a deep level, she'd made him feel threatened.

'How's everything here?' asked Daniel.

'It's truly terrible,' said Welbeck, pulling a face. 'We're cold, miserable, badly fed and bored. The only advantage of this weather is that it makes people think twice about deserting. I do my best to keep them on their toes. Marching them up and down is the one sure way to keep them warm.'

'They'll be warm enough when the campaign season starts.'

Welbeck snorted. 'I don't know which is worse, Dan – dodging the enemy's musket volleys or putting up with the monotony of being in winter quarters. It's a choice between danger and tedium. Each is as bad as the other.'

'I'd choose danger every time, Henry.'

'Does Amalia know that?'

Daniel was taken aback by the question. He considered his reply.

'In a sense,' he said at length, 'I suppose that she does.'

'The one thing I'll say in favour of Rachel Rees is that she understood what soldiering means. She's heard the roar of cannon and seen the ritual slaughter. She's crawled over battlefields in search of booty. She's smelt blood. What about Amalia?' asked Welbeck. 'Does she *really* know what happens when you put on your uniform and go to war?'

'No,' admitted Daniel.

'Then perhaps you should tell her.'

Emanuel Janssen was very careful in his choice of apprentices. Not only did they have to spend a large amount of time under his roof, they had to share his love of his work. Kees Dopff had been an ideal apprentice, attentive, conscientious and possessing real flair. He was also extremely pleasant company. Feeling protective towards him, Janssen treated him like a son. He'd been less certain about Nicholaes Geel at first. The youth had been eager but there was an impulsiveness about him that worried Janssen. It took concentration and patience to produce a good tapestry and, at the start, Geel seemed to have neither quality. Yet he was very personable and had a readiness to learn. As it turned out, he lacked Dopff's instinctive ability but he made up for it in other ways. Janssen had no cause to regret taking him on. Geel had served his apprenticeship and become a valuable member of the team. Whenever physical effort was required, he was always the first to step forward.

'Where shall I put it, master?' he asked.

Janssen pointed. 'Over there in the corner, please.'

'This will keep us going for a long time.'

'It will have to, Nick. Stocks are low in the warehouse. Until ships can sail and imports can come into Amsterdam again, we may have to slow down a little.'

Geel was carrying a heavy bale of wool with comparative ease. Setting it down carefully in a corner of the warehouse, he rubbed his hands together. 'We'll have to start keeping our own sheep,' he suggested.

'If only we had the land to do that!' said Janssen, covetously. 'And if only this war would end, we'd be able to get the finest Picardy wool. That's what I always used when trade with France was unimpeded.'

'We can still get Italian silk. At least, we will when the roads become passable again. I can't see many Italian merchants wanting to travel overland at the moment.'

It was early morning and Janssen had just taken delivery of some wool. Dopff was still finishing his breakfast and Pienaar had yet to arrive. Geel, however, was there ahead of the others and was a willing volunteer. Janssen plucked at his beard as he regarded his youngest employee.

'Do you ever think about the future?' he asked.

'No, master, I never look beyond any particular day.'

'Perhaps you should do so, Nick.'

'But I've no need,' said Geel with a grin. 'I have the best job in the world and the most wonderful master. Working under you is an absolute joy. My life couldn't be any happier. I just want to carry on as I am.'

'So do I,' said Janssen, ruefully, 'but, alas, I can't do that. Old age is taking its toll. I can't go on for ever.'

'You're not old, master. You can still work as long and as hard as the rest of us. Amalia – your daughter, I mean – is always amazed at your energy. I've heard her talking about it to Beatrix.'

'They can't feel how much my body aches.'

'You once told me that work keeps you young,' recalled Geel.

'That's what I used to think at one time. It's not true, Nick.'

'I'll wager that you still have years left in you, master.'

'I certainly hope so,' said Janssen with a smile, 'but I don't intend to spend them all at a loom. Sooner or later, I'll retire.'

Geel was worried. 'Do you mean that this workshop will close down?'

'No, it just means that I'll no longer be in charge. I'll hand over to Aelbert. Tapestries will continue to be made here but not in the same way.'

'I see . . . Have you told this to Aelbert?'

'I don't need to. He can see that I'm gradually slowing down. I don't have the strength or the will to take on an apprentice. So I won't be looking for another Nicholaes Geel to instruct in the magical art of weaving tapestries.'

Geel looked even more anxious. 'If and when you *do* retire, master,' he said, 'what will happen to me?'

'That's what you ought to consider.'

'Won't there be a place for me here?'

'Yes, of course,' said Janssen. 'I'll make that clear to Aelbert. You and Kees can work here for as long as you wish. Kees will certainly stay. He and Aelbert get on well together. But I can't say the same of you, Nick.'

Geel was defensive. 'Yes, you can – Aelbert and I are good friends.'

'Then why has there been friction between the two of you? Oh, I know it's nothing serious and it doesn't affect your work, but the fact is that you find Aelbert rather dull. You're always taunting him about it.'

'I like a joke now and then, that's all.'

'But some of your gibes hurt him deeply. That's why he strikes back at you. All that he wants to do is get on quietly with his work.'

'Conversation doesn't hurt anyone, master. It helps to pass the time. When *you're* not here, I've nobody to talk to. Kees can't speak and Aelbert chooses not to. It's the reason I end up trying to prod him into saying something.'

'Perhaps you should try to leave him alone.'

'What do you mean?'

'Where Aelbert is concerned, you have fences to mend. He'll take my place one day and he won't stand for any mischief-making when he holds the whip hand over you. Can you hear what I'm telling you, Nick?'

'I think so,' said Geel, uneasily. 'Things are going to change.'

'Let me be blunt,' said Janssen. 'You can either look for work elsewhere or stay on here. If you decide to leave, you'll get a glowing testimonial from me. If you stay, however,' he warned, solemnly, 'you'll need to treat Aelbert with a lot more respect. Start doing that now.'

Geel was sobered. He hadn't realised how much his good-natured teasing upset his older colleague. There was nothing malicious in it. Aelbert Pienaar was such a dry and lacklustre companion. While he sympathised with him over the loss of his wife, Geel could never bring himself to like the fellow because they had nothing whatsoever in common. Could he spend most of his life working under such a person? It was a moot point. Until his employer had raised the subject, Geel had never thought about his future, assuming that it was already set out. He'd continue to work for Janssen indefinitely and have the occasional thrill of talking to Amalia. Seeing her more or less every day was a positive delight and he'd hate to forfeit it. While Pienaar brought dark clouds into the house, Amalia radiated sunlight. Geel loved to bask in it. He couldn't bear to lose her.

When he heard the door open behind him, he turned round and saw Pienaar enter the workshop. Glad to be out of the cold, the newcomer looked rather forlorn. Geel manufactured a smile of welcome.

'Good morning, Aelbert,' he said, pleasantly. 'How are you today?'

Out of the corner of his eye, he saw Janssen nod in approval.

Amalia sat near the window as Beatrix brushed her mistress's hair with steady, rhythmical movements. It was late afternoon and light was fading. The servant was in a reflective mood.

'I wonder what it's like to be married,' she mused.

Amalia laughed in surprise. 'Why ever do you wonder that?'

'It's something I'll never enjoy.'

'That's not true, Beatrix.'

'My life is here and I'm happy with it. Besides, what man would look at me twice? Whenever I'm out with you, I might as well be invisible. Men only have eyes for you, Miss Amalia. They ignore me.'

'Aelbert doesn't ignore you,' Amalia pointed out, 'and neither does Nick. They both like you immensely. Nick loves chatting to you.'

'Yes,' conceded Beatrix, 'but what do we chat about? It's not me, I can tell you. The only person Nick is interested in is you. He's always asking after you. In any case,' she went on with a sigh, 'Nick is too young for me.'

'What about Aelbert?'

'He's too old – and he'd never marry a mere servant.'

'You're a lot more to me than that, Beatrix.'

'That's because I brush your hair so nicely. I can't do that for Aelbert because the poor man doesn't have any.' They both giggled. 'Oh, we shouldn't laugh at him,' said Beatrix, controlling her mirth. 'He's still mourning his wife. He doted on her.'

'And I'm sure there's someone who'd dote on you,' said Amalia. 'Given the chance, that is.'

'But they'll never *get* that chance, will they?'

'Don't give up hope.'

'That's the odd thing. I'm not sure that I have any hope.'

'I don't follow.'

'Well, I'm curious to know what being married is like, but I doubt if I'd really enjoy it. I'd hate to share my life with someone then lose them. I couldn't cope with the grief. Look at Aelbert – he'll never get over the death of his wife. And your father is the same, Miss Amalia. I know it was a long time ago but he still misses your dear mother. So do I, for that matter.'

A tear came into Amalia's eye. 'We all miss her terribly.'

'I think it will be safer for me to stay a spinster.'

'Wait until you meet the right man, Beatrix.'

'I doubt that I ever will.'

'You'd make someone a wonderful wife.'

Beatrix was upset. 'Are you saying you wish to get rid of me?'

'No, no, of course I don't.'

'I thought you were very satisfied with my work.'

'I am,' said Amalia. 'I just want what's best for you.'

'Well, I've already got that.'

Having initiated the discussion, Beatrix brought it to an abrupt end. She began to wield the brush more vigorously. Amalia sat back in the chair and said nothing. It was minutes before the silence was broken. Glancing out of the window, Beatrix suddenly froze, holding the hairbrush in mid-air. She looked hard for a few seconds at a rider coming towards the house in the twilight.

'That's him!' she cried. 'I *told* you there was someone out there. That's the strange man who's been watching the house.'

Amalia stood up to look. 'Who are you talking about?'

'The man on the horse – I recognise him.'

'So do I,' said Amalia, letting out a whoop of delight. 'It's Daniel!'

And she rushed excitedly to the front door as fast as her legs would carry her.

CHAPTER SIX

Henry Welbeck had few real friends in the regiment. His abrasive manner and unforgiving nature were more likely to create enemies. Leo Curry was both friend and enemy, allied to him as a fellow sergeant yet in constant verbal conflict with him. The mutual respect between them came and went with almost tidal regularity. With the exception of Daniel Rawson, Welbeck's closest friend was Joel Drew, a grizzled individual in his sixties with short, grey hair and a pockmarked face. Drew was a vivid illustration of the perils of warfare. He'd lost two fingers in one battle, an eye in a second and a limb in a third. Yet, though he was forced to hobble around on his wooden leg and squint at people through his one remaining eye, he had no trace of bitterness or regret. Drew considered himself to be a survivor and was eternally grateful for that. When others bemoaned lesser injuries, he could put them to shame. His cheerfulness and resilience were an example to all.

'What can I do for you today, Sergeant?' he asked.

'Try to make me look pretty,' said Welbeck.

Drew cackled. 'Even the Almighty couldn't do that. The best I can promise is to make you a little less hideous.'

'Then I'll settle for that.'

Unable to bear arms, it had never occurred to Drew to quit the army and return home. In his view, that would be a form of desertion. In spite of its vicissitudes, he enjoyed the life of a soldier. Keen to make a contribution of some sort, he became the regimental barber, cutting the hair of all and sundry with a skill that belied the fact that his eyesight was impaired. Everyone liked Drew. He was wise, experienced, good-natured and always willing to listen to the woes of others without passing judgement. A visit to the barber left people feeling better afterwards.

Welbeck sat down and removed his hat, resting it on his lap. Drew reached for his scissors. They were in a little hut where the barber had set up shop. He asked the same question that he always put to Welbeck.

'Shall I give you a shave as well, Sergeant?'

'No, thank you,' replied the other. 'Much as I trust you, I wouldn't let any man hold a razor to my throat. You know why.'

'Sergeants are never popular.'

'That's why I became one.'

'Do you enjoy being disliked?'

'What I enjoy is being *feared*.'

'Then you hold the right rank,' observed Drew, starting to snip away. 'I worship His Grace, the Duke, and I admire some of his officers, but the only person I ever feared was the black-hearted bastard of a sergeant who made my life a misery when I first joined the army.'

'Did you ever try to get revenge on him?'

'I thought about it. Then I got caught up in a skirmish and realised why he'd been such a merciless tyrant. He'd prepared me for battle. But for him, I'd have been filling my breeches at the sound of an enemy musket. As it was,' said Drew with a chuckle, 'I knew exactly what to do.'

'Did you thank the sergeant afterwards?'

'Oh, no – that would have been too much to ask.'

Welbeck laughed. He was fond of the barber and always took pleasure from his company. At the same time, he felt a twinge of discomfort whenever he saw Joel Drew, wondering if that was how *he* would one day end up. When his fighting days were over, would he become a philosophical old soldier like Drew and find a means of making himself useful in the army? Was that the fate that awaited Welbeck? It was not one that appealed to him. Dismissing such thoughts from his mind, he talked about the prospects for the campaign season and the two of them speculated at length about the resources of the French army.

'We kicked every last turd out of them at Oudenarde,' recalled Drew as if he'd actually fought in the battle, 'and we did the same at the siege of Lille. I don't think King Louis will be able to put a proper army in the field again.'

'Oh, I fancy that he will,' said Welbeck.

'He hasn't got the stomach for a fight anymore.'

'It's not Louis who does the fighting, Joel. It's his soldiers. And no matter how many of them we kill, he somehow manages to recruit more.'

'How can he afford to pay for them? Everyone says that France is bankrupt.'

'So am I but that won't stop me fighting.'

Drew cackled again then stood back to admire his work. He put a hand under Welbeck's chin so that he could tilt his head slightly to the left. As he snipped on, hair fell to the floor and was deftly flicked aside by the barber's wooden leg. They were still chatting happily away when another customer arrived. Welbeck's lip curled.

'What do you want?' he demanded.

'I'm here for the same thing as you, Sergeant,' said Ben Plummer, chirpily. 'Just because we're idle, it doesn't mean we can't be smart.'

'Who told you that?'

'As a matter of fact, *you* did.'

'I'm glad to hear that you actually listened to me for once.'

'I always listen to you, Sergeant,' said Plummer. 'When I first enlisted, you drummed it into us that we had to have self-respect.'

'That's quite right,' Drew put in. 'Self-respect is everything.'

'Having a haircut is part of it – like washing and shaving every day.'

Plummer had changed. He was a tall, gangly man in his thirties with a jaunty air about him. He hadn't volunteered for the army but saw it as the lesser of two evils. Instead of being imprisoned for living off the proceeds of prostitution, he'd accepted the alternative of joining the army. When he'd first met Welbeck, he'd made the mistake of answering back and had his two front teeth knocked out by the sergeant. Yet it hadn't entirely cured him of impudence or wiped the smirk off his face. The change had come in his appearance. He'd joined the army with tousled hair and a tufted beard. Plummer was now clean-shaven and made periodic visits to Joel Drew for a haircut. He prided himself on his smartness.

'Disappear!' ordered Welbeck.

'But I'm a customer,' argued Plummer.

'Come back when I'm gone. I'm not having you watching me.'

Plummer grinned. 'But I'm trying to pattern myself on you, Sergeant, and that means I have to study you.' He scurried out of reach as Welbeck swung a fist at him. 'You see? You taught me to move fast in the event of attack.'

'If you don't vanish, I'll teach you what it's like to have a boot wedged up your backside. Make yourself scarce, you mangy cur!'

'To hear is to obey.'

Plummer's sarcasm got Welbeck off his chair but the kick he aimed at him was well wide of the mark. Sniggering aloud, Plummer had already jumped clear. With a wave of farewell to both men, he left the hut.

'He's a lively fellow, that one,' opined Drew.

'He's far too lively for my taste, Joel.'

'I like a man who's got plenty to say for himself.'

'That depends what he says.' Welbeck sat down again.

'Ben Plummer always has a smile and that goes a long way with me. Most of the people who sit in that chair are so gloomy. All I hear from them is a list of complaints about this, that and the other damned thing. Plummer is different,' said Drew. 'Nothing seems to bother him. And although he's only a private soldier on low pay, he always gives me twice what he's asked.'

Welbeck was pensive. 'Now why does he do that, I wonder?'

'It's because he's pleased with his haircut, of course. Why else?'

'You don't know Plummer as well as I do,' said Welbeck, grimly. 'I've had trouble with him from the start. So when he takes care with his appearance and is generous with money, I'm bound to ask one simple question.'

'And what's that, Sergeant?'

'What exactly is the cunning swine up to?'

Daniel was given an enthusiastic welcome at the Janssen household. He collected a kiss and a loving embrace from Amalia, a warm handshake from her father, a friendly greeting from the three assistants in the workshop and a collective smile from the servants. Beatrix claimed a kiss of her own. Janssen used his arrival as an excuse to break off work an hour early and to send Pienaar and Geel home. Kees Dopff remained and joined the family for a celebratory meal, gazing at Daniel with undisguised admiration. Seated beside his assistant, Janssen knew better than to press their visitor about his movements since they'd last seen him. Prompted by a need for discretion, Daniel would say little about any secret assignment on which he'd been and – for fear of upsetting Amalia – he'd be careful never to reveal the true extent of any dangers he'd encountered. He was thrilled to be back in Amsterdam again, all the more so because he was enjoying a delicious meal in comfortable surroundings and because he was sitting close enough to Amalia to feel the brush of her arm against his.

'I understand that the tapestry is now complete,' he said.

'Yes,' replied Janssen. 'It's ready for delivery.'

'His Grace sent me to inspect it.'

'And I thought you came to see me,' said Amalia with mock annoyance. 'Since when do I take second place to a tapestry?'

'You'd never do so in my mind,' Daniel assured her. 'When the Battle of Ramillies is no longer sitting in the workshop, I'll still keep coming here with the same urgency.' Amalia was pacified. 'But how have you all been in this cold weather?'

Amalia and her father issued a whole stream of complaints, supplemented by Dopff's graphic gestures. Evidently, they'd suffered great inconvenience and continued frustration. Daniel was sympathetic. He'd met with far worse conditions in Paris but chose to say nothing about them.

'How long can you stay?' asked Amalia.

'I'll be here for a few days at least,' he said.

Her face fell. 'Is that all?'

'His Grace will expect a report, Amalia.'

'Then send him one by messenger.'

'I *am* the messenger.'

'You can tell him you were held up by impassable roads.'

Daniel smiled. 'I'd never lie to His Grace,' he said, 'but I don't think he'd mind if I stayed here a week. He's very much aware that Amsterdam holds a lot more for me than your father's tapestry.'

It was not only the chance of seeing Amalia that made him repair to the city with such alacrity. Daniel's mother was Dutch. He'd still been a boy when his English father,

Nathan Rawson, had joined the Monmouth Rebellion and fought against royal forces at the battle of Sedgemoor. In the wake of defeat, he'd been hanged along with many other rebels and his farm had been confiscated. Daniel and his mother had fled to Amsterdam and it was there that he'd grown to maturity. The city therefore occupied a special place in his heart and, whenever he was there, he made a point of visiting his mother's grave. She'd died with an implacable hatred of the Duke of Marlborough because – as Major-General John, Lord Churchill – he'd been one of the commanders of the royal army at Sedgemoor. Juliana Rawson would never have been able to accept the fact that her son now served a man who'd been indirectly responsible for the death of her husband. It was as well that she'd passed away before Daniel joined the British army.

'How was the journey here?' asked Janssen.

'Long and tiresome,' replied Daniel.

'The whole country seems to have ground to a halt.'

'It's just as bad in The Hague as here. There's no sign of a thaw.'

'We must count our blessings,' said Amalia. 'We have a roof over our heads and warm fires to sit beside. Some people lack both. There are tales of poor devils being found in shop doorways, frozen to death.'

Daniel thought of the frozen soldier and his horse.

'Let's not dwell on such things,' suggested Janssen. 'Daniel is here at last and we should savour his visit. The tapestry can wait until tomorrow when it can be seen properly in the daylight. This evening must be given over to merriment.'

Dopff agreed heartily, thumping the table with a fist in approbation. He knew how much Daniel's arrival would lift the whole household and he never forgot the way in which their visitor had risked life and limb to sneak them safely out of Paris when there was an extensive manhunt for them. They ate, drank and revelled in each other's company for several hours. Dopff was the first to retire to bed and Janssen soon followed. Ordinarily, Beatrix would have come into the room to act as a chaperone but Daniel was trusted sufficiently to be left alone with Amalia. As they sat beside each other in the parlour, he held both her hands.

'You look more beautiful than ever,' he said, softly.

'I thought you only came to see the Battle of Ramillies,' she teased.

'I saw far too much of it when it was actually raging, Amalia. I was at His Grace's side for much of the time, so I had a perfect view of what was happening. I can tell you this,' he added, squeezing her hands, 'I'd much prefer to enjoy a perfect view of Amalia Janssen. It's far less perilous.'

She laughed. 'Thank you, Daniel. Have you missed me?'

'You're never out of my thoughts.'

'I've spent every day wondering where you are.'

'That's reassuring to hear.'

'Surely, you don't doubt me?' she said.

'Not for a second,' he promised her, 'and I hope you don't doubt me.'

'I just wish we could spend more time together.'

'Only the needs of war keep us apart. One day, it will be different.'

'One day – God willing!' Looking into her eyes, he tightened his grip on her hands. She wanted to melt into his arms and gave him an inviting smile, moving closer to him as she did so. Daniel was about to embrace her when Beatrix came into the parlour.

'It's wonderful to have you here again, Captain Rawson,' she said, effusively. 'The whole house seems suddenly warmer as a result. It's an omen. Winter is at last coming to an end.'

'Yes,' he said, drawing back reluctantly from Amalia, 'I believe that it is.'

Dopff had been dumb from birth but there was nothing wrong with his hearing. If anything, it was more sensitive than that of the average person. He had a bedchamber at the back of the house and above the workshop. As a rule, he slept soundly but something brought him abruptly awake that night. Not knowing what it was, he sat bolt upright in bed and blinked his eyes. Telling himself that it must have been a dream, he lay down under the blankets again and was soon slumbering peacefully. Ten minutes later, he was awake again and this time he had an inkling of what had prompted him. There were noises from below, faint but discernible noises. They might, of course, be made by Janssen who could have had reason to retrieve something from the workshop. Dopff had known occasions when his master had actually worked through the night by the light of candles. He wouldn't be doing so now. It was far too cold.

There had to be some other explanation. Getting out of bed, Dopff went to the window but it was frosted on the outside and he could see nothing through it. He therefore wrapped a blanket around his shoulders and groped for the candle. Because his hands were shaking so much, it took a moment to ignite it. Shivering all over, he let himself out and crept along the landing. The house seemed eerily calm. He felt somehow threatened, as if a ghost had come to haunt them and was playing games with him. Timid by nature, Dopff was tempted to return to his room and bolt the door, but loyalty to Janssen drove him on. He'd been given work, a home and unstinting affection by his master and could never fully repay him. The least that he could do was to investigate strange noises in the night.

Working his way through the various rooms, he came to the workshop and paused. No sounds came from within but he felt a draught from under the door. Surely, nobody had been foolish enough to leave a window open in there. It was inconceivable. He unlocked the door and let himself in. Almost immediately, a gust of wind blew out his candle and left him in darkness. He knew at once what had happened and it made his blood curdle. Dopff had discovered an appalling crime. Thieves had broken in and left the back door wide open.

The precious tapestry of the Battle of Ramillies had been stolen.

'Stolen!' Marlborough looked at the letter in utter despair. 'My tapestry has been stolen? Who could've done such a thing?'

'We have many enemies, Your Grace,' said Cardonnel.

'Yes, but what malign impulse can be served by such a dreadful act?'

'Someone wishes to stop you glorying in your victory.'

'It was hard won, Adam. We're entitled to take pleasure from it.'

'Does the letter give any details?'

'None at all – that's what's so maddening.'

Daniel had written to Marlborough to apprise him of the crime and to assure him that he'd do everything in his power to solve it. Marlborough's fears were not allayed. He believed that anyone determined to rob him of the delight of looking at a lasting memorial of his triumph would probably destroy the tapestry. It could be woven again but that would take an age and Marlborough was anxious to see it hanging in Blenheim Palace. His wife had seen the design for the tapestry when Janssen had shown it to her and she'd given it her approval. Marlborough knew just how difficult she was to please. As he realised that he'd now have to pass on the terrible news to her, his stomach lurched.

Reading his mind, Cardonnel was quick to supply a suggestion.

'There's no reason why Her Grace should learn of this yet,' he said.

'It can't be kept from her indefinitely.'

'Why not wait until we know that it's beyond recall?'

'Instinct tells me that it already is, Adam,' said Marlborough, disconsolately. 'Whoever took it must have planned the crime with care. They'd know where to dispose of it and they'd do so quickly.'

'You can't be certain of that,' argued Cardonnel.

'I was so looking forward to taking it back to England with me.'

'Have more faith in Daniel Rawson, Your Grace. If anyone can retrieve the tapestry, it's the good captain. He knows Amsterdam well. He'll look into every nook and cranny until he finds it.'

Marlborough shook his head. 'All that he'll find are the charred remains.'

'There's something you're not considering.'

'What's that?'

'Well,' said Cardonnel, thoughtfully, 'this may be nothing whatsoever to do with enemy spite. Supposing that the tapestry was stolen by common thieves? In that event, what would they do?'

'They'd have to sell it to make any profit from the crime.'

'But who would possibly buy it? It's worthless to anybody but you. I don't believe it's been destroyed at all. Why go to such trouble if there's to be no pecuniary advantage?'

Marlborough frowned. 'I'm not sure that I understand you, Adam.'

'It's quite simple, Your Grace,' said Cardonnel. 'Since the one person who really wants it is *you*, the thieves will probably offer to sell it to you.'

Marlborough was stunned. The notion implied a violent assault on his purse.

'Sell me my own property?' he yelled in outrage. 'I'm not going to pay twice for the same thing. That would be insupportable. No thief is going to make money out of a battle in which so many of our brave soldiers gave their lives.' Snapping his fingers, he pointed to the table. 'Write to Captain Rawson at once. Tell him that it's imperative he somehow retrieves the tapestry. He can act with my full authority. I want the Battle of Ramillies back in my possession and I want the rogues who dared to steal it dangling by the neck from a rope.'

Daniel was as shaken as anyone at the disappearance of the tapestry. His immediate response had been to search for clues and possible witnesses. The tapestry was large and heavy. It would have taken at least three men to carry it and a cart would have been needed to take it away. Daniel knocked on the doors of all the neighbouring houses and asked if anyone had heard or seen anything on the previous night. But his efforts were in vain. No help was forthcoming. Janssen was heartbroken. Nothing he'd ever created had given him more pride and pleasure. Endless months of work had gone into it. Yet it had vanished into thin air. He had large posters printed and put them up in strategic places. Janssen was ready to offer a substantial amount of his own money for information that led to the capture of the thieves and the return of his tapestry. He was mortified when nobody came forward. Amalia had never seen him look so despondent. The shock was making her father ill.

After days of fruitless effort, Daniel reached a conclusion.

'The thieves had an accomplice,' he told Amalia. 'They were helped by someone under this roof.'

'That's impossible,' she said, hotly. 'Nobody would dare to betray Father.'

'I'm not saying he was a willing accomplice. It's just that he unwittingly helped the villains. How did they know that such an important and valuable tapestry was here in the first place?'

'They couldn't have known, Daniel.'

'Exactly,' he said. 'Apart from your father, only Kees, Aelbert and Nick knew what they'd been working on and when it would be finished. The thieves bided their time until they knew it was complete.'

'Kees is dumb so we can exclude him at once.'

'Then it has to be either Aelbert or Nick. One of them has a loose tongue.'

'In that case, it must be Nick. Aelbert is laconic at the best of times. He prefers a quiet life. It's Nick who visits a tavern from time to time.'

'Doesn't your father warn him not to talk about his work?'

'Yes,' said Amalia, 'he insists on privacy and all who work for him have sworn to maintain it. Somehow, one of them – Nick, most likely – let it slip out. He'll be cursing himself for doing that.'

'Not if he can remember when and where it happened,' said Daniel. 'If Nick can recall the name of the tavern and the day when he talked about his work, the landlord may be able to remember who else was there on that occasion. Winter's been bad for business. If he had few customers when Nick Geel was there, the landlord should be able to give us their names.'

Amalia was rueful. 'I should've paid more attention to Beatrix.'

'Why?'

'She said that someone was watching the house. I didn't believe her.'

'It proves that nobody here was in league with the thieves,' decided Daniel. 'If they had been, there'd have been no need to take stock of the place and to find out where the workshop actually was. A real accomplice would simply have told them.'

'That's a point,' said Amalia, relieved that the assistants were absolved of any suspicion of being directly involved. 'What will you do, Daniel?'

'I'll speak to each of them in turn – Nick first and then Aelbert.'

'They're both as upset as Father. And so is Kees, of course. He was the one who discovered what had happened. It almost made him sick on the spot.'

'That's understandable.'

Since the crime had come to light, there'd been no activity in the workshop. Janssen had sent two of his assistants back home. The other one, Dopff, was moping in his room, blaming himself for not coming downstairs earlier on the fateful night. Yet nothing had ever been stolen from the workshop before and there'd been no cause to believe that the tapestry was in any danger.

'What do we do?' asked Amalia. 'Do we report the theft to a magistrate?'

'Oh, no,' Daniel said, firmly. 'We don't want the authorities involved. I'll continue to lead my own investigation. One thing is certain – the tapestry is still in Amsterdam.'

'How do you know that?'

'I rode here from The Hague, remember. It was difficult enough on horseback. You'd never get a cart along some of those roads. It's here, Amalia. Someone has hidden it away and I mean to find it.'

'Amsterdam is a big city. You can't search every house.'

'I can eliminate large numbers of them, Amalia. The crime was the work of practised thieves. They got in and out without disturbing anyone except Kees. The vast majority of citizens here are decent and law-abiding. I need to search the haunts of criminals.'

'They could be dangerous, Daniel,' she said, worriedly. 'You're one man against at least three. Are you sure you should be doing this entirely on your own?'

'No,' he admitted, 'I'm not sure. That's why I've sent for help. I've asked Henry Welbeck to come here. He'll jump at the chance to escape the privations of winter quarters. That will make it two against three or four,' he went on with a grin, 'so the odds have tilted very much in our favour.'

They were in the parlour of the Janssen house. So absorbed were they in their discussion that they didn't see a figure walk past the window. Nor did they hear anything being slipped under the front door. It was minutes later when Janssen came in, holding a letter and looking perplexed.

'Beatrix has just given me this,' he said. 'It was put under the front door by someone who obviously didn't want to be seen.'

'Why do you say that, Father?' asked Amalia.

'I think it's from *them*.' He held the letter out so that they could see the names on it. 'It's addressed to me *and* to the Duke of Marlborough. I think you'd better open it on His Grace's behalf, Daniel,' he added, passing the missive over. 'I daren't.'

He watched with trepidation as Daniel opened the letter and read it.

'Your instinct is sound,' said Daniel. 'This is from the

thieves. They're offering you the chance to buy back the tapestry for what looks like a king's ransom.'

Janssen gulped. 'What if we refuse?'

'Then they'll destroy it completely.'

Letting out a cry of pain, Janssen clutched his chest and collapsed to the floor.

Chapter Seven

The Duke of Marlborough was known for his iron self-control and his calm under fire. In the heat of battle, nothing could upset his equanimity. Other commanders could be driven into a panic or forced to make hasty and ill-considered decisions. Marlborough remained aloof from them. With a mingled spite and envy, his enemies accused him of having ice in his veins. Yet there was no sign of that ice now. As he paced up and down like a caged animal, his blood was boiling. Seated at the table, Cardonnel tried to soothe him.

'There's nothing we can do except wait,' he said, reasonably.

'Yes, there is, Adam,' insisted Marlborough, rounding on him. 'We can head for Amsterdam this instant and take charge of proceedings.'

'What purpose would that serve, Your Grace?'

'It would rid me of this debilitating sense of impotence.'

'You're needed here.'

'Not when my tapestry has been stolen.'

'We're dining with our host this evening and you have an appointment with Grand Pensionary Heinsius tomorrow. It could be a significant meeting.'

'Have it postponed.'

'I'd strongly advise against it.'

'For heaven's sake!' snapped Marlborough. 'Do as you're told, man.'

Cardonnel inclined his head. 'Of course, Your Grace.'

Marlborough repented immediately. He never raised his voice in anger at his secretary and had no call to do so now. Cardonnel was irreplaceable. He was the son of Huguenot refugees driven out of France, so he was deeply committed to the war against Louis XIV and all that the French king represented. The secretary had given such invaluable service that Marlborough hoped one day to reward him with high political office when his own influence back in England was strong enough. To berate Cardonnel for offering sensible advice was grossly unfair.

'A thousand pardons, Adam,' said Marlborough with a placatory hand on his secretary's shoulder. 'You are, as ever, quite correct. I have responsibilities here in the Dutch capital. Please forgive my unwarranted outburst.'

'I understand and share your frustration.'

'I know and I'm ashamed I spoke so harshly. But this business is like a dagger in my breast. It gives me no respite.'

'Would charging off to Amsterdam ease the pain?' asked Cardonnel.

'It might.'

'I think not, Your Grace. What could you actually do? This is a not a military situation. Leadership of the kind you offer is not required. I venture to suggest – and I do so with all humility – that you might actually hinder the process of retrieving the tapestry.'

Marlborough flopped into a chair. 'You could be right,' he agreed, taking off his periwig and dropping it on the table, where it lay like a dead spaniel. 'It's just so infuriating to think that someone has stolen my property in order to exact a vast amount of money out of me.'

'We don't know that for certain yet.'

'It's a logical possibility and you were the one to point it out.'

'Thieves seek profit. How else would they achieve it?'

'Quite so, quite so . . .' Marlborough scratched his head. 'I'm terrified at the thought of having to communicate all this to my wife. She has an obsession with money. This predicament will bring her untold grief.'

'Then it's best that Her Grace remains unaware of it.'

'I cannot, in all conscience, hide the truth from her for ever.'

'No,' said Cardonnel, 'I accept that. But it's surely better to send her good news to soften the bad. Who knows? That good news may even now be on its way from Amsterdam. Captain Rawson will not have been sitting on his hands. He's a man of action.'

'That's true. He won't rest until the matter is resolved. Poor Daniel!' he sighed. 'He went there in order to spend time with his beloved. Instead of that, he has to search for a missing tapestry and catch the thieves who stole it. Trouble does seem to have a habit of finding work for him.'

'I think he relishes that, Your Grace.'

'Then the best thing to do is to leave him to it. I'd only get under his feet if I went haring up there. On the other hand,' he said, voice hardening, 'I wish to make one thing clear. In no circumstances will I be prepared to buy back a tapestry from these villains. Draft a letter to that effect. Daniel Rawson must do all he can to retrieve it – but at no financial cost to me.'

Nicholaes Geel was slightly alarmed when Daniel called on him, wondering what his visitor could possibly want. The assistant lived with his parents in a pleasant, narrow-fronted house in the suburbs. He conducted Daniel to the parlour and waved him to a seat. Offered refreshment, Daniel declined it. He told Geel about the demand from the thieves and of its effect on Janssen.

Geel was concerned. 'The master is ill in bed?'

'It's just a precaution, Nick. His nerves are frayed.'

'May I see him?'

'Leave it for a few days. He needs rest. Let me tell you why I'm here,' Daniel went on. 'I'm trying to establish how the thieves *knew* that the tapestry existed and when it was likely to be completed. Somebody must have told them.'

'You're not accusing me, are you?' asked Geel, face reddening. 'I swear to you that I'd never associate with criminals, least of all if they had designs on our tapestry. I'd die rather than do that, Captain Rawson.'

'I'm sure that you would. But there's a difference between acting as an accomplice and inadvertently giving away information. Did you, for instance, ever mention to your friends what you were working on?'

'No, I didn't.'

'What about someone you may have met in a tavern?'

'I'd never divulge secrets to a stranger.'

'Drink can dull our brains sometimes, Nick. When we've had too much of it, we don't always know what we say. Think back. Has there been any occasion recently when you had more than usual?'

'Well,' admitted Geel, 'I did help to celebrate a friend's birthday two weeks ago and I suppose that we did stay drinking until very late.'

'There's no disgrace in that,' said Daniel. 'We've all done it.'

'I had such a headache the following day.'

'Where did you celebrate?'

'It was at the White Swan.'

'And were any strangers there at the time?'

'Yes, I think that there were.'

'So you could – just *could* – have made some incautious remarks about your work on the tapestry and about your illustrious client.'

'It's possible, I suppose. I don't remember.'

'What about your parents? You've told them, I assume.'

'The master forbade it,' said Geel. 'He doesn't like anyone to know details of what we do in the workshop. My parents accept that. They never ask.'

Daniel appraised him. Geel was patently telling the truth. He would never deliberately betray secrets and was horrified to think that he might have done so when he was inebriated. The idea that he might actually have been, to some extent, a culprit made him shudder. Daniel felt sorry for him. Geel was young and impetuous but would have had no cause to boast about his work when he was celebrating the birthday of a friend. It was the friend who would've been the centre of attention that evening.

Daniel changed tack. 'Tell me a little about Aelbert Pienaar.'

'Why?' asked Geel, defensively.

'I have the feeling that you don't altogether like him.'

'Aelbert is an expert at what he does. I admire him greatly.'

'That's not the same thing as liking him, Nick. I could be wrong, of course. Over the years, I've not seen much of either of you. Whenever I *have* been here, however, I've sensed that there's some animosity between you.'

'Well, it's not on my side, Captain Rawson.'

'Has Aelbert been unkind to you or crossed you in some way?'

'No, no – he's too wrapped up in himself.'

'Do you resent that?' pressed Daniel. 'Does it annoy you that he's preoccupied with his own concerns? Do you feel shut out?'

Geel pondered. 'Yes,' he said, eventually, 'I think I do.'

'And how do you respond to that?'

'I taunt him sometimes.'

'From what I've seen of Aelbert, I don't imagine he'd like that.'

'No, Captain Rawson,' said Geel, shamefacedly. 'He doesn't. It hurts him.' He forced a smile. 'But I'm doing my best to be more considerate to him now.'

Daniel waited a few moments before asking his final question.

'Do you think that Aelbert Pienaar could have

accidentally given away details of the tapestry on which you were working?'

Geel was positive. 'No,' he said. 'Aelbert is too secretive by nature.'

Unhappy at being off work and wondering if there'd been any developments, Pienaar called at the Janssen house and was disturbed to learn that his employer was in bed. He was permitted to spend a little time with him and was upset to see the state that he was in. Gaunt and hollow-eyed, Janssen looked as if he was seriously ill and not simply recovering from a bad shock. Pienaar was interested to hear that the thieves had made contact and took comfort from the fact that the tapestry had so far been undamaged. At the same time, however, he doubted if Marlborough would bow to their demands. Even though he coveted his tapestry, the captain-general would surely never reward thievery. It would be against his principles. Having come to the house, Pienaar couldn't resist looking in the workshop. The room seemed so empty and forlorn, its looms silent, its prize possession taken. It was so much more than a place of work to him. It was a second home. Since the loss of his wife, he'd found great solace there. Work was his escape from the brutal realities of life, a tiny world in which he could lose himself and gain a sense of worth. There were irritations, naturally. He wished that Geel was not so talkative and that the workshop was not quite so cold. He also wished that he could stay there for longer hours so that he didn't have to return so early to a house that held painful memories. But these were minor matters. Nothing could compare with the pleasure of working for Emanuel Janssen and producing exquisite tapestries. It gave his life direction and it made him feel wanted.

He went across to Janssen's loom and ran a hand over the smooth timber. It was a paradox that such an ugly and cumbersome machine could create such beauty. A thought popped into his mind and he glanced upwards. If Janssen died – and this latest illness might be a precursor to that – then Pienaar would take charge. His inheritance had been promised in word and confirmed in writing. He loved Janssen far too much to want him to die but the possibility had to be taken into account. What would he do if and when he took over? How could he continue the noble tradition that had been established there? Who could he hire to work on Janssen's vacant loom? Surmounting all these questions was an even more important one. What would he do with Nicholaes Geel?

For the first time in years, Pienaar actually smiled.

Leo Curry didn't recognise him at first. When Henry Welbeck rode towards him in civilian clothing, the sergeant had to look twice to be certain who it was. Welbeck reined in his horse beside the other man.

'Are you trying to desert us, Henry?' asked Curry, jocularly.

'I'd never desert you, Leo. You're the joy of my existence.'

'You've called me a lot worse than that in the past.'

'And I'll probably do so again in the future.'

'Why are you dressed like an undertaker's bloody assistant and sitting on horseback? I thought you hated riding.'

'I do,' said Welbeck, 'but I've urgent business to attend to in Amsterdam.'

'Oh? What is it?'

'I won't know until I get there. Captain Rawson summoned me.'

'Would you like some company on the way?'

'Your place is here, Leo. Someone has to keep the camp in order.'

Curry beamed. 'Unlike you, I do the job properly.'

'That's only because you copy me,' said Welbeck, accusingly. 'You're the laziest sergeant in the whole bleeding regiment. If they gave medals for idling, you'd have rows of them on your chest.'

'I'm never idle!' bellowed Curry. 'I work as hard as any man.'

'The only time you exert yourself is when you open your bowels in the latrine. You'd be useless without me to help you.'

'I don't need your help for anything,' retorted the other, bristling.

'You couldn't find your own prick if I didn't tell you where it was.'

'Get down off that fucking horse and say that again.'

'I don't have the time.'

'In other words, you're too scared.'

'Yes,' said Welbeck, enjoying the exchange, 'I'd be too scared to do you serious damage. You're no match for me, Leo. I'd have you flat on your back in seconds then I'd piss all over you for good measure.'

'Get out of that saddle!' roared Curry.

'Duty calls, I fear. I must obey. It must be something

really important. That's why Dan Rawson sent for me, not for you.'

'He chose you because you're the one who licks his fucking boots.'

'He wants someone he can rely on and not a buffoon like you.'

'I'm not a buffoon!'

'Try looking in a mirror.'

'For two pennies, I'd drag you off that horse,' warned Curry.

Welbeck grinned. 'Pennies are not legal tender in Holland.'

'Don't tempt me, Henry.'

'Then stop being so bleeding stupid.'

Curry brandished a fist. 'You're asking for it, aren't you?'

'Not at all,' said Welbeck, patting him soothingly on the head. 'I only rode this way to bid you a fond farewell. I may be gone for some time.'

'Well, I hope you bloody well stay away.'

'I couldn't do that, Leo. I'd miss you too much.'

'The 24th won't miss you, I can tell you that.'

Welbeck grinned again. 'Won't I get a fanfare when I get back?'

'Not from me,' said Curry before spitting on the ground. 'Good bloody riddance, I say! A sergeant who can't control his men is no fucking use to me.'

'I rule them with a rod of iron.'

'Not all of them – you ask Private Plummer.'

'Why?' Welbeck was checked. 'What's Ben been doing?'

'He's been bothering my men,' explained Curry, 'and I don't take kindly to that. It's the second time I've caught him at it. If there's a third, I'll cut his balls off and feed them back to him in a bowl of porridge.'

Welbeck became serious. Discipline was his watchword. Most of his men were too frightened to disobey him. The few who ignored his strictures suffered severe retribution as a result. After that they soon fell into line. Ben Plummer had been a troublemaker ever since he'd joined the army. Even the horrors of the siege of Lille hadn't tamed him. He was too clever to provoke Welbeck to extremes but he knew how to sting the sergeant from time to time. If Plummer was wandering all over the camp, Welbeck wanted to know why.

'Why was he bothering your men, Leo?' he asked.

'It was because you let the clever bastard off the leash.'

'Did you kick his scrawny arse for him?'

'I was too slow to catch him,' admitted Curry, 'but I'll get him next time. Perhaps you should hurry back to camp, after all. I'm sure you wouldn't want to miss Ben Plummer's funeral.'

Curry stalked off, leaving Welbeck to kick his horse into action. As he rode away, he was troubled. It was an article of faith with him that his men didn't let him down. Plummer was clearly doing that and giving a rival sergeant an opportunity to crow over Welbeck. It was a long ride to Amsterdam. He'd have plenty of time to brood on a suitable punishment for the wayward private.

Since they'd had no children, Pienaar and his wife had lived in a relatively modest house. When he was admitted by a servant, Daniel was struck by its total lack of colour. A man who worked with vivid silks and wool of many hues occupied a rather bland environment. Even the paintings on the walls had a pallid look to them. Daniel was shown into the parlour. Pienaar joined him, surprised at the visit but glad to see him. After they had shaken hands, they took a seat opposite each other.

'How is he?' asked Pienaar with genuine concern.

'He's having another day in bed.'

'When I called to see him yesterday, he looked dreadful.'

'The theft of the tapestry has hit him hard, Aelbert.'

'It's hit us all, Captain Rawson. It was so unexpected. That's why we took no special measures to protect it. Oh, if only we'd done that!'

'It's too late to worry about it now,' said Daniel. 'The doors of the workshop have been reinforced. It won't be so easy to get into the property again.'

'Why exactly are you here?'

'I came to ask you the same question that I put to Nick Geel.'

Pienaar stiffened. 'You went to see Nicholaes first?'

'Yes, I did.'

'But I'm senior to him.'

'Rank doesn't come into this, Aelbert. There's no significance in my talking to him first.' Daniel could see that he was peeved. 'What I put to him was this. In order for someone to steal the tapestry, they had to know that it existed and was about to be completed. Do you agree?'

'I do, Captain Rawson.'

'Neither of you would knowingly reveal such information – you're both too loyal to do that – but it might have come out in an unguarded moment.'

'I don't *have* unguarded moments,' said Pienaar, sharply.

'Everyone else does.'

'I am not everyone else.'

'Your friends are bound to be curious about your work.'

'I've told them that I never discuss it. Besides, I have a very small circle of friends.' He pursed his lips. 'It's even smaller since I lost my wife. Several people seem to have drifted out of my life. A single man doesn't have as many invitations as a married couple. That suits me,' he went on, chin up. 'I prefer to be alone.'

'But even you must have a social life of some kind, Aelbert.'

'So?'

'Has there been a convivial occasion recently?'

'I try to avoid such things.'

'Don't you like a drink from time to time?'

'Yes – but only in the privacy of my own home.'

'Presumably, you invite friends here and offer them a beverage.'

'That's enough, Captain Rawson!' shouted Pienaar, simmering with righteous indignation. 'I can see what you're getting at and I find it insulting. First of all, I have never in my entire life got so drunk that I don't know what I'm saying. Secondly, I don't number common thieves among my friends. Even if I did mistakenly pass on information about my work, they wouldn't use it to plot against me and my employer. Thirdly – and this is something you must bear in mind – Emanuel Janssen is my friend. He's without a peer in the whole of Europe. I idolise the man. I may only have been working for him for a short time but I spent fifteen years waiting for the opportunity to do so. Given all that,' he added, veins standing out on his temples, 'do you *really* think that I'd stoop to betray my master?'

Daniel held up both palms. 'No, Aelbert, I never thought that for a moment.'

'Then why come bothering me?'

'I have to explore every avenue.'

'Talk to the servants. One of them might be the culprit.'

'I've already done that,' said Daniel, 'and I'm satisfied that they're completely innocent. Like you, they're sworn to secrecy. So, of course, is Amalia.'

'Then the finger must point at Nicholaes.'

'He swears that he's revealed nothing about the tapestry.'

Pienaar was unconvinced. 'That's what he'll say when he's sober.'

'Do you have some reason to doubt his honesty?'

'No, he's very honest. I grant him that.'

'Yet you still have reservation in your voice,' noted Daniel.

'Nicholaes has many good qualities,' said Pienaar, choosing his words with care. 'He's a fine craftsman and he works hard. In fact, there have been times when he's worked rather too hard. The strain has been too much for him.'

'In what way?'

'He's needed to bolster his spirits, Captain Rawson.'

Daniel guessed his meaning. 'He took strong drink to work with him?'

'I caught him swigging from a bottle when he thought I wasn't looking. It's strictly forbidden. If the master had known about it, Nicholaes would've been in serious trouble.'

'Didn't you report him?'

'I don't carry tales,' said Pienaar, piously. 'I gave him a

stern warning instead. Since then, he's behaved himself.'

'So it was a solitary incident?'

'No – it just happened to be the first time it came to my notice. He admitted that there'd been other occasions, when the master and I were absent. Can you hear what I'm telling you, Captain Rawson?' he continued. 'Nicholaes has a weakness. My suspicion is that someone may have exploited it.'

'That's a possibility,' conceded Daniel.

'Look at him and not at me. There's no need to come knocking at my door. I have no such weakness. I'd never dream of turning to drink to get me through the working day. I have too much self-respect.'

'I can see that, Aelbert.'

'May I be candid?'

'Please do.'

Pienaar took a deep breath before speaking. 'The very fact that you felt the need to question me on this matter is offensive. It was unnecessary and I found it deeply unpleasant. I'll thank you not to come here again.' He wagged a finger. 'In short, please remove my name from your list of suspects right now. It ought never to have been there in the first place. You've disappointed me, Captain Rawson. I took you for a shrewder man than you are. Remember this.' His eyes blazed for a second. 'I am wholly above suspicion.'

After offering him a polite apology, Daniel excused himself and left the house. The keen air encouraged him to walk briskly. On the journey back to the Janssen house, he had much to reflect on. The real surprise was that Aelbert Pienaar had some fire in his belly. Daniel had never seen any hint of it before. In the past, Pienaar had always been quiet and withdrawn yet there was clearly another side to the man. He had a temper and it was instantly roused by the suggestion that he might unwittingly have provided information about the tapestry to the people who subsequently stole it. Pienaar's defence of himself had been strong and impassioned. Daniel had admired him for speaking out. There was only one problem. Though the man had claimed to be wholly above suspicion, Daniel didn't believe him. Something told him that Aelbert Pienaar would repay close investigation.

Someone who protested his innocence so fiercely had something to hide.

Chapter Eight

Emanuel Janssen couldn't be kept away from work for long. Even though he was still visibly unwell, he insisted on dragging himself out of bed and returning to his normal routine, arguing that that was the best possible medicine for him. Geel and Pienaar were both pleased to resume work after the brief suspension. While they were alarmed to see how frail their employer looked, they understood how important it was for him to be there instead of fretting in bed. It was during a break in work that the three of them were able to have a proper discussion at last.

'How do you feel?' asked Pienaar, solicitously.

'I'm fine, Aelbert,' said Janssen with a weak smile. 'Work is my lifeblood.'

'You mustn't strive too hard.'

'That's what my daughter keeps telling me.'

'She must be very anxious about you,' said Geel, seeing

a chance to talk about Amalia. 'I can't ever remember you taking to your bed before. How did Miss Amalia react when it happened?'

'She feared that I was at death's door.'

'Poor woman – she must have suffered.'

'I'm stronger than I seem, Nick.'

'That's a relief,' said Pienaar.

'The shock of that letter was dreadful. It hit me like a violent blow.'

'What are you going to do about it?'

'Well, there's no way that I can raise the amount of money they demand,' said Janssen. 'I'd have to sell my house and borrow from friends to do that.'

'The Duke of Marlborough could afford it,' Geel put in. 'By all accounts, he's a very wealthy man.'

'That's beside the point, Nick. In theory, he *could* pay but Captain Rawson assures me that he'd never do so. If he can stand up to a whole French army, His Grace is not going to give in to the demands of a few Dutch thieves.'

'In that case, the tapestry is doomed.'

'Not necessarily,' said Janssen. 'We're very fortunate to have Captain Rawson staying here. He's confident that we'll retrieve it somehow. He's taken charge.'

'I know,' said Geel without enthusiasm. 'He came to see me.'

Pienaar was aggrieved. 'He paid me a visit as well,' he recalled, 'and had the gall to suggest that I might have divulged details of the tapestry while in my cups. I was affronted. I know you have faith in Captain Rawson, but I don't share it.'

'You would if you knew him as well as *I* do,' said Janssen. 'Daniel is a very extraordinary man.'

'I'm sure that he is. But being a military hero doesn't mean that he's the ideal person in a situation like this. On the battlefield, you can *see* your enemy, whereas here they're invisible.'

'That's a good point, Aelbert,' said Geel, continuing his policy of being more respectful to his colleague. 'We have no idea where the thieves are.'

'They're bound to show their hand again,' reasoned Janssen. 'They'll want to know our response to their demand so will contact us again somehow.'

'Somebody should watch through a window. The next time a letter is put through the door, they can rush out and grab the person who delivered it.'

'I had the same idea, Nick, but Captain Rawson pointed out its defects. The thieves would never take the risk of coming here in person. They'd pay someone else, a complete stranger who had nothing to do with the theft of the tapestry. In any case,' added Janssen, 'we can't have someone on guard twenty-four hours a day. What's to stop a letter being delivered in the dead of night?'

'In short,' said Pienaar, gloomily, 'there's nothing we can do.'

'Oh yes there is, Aelbert.'

'Then what is it?'

'Leave it to Captain Rawson. He'll devise a plan.'

Henry Welbeck was glad when he finally arrived in Amsterdam. Always an unwilling horseman, he'd begun to feel saddle-sore after the first few miles. But he persevered and rode into the city on what was a comparatively mild day. Daniel had warned him how busy the streets could become and he spent most of his time trying to dodge speeding carts and rumbling coaches. He'd never been to the Janssen house before, so had some difficulty finding it. When he finally tracked it down, he knocked on the door and waited. The door was eventually opened by Beatrix, who looked at him with suspicion. When she learnt who he was, however, her manner changed at once and she gave him a cordial welcome. She called a manservant to stable Welbeck's horse then invited the visitor in.

'Captain Rawson has told us so much about you, Sergeant,' she said.

Welbeck was uneasy. 'I see.'

'He said that you're the best man to have beside him in an emergency.'

'That depends what the emergency is.'

'He'll explain everything . . . My name is Beatrix, by the way.'

'Dan's mentioned you a number of times.'

She was delighted. 'Really? What did he say about me?'

'I forget.'

He remembered very well but found her proximity unsettling and didn't want to prolong the exchange. Welbeck was never comfortable in the presence of women, especially when one of them was being so friendly. In spite of his unsightly features, Beatrix was obviously impressed by him. She was grinning broadly as she took him into the parlour, where Daniel was sitting down. Leaping up from his chair, he came over to pump his friend's hand. Beatrix hovered until she realised that she was in the way. Bestowing a sweet smile on Welbeck, she tripped out.

'What have you been telling her about me?' asked Welbeck, gruffly.

'I told her nothing but the truth, Henry.'

'I didn't like the way she kept grinning at me.'

'Don't worry,' said Daniel, laughing. 'You're in no danger from Beatrix. Besides, you're already contracted to another woman – Rachel Rees.'

Welbeck spluttered. 'Keep that harpy away from me!'

'You made a conquest, Henry, and you should acknowledge it.'

'I'd rather stick rusty pins in my eyes.'

It took Daniel minutes to calm him down. When they were both seated, he explained the situation to Welbeck and told him about the letter from the thieves. The amount demanded in guilders was the equivalent of fifty thousand pounds.

'His Grace will never even consider paying it,' said Daniel.

'He's too bloody tight-fisted, that's why.'

'And Amalia's father simply doesn't have the money.'

'You can't say that about Corporal John,' said Welbeck. 'He must be one of the richest men in England. Think of the income he gets from selling commissions, for instance. And look at all the houses he owns. I don't even own *one*.'

'You don't need to when you're in the army.'

'No – I can freeze to death in a tent.'

'Not when you're here in Amsterdam. This is a very cosy house, Henry. You'll find it an improvement on being in winter quarters.'

'I'm not so sure. At least in camp I don't have women like Beatrix grinning at me like a monkey. Instead I have dozens of miserable bloody soldiers to look at.'

'Not to mention the handsome face of Sergeant Curry.'

'Only a blind man would find Leo handsome.'

'You love a regular tussle with each other. You won't be able to trade insults for a while, I'm afraid. The sergeant must have been sad to see you go.'

'He was frothing with jealousy, Dan. While I escape the camp, he's stuck there with nothing to do. However,' said Welbeck, 'let's come back to the problem in hand – and it seems to be a very big problem. If nobody is ready to pay what the thieves are asking, you'll never see the tapestry again.'

'Yes we will, Henry.'

'How?'

'We accept their terms.'

Welbeck was taken aback. 'But you can't drum up that amount of money.'

'*We* know that,' said Daniel, 'but they don't. We have to pretend to accede to their demand. It's the only way to draw them out into the open.'

'I never thought of that.'

'Ideally, of course, it would be wonderful if we could catch them *before* we get to that stage. We can certainly buy some time to continue the search. When they next make contact, we can tell them that His Grace is gathering the money together in The Hague and will send it in due course. That should give us precious extra days.'

'How can we make best use of them?'

Daniel told him about the way he'd questioned the two assistants and how each had responded. While he didn't rule out Geel as the possible source of an unintentional leak of information, he was more interested in taking a closer look at Pienaar. He confided his suspicions to Welbeck and asked him if he'd tail the man when Pienaar left at the end of the day.

Welbeck was mystified. 'Why don't *you* follow him, Dan?'

'Because he knows me,' replied Daniel. 'If he caught sight of me, he'd have another fit of pique. You're a stranger to him. It would never cross his mind that you were trailing him.'

'Do you think the effort could be worthwhile?'

'Yes, Henry, I do. There's something about the man that jars with me.'

'So all I have to do is to follow him home?'

'No,' said Daniel, 'you simply have to make sure that that's where he's going. My guess is that we may be in for something of a surprise.'

Now that he knew the amount of money being demanded, Marlborough was even more irate. He would never hand over the sum of fifty thousand pounds in Dutch currency for property that was rightly his own. It was unthinkable. He was not unused to demands for money or, indeed, for making them. Holding prisoners of war to ransom was a common and very lucrative practice. If he was unable to organise a prisoner exchange, he'd willingly paid large amounts for the return of senior British officers who'd fallen into enemy hands. There was nothing ignoble in that. It was in the nature of warfare. He could always recoup such expenditure in due course. The situation here was different. Thieves had stolen something that held immense emotional value for him. Ramillies was a stirring victory that confirmed his position as a supreme military strategist. To have a tapestry of the battle hanging in Blenheim Palace meant that he had a permanent reminder of his triumph.

It was his wife who troubled him most. Sarah, Duchess of Marlborough, was an authoritative woman with a truculent streak. If he told her about his dilemma, she would explode with rage and he desperately wanted to avoid that. As it was, her most recent letters had fury coursing through every line. She complained bitterly about the way that her close friendship with Queen Anne had been systematically undermined by Abigail Masham, a member of the royal retinue for whom she retained the most utter detestation. Ousted from royal favour, the Duchess sought consolation in supervising the construction of Blenheim Palace, but there was more vexation than consolation. Money was inevitably the root cause. She was forever haggling with the architect over costs and trying to make craftsmen take less for their services than they were asking. Every detail of her financial skirmishes was dashed off in letters to her husband and he'd been almost relieved when ice in the Dutch ports brought a halt to her correspondence. He loved her dearly and missed her greatly, but there were times when he was actually glad to be apart from her. This was one of them.

Yet she would have to know the ugly truth one day. Marlborough prayed that the situation would have been resolved by then. He wanted to be able to return to England with the tapestry. Having to admit to her that it had been destroyed by thieves in an act of malice would rouse her to a pitch of anger. Once infuriated, she couldn't easily be pacified. The fact that Marlborough had refused to part with any money wouldn't moderate her wrath in any way. The Duchess had been shown the design for the tapestry by Janssen himself and she'd given it her seal of approval. She'd already waited a long time to see the finished work. To be told that Janssen and his assistants would have to start all over again would be intolerable to her. Though none of it was his fault, Marlborough would be made to feel obscurely responsible. Only his wife was capable of doing such a thing to him.

His one hope lay with Daniel Rawson. Having employed him on a number of dangerous assignments, Marlborough knew about his almost limitless capabilities. But his previous work had always had a military aspect to it. He'd never before been engaged to solve such a crime and recover property. Marlborough was bound to wonder if even Daniel's resourcefulness was equal to the task.

'It's a waste of time, Dan,' protested Welbeck. 'I've followed him twice now and he went straight home. Pienaar is not the man we're after.'

'Don't give up, Henry,' said Daniel. 'Trail him again this evening.'

'What's the point?'

'I have this worry about him.'

'And so do I,' said Welbeck, bitterly. 'My worry is that he does nothing but come to work and return home day after bloody day. That's his entire life.'

'Try just once more.'

'It's *cold* out there.'

'Do it as a favour to me, Henry.' Welbeck could not

refuse such an appeal but he continued to grumble. It was a long walk to Aelbert Pienaar's house and, on the first occasion, he'd got hopelessly lost on his way back. There was always the possibility that Pienaar went home, had a meal and later went out, but Welbeck doubted it. The man had trudged all the way to his house and entered it as if eager to collapse into a chair by a warm fire. He didn't give the impression of someone intent on revelry. Everything about him – his sober attire, his hunched walk, his air of sadness – suggested that Pienaar led a very private existence. Such a person would hardly associate with criminals.

Notwithstanding his objections, Welbeck responded to Daniel's request. When Pienaar finished at the end of a long day, he put on his coat and hat before letting himself out into the darkness. Welbeck was ready. After watching him through the window, he left the house and fell in behind him. Because he felt in no danger of being discovered, he stayed fairly close to him. On neither of the two previous occasions had Pienaar bothered to look behind him. He was too intent on getting home. When the man took the same route as usual, Welbeck groaned inwardly and braced himself for another fruitless plod through the streets of Amsterdam. Then Pienaar suddenly turned off his familiar path and headed down an alleyway. He was more cautious now, pausing to look over his shoulder before continuing. Keeping to the shadows, Welbeck allowed more space between them. He was excited by the change in routine, wondering if Daniel's distrust of Pienaar would, after all, prove justified.

A stranger to the city, Welbeck was nevertheless aware that they were now moving into one of its less salubrious districts. They passed rowdy taverns and groups of men lounging on street corners. Stray dogs were roaming. The quality of the housing declined. Pienaar eventually stopped outside a house and looked in both directions before knocking on the front door. Confident that he hadn't been seen, Welbeck took up a position on the opposite side of the road. He was unsure what to do. He certainly had no inclination to wait indefinitely on such a raw evening. If he was visiting relatives, Pienaar might even stay the night. Yet it didn't seem to be the sort of place where such a respectable and fastidious man would care to spend time. Buildings nearby were almost ramshackle and there was a faint hint of danger in the air. Welbeck was persuaded to linger where he was.

His patience was rewarded. Twenty minutes later, the door of the house opened and two people appeared. A man embraced a woman and kissed her full on the lips before rolling drunkenly down the street and singing to himself. After waving to him, the woman closed the door. There'd been enough candlelight for Welbeck to get a good look at her. He'd seen enough. It was time to go.

Amalia was surprised to see a light under the door of the workshop. Her father had finished work for the day, Dopff had gone off to his room and, she assumed, the other assistants had gone home. When she opened the door and peeped in, she saw that Geel was still there, brooding beside his loom. The sudden noise brought him out of his reverie.

'Oh!' he exclaimed, turning round. 'You surprised me.'

'What are you doing, Nick?'

'This and that . . .'

'I thought you'd left over an hour ago.'

'No, no, I had some work to finish and some thinking to do.'

Amalia backed away. 'Then I won't disturb you.'

'Please don't leave,' he said, going across to her. 'I need to share my thoughts with someone. I can't keep them bottled up.'

'Whatever they are,' she said, noting the anxiety in his face and voice, 'they're obviously troubling you.'

He bit his lip. 'They've kept me awake night after night.'

'Why is that?'

Her sympathetic smile encouraged him. He couldn't bring himself to confide in Janssen and Pienaar was unapproachable. Doff, too, was not a person to whom he could turn. Amalia, however, was the ideal person. Simply to be alone with her was a thrill for him. To be able to engage her interest was an added bonus.

'I keep wondering if I was to blame,' he confessed.

'For the theft, you mean?'

'Yes.'

'What possible grounds do you have for saying that?'

'I don't know, Miss Amalia, but . . . I have this feeling of guilt.'

'We all have that,' she told him. 'I feel guilty that I didn't wake up that night when thieves broke in here and stole the tapestry.'

'Thank goodness you didn't! They'd be far too dangerous to confront. My fear,' he went on, 'is that I somehow helped them. I can't honestly think of a time when I spoke about my work here but I can be boastful. I do blurt things out without really meaning to. Did I drink too much one night and say something that I shouldn't have said? Did I accidentally betray your father?'

'You didn't do it accidentally or deliberately.'

'How can you say that?'

'I *know* you, Nick,' she reminded him. 'Over the years, I saw you change from a keen, young apprentice into an expert weaver. You love working here and would never do anything remotely disloyal.'

He was heartened. 'Do you believe that, Miss Amalia?'

'Yes, I do. Father would say the same about you.'

'Then why do I have this lurking sense of blame?'

'I can't answer that. In my opinion, your conscience should be clear. Daniel questioned you and found no reason whatsoever to suspect you.'

He grimaced. 'It was Captain Rawson who first planted the seed of doubt in my mind. Until then I'd never even considered that I might have been the culprit. I wouldn't have you think that it happens very often, Amalia,' he added, keen to avoid her disapproval. 'In fact, in the last few months, there's only been the one occasion when I might have had too much to drink. I'm quite abstemious, as a rule.'

She could see how distressed he was. Having known him for so long, however, she couldn't believe he'd be indiscreet about his work to anyone. Had he been likely to boast about what he did, he'd have done so years before now and, if the information had got into the wrong hands, they might have had valuable tapestries stolen much earlier.

Aware of his shortcomings, she knew that they were greatly outnumbered by Geel's many virtues. Introspection had turned him into a nervous and penitent young man. He needed reassurance.

'Go home, Nick,' she said, putting a comforting hand on his arm.

'Yes, I will.'

'And stop worrying – you weren't to blame.'

'No,' he said, gratefully. 'Thanks to you, I don't need to accuse myself.'

He beamed at her. Amalia had offered him friendship and affection. It was a moment that he'd cherish. When he set off for home, he was sustained by a feeling of exhilaration. The woman on whom he doted had attested his innocence. In convincing him that he was no longer a possible culprit, however, Amalia had raised an obvious question. If Geel didn't alert thieves to the whereabouts of the tapestry, then who *did*?

Daniel didn't believe in delay. As soon as he heard Welbeck's report, he set off into the night with his friend. Surprised to hear that Pienaar had visited a brothel, he was quick to see it as a potential place of betrayal, albeit inadvertent. Welbeck had memorised the way carefully. Having got lost on an earlier expedition, he'd taken care to note every turn that he'd made as he'd followed Pienaar. They pursued the same route until they came to the house that the man had entered. Given the amount of time it had taken for Welbeck to go back to the Janssen home, and to make a return journey with Daniel, it was felt unlikely that Pienaar was still inside the brothel. They could therefore approach it without any fear of meeting him there. Welbeck was quite certain that it was a disorderly house. He'd rousted enough lustful young soldiers out of brothels in his time. It had only served to intensify his dislike and distrust of the female sex.

On this occasion, he was happy to leave it to Daniel to enter the premises. Welbeck stayed close to the house in case his friend needed to call for assistance. Daniel knocked on the door and waited until it was opened by a fleshy woman in her fifties daubed in powder and giving off a powerful aroma of perfume. When she saw her visitor by the light of the candelabra she held, her lips parted to reveal a row of uneven teeth. She gave a low, throaty chuckle. Daniel was evidently much younger and more handsome than her usual clients.

'Can I help you, sir?' she asked, running an appreciative eye over him.

'I came on the recommendation of a friend,' he told her.

'Oh – and who might that be?'

'Aelbert Pienaar.'

'Ah, yes,' she said. 'Dear, dear Aelbert – he comes here once a week. In fact, it's not long since he left, but he probably warned you that he'd be here today.' She stood back to let him step into the hall and closed the door behind him. 'He comes to see Gerda – always Gerda. Nobody else will do.'

As he looked around the dingy interior with its fading walls, tattered carpet and abiding smell of damp, Daniel didn't condemn Pienaar. If the man was driven by grief and loneliness to seek comfort in the arms of a woman, he deserved pity rather than censure. All that

Daniel was there to establish was whether or not Pienaar had been drawn into revealing confidential information. The madame of the brothel was still feasting her gaze on him. Her smile broadened into a grotesquely frank grin. As he nodded back at her, he was aware that they were not alone. Lurking at the far end of the hall was the hulking figure of a man. A gesture from the woman dismissed him and he slunk off into a room. At a glance she'd decided that she needed no protection from her latest client.

'We have several ladies to choose from,' she said, sidling closer. 'All of them are skilled at satisfying your every desire. There is Anneka, Brigitte, Magdalena . . .'

'Gerda,' said Daniel. 'I'd like to see Gerda.'

She was surprised. 'Gerda is very popular this evening.'

'Is she available?'

'At a price – she does not give her favours away.'

Daniel paid the amount requested. He was then ushered up the staircase and along a passageway. They stopped outside a door. The woman knocked, opened the door and went in alone. Seconds later, she emerged to tell Daniel that he could enter. Gerda would be happy to accommodate him. When he went into the room, he closed the door behind him. The odour of perfume was almost overwhelming and helped to hide the stink of damp. There was a fire in the grate but the room still felt cold. Gerda was seated on the edge of the bed in a provocative pose. Daniel could see why the woman had been surprised at his choice. Gerda was at least fifteen years older than him, a thin, raddled, angular woman with the remains of a youthful prettiness all but obliterated.

Candles were artfully arranged so that too much light didn't fall on her. She wore a taffeta dress that exposed her arms and dipped at the front to display most of her wrinkled bosom.

There had to be much younger and more appealing prostitutes in the house. It seemed strange to Daniel that Pienaar had selected this particular one. There was nothing alluring about her.

'What is your wish, good sir?' she asked.

'I'd like to talk to you, Gerda,' he replied.

She was disappointed. 'We can do that afterwards.'

'I understand that Aelbert Pienaar is one of your regular clients.'

'Yes, Aelbert comes here every Friday. Why do you ask?'

'He told me how much he enjoyed his visits here.'

'He enjoys them more than I do,' she said, tartly. 'All that Aelbert wants to do is to talk. In the months that he's been coming here, he's never laid a finger on me.' She gave him an open-mouthed smile. 'I can see that you're much more of a man than he is. You want what you paid for, don't you, sir?'

'Tell me about Aelbert first.'

She frowned. 'Why bother about him when we have each other?'

'Why does he always come to *you*?'

She sighed. 'I'm the only one with the patience to listen to him.'

'There must be another reason.'

'There is,' she said, rising to her feet and coming to stand close to him. 'Take your pleasure first and I'll tell you what that reason is.'

When she reached out for him, Daniel caught her wrists and held them.

'Tell me now,' he insisted. 'Why does Aelbert spurn everyone else? What is it about you that brings him here every Friday?'

'It's sheer accident,' she said with a shrug.

'Go on.'

'He says that I remind him of his dead wife.'

CHAPTER NINE

Daniel didn't stay there for much longer. Less than ten minutes after he'd arrived, he left by the front door. Welbeck was waiting for him outside. On the way to Pienaar's house, Daniel gave his friend details of what he'd learnt in the brothel. Welbeck reached an immediate conclusion.

'I think she teased the information out of him,' he said.

'No,' said Daniel. 'She's not that cunning. It's far more likely to have come from him. Gerda simply let him do the talking and he rambled on. It was as if Aelbert Pienaar was sitting at home with his wife.'

'I can't believe that his wife worked in a dreadful place like that.'

'I'm sure that she didn't, Henry. There was a resemblance between the two women, that's all. Or, at least, that's what Pienaar thought. In the subdued lighting, he'd never have been able to see Gerda properly. He *needed* her to be his wife and that's what she became.'

Welbeck snorted. 'It must have been a strange kind of marriage.'

'You're wrong. It was a loving union. They were very close.'

'Then why betray his wife's memory by visiting a bawdy house?'

'In his view,' said Daniel, 'that wasn't what he was doing.'

Their footsteps eventually took them into a more prosperous district with better houses and cleaner streets. Nobody lingered in the gloom. They felt quite safe being abroad at night. It was Welbeck's third visit to the Pienaar residence. This time at least, he told himself, he'd be able to go inside it. That assumption was thrown very much in doubt when a servant opened the door. As soon as Daniel gave his name, Pienaar hurtled out of the parlour and demanded to be left alone. He was fuming. If Welbeck hadn't put his foot in the way, the door would have been slammed in their faces. It was Daniel who produced the key that gained them entry.

'We've just come from Gerda,' he said, pointedly.

Pienaar was speechless. His cheeks paled and his eyes were pools of remorse and embarrassment. He rocked unsteadily on his feet. All the anger drained out of him. He looked so pathetic and defenceless that even Welbeck felt sorry for the man. Daniel suggested that they should continue their discussion inside the house and Pienaar agreed, stepping back to admit them. Once in the parlour, he more or less collapsed into his chair. His visitors sat opposite him. Since he had an uncertain grasp on the Dutch language, Welbeck let Daniel do the talking.

'Let me begin by introducing Sergeant Welbeck,' said Daniel, indicating his companion. 'Because he was a stranger to you, I asked him to follow you after work. This is the third evening he did so. You'll know what he found.'

Pienaar could barely manage a nod. He was writhing with humiliation. The most secret and sensitive part of his life had been exposed to public view. Daniel explained that he'd met Gerda and learnt why Pienaar had been making a weekly visit to the house. He asked how he'd met the woman in the first place. It was minutes before Pienaar was able to summon up an answer. Face taut and hands clasped together, he spoke in a low, apologetic voice.

'Please don't judge me harshly,' he began. 'I can guess what you must have thought when you saw that house. It's not the sort of place I ever dreamt of visiting. I was happily married. I never sought or needed what they offered there. To be honest, I wouldn't even have known where to find such an establishment.'

Daniel believed him. Pienaar might be highly competent as a weaver but there was something unworldly about him. He was a deeply religious man brought up to respect the sanctity of marriage. He had a blend of maturity and innocence that regular visits to a brothel had somehow failed to dispel. Until they'd knocked on his door, he'd persuaded himself that what he was doing was harmless. Now he was squirming with guilt A reassuring weekly event in his life had suddenly been turned into something unwholesome and despicable. The pain was almost unbearable.

'I met her in the street,' he said, eyes on the floor. 'It was a complete accident, I swear it. I thought it was her, you see. When she walked along the pavement towards me, I really did think for a second that it was my dear wife.'

'Did you speak to her?' asked Daniel.

'No, I was too overwhelmed to say anything. But she spoke. I was staring at her so hard that she could see she'd aroused my interest. She told me her name was Gerda. I didn't realise at the time what she did for a living, of course. Had I done so,' Pienaar insisted, 'I'd have walked away in disgust.'

'But you didn't,' said Daniel. 'She engaged you in conversation. It's what women like that do. They can be very ingratiating.'

'She was so friendly and so like my Johanna. I was spellbound.'

Gerda had failed to cast any spell on Daniel. He'd seen her in her true colours. As he recalled her gaunt features and skeletal frame, he decided that Pienaar's wife must have died of consumption or a similar wasting disease. It would have eaten away at her and left her as decayed and fragile as Gerda. Daniel didn't want to upset the man further by pressing for details of his wife's death. The point was that a chance resemblance had hooked Aelbert Pienaar. It was enough to entice him to a brothel, although, Daniel surmised, Pienaar wouldn't have understood the true nature of what went on there at first. By the time that he did, the pleasure of being with Gerda outweighed his natural revulsion. She was the one person able to soften his bereavement.

'I won't ever go there again,' asserted Pienaar. 'I promise you that.'

'I'm more interested in the visits you've already made there,' said Daniel. 'Did you – in the course of your conversations with Gerda – ever mention anything about your work?'

'I don't think so, Captain Rawson.'

'Does that mean you don't remember?'

'We just talked. That's to say, I came home to my Johanna and told her what sort of a day I'd experienced. There's nothing wrong in that, is there?'

'That depends who was listening.'

'Johanna – Gerda, that is – was the only person there.'

'She may have been the only person in the room,' said Daniel, 'but I suspect that someone may have been listening outside the door. Did you, for instance, ever notice a man lurking in the background?'

'No, I didn't.'

'Who let you into the house?'

'It was Gerda. I always arrived at the same time on a Friday. She'd be waiting for me and took me straight to her room. There was another woman there but, when I paid her, she left us alone.' Pienaar pondered. 'I may have made a casual remark about my work, I suppose,' he admitted at length, 'but I don't recall doing so. I have confided things to Johanna in the past because I trusted her implicitly. She'd never breathe a word of what I said to her.'

'But you weren't talking to your wife.' Daniel reminded him. 'The woman listening to you was Gerda. In return for money, she gave you what you wanted from her and that was companionship.'

Pienaar was earnest. 'It was, Captain Rawson. That's *all* it was.'

'What's he saying, Dan?' asked Welbeck.

'He can't be certain,' said Daniel, speaking in English

for his friend's benefit. 'He *might* have mentioned the tapestry in an unguarded moment. My guess is that when he starts talking to Gerda, he isn't sure what he says. He's so desperate for the intimacy of a marriage that the words just tumble out.'

'Men always leave their brains outside when they step into a brothel.'

Daniel smiled. 'Fortunately, I didn't.'

'There was one strange thing,' said Pienaar, searching his memory. 'It must have been weeks ago now.'

'Go on,' encouraged Daniel.

'Well, when I arrived there one evening, Johanna asked me how far I'd had to come. My wife knows. Why did she want the address?'

'Did you give it to her?'

A hunted look came into Pienaar's eye. 'I must have,' he said, putting his hands to his head in a gesture of despair. 'How stupid of me!' he exclaimed. 'I betrayed my master. It's my fault that the tapestry was stolen. I'll never be forgiven for that. Emanuel will dismiss me.'

When Pienaar burst into tears, Welbeck needed no translation. He exchanged a knowing glance with Daniel who put an arm around the distraught weaver.

'There's no reason why Emanuel should ever know about this,' said Daniel, soothingly. 'He won't blame you – especially if you help us to catch these men and reclaim the tapestry. *Will* you help us, Aelbert?'

Pienaar looked up hopelessly. 'What can *I* do?'

Work had enlivened Emanuel Janssen. When he was at his loom, he could block out any horrible thoughts and concentrate on the job that he loved. Once he finished work, however, doubts and fears rushed in again and made his shoulders sag. As he sat in the parlour of his house, he looked sick and careworn. Amalia was troubled.

'You should go to bed, Father,' she said.

'I feel much better now.'

'You look ill. There's no point in forcing yourself to stay up.'

'I want to hear if they found anything out.'

'Daniel will come up to your room to tell you.'

'I'm staying here, Amalia.'

'Have you taken your medicine?'

'No – it only makes me feel drowsy.'

'You need your sleep.'

Janssen was determined. 'I want to stay down here,' he said. 'I want to know what's going on.'

Amalia could see that her advice was in vain. Nothing could make her father rest. If he went to bed, all that he did was to brood on the situation. Being with her at least gave him some moral support. Distressed at the theft of the tapestry, she was far more concerned about its effect on him. It was an open wound that was still bleeding. The only consolation was that Daniel was staying with them. His presence gave them a chance of recovering the tapestry. Had he been hundreds of miles away on a battlefield, they'd never have been able to survive the crisis. Its impact on Janssen would've been far worse, even fatal. Amalia shuddered at the thought.

'Where have they gone?' asked Janssen.

'I've no idea, Father,' she replied.

'Sergeant Welbeck worries me.'

'Why?'

'I'm not sure. How well do you know him?'

'Not very well – but Daniel has the highest opinion of him.'

'The fellow always looks so uncomfortable.'

'He's a soldier. He's used to life in camp.'

'He creeps around the house as if he's imprisoned here.'

'That's just his way.'

'I'd love to know where he is now.'

Amalia sat up as she heard the front door open. 'That could be them now,' she said, hopefully. After a few seconds, the door was shut again and locked. 'No, I'm afraid that it wasn't.'

There was a tap on the parlour door and Beatrix entered the room.

'This came for you, sir,' she said, handing a letter to Janssen. 'When I saw it being slipped under the door, I tried to catch the person who delivered it but I was too late. All I saw in the street was a boy running away.'

'Thank you for trying,' said Amalia. She turned to her father who was reading the letter. 'Is it from them?' He nodded. 'What do they say?'

'They want their money within two days,' he told her. 'I have to reply to them on behalf of myself and His Grace, the Duke of Marlborough.'

'How do you get in touch with them?'

'They mention a place where a letter can be left tomorrow. There's a warning,' he added. 'If anyone tries to follow me when I deliver my reply, they'll destroy the tapestry. In other words, they'll be watching, Amalia. There's nothing we can do.'

'Daniel will think of something.'

'You've been saying that for days.'

'Don't lose faith in him, Father.'

Janssen was agitated. 'I have the greatest respect for the captain,' he said, running a nervous hand through his hair, 'but even he can't help us this time. He has absolutely no idea who these people are.'

The burly man with the fringe beard let himself into the tavern and peered through the fug. His friend was seated alone at a table. After buying a drink, the newcomer joined him. Frans Tulp gave him a nod of welcome. Tulp was a small, slight ferret of a man with a pointed snout and oily hair slicked back over his head to reach his shoulders. His eyes were always on the move in self-defence. Jan Dekker, by contrast, half Tulp's age and twice his size, had a strong man's fearlessness. Nobody would dare to attack someone of his bulk. He took a long slurp of his beer.

'Did you deliver the letter?' he asked.

'I paid a lad to do that.'

'When do we get a reply?'

'Tomorrow,' said Tulp.

'What if they refuse to pay up?'

'There's no danger of that happening.'

'You never know, Frans.'

'They want that tapestry back. They'll be dying to pay. All we have to do is to share the money between the three of us.'

'What about Hendrika?'

'What about her?'

'She first heard about Emanuel Janssen.'

'But *you* were the one who hid in Gerda's room after that. Without the details that you picked up from that fool, we'd have got nowhere.'

'Hendrika deserves something.'

Tulp smirked. 'Then spend the night with her.'

'She's too old for me. She's more your age, Frans.'

'I like my women fresher than Hendrika. Forget her. She's happy enough running the house. When we've got our money, we'll quit Amsterdam altogether and leave her to it.'

Dekker had scruples. 'That'd be unfair.'

'Fairness doesn't matter. We stole that tapestry – you, me and Teunis. We should get the reward.'

'I might give Hendrika a gift of some kind.'

'That's your business. The old sow will get nothing from me.'

Tulp was a hard man. He'd planned the crime and therefore expected to get a larger share of the ransom. Neither Dekker nor the other accomplice argued about that. Tulp was their acknowledged leader. He was more artful and intelligent than either of them. All that they could provide was physical energy. It was Tulp who supplied control and direction. Thanks to him, they had a chance to make a fortune.

'How's everything at the house?' asked Tulp.

'Much the same,' replied Dekker, downing some more beer.

'Was he there again?'

'Yes, Pienaar came at the usual time.'

'Of all the women there,' said Tulp with a sneer, 'he chooses Gerda. She's nothing but skin and bone. I wouldn't touch her if you paid me.'

'*He* doesn't touch her either.'

'Can you blame him?' They shared a crude laugh. 'She must have every disease under the sun. And look at the way she scratches – that means fleas.'

Dekker laughed again. Employed at the house to protect the prostitutes, he'd long ago learnt that they could take care of themselves. Most of them had daggers hidden in their rooms and Hendrika, the madame, had a pistol she was more than ready to use. Dekker had only ever had to throw two awkward clients out of the house. Disposing of the body of an elderly man who died in flagrante had been rather more problematical. It was yet another occasion when Tulp's advice had been invaluable.

'Oh,' said Dekker as a memory stirred lazily at the back of his mind, 'there's something I should tell you. We had a stranger there this evening. He said he was a friend of Pienaar. He asked for Gerda.'

'Was the fellow *blind*? Nobody in his right mind would choose her.'

'This one did, Frans.'

'What manner of man was he – old and decrepit?'

'No, he was not much above my own age. Some would call him handsome.'

'Then why did he want to fuck that crone?'

'That wasn't what he was after,' said Dekker. 'Gerda moaned about it afterwards. He never even lifted her skirt to feel her. He just talked.'

Tulp was wary. 'What about?'

'I don't know. I couldn't hear them clearly through the door.'

'How long did he stay?'

'He was in and out quite fast. What a waste of good money!'

'I wonder,' said Tulp, chewing a lip.

'If you ask me, I think he lost his nerve. It often happens. They either change their mind at the last moment or they get too excited and soil their breeches before they even get their pizzle out. I don't think we need worry about him, Frans,' said Dekker, airily. 'He was harmless.'

'I'm not sure about that. Tell me exactly what happened, Jan. Who let him in? What did he say about Pienaar? Why did he pick Gerda?' As Dekker was about to take another drink, Tulp grabbed his friend's arm to stop him. 'This could be important. Tell me everything.'

Daniel kept his promise. When he and Welbeck returned to the Janssen house, they said nothing about Pienaar's visits to the brothel. Nor did they explain that the man had been followed by Welbeck for three days in a row. Daniel felt it would be wrong to alarm Janssen by suggesting any distrust of a loyal employee. He simply told Amalia and her father that their search that evening had been fruitless. An anguished Janssen waved the letter at them. Daniel read it first then translated it for Welbeck.

'What do we do?' asked Amalia.

'Your father must reply and deliver the letter in person,' said Daniel. 'The thieves must be given the impression that he's obeying their orders.'

'We have no money to give them.'

'We won't need any, Amalia. We must slow them down. The letter will say that the money will be on its way from The Hague in a few days but that it will not be handed over until we have clear proof that the tapestry is undamaged.'

Janssen gasped. 'Do you think they've already destroyed it?'

'No,' said Daniel. 'Without it, they'd have nothing with which to bargain. But we must insist that someone verifies its existence. It will show them that we can't be rushed into paying any ransom. And,' he went on, 'it will give us an idea of the whereabouts of the tapestry.'

'They won't *show* us where it is, surely?'

'Of course not – they'll probably insist on blindfolding someone before taking him to the hiding place. But whoever inspects the tapestry will be able to pick up some clues.'

'I'll go,' volunteered Janssen.

'No, Father,' said Amalia in dismay, 'it's too dangerous.'

'I know that tapestry better than anyone.'

'Let Daniel go – he helped you with the design, after all.'

'It's my duty, Amalia.'

'You'd get too upset,' she argued. 'I'm afraid that seeing it again will be too much of a shock for you. We have to put your health first.'

'I agree with Amalia,' said Daniel. 'Someone else must go.'

Janssen was hurt. 'It's my right.'

'Then it's one that should be waived. When you see the tapestry again, it's bound to arouse your emotions. You'll be so distracted that you won't be able to look and listen for clues as to your whereabouts. This is work for someone else.'

'That means you, Daniel,' said Amalia, 'or even Sergeant Welbeck. The thieves are desperate criminals. You could stand up to them.'

Daniel shook his head. 'That won't be necessary, Amalia.'

'Oh – why is that?'

'It's because neither I nor Henry will be involved.'

'*Somebody* must make sure the tapestry is unharmed,' said Janssen.

'I know the ideal person for the assignment.'

'And who might that be?'

'A man who worked beside you on the project,' said Daniel. 'It's someone with the same desire and urgency to recover the tapestry. He'll be able to cast an expert eye over it to see if it's been blemished in any way.'

Janssen was puzzled. 'Are you talking about Kees or Nick?'

'I'm talking about Aelbert Pienaar.' Daniel smiled as he thought of the man's likely reaction to an early chance of redemption. 'I have a feeling that he'll jump at this opportunity.'

Everything went according to plan. As they watched from their hiding place, Tulp and Dekker saw the letter being delivered by Emanuel Janssen. Nobody was with him and he'd not been followed from the house by any friends. The thieves were certain of that because Dekker's brother, Teunis, had been stationed opposite the Janssen home to make sure he complied with his orders. He'd then trailed Janssen all the way to the quayside where the letter was deposited. A signal from their accomplice told Tulp and Dekker that no subterfuge was involved. After placing the missive where he'd been told, Janssen turned on his heel and hurried away. A boy ran over to retrieve the letter. Taking it from him, Tulp slipped him a coin and sent him on his way. Dekker was illiterate, so he had to wait for Tulp to read the letter.

'What does it say, Frans?' he asked. 'Will we get our money?'

'Not for a few days,' replied Tulp, irritably.

'We told him to hand it over tomorrow.'

'It's coming from The Hague. That's where the Duke of Marlborough is staying. But we won't get anything until they know that the tapestry is still in good condition.'

'Tell them that it is.'

'They want proof.'

Dekker was aggressive. 'They'll have to take our word for it.'

'That's not good enough, Jan. To be honest, I don't blame them. I wouldn't hand over that amount of money until I was certain that I was getting something in return. We'll have to agree.'

'But if we show them the tapestry, they'll know where it's hidden.'

'Not if we're careful. We'll take one of them there by night and make sure he's blindfolded. First, we'll take him around Amsterdam to confuse him.'

Dekker was impressed. 'I'd never have thought of that.'

'That's why you should leave the thinking to me.'

'Where will we go when we get the money?'

'Let's make sure we get it first.'

'I've always wanted to see The Hague.'

'We'll be able to go further afield than that, Jan.'

'Teunis has a family. He's going to stay here.'

'That's his decision. I want to get far away from this city. There are too many people looking for me here. I need to start a new life somewhere else.'

'The same goes for me.'

Tulp grinned. 'I thought you liked living with all those whores.'

'I did at first,' said Dekker, 'but I got bored. I've had all they can offer.'

'Well, keep your wits about you while you're still there,' said Tulp. 'Make a note of any strangers who turn up. The man who came there yesterday worries me. Why should he pay all that money just to talk?'

'He learnt nothing, Frans. What could Gerda possibly tell him?'

'Ask her.'

'I did, but she told me to mind my own fucking business.'

'You should have beaten an answer out of her.'

'Hendrika doesn't like me hitting any of them. If I do, they can't earn their keep. Who wants a whore with a broken arm?'

'Tell Gerda you want to know everything that stranger said to her yesterday. Give her a slap to jog her memory. If she still won't tell you,' warned Tulp, raising a fist, 'I'll break every bone in her rotting old body.'

Chapter Ten

For the whole time that her father was out of the house, Amalia was on tenterhooks. She was terrified that he might come to some harm or that his health would fail him. When he dragged himself out of bed that morning, he'd been fatigued, having spent a sleepless night agonising over the fate of his tapestry. As he went off to deliver the letter, his gait had been so unsteady that Amalia was profoundly disturbed. Daniel wasn't there when Janssen left and it was several minutes before he was able to join Amalia in the parlour.

'I should have gone with him,' she said, anxiously.

'It was something he had to do on his own, Amalia.'

'You saw how ill he looked this morning.'

'Yes,' said Daniel, 'but I also saw that letter from the thieves. Their warning was quite specific. Your father was to go alone. Had he been seen with anybody else – even with his daughter – it might have jeopardised our chances of recovering the tapestry.'

'I just can't bear the thought that Father is in danger.'

'He's perfectly safe, I promise you.'

'I wish that I could believe that.'

'The thieves want their ransom,' he pointed out. 'If they were stupid enough to harm your father, they know they'd never get any money.'

Daniel continued to reassure her but Amalia was inconsolable. Though she didn't voice her concerns, she was beginning to doubt his ability to identify the thieves and to reclaim the tapestry. It was a salutary moment for her. Because he'd never let her down in the past, she'd come to think that Daniel was infallible. Even with Welbeck at his side, however, he appeared to have made no headway in solving the crime. Could it be that he was finally out of his depth? Was he about to fail? She tried to stifle such thoughts and remembered instead how he'd dashed all the way from Lille to Oxfordshire in order to save her from the clutches of an obsessive admirer. Sensing her fears, Daniel was waiting until Janssen had returned before showing her that he and Welbeck had indeed made progress.

Amalia's patience soon wore thin. Instead of standing in the window, she put on a coat and went out into the street to wait for her father. When he finally came around a corner, she ran to greet him and enfold him in her arms. She supported him all the way back to the house then helped him take off his hat and coat. Since it had obviously been an ordeal for Janssen, Daniel made sure that the older man had time to recover before he was plied with questions.

Amalia sat beside her father, troubled by the pallor of his cheeks and the way he struggled for breath.

'Are you ready to tell us what happened?' she asked, softly.

'I think so, Amalia.'

'Was anybody waiting at the quayside?'

'Nobody at all,' said Janssen. 'I came straight back home.'

'Did you see the man who was following you?' asked Daniel.

Janssen was shocked. 'No, I didn't. Was there someone?'

'He was waiting at the corner for you.'

Amalia was surprised. 'How do you know that, Daniel?'

'I watched him from the attic through a telescope. He was very clever. He let your father get well ahead of him before he went after him.' He turned to Janssen. 'The man wasn't only there to follow you. He wanted to make sure that nobody from here did the same thing.'

'I was completely unaware of him,' admitted Janssen, 'but then, I was in such a state that I wouldn't have noticed if a troop of cavalry had been at my heels. All that I could think about was delivering that letter to the place I was told. My hand was trembling when I put it down.'

'I hope that makes you think twice about going to see the tapestry,' said Amalia. 'You shouldn't have to suffer like that again.'

'I agree, Amalia. It's not a job for me.'

'That's settled, then.'

'But I do wonder if it's fair to foist it on to Aelbert.'

'It's fair and it's appropriate,' said Daniel.

'Will he be able to cope?'

'I'm certain that he will. He has as much incentive as anybody.'

'Nick is younger and more resilient.'

'That doesn't matter. Aelbert has seniority. I fancy that he'd feel hurt if someone else went in his place.' Standing at the window, Daniel caught sight of a stocky figure approaching the house. 'Ah, here's Henry at last,' he said. 'I thought he'd be back before too long.'

'Where has he been?'

'And why didn't we see him for breakfast?' added Amalia.

'He was ready to make sacrifices,' explained Daniel. 'It's something we do as a matter of course in the army. Henry left before dawn so that he could get down to the harbour and find somewhere to hide. Nobody could have seen him leave the house or been aware of his presence near the spot where the letter was left.' There was a knock on the front door. 'But I'll let him tell his own story.'

They heard the front door opening then shutting. Seconds later, Welbeck came into the room wearing a hat that concealed his face and a thick coat. He removed the hat with a flourish and sidled across to the fire.

'It's getting no warmer out there,' he said.

'I didn't even notice the weather,' said Janssen in English.

'Well, I noticed and felt it – especially before the sun came up.'

'It was very noble of you, Sergeant Welbeck,' observed Amalia.

Daniel helped him off with his coat. 'What did you see, Henry?'

'I saw lots and lots of seagulls,' said Welbeck. 'They sounded as cold and hungry as I did. But I stayed where I was and eventually I saw them moving into position. There were two of them – a big, hefty character with a fringe beard and an older, shorter, skinnier man who seemed to be in charge. They waited until the letter had been placed on the wall, then they let a boy pick it up. The lad was paid and sent on his way. They read the letter and looked perplexed. It was obviously not what they expected. They didn't realise you'd want to make sure that the tapestry was intact.'

'Then what happened?'

'They were joined by a third man.'

'It must have been the one who followed me,' said Janssen.

'It was,' confirmed Welbeck. 'As you walked towards the quayside, I saw him stalking you. He had the same build and features as the big man. I'd say that they might even be brothers. After a while, they split up and went their separate ways. I came back here.'

'You did well, Henry,' said Daniel. 'At least we have a clearer idea of what we're up against. All we can do now is to wait for their response. Oh,' he added with a grin, 'there's something else for which we must wait.'

'What's that, Daniel?' asked Amalia.

'We must tarry until a large amount of money has been sent from The Hague by His Grace, the Duke of Marlborough.'

Even Janssen joined in the ironic laughter.

One of Dekker's few virtues was that he knew how to obey orders. After leaving the others at the harbour, he walked back to the house he shared with seven prostitutes. Tulp had told him to question Gerda closely and that's what he intended to do. Even though she was fast asleep at that time of the morning, Dekker didn't mind. He barged into her room and shouted to wake her up. When the woman didn't stir, he grabbed her by the shoulder and shook her violently. Gerda came awake with a string of expletives pouring out of her mouth like hot steam. Rubbing her eyes, she peered at her visitor.

'Get out, Jan!' she snapped.

'I need some answers,' he said.

'And I need my sleep.'

When she turned her back on him and pulled the blankets over her head, Dekker was furious. Seizing the blankets, he pulled them off her and tossed them on to the floor. She sat up and shivered in the cold.

'I'm freezing,' she howled. 'Give me those bleeding blankets.'

'You get nothing until I get answers.'

'Give them here, you bastard!'

'Tell me what I want to know or I'll throw you out into the street stark naked.'

'This is my room – get out!'

Hauling herself out of bed, Gerda tried to retrieve her blankets but Dekker stood in her way. Another torrent of abuse poured from her lips. She pummelled his chest with her puny fists only to enrage him the more. Dekker was merciless. After slapping her hard across the face, he grabbed her by the hair and swung her across the room until she collided with a wall. Dazed and in great pain, Gerda didn't even have enough strength left to curse him. Dekker stood over her.

'Tell me about that stranger,' he demanded.

'What stranger?'

'That man who came here yesterday. He said he was a friend of Pienaar.'

She was confused. 'Did he?'

'I was here when Hendrika let him in. He asked for you.'

'You hurt me,' she said, rubbing her arm.

'I'll hurt you even more if you don't tell me the truth.'

'There's nothing to tell.'

He kicked her. 'Don't lie to me.'

'It's true, Jan,' she whimpered, recoiling from the blow. 'He was just like Aelbert. All he wanted to do was to talk.'

'I know that – but what did he *say*?'

'Who cares?'

He kicked her harder this time and she screamed in pain. Taking her by the throat, he lifted her up and pinned her against the wall. She began to splutter.

'I'll ask you one last time, Gerda. What did that man say?'

Unable to fight back, she spat defiantly into his face. Dekker went berserk, banging her head repeatedly against the wall before hurling her on to the bed like a rag doll. He was just about to administer further punishment when he felt something hard against the back of his skull.

'If you touch her again,' warned Hendrika, holding the pistol firmly, 'I'll blow your brains out.'

Dekker froze. He knew Hendrika well. She wasn't given to making idle threats. If need be, she'd pull the trigger without hesitation. In assaulting Gerda, he'd gone too far. The woman might be old and spindly but she was one of Hendrika's charges. Thanks to him, Gerda had been badly hurt and was lying unconscious on the bed. She'd be unable to work for some time. Instead of being a source of income, she was a liability.

Still aiming the pistol at him, Hendrika stepped across to the open door. 'Get out of my house!' she ordered.

'But I work here,' he said, piteously.

'Not anymore, Jan.'

'All I wanted from Gerda is a few answers.'

'You've no business here now,' she said, motioning with her pistol. 'Get out and stay out. And the same goes for that little rat, Frans Tulp. If I see either of you near this house again, I'll bite your pricks off and feed them to the dog.'

Dekker tried to plead with her but his entreaties fell on deaf ears. Hendrika was finished with him for good. After glowering at Gerda, he accepted defeat and stormed out of the house. The cold air sobered him and allowed him to view his situation more calmly. It was not as bad as it seemed. Being ejected from the house was no punishment because he was in any case planning to leave it very soon. Once he had his share of the ransom, he'd flee from the city with Frans Tulp. He might have failed to get the truth out of Gerda but his friend wouldn't know that. All that he had to do was to tell Tulp a simple lie and the whole matter would be forgotten. Hendrika, Gerda and the others belonged to his past. In a couple of days, he and Tulp would be rich men, able to pay for any pleasures they sought.

There was danger involved. Daniel made no attempt to disguise that. They were dealing with criminals. If Pienaar made a false move, they'd have no compunction in turning on him. Daniel foresaw another problem. His visit to Gerda might well have aroused suspicion. Since there was a link between the thieves and the brothel, they might have been made aware of what Daniel had asked the woman. In case he was questioned about it, Pienaar needed to have a plausible explanation for Daniel's appearance at the house. They discussed the possibilities at length.

As Daniel had assumed, Pienaar was delighted to be given the opportunity to redeem himself. If he could be instrumental in helping to catch the thieves, it would assuage the sense of guilt smouldering inside him. He was pathetically grateful for Daniel's discretion. Pienaar had been terrified that Janssen and the others would learn of his visits to a prostitute. As well as blaming him for the theft of the tapestry, they'd be disgusted by the revelation that he'd entered a brothel. Pienaar's career would have been over and there would have been a total loss of dignity. Because of Daniel, that had not happened. Instead of being exposed to condemnation, he was being offered the chance to gain the admiration of his employer. That meant everything to Pienaar.

'Why didn't you choose Nick?' he asked.

'I couldn't rely on him,' said Daniel. 'He's likely to make a slip of the tongue when put under stress. You have more self-control.'

'What must I do, Captain Rawson?'

'Commit everything you can to memory. If they blindfold you – as I'm sure they will – try to remember in which direction they take you. Listen for any noises that might give you clues as to where you are – the chiming of a clock, for instance, or the ringing of church bells. Breathe through your nose so that you can detect smells. If they take you anywhere near the fish market, you'll know it immediately.'

Pienaar listened to his instructions and resolved to follow them. He was very nervous about his assignment but more than willing to accept it. Another letter had arrived from the thieves, agreeing to let Janssen view the tapestry but imposing strict conditions. He was to leave the house alone at a given time that evening and walk in the direction of the harbour until it was clear that he was not being followed. He'd then be taken to the place where the tapestry was stored. Pienaar wondered if it might actually be kept in the brothel.

'I doubt it,' said Daniel. 'For one thing, it's too far away. Before they stole it, they would have arranged for a hiding place much nearer.'

'They'll be expecting Emanuel. What will happen when I turn up instead?'

'You explain that he's too ill to come and sent you in his stead. They know you by name, Aelbert, so they'll trust you.'

'I hope so.'

'They're not men of great intelligence. Look at the letters they've sent us. They were scrawled by an uneducated hand. What they have is low cunning. They'll always be trying to get an advantage.'

'And thanks to me,' said Pienaar, penitently, 'they got one.'

'Put that out of your mind.'

'But I was the one who told them about the tapestry.'

'You weren't to know that,' said Daniel. 'It was unintentional.'

'I'd have cut my tongue out before I'd have given them the information voluntarily.' He gritted his teeth. 'Oh, if only that damned woman hadn't looked like my Johanna!'

They were alone in the parlour of the Janssen house and it was fast approaching the time when Pienaar had to leave. Somewhere outside in the darkness, one of the thieves would be watching. Daniel was bound to have qualms. He wasn't entirely sure that Pienaar was equal to the task but there was no alternative. Of Janssen's assistants, he'd be the most acceptable to the thieves because he was already known to one of them. He posed no physical threat and would be viewed as a sad old man who paid money every Friday simply to talk about his wife to a whore.

Daniel looked at the clock on the mantelpiece. 'Are you ready?'

'I think so,' said Pienaar, swallowing hard.

'Off you go, then – and good luck.'

Dekker was relieved. Tulp had accepted his assurance that the stranger who visited Gerda posed no problem to them. He boasted that he'd beaten the woman to get the truth out of her, omitting to mention that he'd then been forced out of the house at gunpoint. They were skulking in a doorway some distance from the Janssen house, waiting for him to arrive. A lantern flickered in the darkness. It was the signal that their target was on his way and that he wasn't being followed by anyone from the house. As footsteps approached along the pavement, the thieves were poised in readiness. The moment that Pienaar drew level with them, Dekker grabbed him and pulled him into the doorway.

Tulp lifted up the lantern he'd been shielding and held it to the newcomer's face.

'Where's Janssen?' he demanded.

'He's too ill to come,' replied Pienaar. 'He sent me in his place.'

Tulp was circumspect. 'This could be a trick.'

'I worked on that tapestry beside Emanuel Janssen. That's why I'm here.'

'He's right, Frans,' said Dekker. 'This is Aelbert Pienaar, the idiot who spends his Friday evenings talking nonsense to Gerda.'

'Is that true?' asked Tulp, prodding the man.

Pienaar was embarrassed. 'It's true that I visit a certain house on a Friday,' he confessed, 'but I don't talk nonsense.'

'Yes you do,' jeered Dekker. 'I've heard you.'

'Shut your mouth, Jan,' ordered Tulp.

'But I was hidden in the room at the time.'

'That's neither here nor there. We have business with this man. Let's get on with it.' Dekker took out a blindfold and put it on Pienaar. 'This is to make sure you don't see where we're going,' explained Tulp. 'Don't you dare to take it off.'

'I won't,' said Pienaar, wincing as it was tied very tightly.

Taking an arm apiece, the thieves hustled him along the pavement and around a corner. A horse and cart stood waiting. Dekker lifted the weaver bodily and sat him on the back of the cart, climbing up beside him. Tulp clambered into the driver's seat. Snapping the reins, he set the horse in motion. It rattled through the streets. Pienaar tried to memorise the route but soon realised that it was impossible. The cart was deliberately zigzagging its way through the city in order to confuse him. Sitting in the back of it, Pienaar had an uncomfortable ride, bouncing about and being held in an iron grip by Dekker. It seemed like an eternity before they reached their destination.

Henry Welbeck was becoming increasingly pessimistic. He and Daniel were alone in the parlour, awaiting the return of Pienaar. Welbeck glanced at the clock. 'He's been gone for over an hour,' he said.

'I can tell the time, Henry.'

'I think he might crack. You're asking too much of him, Dan. There's every chance that he'll break down and then where will we be? If they learn that there's no intention of paying the ransom, the tapestry will be destroyed and Pienaar's life will be at risk. You were wrong to send him.'

'I know the man better than you,' said Daniel, 'and I have faith in him.'

'You should have let me go.'

'It needed someone who spoke Dutch.'

'Then *you* should have gone.'

'Aelbert was far and away the best choice,' insisted Daniel. 'After what we discovered about him, it was only fair to let him atone for what he did. The thieves won't harbour suspicions about someone as old and patently harmless as Aelbert. It would have been a different matter if you or I had gone in his place.'

Welbeck got to his feet and walked up and down to relieve his tension. He was a man of action who hated to be idle in the face of a threat. He wanted to grab a weapon and take the fight to the enemy. Since that was impossible, he fretted at the delay. Welbeck wanted the problem resolved swiftly. Comfortable as the house was, he yearned to be back in the familiar surroundings of an army camp where he could speak his own language to everyone around him. In the middle of Amsterdam, he felt like an interloper. Even mischievous soldiers like Private Ben Plummer were preferable to the dour Aelbert Pienaar, the ebullient Nicholaes Geel and the silent Kees Dopff. Again, he missed the lively exchanges with Sergeant Curry, and while he was glad to be with Daniel at first, Welbeck knew that Amalia would always take priority over him.

After pacing the room for several minutes, he came to an abrupt halt.

'He's given the game away,' he decided. 'I feel it.'

Daniel smiled indulgently. 'You're getting impatient in your old age, Henry.'

'He's probably lying somewhere with his throat cut.'

'Stop fearing the worst.'

'He's not experienced, Dan. We've been trained to cope with danger but Pienaar hasn't. When he's alone with the thieves, he'll be a bag of nerves.'

'I think he has more steel in him than that.'

'Well, I've seen no sign of it. I'm used to judging a man's character. I do it all the time when I have new recruits to knock into line. When I look at Pienaar, what I see is a weak, pitiable, vulnerable man.'

'Then he's going to surprise you, Henry.'

'Would you care to have a wager on that?'

'No,' said Daniel, laughing. 'It would be cruel to take your money.'

He was suppressing his own doubts. Convinced that the tapestry was stored reasonably close to the house, he was worried at the length of time it was taking for Pienaar to return. Once he saw the tapestry, the weaver would assess its condition within minutes and be on his way back to the house. What was delaying him? It was unsettling. Welbeck remained sceptical and Daniel continued to make futile attempts to reassure him. They were still arguing when they heard a knock on the door. Daniel was the first to reach it, opening it to let Pienaar come into the house. Amalia and her father also came rushing to greet him. They shepherded Pienaar into the parlour and across to the fire, letting him thaw out before he spoke. Daniel winked at Welbeck.

'I was wrong,' conceded his friend.

'Would you still like to make that wager?' asked Daniel.

'Let's hear what he has to say first.'

Pienaar was grateful to escape from the freezing temperatures outside. Warmed by the fire, he was further revived by a glass of brandy from Janssen. It helped him to find his voice again.

'It was as Captain Rawson predicted,' he said. 'I was followed from the house then accosted by two men some distance away. I was blindfolded and lifted on to a cart by a man named Jan. He sat with me as we drove endlessly through the streets. There were so many twists and turns that I had no idea where we were. Eventually, we bumped down a cobbled hill and pulled up. I was hauled off the cart and marched into some kind of storehouse, though they made sure that I didn't see what was being stored there.'

'What about the tapestry?' pressed Janssen. 'Was it there?'

'Yes, it was safe and dry, rolled up under a tarpaulin.

They took off my blindfold and let me have a good look at it. There was no damage.'

'Thank God for that!'

As Pienaar continued with his narrative, Daniel translated the Dutch so that Welbeck could understand exactly what had happened. Some clues had emerged. Pienaar had learnt three names. Jan was the sturdy man who'd manhandled the weaver, Frans was the smaller, older man who gave the orders and they'd been joined at the storehouse by an accomplice named Teunis. Pienaar had only got a glimpse of his face but saw enough to notice his close resemblance to Jan. When he heard the details in translation, Welbeck snapped his fingers.

'It's the same three men I saw at the harbour,' he said.

'We have to be careful,' warned Pienaar. 'They're evil men. If they discover a ruse, they'll turn nasty. Somebody could get hurt.'

'What did you tell them about the money?' asked Daniel.

'I repeated what you told them, Captain Rawson. I said that it would be arriving by courier from The Hague the day after tomorrow. They complained bitterly at the delay but accepted it in the end. Then they blindfolded me again, bundled me on to the cart, and drove me back by a different route. I was dropped off a few hundred yards from here.'

Amalia was disappointed. 'So you've learnt nothing of real use.'

'He learnt that the tapestry is unharmed,' Janssen pointed out.

'He also discovered their names,' noted Daniel, 'and the fact that two of them are probably brothers. That confirms Henry's observation.'

'But we still don't know who or where they are,' she said.

'That's not true,' countered Pienaar, taking care to give no details. 'I think I may have come across the man named Jan before.'

'Then your ordeal has paid a rich dividend,' said Daniel, realising that Jan must have been employed at the brothel. 'If you can remember *where* you saw him, Henry and I can pay him a visit.'

'It's slipped my mind at the moment, Captain Rawson, but I'm sure that it will come back in time.' He smiled at Amalia. 'It was a cold and miserable journey but it wasn't a waste of time, I assure you. See for yourself.'

He turned round to reveal white patches on the back of his coat.

'Is it snowing outside?' asked Amalia.

'No,' said Pienaar, facing her again. 'The white marks came from the cart.' He put a hand into his pocket and took something out. 'I picked up a handful of it when nobody was looking.' He offered it to Daniel. 'Taste it.'

Daniel wetted his finger and put some of the powder on his tongue. 'Salt,' he said, identifying it at once. 'It's a salter's cart.'

CHAPTER ELEVEN

After the long and tedious wait, there was a flurry of action. Daniel and Welbeck armed themselves, then saddled their horses before riding off together in the direction of the brothel. Daniel had taken care to speak to Pienaar alone to glean further details about Jan's identity. He discovered that the man had actually hidden in the room when the weaver talked to Gerda on his Friday visits to the establishment. Having learnt about the significance of the tapestry, Jan had obviously passed on the information to his accomplices and a plot had been hatched. Daniel's faith in Pienaar had been vindicated. The weaver had returned with evidence that led directly to one of the thieves. Welbeck acknowledged that his friend had been right to entrust the task of meeting the thieves to Pienaar. It had at last given Daniel and him their cue to launch an attack.

The sergeant raised his voice above the clatter of hooves.

'What else did Pienaar tell you, Dan?' he asked.

'It was what he *didn't* tell me that pleased me,' replied Daniel. 'He made no mention of the fact that I'd visited the place on Friday after he did. That means they didn't ask him why he'd recommended it to me or try to find out what I said to Gerda. If they'd done either of those things, Aelbert would have had to talk himself out of an extremely awkward situation.'

'He did well – much better than I dared hope.'

'Tell him that, Henry. He'd appreciate it.'

'Let's round up these villains first.'

Daniel chuckled. 'That's why I brought you to Amsterdam. I wanted to ride into battle with you once more. It will be just like old times.'

'Except that I'm an infantryman. I prefer to fight on foot.'

'You'll have your chance to do that,' promised Daniel.

As the two of them rode side by side down a long lane, the clacking of hooves reverberated off the walls. At the end, they turned into the street where the house was located. It was no time to stand on ceremony. After tethering their horses, they marched to the front door, hands on their swords. Daniel banged on the timber with a peremptory fist. The door was soon opened by Hendrika, holding a candelabra and beaming at them.

'Good evening, gentlemen,' she said with professional sweetness. 'You're most welcome.' When she squinted at Daniel, she recognised him. 'If you've come back to talk to Gerda,' she apologised, 'I'm afraid that she's not available, sir, but we have other delights to offer you and your friend.'

'I didn't come to see Gerda,' said Daniel, pushing past

her and looking around. 'We're here to speak to Jan.'

Her face hardened. 'Then you're wasting your time,' she snarled. 'He's not here.' Angered by the sudden intrusion, she drew out the pistol from beneath the folds of her dress. 'So I'll thank you both to leave my house at once.'

Welbeck reacted swiftly. Almost as soon as he saw the pistol, he jumped forward, grabbed it by the barrel and twisted it expertly from her grasp. Hendrika shrieked at him but the words died on her lips when she found the weapon turned on her. Instantly, she became more amenable.

'There must be some mistake here, sirs,' she said, forcing a smile. 'Why don't we step into my parlour and take a glass of something to warm us up?'

'We want Jan,' insisted Daniel.

'I told you. He's not here.'

'Then where is he?'

She was rancorous. 'I don't know and I don't care. I threw him out when he tried to kill Gerda. She's still laying half dead in her room. I'll get no money out of her for weeks. It was *your* fault,' she went on, pointing an accusatory finger at him. 'Jan wanted to know what you said to Gerda. When she wouldn't tell him, he set about her. If I hadn't held a pistol to his head, he'd have murdered her.'

Daniel was overcome with remorse. As a result of his conversation with her, Gerda had endured a terrible beating. The fact that she hadn't told Jan about her conversation with Daniel was no consolation to him. She was an innocent victim. An already frail woman had been assaulted by a man who was reportedly big and powerful. It served to spur on Daniel to seek retribution.

'Where is he likely to be?' he demanded.

'He's probably in a tavern,' she said, 'or between the thighs of some doxy.'

'What's his full name?'

'Jan Dekker.'

'Does he have a friend called Frans?'

'That little fart,' she said, derisively. 'Frans Tulp is a nasty creature. I've let him hide here a couple of times when officers of the law were after him. He pays well but he treats my ladies badly. I won't have him in here again.'

'What does he do for a living?'

'He steals.'

'Where could I find him?'

'He's with Jan, most likely.'

'Let's go back to Dekker. Does he have a brother?'

'Yes, he does,' she said. 'Teunis – why do you ask?'

'It's because I think I know what he does for a living,' said Daniel. 'Would he, by any chance, be a salter?'

'As a matter of fact, he is,' she replied.

'Do you happen to know where he lives?'

Hendrika sniffed profit. 'How much is the information worth?'

'This much,' said Welbeck after Daniel translated the question for him.

And he let the barrel of the pistol rest gently against her forehead.

Teunis Dekker was a brawny man with the same limited intelligence as his brother. Struggling to make a living as a salter, he'd grown to hate the monotonous work of salting meat and fish in order to preserve it. Winter had made it difficult for him to get supplies of salt. The stocks in his storehouse were dwindling. With a wife and three small children to feed, he needed to get money from another source, so he jumped at the offer made by Tulp and by his own brother. Taking part in the theft of the tapestry would solve all his problems. All that he'd had to do was to steal something, hide it in his storehouse and act as an occasional lookout. Once the money had been handed over by Janssen, he could take his share, sell his business and move to a better district. The salter was sitting alone beside the fire with a tankard of beer in his hand. His wife was upstairs, putting the children to bed. When he heard a knock on the front door, he got grumpily to his feet and ambled out. Opening the door, he was confronted by a stranger.

'Are you Teunis Dekker?' asked Daniel, politely.

'Yes,' replied the other. 'What do you want?'

'I just passed your storehouse and it looks as if someone has broken into it.'

Teunis was roused. 'Are you sure?'

'The door is wide open.'

'Wait here.'

The salter vanished into the house to get his coat. Daniel had taken note of his size and muscularity. Thanks to directions from Hendrika, he and Welbeck knew where the man lived and found his storehouse nearby at the bottom of the cobbled hill mentioned by Pienaar. The name of Teunis Dekker was painted in bold letters on the door. Emerging with his coat and hat on, the salter carried a lantern. He and Daniel walked down the hill until they reached the storehouse. The open door was flapping in the wind. The salter was furious. He charged into the building to see what had been taken. Welbeck had been waiting behind the door to ambush him. Sticking out a foot, he tripped the man up. Teunis Dekker roared with anger and tried to get up to exact revenge but he found the point of Welbeck's sword at his throat. Daniel snatched up the lantern and held it over their captive.

'Who the hell *are* you?' shouted the salter.

'We're friends of Emanuel Janssen,' explained Daniel, 'and we've come to reclaim his tapestry. Since you helped to steal it, you can help to load it back on to your cart so that we can take it back to its rightful owner.'

'It wasn't my idea,' pleaded the other. 'It was all Frans Tulp's doing.'

'We'll come to him in due course. The tapestry has to be returned first. Before you get to your feet,' added Daniel, 'let me give you a word of warning. Sergeant Welbeck fought in the battle of Ramillies as depicted on the tapestry. If he's given the slightest excuse to kill one of the thieves who stole it, he'll take it.'

He nudged Welbeck who pricked the man's throat with his sword and drew blood. The salter quailed. There was no escape.

Dekker and Tulp had been celebrating in their favourite tavern. Now that they'd met Janssen's demand for proof that the tapestry was undamaged, they simply had to wait until the ransom was handed over. It pleased Tulp that the money would come from the Duke of Marlborough himself.

'This is one battle that he *didn't* win,' he boasted. 'I achieved something that even the French army couldn't manage.'

'You always did have brains, Frans.'

'That's why I get the lion's share of the ransom.'

'I agree, and so does Teunis.'

'As for Hendrika, she gets nothing from me.'

'Nor from me,' said Dekker, bitterly. 'I'm done with her. I hope I never see the old bitch again.'

'I thought you wanted to leave her a gift.'

'She doesn't deserve it. I walked out of that house for good.'

Fearing his reaction, Dekker hadn't told his friend that he'd been evicted or that he'd left one of the women unconscious after failing to get information out of her. That was irrelevant now. Liberated from his duties at the brothel, he could pass the time planning how he'd spend his wealth.

Tulp was pensive. 'We made only one mistake, Jan.'

'What was that?'

'We should have asked for more.'

'Could the Duke have afforded it?'

'The old bastard could afford ten times that amount.'

Dekker smiled dreamily. 'What's it like to have so much money?'

'Stay close to me and you may one day find out.'

They were sitting in a corner of the bar. Tulp had his back against the wall so that he could keep an eye on anyone who entered the tavern. Even in a place where they were well known, he was always on guard. Dekker, however, was not. After several tankards of beer, he was in a jovial mood. When someone stepped into the bar, he was completely unaware of him. Tulp, however, spotted Daniel at once. Sensing danger, he immediately put down his tankard and moved a hand to his dagger.

Dekker noticed the way that his friend had suddenly tensed.

'What's the matter, Frans?' he asked. Turning round, he saw Daniel bearing down on him. Dekker blinked. 'I've seen you before.'

'I've come to deliver a message from Gerda,' said Daniel, punching him hard on the jaw and knocking him to the floor. 'Get up so that I can give it to you in full.'

Dekker was inflamed. Rubbing his jaw, he scrambled to his feet and took a wild swing at Daniel. It completely missed its target. Ducking beneath the huge fist, Daniel replied with two searching punches to the stomach that took all the breath out of Dekker and made him bend forward. Daniel pounded his face until blood surged from his nose then put all his strength into an uppercut that felled the man. After a weak attempt to haul himself up, Dekker slumped back to the floor. Other patrons of the tavern had cleared a space for the fight to take place. Now that it was over, they closed in on Daniel.

'Stand back!' he warned, whipping out a pistol. 'This man is under arrest for a number of crimes. He will be handed over to a magistrate. If any of you would like to join him behind bars, please step forward.'

The note of authority in Daniel's voice was enough to disperse the threat. Everyone backed away at once. Still holding the pistol in one hand, Daniel took Dekker by the scruff of his neck and dragged him out of the tavern.

Tulp hadn't stayed to watch the fight. An instinct for self-preservation told him to take to his heels. He abandoned his friend to Daniel and darted out through the rear door of the tavern, only to run straight into the solid frame of Henry Welbeck. Before he could even reach for his dagger, Tulp was thrust against a wall, kicked in the shins and swiftly disarmed. Welbeck pinned him against the cold bricks.

'You must be Frans Tulp,' he said with a grim smile. 'His Grace, the Duke of Marlborough, has sent this gift for you.'

One fearsome punch sent the thief into oblivion.

The whole household was assembled to view the tapestry and to congratulate those who'd recovered it. Pienaar was embarrassed by the praise he was receiving but it was the evidence he'd gathered that had proved vital. Janssen couldn't thank him enough. Amalia reserved most of her acclaim for Daniel and for Welbeck. They'd actually captured the three thieves and handed them over to a magistrate. Such a feat was well beyond Pienaar.

'It's fortunate that Aelbert had seen one of the men before,' she said.

'He's got a sharp eye and a good memory,' said Daniel.

'Where had he met such a rogue?'

'What does it matter, Amalia? The fact is that he was able to give us an idea of where we might track down the villain.'

Establishing that Jan had worked at the brothel had been the crucial piece of evidence gathered by Pienaar. Daniel wasn't going to betray a confidence by telling Amalia what the weaver did on his Friday evenings. Pienaar was being hailed as a hero and Daniel felt that that was appropriate. The man's bravery and vigilance had more than compensated for the unintentional lapse made in conversation with a woman who resembled his wife. Pienaar would be making no more visits to the house.

It was cold in the workshop, so they folded up the tapestry and left it in a corner. Now that the rear door of the house had been reinforced, they felt it was safe to leave it there. Janssen led the way into the parlour where they could bathe in some warmth. Drink was flowing and Beatrix was offering light refreshment on a platter. When she came to Welbeck, her eyes were sparkling with admiration. She knew enough English to compliment him.

'You're a hero, Sergeant Welbeck,' she said.

'Thank you, Beatrix.'

'We owe you a lot.'

'I was happy to be of help.'

'It's so good to have a soldier in the house.'

'You've had two of us.'

'Do you like it here?'

'Yes, I do.'

Welbeck was surprised at his answer. Earlier that day, he'd been regretting his decision to come to Amsterdam because he felt out of place. The chance of action, however, had exhilarated him and he felt quite comfortable joining in the celebrations with the rest of them. Beatrix was largely responsible for that. Every other person in the house had been unfailingly cordial towards him but it was Beatrix who'd shown most interest in him. Yet she was in no way intrusive. She simply appeared when he had need of a servant. In the course of his stay, his antipathy towards women had been slowly eroded. But for the crisis that had brought him there, the Janssen household was supremely contented and Beatrix occupied a prime place in it. While he had no wish to prolong a domestic existence, he'd been forced to admit that it had its appeal. And in Beatrix, he'd finally found a woman whose company he could endure without feeling threatened.

'I hope you'll stay as long as you wish, Sergeant,' said Janssen.

'Thank you – but I have to get back to my regiment.'

'It's been a pleasure to have you here.'

'The pleasure has been mutual,' said Welbeck.

'I never thought to hear Henry saying that,' teased Daniel, joining the two men. 'You've tamed him at last. Until he came here, he was happiest when living under canvas. He's at last discovered the joys of civilised life.'

'Yet I still prefer to return to winter quarters, Dan.'

'Tarry a little in Amsterdam.'

'Yes,' added Janssen. 'My house is at your disposal.'

'It's a kind offer,' said Welbeck, 'but I've done what I was asked to do. It's time to leave.' He caught Beatrix's eye and had a momentary pang of regret. 'I'll bid you all farewell in the morning.'

'Remember that you're always welcome here, Sergeant.'

'I appreciate that.'

'Actually,' said Daniel, 'I can't let you ride back to winter quarters. There's some unfinished business for us to complete first, Henry.'

'Is there?'

'The tapestry belongs to His Grace. We must deliver it to him.'

'Yes,' agreed Janssen. 'I'll write to tell him how it was retrieved and how much we owe to two of his finest soldiers. You can bear the letter with you.'

'We'll be glad to do so.'

Amalia was saddened. 'Do you really have to go so soon, Daniel?'

'I'm afraid so. His Grace has been waiting a long time for his tapestry.'

'Let him wait a few more days at least.'

'I'm sorry, Amalia. I'll be back as soon as I possibly can.'

'I'll hold you to that.'

'And so will I,' said Janssen. 'This is your second home.'

'Then I'll make sure that I don't stay away from it for long,' promised Daniel. 'Tomorrow we'll hire a cart to take the tapestry to The Hague. As soon as this cold spell ends, His Grace will want to take it back to England with him.'

Amalia was distressed. 'I hope that you won't go with him.'

'That decision doesn't lie in my hands, Amalia. I have to obey orders. Whatever His Grace has in mind for me, I must perforce do it. That's how we first met, after all. On that occasion, too,' Daniel recalled, 'it was a tale of a tapestry, a rescue and a beautiful young lady. That's why I feel so indebted to the British army.'

Marlborough pored over the map and wondered which would be the most likely theatre of war once the campaign season resumed. Though there was a desire on all sides to achieve an equitable peace settlement, he had grave doubts that it could be achieved. Negotiations had been opened time and again, only to falter when the terms on offer were rejected. France might be on its knees, but whenever there was a military threat it always showed remarkable resilience.

He was confident that Louis XIV would be capable of raising yet another army and of finding a man worthy of leading it. With its wealth, driving ambition and expertise on the battlefield, France had dominated Europe for over forty years. In spite of major defeats inflicted by Marlborough, its army hadn't lost its sense of entitlement. It still expected to win as of right.

A sudden pain shot through his head, forcing Marlborough to push the map aside and sit up. He feared the onset of yet another migraine but the pain faded away in minutes. Even though hostilities had temporarily ceased, there'd been no real improvement in his health. He was still racked by fatigue, dizzied by headaches and liable to bouts of fever. Inertia also took its toll, leaving him bored and fretful. In previous years, he'd spent the winter back in England, where a busy social round partially compensated for the lack of action in the field. Time spent with his family, friends and political allies always revived him for the struggles that lay ahead in a forthcoming campaign season. That was not the situation here. Though he and his retinue were living scot-free in a mansion, the delights of The Hague had long since started to pall. He felt increasingly homesick.

Cardonnel entered the room to find him in a familiar pose, both hands to his head as his elbows rested on the table. The secretary crossed over to him.

'What ails you?'

'*Everything* ails me, Adam,' said Marlborough, looking up. 'The war, the winter, the endless haggling with our partners in this venture and these splitting headaches sent to torment me.' He lowered his hands. 'And that's only the beginning of it.'

'Then let me give you some good news for once.'

'Is there such a thing?'

'A thaw is setting in. Reports suggest that the ports will soon be open again.'

'You call that good news?'

'Of course, Your Grace – it will enable us to sail to England.'

'Where I will have to face the wrath of my dear wife,' said Marlborough with a sigh. 'Think of all the bile she'll have stored up during the time when she was unable to write to me. I'll be drowned in a veritable waterfall of it. I answer to Her Majesty yet my wife despises the woman. Each day brings a new perceived slight about which to complain. Nobody can hate with the passion of a woman.'

'I'm sure that Her Grace will be delighted to see you again.'

'But how long will that delight last?'

'I don't follow.'

'When she hears that our tapestry has been stolen, she'll blame me for not having it guarded properly. Sarah has seen the design and met its creator, remember. Emanuel Janssen actually went to Blenheim Palace last year to view its progress.' He rolled his eyes. 'There'll be a large blank wall where the Battle of Ramillies should be and my wife will not let me forget it.'

'The tapestry may yet be recovered, Your Grace.'

'Then why have we heard nothing from Amsterdam?'

'I have no answer to that,' admitted Cardonnel.

'When was the last communication?'

'It was over a week ago. Captain Rawson wrote to advise you that he'd sent for Sergeant Welbeck of the 24th Foot to assist him. They make a formidable team, Your Grace, and have proved themselves time and again.'

'Granted – yet I sense that they have at last failed.'

'I remain more sanguine.'

Marlborough rose to his feet. 'God bless you, Adam!' he said, patting the other man's arm. 'You're my saviour. Whenever I look into the pit of despair, you're there to pull me back from the edge.'

'It's something I learnt from you, Your Grace. No matter how bad the omens, never give up. Stay true to yourself and you'll win through.'

'It's a lesson I need to relearn for my own benefit. So,' he went on, making an effort to strike a more cheerful note, 'there's a thaw setting in, is there? That should gladden the heart. The Dutch are staunch allies but I miss the company of my fellow countrymen. Compared to England, this is such a dull and prosaic nation. And even though I may fear the ferocity of my beloved wife, I yearn to be with her once more and to remind myself what a fortunate husband I am.'

'Being at home again will surely improve your health.'

'That will be an additional bonus.'

'And you'll be able to discuss your position with Her Majesty.'

Marlborough scowled. 'I look for no favours from that quarter.'

There was a tap on the door and, in response to a barked command from Marlborough, it was opened by a uniformed lieutenant.

'Apologies for this intrusion, Your Grace,' he said, 'but Captain Rawson presents his compliments and requests a meeting with you.'

'Send him in,' urged Marlborough, 'send him in.'

'I told you that he wouldn't let you down,' said Cardonnel as the man bowed himself out. 'He's here in person to trumpet his success.'

'He could equally well have come to report failure, Adam. Unable to squeeze any money out of us, the thieves may have destroyed the tapestry out of sheer spite.'

'I incline to a more optimistic view.'

Marlborough gave a hollow laugh. 'I'm glad that one of us does.'

'Failure isn't a word in Captain Rawson's lexicon.'

'We shall see.'

There was a knock on the door. Daniel opened it, stepped into the room and exchanged greetings with them. His face was impassive.

'The tapestry is no longer in Amsterdam,' he announced.

'I knew it,' said Marlborough, gloomily. 'Those devils have destroyed it.'

'Let's hear the full details,' cautioned Cardonnel.

'I'll have them roasted alive for this.'

'The tapestry is no longer in Amsterdam,' repeated Daniel with a slow grin, 'because it's here in The Hague. At this very moment, Sergeant Welbeck – who helped me to retrieve it – is standing guard over it.'

'By Jove!' exclaimed Marlborough, embracing him. 'This is joyous news.'

Cardonnel was laughing. 'Allow me to congratulate you, Captain Rawson.'

'Sergeant Welbeck deserves as much credit as I do,' said Daniel, 'and we owe a debt to the bravery of Aelbert Pienaar.'

He gave them a full account of the recovery of the tapestry and the capture of the thieves. Pienaar's link with the brothel was the only important detail omitted. That information would never be shared with anyone else. Daniel stressed that the tapestry was unharmed, and was pleased to be handing it over into Marlborough's custody.

'There you are, Your Grace,' Cardonnel pointed out. 'It looks as if you've won the Battle of Ramillies for the second time.'

'There won't be a third time,' vowed Marlborough. 'As soon as humanly possible, it will travel to England with me – and you, Daniel, will accompany me to tell your tale to my wife.'

Daniel was dismayed. 'Do you really *need* me, Your Grace?'

'There's always work for you at my side.'

'I'd endorse that,' said Cardonnel.

'And I daresay that you'd like to be on English soil again.'

Daniel straightened his back. 'Yes, I would.'

Concealing his misgivings, Daniel tried to sound pleased. Returning to England meant putting the North Sea between him and Amalia. There'd be no hope of seeing her again until Marlborough was ready to return to the Continent. It was disappointing and yet another illustration that his duties as a British officer surpassed all else. He didn't relish the notion of writing to Amalia to inform her of his departure. Their time together in

Amsterdam had been marred by the crisis over the stolen tapestry and he'd been hoping for a chance to make amends by visiting her again. It was not to be. Daniel would sail for England with Marlborough. The real Battle of Ramillies had kept him and Amalia far apart. Its depiction on the tapestry was about to do exactly the same thing.

CHAPTER TWELVE

The main advantage of a return to England was that it allowed Daniel to pay a visit to his father's grave in Somerset. It was an event that always generated contradictory emotions. While he felt a surge of pride for a man he'd loved and admired, he was forced to remember the tragic circumstances of his death. Defeated and captured at the Battle of Sedgemoor, Captain Nathan Rawson had met the fate of so many other rebels and dangled from the gallows in front of a large crowd. A mere boy at the time, Daniel had never forgotten the sight. It was seared into his brain. Under cover of darkness, he'd helped to cut his father down and spirit him away to the parish church, where he was buried furtively in an unmarked grave. It was years before Daniel was able to return to the spot and arrange for his father's remains to be exhumed then interred after a Christian burial service. That gave him a sense that justice had been done.

As he knelt beside the grave, he thought – not for the first time – how different it would all have been if the rebellion had succeeded. His father would have retired from the makeshift army gathered around the Duke of Monmouth and become a farmer once more. Daniel would have worked alongside him and, in time, have taken charge of their broad acres. By now, he'd certainly have been married and been blessed with children whom he could regale with stories of how their grandfather had been a military hero assisting the overthrow of an unpopular Stuart king. Daniel's life, however, had taken a very different course. When their farm had been confiscated, he and his mother fled to Holland and he'd led an urban existence in Amsterdam until he was old enough to join the army. The new English king, William of Orange, achieved what the Monmouth Rebellion had failed to do and replaced a Roman Catholic monarch with a stern defender of Protestantism.

Daniel was bound to reflect on the fortunes of the man he now served. John Churchill had been one of the leaders of the royal army at Sedgemoor but deserted King James II during the extraordinary events of 1688. Though he fought in Ireland under the banner of William of Orange, capturing Cork and Kinsale, he never enjoyed his new master's full confidence and had to watch Dutch officers of lesser ability promoted over him. The Earl of Marlborough, as he then was, suffered the unjust humiliation of being dismissed in 1692 and imprisoned briefly in the Tower. Yet here he was, years later, leading a vast coalition army as captain-general and towering above any other commander in Europe. Such were the changes brought about by the whirligig of time. Notwithstanding the fact that his father had fought against John Churchill, Daniel was proud to be part of Marlborough's personal staff.

There were moments, however, when Daniel worried about him.

'How was your journey?' asked Marlborough.

'It was uneventful, Your Grace,' replied Daniel.

'Then that sets it apart from almost every other journey you've made.' He turned to his guest. 'Look on the face of this fellow, Sidney. You'll never have seen a more singular soldier. Every time that Captain Rawson is sent on an assignment, he's confronted by the most appalling perils. Yet somehow he always survives. Extreme danger is his natural habitat.'

'I'm familiar with the captain's adventures,' said Godolphin with an approving nod. 'I'm told he's become a legend in his regiment.'

'He has – and with justification.'

'Your Grace exaggerates,' said Daniel, modestly.

'I know your worth better than any man alive.'

Godolphin smiled. 'It's good to have such valiant men in our army. Valour is not a quality one often finds in politicians, alas.'

'I agree, Sidney. By and large, you're a rather insipid, overcautious breed. Though there are exceptions,' he added with distaste. 'We all know who those busy, conniving, power-hungry politicians are.'

The three men were at Holywell, the Hertfordshire residence favoured by Marlborough. It was in that same house, five years earlier, that Daniel had first met the Earl of Godolphin and found the Lord Treasurer a pleasant if rather uninspiring companion. Now well into his sixties, he'd been in a position to organise the finance of the war and had supported Marlborough loyally against his many critics. The two men were not simply bonded by close friendship. Marlborough's daughter, Henrietta, was married to Godolphin's son, Francis, thus uniting two highly influential families. Daniel noted that the burdens of office had gouged even deeper lines out of the Lord Treasurer's face and made his shoulders stoop even more. But it was Marlborough's appearance that alarmed Daniel. Looking ill and beleaguered, he seemed to have shrunk in size and lost any real authority from his voice.

'We all hope for peace,' Marlborough began, 'but what will happen if the negotiations fail and we take up arms once more?'

'Then we'll lose even more friends in Parliament,' warned Godolphin.

'I didn't know that we still had any.'

'Don't be so downhearted. There are still many who revere your name and boast of your triumphs. Set against them, however, is a growing number of mealy-mouthed individuals who deplore the cost of the war and demand a resolution to the conflict.'

'Then perhaps they should join the army and fight for it,' said Daniel.

Marlborough nodded. 'You echo my sentiments, Daniel.'

'It's nothing short of cowardly to hide behind the barricades of Parliament while condemning men who bravely put their lives at risk. They should back us to the hilt, not quibble endlessly over money.'

'Quibbling is in a politician's nature,' said Godolphin with a dry smile. 'Not without reason, they argue, they're entitled to see a return on the massive investment.'

'Then let them repeat the names of Blenheim, Ramillies and Oudenarde,' said Daniel with passion. 'Are not they amazing profits? Add the successful siege of Lille to the list and you'll see what a magnificent record His Grace has delivered.'

Godolphin held up both hands. 'I need no convincing, Captain Rawson.'

'Too many people do,' complained Marlborough. 'Unfortunately, one of them happens to be Her Majesty. She's been listening to too many whispers.'

'Have you spoken with her?'

'I tried to, Sidney, but it was to no avail.'

'She's still distracted by the death of her husband.'

'It was my dear wife who provided the distraction on this occasion. I simply had to mention Sarah's name and Her Majesty became distant towards me. It was a most distressing interview.'

There was an air of defeatism about him that Daniel had never seen before. Working so closely with Marlborough, he was keenly aware of the great diplomatic and military skills he possessed. Given what the captain-general had achieved in all manner of adverse circumstances, Daniel believed that he should be greeted with an ovation every time he set foot in England. Instead, he was at the mercy of sniping politicians and a queen whose attitude towards him had become rather lukewarm. At the peak of his power, Marlborough had forged what amounted to a ministry with Godolphin, soldier and statesman in perfect harmony, one fighting a war while the other raised funds to support it. The partnership had lost its effectiveness and it saddened Daniel to see two such able men struggling to maintain their influence. He began to fear for the future.

'What else did you do in Somerset?' wondered Marlborough.

'I visited our old farm,' replied Daniel.

'Has it changed in any way?'

'It's done so beyond all recognition. It's much larger now and run very differently. They have less stock than we did and grow far more crops. My father would never have done that.'

'Why not?'

'He believed that sheep and cattle could be nursed through a bad winter, whereas an arable farm could be ruined by it. We grew enough to feed ourselves and our animals. What was left was sent to market. Our major source of income was our stock.' Daniel smiled nostalgically. 'There's a real joy in animal husbandry.'

'He has a farmer's instincts,' observed Godolphin. 'If you're not careful, you'll lose one of your best soldiers to the land.'

Marlborough was melancholy. 'We might all be turned out to pasture before long, Sidney,' he said. 'Daniel is clearly made of prime beef but what sort of price would a stringy old goat like me fetch at market?'

Godolphin laughed and Daniel felt obliged to smile. Deep down, however, he was disturbed. It hadn't been a joke. Marlborough had spoken with calm sincerity.

Alone in the Janssen house, Nicholaes Geel was glad of Daniel's departure. As long as he and Sergeant Welbeck had been there, Amalia was wholly preoccupied. She hardly noticed Geel and that pained him. Adding salt to the wound was the fact that Aelbert Pienaar was now being treated like a hero because of the way he'd assisted in the recovery of the tapestry. Amalia never passed the older man without giving him a word of praise. That rankled with Geel. But he continued to work sedulously and even joined in the general adulation of Pienaar. Gradually, he came to Amalia's attention again and they began to have snatched conversations. While they meant nothing to her, they were manna to the lovelorn weaver. They kept hope alive. There was always the possibility – distant as it might be – that Daniel would come to grief on the field of battle or perish while spying behind enemy lines. Amalia would be utterly distraught, presenting him with the opportunity of being a sympathetic friend who would slowly edge his way into her affections.

When he arrived for work that morning, he had a chance meeting with her in the hall. Though they merely exchanged comments about the improvement in the weather, it was a significant conversation to him. Trying to prolong it, he was thwarted by the arrival of the mail. Beatrix was on hand to take it from the courier and to identify the sender of one letter.

'It's from Captain Rawson,' she said, excitedly.

Amalia was thrilled. 'Let me have it,' she cried, taking it from her.

'When is he coming back to Amsterdam?'

'I haven't even opened it yet, Beatrix.'

Geel looked on with despair seeping into his soul. Amalia had forgotten him.

'Daniel's been to see Blenheim,' declared Amalia, reading the missive. 'He thinks it will be sumptuous. That's what we felt. We'd never seen anything so opulent.'

'Did he meet Her Grace, the Duchess?'

'There's no mention of her.' She turned to the second page. 'Daniel has been to Somerset and visited his old farm. It brought back lots of memories for him.'

Amalia fell silent as she read two paragraphs written solely for her eyes. Geel winced as he saw how moved she was. He longed to be able to write something that would have the same effect on her but it was beyond him. He was no gallant soldier like Daniel. All that he could do was to weave tapestries. Yet it was a man with the same occupation who'd won the heart of Amalia's mother and he'd heard many times from Janssen that his daughter had inherited her beauty from her mother. It was wrong to have such low self-esteem. Geel had qualities that could impress a woman but, unfortunately, Amalia wouldn't spare them a glance while Daniel still lived.

'Go on,' encouraged Beatrix. 'What else does Captain Rawson say?'

'He sends you his warmest regards.'

The servant bubbled with joy. 'How kind of him to remember me!' she said. 'Is Sergeant Welbeck with him?'

'No, Beatrix, he went back to winter quarters.'

'I'm sorry to hear that.'

'But the best news of all,' continued Amalia, reaching the final paragraph, 'is that Daniel will soon be sailing for Holland. He and His Grace have business in The Hague. Isn't that wonderful? Daniel will be back at last.'

'I rejoice in the news,' said Beatrix, clapping her hands.

'Yes,' said Geel with false enthusiasm, 'so do I.'

But the letter had just slipped a red-hot knife between his ribs.

It was demeaning. It upset Daniel that he felt the snub more keenly than Marlborough himself. At the formal peace negotiations held at The Hague, there were two British plenipotentiaries and – in spite of his central role in the war – Marlborough was only the junior partner. It angered Daniel that the Whig Junto ruling England had appointed its own man above the captain-general. Charles, Viscount Townshend, still in his thirties, had neither the military experience nor the long association with French diplomacy that Marlborough enjoyed, yet he was given the senior role. To all intents and purposes, Marlborough was effectively an observer at the various sessions. Daniel, whose fluency in Dutch and French earned him a position as an interpreter, had to watch him being consigned to a secondary role. It made Daniel resentful.

There was never a better time for the Allies to enforce their demands. The harsh winter that had crippled France had been followed by a continuously wet spring, causing further disaster to French agriculture. The country was on the verge of collapse. As a result, the Marquis de Torcy, its foreign minister, seemed ready to concede anything to bring a ruinously expensive war to an end. So confident was he of the outcome that Marlborough was able to write to Godolphin, assuring him that '*M. Torcy has offered so much that I have no doubt it will end in a good peace*'. Daniel took the same view. The enemy had been beaten by a combination of superior military tactics and devastating weather. He fully expected that the War of the Spanish Succession would finally cease and that he would be able to see more of Amalia instead of having to prepare for yet another campaign season.

After long discussions, the Allies presented Torcy with their demands at the end of May. There were forty conditions in the catalogue and Louis XIV was given an ultimatum that he had to accept the formidable terms within a week or the war would resume. In a private moment with Daniel and Cardonnel, Marlborough was still anticipating success, in spite of the severity of the demands made on the French.

'Louis will accept,' he asserted. 'He has no choice but to accept.'

'I wish that I could feel more certain of that,' admitted Cardonnel.

'So do I,' said Daniel, beginning to have reservations. 'Will the French *really* cede the entire Spanish Empire without a fight? And can we imagine that they will agree to yield up fortresses in Flanders and on the Rhine as a gesture of good faith? I doubt it, Your Grace. It's simply not in their nature to make such enormous concessions.'

'We are asking too much of them.'

'We have to press home our advantage, Adam,' said Marlborough. 'When you have an enemy by the throat, you must squeeze hard with all your might.'

'French pride is at stake. It might yet wreck the negotiations.'

'Then why do I feel so strangely optimistic?'

'I hope that your optimism is not misplaced,' said

Daniel. 'I know that the French have given ground time and again at the conference table but on one condition they will surely make a stand. I refuse to believe that they'll make King Philip abdicate within two months or remove him by force if necessary. Think how such a condition will be viewed at Versailles, Your Grace. Louis would never inflict such humiliation on the beloved grandson he placed on the Spanish throne.'

'I own that that condition is perhaps ill-conceived,' said Marlborough. 'If it were left entirely in my hands, such a demand would be removed lest it arouse defiance. Nevertheless,' he went on, 'I still contend that the French will bow to our terms. I'm so convinced of it that I've ordered Cadogan to prepare a number of regiments for transfer back to England. The dove of peace is fluttering its wings.'

'Let's pray that it takes flight,' said Daniel.

'It must, Daniel. Miss this chance and the war will continue for years on end, destroying towns, scarring the countryside and killing thousands more men. Louis understands that. He doesn't want any more carnage.' He lifted his chin. 'That's why I feel so buoyant,' continued Marlborough, shaking off his weariness for once. 'France will submit. We have won a gruelling war. Peace is our reward.'

After drilling his men for a couple of hours, Henry Welbeck dismissed them and headed for his quarters. He was smouldering with discontent. On the way, he encountered Leo Curry, who was in an equally disgruntled mood.

'I thought the fighting was over,' he complained.

'So did I,' said Welbeck, 'but the bleeding politicians let the chance of peace slip through their stupid fingers. We're off to the battlefield once more, Leo.'

'What went wrong?'

'I just told you. Our politicians are to blame.'

'There's more to it than that,' said Curry, sourly. 'According to you, Captain Rawson was at the negotiations. Hasn't he told you why they broke up?'

'I haven't had chance to speak to him yet.'

'I heard that Corporal John was the culprit.'

Welbeck stiffened. 'That's arrant nonsense.'

'He needs the war to continue so that he can carry on strutting like a peacock across Europe. Over here, he has power. In England, he has none.'

'Who told you that?'

'It's what a lot of people are saying, Henry.'

'Then they're talking through their buttocks,' retorted Welbeck. 'Corporal John would do anything for peace. He's old, ill, exhausted and fed up with spilling blood over the same sodden ground year after year. Anyone who says that he wants this war to carry on is a fucking idiot.'

Curry squared up to him. 'Are you calling me an idiot?'

'I don't need to, Leo. It's clear for all to see.'

'He's fighting this war for his own benefit.'

'Listen, you mutton-headed fool,' said Welbeck with contempt. 'Ask yourself one question. If Corporal John wanted to take up arms again, why hasn't he made any preparations to do so? He thought the war was over. No commander would be eager to take to the field again when there's such a shortage of forage. Do you agree?'

As Curry pondered, his eyebrows formed a chevron. 'I don't know.'

'That ought to be your motto. *I don't know.* Get it translated into Latin, Leo, because it sums you up perfectly. You don't know a thing yet you still open your big bleeding mouth on any and every subject.'

'I'm entitled to my opinion.'

'And I'm entitled to tell you what to do with it.'

'You think you're so high and mighty because you went off to Amsterdam and caught a few thieves with Captain Rawson. While you were having your little holiday, I was doing proper military duties here.'

'Drinking beer and boring the balls off anyone mad enough to listen to you.'

Curry's eyes flashed. 'Don't tempt me, Henry.'

'I won't. I'd be afraid you'd fall over.'

'You're asking for a punch on the nose.'

Welbeck shoved him away. 'Go back to the madhouse you escaped from.'

'Say that again!' challenged Curry.

'You heard the first time.'

Curry tried to grab him but Welbeck was far too quick. Stepping to one side, he dodged the outstretched arms and clipped one of Curry's ears. The other man roared. Before he could turn on Welbeck once more, however, he was halted by the arrival of a smirking Ben Plummer.

'Are you two at it again?' he asked, derisively.

'Shut your gob, Plummer!' snapped Welbeck.

'I thought you were supposed to be on the same side.'

'We are. If you're not careful, Sergeant Curry and I will

prove it by tearing you limb from limb together.'

'Yes,' said Curry, 'then we'll bury what's left of you in a pile of horse shit.'

Plummer was unabashed. 'Thank you for being so caring towards me.'

'Sarcasm will get you nowhere.'

'Except flat on your back, that is,' warned Welbeck. 'Show more respect to your superiors or you'll be in serious trouble.'

'I hear and obey,' said Plummer, giving a mock salute. A blow from Welbeck sent him reeling but didn't dislodge his smirk. 'I'll let you fight on.'

He caught a punch from Curry this time but shrugged it off and walked away. Their dispute over, the two sergeants looked after him.

'Did he cause any trouble while I was away?' asked Welbeck.

'He had the sense to steer clear of me, Henry.'

'I still think he's gone back to his old trade.'

'You mean that he's keeping women somewhere?'

'It's what he did before he was forced to join the army. He's a scurvy pimp. Plummer made the women do all the work while he lived off the profits.'

Curry was envious. 'Dirty devil probably had a different one of them in his bed every night.'

'They'd have been the ugliest drabs in Christendom.'

'A woman is a woman, Henry. We all have needs.'

'Speak for yourself.'

'If he's gone back to his trade, where does he keep his whores?'

'I don't know, Leo,' said Welbeck, 'but I intend to find

out. I'm not having my men infected by a pack of mangy harlots. We need to have them fighting fit, not walking around in circles scratching their burning pizzles.'

It had all happened so swiftly. In mid-May, the prospects for peace seemed very rosy. A month later, two armies had been assembled for combat. The Allies had mustered one hundred thousand men in Flanders comprising one hundred and fifty-two battalions and two hundred and forty-five squadrons with substantial reinforcements still awaited. Marlborough had displayed consummate skill in persuading allies like the King of Prussia to send more mercenaries by praising the quality of those dispatched in earlier years. When he joined the army near Ghent in the company of Prince Eugene of Savoy, the captain-general found it equipped with one hundred and four canon, twenty-four mortars and forty-two pontoons, as well as ancillary weapons. Fodder remained in short supply but that didn't deter the two commanders. They were eager to fight the enemy under its flamboyant new leader, Claude Louis Hector, Duc de Villars and Marshal of France.

While the French army might be dispirited, it had to be respected now that it was under the command of Villars. He was a brilliant soldier with an impressive record of success. He'd won a comprehensive victory over the Margrave of Baden at Friedlingen in 1702, then defeated a Hapsburg army at Hochstadt the following year. In 1705 he inflicted the first strategic reverse sustained by Marlborough by his clever defensive tactics on the Moselle. But it was his ability to inspire his men that made him so dangerous an opponent. His soldiers feared his quick temper but they

admired his bravery and were uplifted by his unshakable
conviction that he was destined for victory. Unlike other
French commanders, he scorned defensive warfare and
believed that only a major battle could destroy the coalition
army. With his gift for rhetoric, he inspired his men with
the notion that they were taking part in a glorious crusade.

Daniel considered Villars to be the one French soldier
capable of matching Marlborough and Prince Eugene.
Even with numerical superiority, the Allies were not assured
of outright victory. When he was sent to carry out a full
reconnaissance, Daniel was given the opportunity to see
the effect that the new commander had had on the French
army. In order to travel with a degree of impunity, he was
disguised as a peasant and drove a battered old cart. After
a week without shaving, he'd acquired a rough beard. He'd
also dirtied his face and hands. With a hat pulled down over
his forehead, even his closest friends needed a second look
to identify him. Progress over roads still sodden from rain
was slow but Daniel was in no hurry. His leisurely journey
gave him plenty of time to take stock of the terrain. When
he eventually came in sight of the French army, they'd drawn
up defensive lines between St Venant and Douai. Daniel
studied them through a telescope. The fortifications were
impressive, with earthworks supplemented by a series of
water obstacles. Additional supplies of timber were arriving
and the thud of axes could be heard as it was cut to size.
Of more interest to Daniel was the fact a long column of
soldiers was moving towards the lines. Unlike some of those
he could see on the ramparts, they were all in uniform and
moving with the discipline of a well-trained force. Having
spent so many years in the army, Daniel could gauge

numbers at a glance. He estimated that the reinforcements amounted to at least three thousand. Judging by the direction from which they came, he surmised that they must have been withdrawn from the garrison at Tournai.

From his vantage point in a copse, Daniel made a detailed mental note of everything he saw. With his cart hidden by the trees, he felt safe from discovery. So intent was he in peering through his telescope that he didn't realise he had company until it was too late. A horse whinnied behind him and he turned to see a mounted French soldier looking down at him with his sword drawn. Daniel was annoyed with himself for being caught off guard. It was a rare lapse and it put him in jeopardy. The concealed dagger he carried was no match for the sword. He had to rely on bluff.

'What are you doing?' demanded the man.

'I found this on the ground,' replied Daniel, holding up the telescope, 'and I was just looking through it. Here – take it.'

He offered it to the soldier who knocked it from his grasp with the sword.

'Don't lie to me,' he snarled, 'or I'll cut you to shreds.'

Daniel crouched submissively. 'I mean no harm, sir,' he said. 'I'm only a poor, humble peasant.' He pointed a finger. 'I farm some land close to here. Your army took what little food we have. I came to see what you were doing.'

'You came to spy on us.'

'No, no, I'd never do that.'

'You're in the pay of the enemy and that's a death sentence.'

'Spare me,' pleaded Daniel, looking for a means of escape

as he did so. 'I've done no wrong, I swear it. Don't kill me. I have a wife and family.'

'Then they can come and bury your stinking carcass.'

Urging his horse forward, the soldier raised his sword. He showed no mercy as he hacked at his prisoner. Dodging the murderous slash of the blade, Daniel tried to run off through the undergrowth but his plan soon faltered. He tripped over a root half hidden by the grass and plunged forward on to his face. The soldier caught up with him, dismounted and lifted his sword to strike.

'Stop!' yelled a female voice.

Surprised at the intervention, the man looked over his shoulder at a plump woman in her thirties seated astride a bay mare carrying a series of bags and pouches. In her hand was a pistol and it was aimed at the soldier. The momentary delay was all that Daniel needed. Pulling out his dagger, he leapt to his feet, disarmed his attacker then slit the man's throat without compunction. Only when the soldier lay dying on the ground did he turn towards his rescuer. Inured to the sight of hideous deaths, she was unmoved by what she'd just witnessed. When he recognised her, Daniel laughed with gratitude.

'Rachel!' he cried. 'It's Rachel Rees.'

Puzzlement creased her face. 'How do you know my name?'

'Thank heaven you came when you did!'

She stared at him. 'You sound just like Captain Rawson,' she said, 'but you don't look anything like him.'

'I'll explain why on the way back.'

'It *is* you, then, Daniel, is it?'

'Yes, it is.'

'What on earth are you doing here?'

'I might ask the same of you. I thought you went off to Wales.'

'I did – but I missed army life.'

'Well, it's wonderful to see you again – especially at a moment like this. I owe you heartfelt thanks. That pistol of yours saved my life.'

She held the weapon up. 'I'll let you into a secret – it's not loaded.'

'It did the trick, Rachel. That's all that matters.'

'Who'd have thought it?' she asked, cackling merrily, her ample bosom heaving up and down. 'I save someone from the French and he turns out to be none other than one of my husbands – or, at least, a man who once *pretended* to be my husband. I call that a happy coincidence.' She slapped a chubby thigh. 'This is what brought me back, you see. It's the beauty of warfare. Strange things always happen. Wonders never cease.'

CHAPTER THIRTEEN

Marlborough never enjoyed councils of war because the Allied generals were inclined to block his bold schemes in favour of less ambitious projects. The Dutch were particularly cautious, often delaying a course of action until it was no longer viable. Years earlier, Marlborough had been glad to get rid of General Slangenburg, the contentious Dutchman, who always opposed his ideas. More recently, he was deeply saddened by the death of the Dutch commander, Field Marshal Overkirk, who invariably supported them. As yet another council gathered around a table in Courtrai, laid out in front of them was a detailed map of Flanders together with a drawing that Daniel had made of the location and disposition of the French defences. Daniel himself was there to act as an interpreter while Cardonnel took detailed notes of the meeting. There was a collective mood of disappointment.

Everyone present had believed that peace was definitely in the offing. The abandonment of negotiations was a bitter blow to them.

After the initial exchange of greetings, Marlborough took charge.

'France is slowly expiring,' he announced, 'but will not yet lie down. Reports from our agent at Versailles speak of widespread misery and deprivation. People were recently seen fighting over fragments of a dead horse on the Pont Neuf. Crowds of angry workmen scour the capital in search of employment that doesn't exist. Beggars die of starvation every day. Those wealthy enough are preparing to flee the country and the King's guards sleep booted and spurred in case of insurrection. Yet somehow,' he continued, 'Marshal Villars has achieved the miracle of assembling a sizeable army and firing it with self-belief. As you will see from the drawing provided by Captain Rawson, the enemy is camped in a favourable position and its fortifications are sound. Since they anticipate an attack, I urge that we deny them their wish.' He indicated the map. 'My plan is to march the bulk of the army to Ypres, covered by an inland feint, with the intention of piercing the French defences on the coast near Dunkirk. This will be a first move towards the River Somme and it will receive naval support in the shape of a descent from the sea against Picardy.'

He paused to let his words sink home. Studying the faces around the table, Daniel could see that the notion hadn't found support. Essentially, it was the plan that Marlborough had advanced almost a year earlier, only to see it rejected for being too audacious. Before anyone actually voiced it, Marlborough sensed opposition and sought to remove it.

'Ypres should be invested,' he argued. 'It's the French weak point. While they are hiding behind their defences further south, we should move fast and lay siege to Ypres. It will be a valuable prize.'

'Nobody disputes that, Your Grace,' said Prince Eugene, 'but there are equally valuable prizes waiting to be secured. Your advocacy of a feint is sensible but we should choose a different objective.'

'Where did you have in mind, Your Highness?'

'Tournai. The admirable Captain Rawson has ascertained that the garrison there has been depleted and left more vulnerable. If we move our artillery train to Menin, it will give the French some jealousy that our design is upon Ypres. Villars will respond accordingly and move his troops in the wrong direction.'

'It's certainly worth considering,' admitted Marlborough.

But the plan had already aroused interest. There was a loud murmur of approval. After the long, expensive and blood-soaked siege of Lille, nobody was keen to invest another French stronghold but it seemed a better option than an attack on the defensive line that Daniel had reconnoitred. The more they discussed it, the more support the plan garnered. Marlborough was forced yet again to shelve his own project and he did so with his usual graciousness. The decision had been made.

'We move towards Menin,' he declared, 'until Villars takes the bait. Our army will have six days' rations. When they least expect it, we'll swing south and east to invest Tournai. The decoy will have served its purpose.'

'I trust that Tournai will not be a second Lille,' said a dissentient general.

'There's no danger of that. It has no Marshal Boufflers to withstand a siege.'

Daniel was of the same mind. Like Marlborough, he would have preferred a decisive battle to a time-consuming siege that would sap their resources, but Villars would be under orders not to engage the Allied army in the field. The French wouldn't dare to risk another resounding defeat so early in the campaign. Daniel remembered Lille well. While he regretted the terrible losses sustained there by the Allies, he could point to the fact that it had eventually surrendered. He knew that Marlborough had an excellent record with regard to sieges. Whether it was Ypres or Tournai, Daniel felt that the result would be the same. An enemy stronghold would be secured and a clear message would be sent to the enemy that the Allies had drawn first blood and outfoxed the new French commander. Tired, unwell and lacklustre, Marlborough might be unable to muster great enthusiasm for the project but Daniel had faith in it. Tournai would fall.

Henry Welbeck was less enamoured of the plan and expressed himself forcefully.

'Another bleeding siege?' he exclaimed. 'Has Corporal John taken leave of his two remaining senses? We lost some of our best fucking men at Lille. Has he forgotten that? It's madness to invest Tournai.'

'It was not His Grace's choice,' said Daniel.

'Then he's got some brains, after all.'

'He wanted us to lay siege to Ypres.'

'And bury even more of our men?' complained Welbeck with a despairing flap of his arms. 'Tournai or Ypres – it makes no difference. Either of them will drain the lifeblood out of us. Doesn't Corporal John realise that?'

'Now then, Henry,' said Daniel, sharply. 'Let's have more respect for His Grace. He's earned it by the way he's led this army.'

'Granted – but I think he's losing his grip, Dan.'

'Then you're grossly misinformed.'

'I'll wager that Prince Eugene wanted to do what I want to do and that's to attack the French army where they are and kick the French shit out of them.'

'Prince Eugene believes that we should invest Tournai.'

Welbeck goggled. 'After what happened at Lille?' he asked. 'He damn near got his head blown off and had to retire from the fray altogether. Hasn't he learnt any lesson at all from the siege?'

They were in Daniel's quarters where he confided the decisions taken at the council of war to his friend. Knowing that the sergeant was completely trustworthy, he talked openly. Welbeck might express his objections but he would never vouchsafe a single word of their discussion to anyone else. It was the first time they'd met since Daniel had returned from his reconnaissance. While he told his friend what he'd discovered about the enemy, he said nothing about his encounter with a French soldier or about his rescue by Rachel Rees. The woman's name was enough to make Welbeck froth with displeasure and he was already agitated enough. Daniel turned to more practical matters.

'Are the men in good heart, Henry?'

'No, Dan, they hate this rain that keeps pissing down on them.'

'The promise of action will revive them.'

'Not when they learn we're heading for yet another siege. Tournai could hold out for another two or three bleeding months. That might mean an end to all hostilities for this year. And what will we have achieved?' he added, scornfully. 'Bugger all. Villars can go back to Paris with his whole army intact.'

'Oh, no,' said Daniel, seriously. 'That will never happen. Marshal Villars won't walk away without an encounter of some sort. He's a man spoiling for a fight. Sooner or later, we'll give him one and you, Henry Welbeck, will be forced to eat your own words.'

Welbeck's nose wrinkled. 'It will be like eating week-old turds.'

'Or even worse – eating army food.'

Their laughter took all the tension out of the air. Putting a hand on his friend's shoulder, Daniel led him out of the tent. He was now clean-shaven, well groomed and back in uniform. All traces of peasantry had gone. He chatted with Welbeck for a few minutes and was about to go back into his quarters when he saw someone riding towards them on a bay mare. Daniel gave her a smile of welcome. Welbeck, however, gurgled in horror.

'It's Rachel bleeding Rees!' he yelled. 'What the hell is *she* doing here?'

'She's probably come to see how I am after my narrow escape,' said Daniel. 'What I didn't tell you earlier is that she saved my life.'

'She may have saved *your* life but she's the bane of mine.'

'Play the gentleman for once. It won't cost you anything.'

'I loathe the woman.'

'Henry!' called Rachel, waving to him. 'This is a double treat. I'm here to see Captain Rawson and I find my favourite sergeant here as well.'

Welbeck eyed her malevolently. 'What's this about you saving Dan?'

'Oh, that was pure luck.'

'It's true, then?'

'As true as I stand here,' affirmed Daniel.

He gave Welbeck a short account of what had happened and how Rachel's arrival had been timely. Untroubled by modesty, she supplied additional details that showed her in a good light. Welbeck was reluctantly impressed.

'Why on earth did you come back to haunt us?' he demanded.

She cackled. 'You always did like to tease me.'

'Wales is the only fit place for a mad Welsh hag like you.'

'Well, you wouldn't have said that if you'd come to Brecon with me. There was no life to the place. All my family had died off and my friends had had the sense to leave. I stuck it through the winter then boredom got into my bones. I wanted to be with soldiers once more and I longed to see your lovely old face.'

'You've seen enough of it for one day,' said Welbeck, gruffly. 'Keep her away from me, Dan. Shackle her, if need be. She unnerves me.'

Spinning on his heel, he walked quickly away. She wasn't dismayed.

'He's delighted to see me, really,' she said, beaming. 'I can always tell.'

'Have you met any of the other sutlers yet?'

'Yes – they were glad to have me back again.' She patted the bags and pouches. 'I've lost my waggon but I can carry a lot of provender on my horse.'

'Don't sell it all at once,' advised Daniel, 'or you'll have a difficult job finding fresh supplies.'

She was confident. 'Oh, there are always places where you can buy what you want if you know where to look. I've been at this game for years, remember.' She gazed after Welbeck. 'He's mellowed since we last met.'

Daniel shook his head. 'I wouldn't put it quite like that, Rachel.'

'In his heart, he's been pining for me. That's understandable, I suppose. It must have been a long, cold, miserable, lonely winter for the poor devil. Henry needs cheering up.'

'You do that best by giving him some breathing space.'

'Oh I will,' she said, happily. 'I'll let him pine for me a little more. It's wrong to let a man think he has you at his beck and call. When he reaches the point of desperation, mind you, I'll pop up in front of him like a fairy queen.'

'I see,' said Daniel, amused by the image that formed in his mind. 'Allow a long passage of time before you do so, Rachel,' he cautioned. 'Somehow I don't think that Henry is quite ready to meet royalty.'

Put into effect, the plan worked perfectly. When the Allied siege train headed towards Menin, the French were fooled into thinking that Ypres was in danger. More soldiers were swiftly withdrawn from the garrison at Tournai to reinforce the area under threat. Marlborough promptly changed direction. Covered by a Dutch force under Count Tilly, the captain-general and Prince Eugene executed a rapid march through the night, squelching along muddy roads in darkness. The operation was a complete success. Tournai was surrounded and the French were left with red faces. The very town from which they'd taken soldiers was now under siege. It was isolated and undermanned.

Yet its capture posed severe problems. Designed by the famous engineer, M. de Maigrini, it had a five-bastioned citadel that was held to be invincible. Tournai's governor, the Marquis de Surville-Hautfois, was an experienced officer and still commanded a garrison of seven thousand seven hundred soldiers. What he lacked were enough troops to defend the town itself but he nevertheless put up stern resistance at first. When the Allies opened the trenches against three sectors of the defences, the garrison fought back with unexpected ferocity. They were confident enough to mount frequent sorties against the encircling army. Casualties among the Allies began to rise ominously. It was starting to feel uncomfortably like the siege of Lille.

'Is there any news of Captain Rawson?' asked Geel, solicitously.

'Yes,' replied Amalia. 'His last letter was sent from Tournai. It seems that they've invested the town and will wait until it falls before moving on to the next stage in the campaign.'

'Did he say *when* it would succumb?'

'That's impossible to predict. Daniel hopes that it will

not be too long but he says that the town is well defended.'

'So there'll be losses on our side.'

Amalia sighed. 'There are always losses, Nick.'

Geel had waited for days for an opportunity to intercept her on her own. His chance finally came when she entered the workshop in search of her father and found only the youngest of his assistants there.

'So we'll not be seeing the captain for some time,' he concluded.

'I fear not.'

'That's a shame,' he said, screening his envy behind a sad smile. 'He always brings such life into the house. Not that it's dull or listless,' he added, quickly. 'No house containing you could be anything but a delight.'

'Thank you,' she said, taking the compliment in her stride.

'I'm so glad that Captain Rawson was here when the tapestry was stolen.'

'So am I – without help from Daniel and Sergeant Welbeck, we might never have recovered it. Aelbert did his share, of course, but he could hardly tackle the thieves and overpower them. That was a job for trained soldiers.'

'If I'd been called upon,' said Geel, trying to engage her interest, 'I'd have been very willing to lend my assistance. I'm young, strong and very able. I'm sorry that Aelbert was chosen ahead of me.'

'You'd have done the task equally well, Nick,' she assured him.

He grinned. 'Do you think so?'

'Nobody doubts your courage.'

'My only regret is that we let the tapestry get stolen in the first place. Had I realised that it was under threat, I'd have slept here all night to protect it.'

'That's very noble of you.'

'I'd have guarded the tapestry with my life.'

'Then I'm glad that you didn't stand sentry over it,' she said in alarm. 'I hate the thought that you might have been injured – even killed – defending the tapestry. You'd be a terrible loss to us.'

He grinned again. 'Do you *mean* that, Miss Amalia?'

'Of course – Father was praising you to me only yesterday.'

'It's a joy to work under this roof.'

'I think that it must be,' she said, smiling, 'for you always stay much longer than the others. Aelbert left half an hour ago and, as I was coming downstairs, I saw Kees going up to his room. Yet you're still here at your loom.'

'It's the place where I feel happiest.'

Gazing deep into her eyes, Geel tried to convey his feelings but his smile froze when Janssen suddenly bustled into the workshop.

'Goodness!' he said. 'Are you still here, Nick? You should have gone ages ago. Why are you hanging about in the workshop?'

The reason was standing beside Geel but he wasn't about to admit that. He'd lingered on the off chance of seeing Amalia and he'd been lucky. She'd found him alone and he'd basked in their conversation. It was something on which to build.

'I was just about to leave, master,' he said, moving

towards the door, 'but I'll be back first thing tomorrow. I bid you farewell.'

He gave them both a cheerful wave but his eyes were solely on Amalia.

By the middle of July, the Allies had one hundred guns and sixty mortars booming away at the walls of Tournai, concentrating their firepower against the Porte de Valenciennes. Allied siege works were strong and their assault seemed to be bearing fruit. After three days of bombardment, they were battering a breach in the main enceinte and were pleased with their progress. It came to an abrupt halt when the French exploded a large mine that damaged one of the four main Allied batteries and claimed many lives. Encouraged by this success, the garrison launched another sortie and wrecked sections of the foremost siege works. It was daunting. During a fortnight or more of intense fighting, the Allies had sustained over three thousand casualties and seen six hundred men desert their ranks. Nothing seemed to have been gained in return.

Observers from the main French force watched from a distance and sent regular reports back to Villars. The commander read them with satisfaction.

'Tournai is holding out,' he said, chuckling. 'Marlborough's army is being given a bloody nose. He's made a gross error of judgement. Had he applied the principles of war, he should have invested Tournai *before* turning to Lille. Instead of outwitting us, he's mired in the mud trying to do something that he could have achieved last autumn.'

'It's a mistake that bodes well for us, Your Grace.'

'The great captain-general will make many more before we're done.'

Villars was in his quarters with Lieutenant-Colonel Morellon, one of the most trusted members of his entourage. The French commander was a striking figure, immaculately attired to the point of vanity and resolutely straight-backed. He strutted up and down with an air of self-importance. Now in his mid-fifties, he showed none of the signs of fatigue that Marlborough was exhibiting. Villars was pulsing with energy and driven by an inner conviction of superiority.

'The Governor of Tournai will not thank us for draining his garrison,' he said, 'but our need is the greater. Even with reduced numbers, he's fighting valiantly.'

'Is there no chance of going to his aid?' asked Morellon.

'Not in the present circumstances. The enemy has completed its lines of circumvallation and is being covered by an army led by Prince Eugene. The place to attack them is not in the environs of Tournai.'

'Then it must inevitably fall.'

'Why, yes – but only after it's taken its toll of the enemy.'

'Reports speak of heavy Allied casualties.'

'The longer the siege goes on, the lower their morale will sink.'

'And the more deserters they'll have,' said Morellon, complacently.

He was a tall, square-shouldered man in his forties with sharp features. A great admirer of his commander, he'd retained his favour by agreeing with him at all times. Senior officers who attempted to argue with Villars found themselves at the mercy of his vile temper. Morellon had learnt never to provoke it.

'If only we had more men, more food and more money,' said Villars.

'You've done wonders with meagre resources, Your Grace. You've turned a rabble into a semblance of an army.'

'There's still a long way to go, Charles. That's why I delayed assembling the men until the last moment. They were simply not ready. At least they now have bread in their stomachs and – in most cases – uniforms on their backs. They're now starting to look like an army.'

'Under your command, anything is possible.'

'Anything but defeat, that is,' said Villars with a harsh laugh. 'But I don't mean to fight from behind barricades. What I yearn for is *la grande guerre*, a war in which a solution takes place on a battlefield strewn with enemy corpses.'

'Yet your hands are tied. Versailles has forbidden an outright assault.'

'They should have more faith in me.'

'The men have faith in you, Your Grace,' said Morellon. 'You've rallied them in a way that seemed impossible after the surrender of Lille. They've started to hold their heads up high again.'

'They just needed to be reminded of France's destiny.'

'They've fought with honour.'

'Yes,' said Villars. 'The raiding parties I've sent out have so far been very successful. They've kept the enemy on their toes. What we've not done, of course, is to test the entire army. That will only happen when the King gives me free rein.'

'When do you suppose that will be, Your Grace?'

Hands on hips, Villars struck a pose. His voice had a rasping impatience.

'The sooner, the better – I was born to confront Marlborough in the field. I mean to teach him that he has too good an opinion of his own abilities.' He bared his teeth. 'It will be a lesson that he'll never forget.'

Daniel hated to see men hanging from the gallows. It reminded him of his father's execution. Yet he accepted that desertion had to be punished in a sufficiently public way to deter others from following their example. Three men swung in the wind from the rudimentary gibbet. He was upset to learn that one of them had been from his own regiment. A large crowd had been assembled to watch the execution. It had now dispersed, leaving only a handful of people still standing there. Daniel recognised two of them as Henry Welbeck and Ben Plummer. He crossed over to the pair and spoke above the thunder of distant artillery.

'Was he one of your men, by any chance, Sergeant?' he asked.

'Yes,' replied Welbeck. 'His name was Jake Abbot and I'd have strangled him with my bare hands if I'd had the chance.'

'So would I,' piped up Plummer. 'Jake owed me money.'

'Be warned, Plummer.' Welbeck pointed at the trio on the gibbet. '*That's* what happens to deserters.'

Plummer glanced towards the rows of crosses on nearby mass graves. 'And that's what happens to those of us who stay here,' he said, forlornly.

'The town will surrender eventually,' said Daniel.

'I'm sure that it will, Captain Rawson, but will I be here to see it?'

'If you're not,' warned Welbeck, 'you'll answer to me.'

'I won't be able to speak when I'm six foot underground, Sergeant.'

Shoulders hunched, Plummer moved away disconsolately. His characteristic insolence had vanished. In winter quarters, he'd been spry and impudent. Now that he was bearing arms in action again, he was a very frightened soldier.

'He's like so many of them, Dan,' said Welbeck, lapsing into a more familiar tone. 'They watch their comrades falling like flies and they ask what, in the name of God, we're actually doing here.'

'We're obeying orders, Henry.'

'We're obeying *bad* orders, you mean.'

'The plan is sound. When we capture Tournai, we have yet another feather in our cap. The French will be shaken by the fact that it fell into our hands.'

'There's no sign of that fall as yet.'

'They can't hold out much longer. His Grace is conducting the siege well. After a series of assaults, we've secured a ravelin on the bank of the Scheldt hard by the Porte de Valenciennes. It's only a matter of days before the governor seeks an armistice. My guess is that he'll surrender the town and retreat into the citadel.'

'So the fight simply shifts to a different bleeding target.'

'Sieges take time, Henry. You should know that by now.'

'What I know is that my men are unhappy. I've lost a dozen of them in a failed assault and seen two of the buggers turn tail. Soldiers are leaving us every day, Dan.'

'Tournai has its casualties as well,' noted Daniel, 'and the desertions are not confined to our army. It might interest you to know that an entire Irish regiment has deserted the French and thrown in its lot with us.'

Welbeck was contemptuous. 'Never trust the Irish,' he said. 'They change sides whenever they think they can gain an advantage.'

'In this case, they're right to do so. We offer better pay than the French and a far better chance of ending up as victors.'

'I didn't feel like a victor when I buried my men yesterday.'

'Think of all the dead and dying inside the town,' said Daniel. 'And they'll increase steadily in number. Listen to the cannon pounding away relentlessly. We have superior artillery and more ammunition. As their stocks slowly diminish, they'll be forced to accept the inevitable.'

'I still think another siege was a hideous mistake.'

'Suspend judgement until it's over, Henry.'

They were well behind the trenches but could see and hear the continuous bombardment. Artillery fire from inside Tournai was more sporadic but accurate enough to claim victims. They could hear screams of pain and howls of anguish. Their attention was soon diverted away from the action. Rachel Rees was walking towards them, wearing a bloodstained apron and an expression of resignation.

'At least I was safe in Brecon,' she said, wearily.

'Then why didn't you do us all a favour and stay there?' asked Welbeck, drily.

'I was needed here, Henry. Someone has to tend the wounded.'

'Ignore him, Rachel,' said Daniel. 'We're very grateful for your help.'

'It's just like being back at Lille – blood and broken bodies everywhere.'

'It will all be over much sooner than at Lille.'

She heaved a sigh. 'One siege is much like another.'

Welbeck noticed the blood on her hands and arms. Even her face had been spattered. Rachel was doing what most of the women who were camp followers had done. She was working as a nurse and, judging by the dark rings beneath her eyes, had been doing so all night. Daniel saw the look of grudging approval in his friend's face. Welbeck had finally found something about the Welsh woman to admire.

'This noise is deafening,' she complained. 'I can't hear myself speak.'

'I wish that *I* couldn't,' sniped Welbeck.

She cackled. 'Away with you,' she said, 'you rotten old tease.'

'That's a good suggestion. She's all yours, Dan.'

Welbeck marched off at speed and left them there together.

'He's just like my first husband,' she confided. 'Will Baggot used to run away from me like that. But I tamed him in the end. It will be the same with Henry.'

'I doubt that, Rachel.'

'I've made a lifetime's study of men. I can read them like a book.'

'And what have you learnt about the sergeant?'

'He's shy,' she decided. 'Because he's not at ease with a woman, he pretends to hate the lot of us. It's a way of keeping us at bay so that we won't find out how shy and inexperienced he is. I know better.'

'There's rather more to it than that in Henry's case,' said Daniel.

'We'll see. I intend to follow your example.'

'What do you mean?'

'I'll do what you're doing to Tournai. I'll lay siege to him.'

He was worried. 'I wouldn't advise that.'

'I know what I'm doing, Daniel.'

'He wants no distractions at a time like this.'

'He'll get none. I can wait for the right moment.'

'Then be prepared for strong resistance.'

'Oh, there'll be noise and protestation at first,' she said, airily, 'and there might even be violence. I can cope with all that. I could never love a man who didn't fight back at me. In the end, however,' she went on, 'the results will be the same.'

'What results are you talking about?'

'Tournai is doomed,' she prophesied, 'and so is Henry Welbeck.'

While they were talking about him, Welbeck had walked back through the camp until he came to his tent. Lifting the flap, he stepped inside and removed his hat. Before he sat down, he spotted a small bottle on the table in the corner. Picking it up, he uncorked it and sniffed. It smelt like rum. He took an exploratory sip and his guess was confirmed. It was rum of good quality. Welbeck was just about to take a second sip when he realised who might have left it there. His first impulse was to pour it on to the ground before throwing the bottle away but he had second thoughts. It was perverse to spurn such a gift. No obligation was felt on his part. If Rachel Rees gave him some alcohol, she'd get no thanks from him. He'd not even accord her the courtesy of an acknowledgement. Popping the cork back in place, he set the bottle back on the table and admired it. In times of stress, a nip of rum was a godsend. And there would be an enormous amount of stress to come.

Chapter Fourteen

There was no respite. Under Marlborough's direction, the Allied army subjected Tournai to a sustained bombardment, concentrating its fire on specific targets. The noise was ear-splitting. Breaches were made in the walls and rubble lay everywhere. Sorties were almost daily events. Though the French fought back courageously, casualties inside the town increased remorselessly. Soldiers and civilians were being killed indiscriminately. Fear spread rapidly and the townspeople begged the governor to deliver them from the furious onslaught. They were afraid that the whole town would be destroyed along with most of its inhabitants. Assessing the situation, Marlborough judged that it was time for a more concerted attack.

When he saw that the Allies were marshalling their troops for a general assault, the governor beat the *chamade*, the signal for a parley. The bombardment ceased at once. There was a formal exchange of views between de Surville and Marlborough, carried out with measured politeness and resulting in an armistice. On the last day of July, three hundred wounded were evacuated to Douai and the remaining members of the garrison – almost four thousand five hundred in number – were allowed to withdraw into the citadel before the second stage of the siege began. During the negotiations, Marlborough had sought to persuade the French to extend the armistice until September and to surrender on that date if they hadn't been relieved in the interim. Much bloodshed, he argued, would be saved as a consequence. Unable to make the decision of his own accord, de Surville referred the terms of the convention to Versailles. A reply soon arrived.

Daniel Rawson was present when the captain-general opened the letter in his quarters. He and Cardonnel looked on as Marlborough read the missive with a blend of irritation and amusement. Clearly, the offer had been rejected.

'Louis is up to his old tricks,' said Marlborough.

'What does he say, Your Grace?' asked Cardonnel.

'He refuses to entertain the terms unless the armistice is linked to a ceasefire throughout the whole of Flanders.' He handed the letter to his secretary. 'Read it for yourself, Adam. I suppose that it's no more than we should have expected of him.'

'It's a form of insult,' opined Daniel. 'King Louis can surely not have believed you to be so gullible as to comply with his wishes. In effect, he's sacrificing Tournai as if it's a gift to us rather than a conquest. *We* are in the position of power. Instead of making demands, he ought to be seeking a compromise.'

'It's a typical subterfuge, Daniel.'

'He only talks of a ceasefire because he lacks confidence in his army. He knows that they're unable to relieve Tournai and is too afraid to let them close with us in a decisive battle because he can foresee the outcome.'

Cardonnel put the letter down. 'Will you draft a reply, Your Grace?'

'It will be a very short one,' said Marlborough.

'A copy of this will have been sent from Versailles to the governor.'

'Then he'll realise that the siege must continue. Louis's offer is ludicrous.'

Cardonnel grinned. 'Will you tell the King that?'

'Yes – but I'll phrase it more obliquely.'

'That was ever your way, Your Grace.'

'Louis and I have had an interesting correspondence over the years,' said Marlborough with a nostalgic smile. 'I've become closely acquainted with that devious mind of his. It's a labyrinth of unadulterated guile.'

His secretary was realistic. 'The citadel will be a tough nut to crack.'

'We have no illusions about that, Adam, but it will nevertheless fall. Our task would be much easier, of course, if we had detailed plans of the fortifications. When we invested Lille – thanks to Captain Rawson – we knew exactly what we were up against because he got inside the place and stole the relevant plans.'

'It's rather too late to ask him to do that here.'

'It most certainly is,' agreed Daniel. 'The best time to

enter a town is *before* it comes under attack. It would be suicidal to try to slip in there at the moment.'

'You'd be blown to pieces by enemy artillery.'

'Heaven forbid!' exclaimed Marlborough.

'Or you'd be picked off by a marksman.'

'The main problem,' said Daniel, gazing at the rough sketch on the table, 'is that we face hidden problems. By all accounts, there's more work below ground than above it. The engineer who designed it – the Marquis de Maigrini – has a passion for mining. There are secret passages and galleries everywhere. What is more,' he added, looking up, 'the Marquis is rumoured to be inside the town even as we speak. That will be a great help to them.'

'He'll be able to see his work tested to the limit,' said Marlborough, 'because we'll hammer away with all our might until the citadel cracks apart.' Sitting at the table, he picked up the letter from Versailles then immediately put it aside. 'No, let Louis wait for his answer,' he decided. 'Others take precedence – the Lord Treasurer and the Secretary at War, for instance. Before either of those august gentlemen, it goes without saying, must come Her Majesty.' He picked up his quill and dipped it into the inkwell. 'It may only be a partial capitulation but it's an achievement that needs to be recorded.'

Daniel watched him as he began to write. Having spent so long in England with him, he was more aware than most of the widening rift between the Duchess of Marlborough and the Queen, and of the predicament in which it left the captain-general. When he'd visited Queen Anne, he'd been given a frosty reception. It came in sharp contrast to the welcome he'd been accorded after his return from the triumph at Blenheim in 1704. He'd been hailed as the saviour of Europe then. The Queen had rushed to load him with honours. Of all the spoils of war, none was dearer to Marlborough's heart – and to that of his wife, Sarah – than the acquisition of Blenheim Palace, set in sixteen thousand acres of Oxfordshire and funded at public expense. It would give them almost monarchical status.

To ensure its future, however, royal favour had to be retained or grants from the Treasury might not be so forthcoming. Back in England, Marlborough's political enemies were using the Queen's estrangement as a stick with which to beat him. The only way to win back her support was to achieve victory in the field. For that reason, every scrap of good news from the front had to be communicated to her. Daniel knew that the surrender of the town was only a prelude to the much more difficult task of capturing the citadel. Yet it was a definite mark of progress and, as such, it deserved recognition. Once the letter had been written and dispatched, the real battle for Tournai could begin.

'Marlborough has bitten off more than he can chew,' said Villars, smirking. 'The siege is not going quite as he would have wished.'

'No, Your Grace,' said Morellon. 'His army has been given a rough welcome and we've been given priceless time in which to organise our defences.'

The two men were in Villars' quarters, enjoying a glass of wine and the latest report from Tournai that the citadel was resisting all attempts to storm it. Villars was pleased that he'd finally wrung a concession out of Versailles. In the event that either Valenciennes or Conde was threatened, he'd been given grudging consent to extend his lines eastwards to include Denain. He'd promptly done so. At the same time, he pursued his policy of sending out patrols to harass the enemy on its flanks.

'Tournai may yet hold out,' said Morellon.

'That's too much to hope for, Charles. Marlborough has time and superior force on his side. He's also a master of siege warfare. The citadel must and will eventually capitulate.'

'I spoke to some of the wounded at Douai. They had grim tales about the extent of the damage done to the town.'

'It was to his credit that Marlborough released them as part of the armistice.'

Morellon was less impressed. 'Was that an act of graciousness on his part or a sign that he wasn't strong-willed enough to keep them in Tournai where they'd probably have died for lack of medical care?'

'You do him wrong,' snapped Villars.

'Then I beg his pardon.'

'He's a true soldier and I salute him for it. He showed compassion. The Duke of Marlborough is a worthy adversary. However,' he went on, 'he has too good an opinion of his own abilities and that's a weakness I mean to exploit. He was lucky at Oudenarde. The odds were against him. By rights, he should have been soundly defeated. His good fortune has now run out. He's facing *me*.'

Morellon raised his glass in tribute. 'You will succeed where others failed.'

'There's no doubt about that.'

'If only you had complete freedom of action, Your Grace.'

'That will come in time. It must.'

'The King is too cautious.'

'Events will force him to become bolder.'

'He should come and see what's happening with his own eyes,' said Morellon, irritably. 'It all looks so different from Versailles.'

'His days in the saddle are over, Charles – unless he's riding a woman, that is.' Villars chortled. 'Only death will rob him of that particular pleasure.'

'Yes, he's been a lusty monarch, no question about that.'

'In that respect, he's been a true French king and should be applauded. As for our immediate future,' he went on, becoming serious, 'we continue the good work I've already initiated. We strengthen our defences, build up our supplies by foraging further afield, keep a close eye on developments at Tournai and send out more raiding parties to inflict casualties on the enemy and to attract their attention.'

'What happens when Tournai falls?'

'One can only guess.'

'What would *you* do in his position, Your Grace?'

Villars sipped his wine. 'I'd have no hesitation in investing Ypres,' he said. 'We must hope that Marlborough doesn't harbour the same intention. That would be a disaster for us,' he admitted, facial muscles tightening. 'King Louis is more concerned about the fate of Mons. Should it fall in the wake of Tournai, he believes that our case is undone. That's why he urges us to use every means to relieve the garrison. The cost is not to be considered.'

'Does he mean the cost in terms of money or the cost in terms of blood?'

'Both – the salvation of France is at stake.'

Morellon's smile was obsequious. 'Then it's as well we have a true saviour leading us,' he said. 'I know it, the army knows it and, very soon, the Duke of Marlborough will come to recognise it.'

Basking in the praise, Villars drained his glass with a decisive gulp.

Regiments engaged in the protracted siege of Lille had blithely assumed that Tournai would prove less problematical. They were soon disillusioned. As in the case of the former town, the siege settled into a battle of attrition. The Allies had to fight tooth and nail to gain ground then struggle to hold it. Every time they advanced their trenches, they were pounded mercilessly by cannon mounted on the ramparts of the citadel. But it was underground that the most savage encounters took place. Sappers digging tunnels to undermine the stronghold had to contend with enemy bombs, burning straw and sudden collapses of the earth above them. When their tunnels met those already built as part of the defences, they found themselves fighting in confined spaces with pickaxes and shovels. Horror stories about gruesome deaths underground did nothing to boost the confidence of Allied soldiers. After hearing about those who'd been blown to bits, burnt to a cinder or buried alive, they were reluctant to enter the tunnels and had to be more or less forced to do so.

Henry Welbeck faced the same difficulties as other sergeants. When he met Leo Curry that morning, he was able to compare notes with him.

'How many have you lost, Leo?' he asked.

'Far too many – the bravest of them died underground

and, rather than obey orders, the cowards deserted.'

'Going into the tunnels is like entering the mouth of hell.'

'I like to fight in the open,' said Curry, 'where you can *see* the enemy.'

'I'm of the same mind. Fighting in the dark is a bleeding ordeal. I've lost count of the mouthfuls of earth I've had to swallow and the dirt has made my uniform filthy. You never know what to expect. The French exploded a mine yesterday and carried off four of my best men. They didn't stand a chance.'

'This is as bad as Lille.'

'In some ways, it's even worse,' said Welbeck. 'If the enemy doesn't kill us, this damned pestilence will. I've already had to bury some of its victims. I'd rather die quickly with a bullet in my brain than perish slowly with a raging fever.'

'So would I, Henry.'

While their artillery continued to open cracks in the citadel, the Allies had suffered a number of reverses. Early in August, they'd tried to storm the walls and lost one hundred and fifty men in the process. Havoc was created underground when a double mine buried all of three hundred soldiers. As the casualties mounted, so did plague victims. Regimental surgeons worked at full stretch to cope with the constant stream of the badly wounded and the fatally infected. There was a pervasive mood of melancholy. Allied soldiers were on reduced rations, fighting in bad weather and ordered to risk their lives in gloomy tunnels that were positive death traps. Inevitably, there were those who succumbed to despair.

Ben Plummer's attitude to the situation was typical. As he joined the two sergeants in the section allocated to the 24th Foot, he was caked with mud and trembling with apprehension. There was a look of panic in his eye.

'Don't send me into one of those tunnels again, Sergeant Welbeck,' he pleaded. 'I'll *pay* you to keep me out of there.'

'You'll do as your bleeding well told,' said Welbeck, sternly. 'Anyway, I didn't *send* you underground. I led you there. What you endured, so did I.'

'I had rats running over my feet yesterday.'

'They probably recognised you as one of their own.'

'How much will it cost to keep me out of there?'

'You can't buy your way to safety, you spineless runt.'

'Besides,' said Curry, 'how can you offer a bribe on army pay? It's barely enough to keep body and soul together.'

'I have plenty of money,' said Plummer with a sly smile.

'Where did it come from?'

'That would be telling, Sergeant Curry.'

'Then try telling us,' said Welbeck, taking him by the collar and shaking him. 'Are you plying your old trade again, Ben? Are you selling powdered women with their legs apart?'

'I've been too busy digging men out of those fucking tunnels,' replied Plummer, resentfully. 'What chance do I have of finding any women here?'

'You got all that money from somewhere.'

'An uncle died and left it to me in his will.'

Welbeck released him. 'Expect me to believe that, you lying turd?'

'You can believe what you like but please assign me to other duties.'

'Next time we go underground, you'll be *first* in line.'

'I'd rather face a firing squad.'

'Is this how you train your men, Henry?' taunted Curry. 'Are they all snivelling cowards like Plummer?'

'No,' retorted Welbeck, 'they're brave men on the whole because I've instilled the bravery into them. Ben Plummer is the exception to the rule.'

Plummer sniggered. 'That's what you think, Sergeant.'

'My men will follow me to the end. I know that it's hard. I know that we seem to be making little headway, but that's not true. We kill more and more of the enemy every day. It may interest you to know that I spoke to Captain Rawson earlier.'

'Can *he* rescue me from this nightmare?'

'No – but he might bring you some hope.'

'How?'

'It seems that two deserters sneaked out of the citadel yesterday,' replied Welbeck. 'According to them, the garrison is brought to the verge of collapse. They're crippled with fatigue in there. Their bread is foul and their water is bad. They're so short of food that they're killing their horses.'

Curry rallied. 'This is cheering news, Henry.'

'The end may yet be in sight. Do you hear that, Plummer?'

'Oh, I hear it loud and clear,' said the other with a sneer. 'I just don't believe it. Listen to their cannon booming away. Look at those muskets firing at us from the ramparts. Crawl in one of those murderous tunnels and taste the earth that keeps falling over your head. There's a long way to go yet. Captain Rawson may sniff victory in the air but the only thing I can smell is death.'

* * *

Rachel Rees didn't only devote her energies to nursing the wounded. She had an occupation. Like any sutler, she had an instinct for a commercial opportunity. As soldiers surged forward to capture new ground, she went after them to sell tobacco or flasks of rum and gin. In such critical situations, men needed something to calm their nerves. Ignoring the pandemonium all round her, Rachel risked her life to bring a modicum of comfort to the troops and to make a small profit in the process. When Daniel finally managed to locate her, she'd just returned from an hour of crawling on her hands and knees in a tunnel. Her face and clothing were besmirched.

'Daniel!' she said. 'I was hoping I'd see you before too long.'

'Where have you been?'

'I was supplying ammunition to the men. Mostly, it came out of bottles.'

Daniel was tolerant. 'We don't want drunken soldiers,' he said, 'but a tot of rum hurts nobody and does wonders for one's courage. You probably have one yourself before you follow the men to the trenches.'

She cackled. 'I have to taste it to check its quality.'

'That's what any good wine merchant would do. I should know. I've posed as one often enough.'

They were in an area reserved for camp followers. Though travelling on a horse, Rachel had plenty of items to sell and had somehow got hold of a small tent. Daniel marvelled yet again at her ability to survive and prosper.

'Has Henry been asking after me?' she wondered.

'He's been too preoccupied with leading his men.'

'I daresay he's been *thinking* about me, anyway. I've made a conquest there.'

'Don't be too sure of that, Rachel,' he warned. 'The only thing on his mind at the moment is how we force the French to surrender.'

'This siege has been going on for ages.'

'There are signs that they won't be able to hold out indefinitely. Once they capitulate, we'll have to turn our attention elsewhere. In fact,' said Daniel, 'that's why I'm here. How would you like to get away from Tournai for a while?'

Her eyes kindled. 'Will I pretend to be your wife again?'

'Not this time,' he told her, 'but I do have a role for you to play. There are dangers involved. I can't hide that from you. But you'd be performing a valuable service and our commanders would be very grateful.'

'Is it something that would impress Henry?'

'It couldn't fail to do so, Rachel.'

'Then I'll do whatever you wish.'

'You haven't heard what it is yet.'

'I don't need to,' she said with a cackle. 'It will draw me closer to the two men I love most – my pretend husband, Captain Rawson, and my future husband, Sergeant Welbeck. To please them, I'd walk through fire.'

To many people in England – especially those outside London – the war seemed like a distant event that involved a confusing mixture of combatants. Regular reports were printed in newspapers like the *Tatler* but they had a limited circulation. The fate of the Allied army didn't dominate national gossip on a daily basis. It was very different in Holland, a country with a long and uneasy relationship with France. There were times when Dutch boundaries were under threat and families in all the major cities mourned sons who'd given their lives while serving in the coalition force. War had a worrying immediacy for the Dutch. Newspaper reports of any action were therefore read with eagerness and discussed at length. Nicholaes Geel had a particular reason for keeping abreast of developments. When he arrived for work that morning, the first thing he did after greeting Aelbert Pienaar was to talk about the siege.

'Have you heard the latest news from Tournai?' he asked.

'Only that the fighting seems to be going on and on.'

'Over three dozen Dutch soldiers were buried alive when two mines exploded in the tunnel where they were working. What a hideous way to die!'

'I know,' said Pienaar, sympathetically. 'It doesn't bear thinking about.'

'British soldiers have also been killed in large numbers.'

'That's no consolation to the families of Dutch casualties.'

'I'm beginning to have qualms about Captain Rawson's safety,' said Geel. 'He does have a fondness for daring exploits.'

'He also has a gift for coming through danger unscathed.'

'His luck is bound to dry up in the end.'

'It's not only a question of luck,' said Pienaar. 'He's an outstanding soldier with years of experience behind him. Well, you saw how he caught those thieves who stole the tapestry. I was terrified when I met them face to face but he and Sergeant Welbeck overpowered them with ease. They knew exactly when and how to strike.'

Geel wasn't happy to be reminded of the incident. Apart from conferring a halo of heroism on Pienaar that his colleague secretly envied, the capture of the three criminals had shown the marked superiority – in Amalia's eyes – of her beloved over any other man alive. Measured alongside Daniel Rawson, the youngest of the weavers fared badly. Only when military duties called Daniel did Geel have any chance to endear himself to the woman he revered.

'It must be a terrible strain on Miss Amalia,' he observed.

'She copes with it remarkably well, Nick.'

'But what if something should happen to him – a serious injury, perhaps?'

'Then he'd be nursed devotedly,' said Pienaar, thinking of his wife. 'Love is only strengthened by adversity. A marriage binds two people indissolubly together and they vow to care for each other in sickness and in health.'

'Yes,' conceded Geel, 'but Miss Amalia and Captain Rawson are not actually married, are they?'

'Can anyone doubt that they will be?'

'I was talking to Beatrix yesterday and she feels that a wedding is out of the question until the war is over. That could take years and years. Beatrix says that—'

'That's enough,' said Pienaar, interrupting him. 'I don't want to hear any servants' tittle-tattle. We're employed as weavers. Remember that, Nick. The family doesn't want us poking our noses into their business. I suggest that you leave Miss Amalia to her own devices. You've no right to intrude on her privacy. In short,' he went on, pointedly, 'do the job you're paid for and stop trying to look through a keyhole into the affairs of the Janssen household.'

It was a stinging reproach and Geel was hurt. He'd been well and truly put in his place. The man who'd chastised him would one day be in charge of the workshop. It was therefore imperative that he kept on good terms with

Pienaar. Geel blamed himself for wearing his heart on his sleeve. He was far too open. In future, he vowed, he'd be more circumspect. And he'd keep track of the casualty figures in the British army. Captain Daniel Rawson had achieved renown during the war. If anything untoward happened to him, it would surely be reported in the newspapers. That was the time when Geel's opportunity might at last come.

They left at night, stealing away from the camp in the dark and, when clear of the Allied lines, evading the French soldiers keeping Tournai under observation. Mons was well over forty miles to the south-east and couldn't be reached in a day. The roads were, at best, muddy tracks and, at worst, veritable quagmires. Daniel and Rachel Rees would have to make the journey in stages. Marlborough had asked him to reconnoitre Mons with a view to a secondary siege. Daniel had been offered a patrol by way of protection. However, he felt that he could achieve more if he had only one companion. His movements would be less conspicuous and unlikely to arouse suspicion. Rachel was his preferred choice. She was a very competent horsewoman and, after years of following an army, was unusually alert. Nor would she panic under severe pressure. She was resourceful and self-possessed. Daniel had the utmost faith in her.

For her part, Rachel was taken aback when he came to fetch her. She'd assumed that they'd be travelling together as a man and wife working as sutlers. That was how they'd entered Lille and, although their 'marriage' had never been consummated, she'd found living in proximity to him very exciting. This time there was no hope of sharing a room with Daniel because he was disguised as a parish priest, a

Roman Catholic curé who'd taken a vow of celibacy. She was to be his sister and they were ostensibly heading for Mons to console their mother after the death of their father. As they rode along, they rehearsed the parts they had to play. If they were accosted, it was agreed that Daniel would do all the talking and Rachel would pretend to be too grief-stricken to speak.

The rain had at last relented but puddles from the previous day's downpour lay everywhere. They squelched their way along at a fairly sedate pace. Knowing that she could keep a secret, Daniel had confided the purpose of their mission.

'How long will it take the army to march to Mons?' she asked.

'That's one of the things I have to assess,' he replied. 'At a guess, I'd say it will be over a week in this weather – eight or nine days.'

'It's the artillery that slows you down.'

'We can't manage without our siege train, Rachel.'

'Why choose Mons?'

'It's strategically placed,' he explained, 'and offers us the chance of a wider looping movement around the enemy's lines.'

'Won't the French rush to defend it?'

'Not if we deceive them about our intentions.'

'How will you do that?'

'I leave it to His Grace. He's adept at misleading the enemy.'

'I don't understand this war,' she admitted. 'We seem to have spent years fighting over the same ground. We win it, lose it, then win it back again. It must be terrible for ordinary people who live in Flanders. They've been caught up in it all.'

'Yes, Rachel. War always produces innocent victims, alas.'

They broke their journey at midday to rest the horses and to take refreshment. It was also an opportunity for them to relieve themselves behind some bushes. No sooner had they finished their meal than they heard the sound of hooves approaching. A French patrol came into sight. Rachel immediately began to sob and took out a handkerchief to dab at her tears. They were soon surrounded by soldiers. The captain in charge of the patrol interrogated Daniel and asked to see evidence of their identity. The forged papers were backed up by his plausible tale of the bereavement that he and his sister had suffered. After expressing his condolences, the captain apologised for detaining them and led his patrol on their way.

Daniel was struck by Rachel's ability to produce tears so readily. She'd seemed to be genuinely distraught. She, in turn, was amazed by the way that he'd settled convincingly into his role. His voice, his manner, his appearance and his patent humility had fooled the patrol completely. The intrepid Captain Rawson had died and been reborn as a devout Roman Catholic priest, his red coat replaced by sombre black attire and a black hat. It was a complete transformation. They spent the night in separate rooms at a wayside inn, where they were treated with great respect by the landlord and his wife. Daniel felt a twinge of guilt at having to mislead such kind people but Rachel revelled in the deceit and had no qualms about it. When they left early next day, they did so with food and drink pressed upon them by their hosts.

'I'm glad that you're the one in holy orders,' said Rachel.

'Why do you say that?'

'I could never pretend to be celibate. It would go against my nature. If you'd asked me to dress as a nun, I'd have refused. I need to feel like a real woman. I wasn't put on this earth to deny myself its joys.'

Daniel was amused. 'Don't you believe in self-sacrifice?'

'Only if there's a profit at the end of it,' she replied, honestly. 'I made all sorts of sacrifices to ensnare my first husband. I even followed Will Baggott into battle and had my hat shot off my head. I almost sacrificed my life for him. It was the same with Ned Granger, my second husband. Henry may turn out to be the most difficult of the three. I'm ready to make any sacrifice for him.'

'It could all be in vain, Rachel. Besides, you once told me that you'd never marry again because you'd already buried two husbands and didn't want to see a third lowered into the ground.'

'Henry changed my mind.'

'How did he do that?'

'I don't know, I just felt drawn towards him.'

'I've never heard a woman say that about him before.'

'Well, you've heard one say it now.'

When she was not feigning anguish over the death of a non-existent father, Rachel was a jovial companion. Daniel was fascinated to hear about her adventures. In spite of many setbacks and disappointments in life, she'd retained an unassailable optimism. She'd endured all the privations of camp life and was ready to continue to follow in the footsteps of the army. Whether it would be in the company of Henry Welbeck was an open question. Daniel believed that even her stratagems would fail to win over his friend. The sergeant's misogyny was like granite.

A persistent drizzle made the ride unpleasant but they pressed on regardless. After the best part of a day in the saddle, they were still almost ten miles short of Mons. As the sky began to darken, they looked for accommodation for the night. The track took them into a wood and its canopy robbed them of further light. Riding side by side, they came into a clearing and were halted by a peremptory command.

'Stop there!' yelled a voice.

Daniel tugged at the reins then looked around. Nobody was in sight.

'Show yourself, my friend,' he said, mildly.

A French soldier emerged from the undergrowth with a pistol in his hand. A second man came up behind them and a third stepped out from behind a tree. All three were unshaven and unkempt, their uniforms spattered with dirt. Daniel knew at once that they were deserters.

'Have you any food?' demanded the man with the gun.

'Yes,' said Daniel, 'and you're welcome to share it.'

'Give it here – we haven't eaten for days.'

As soon as Daniel took the bread from his saddlebag, it was snatched from him. The three men grabbed a piece each and gobbled it down. When Daniel took out a flask of wine, that too was seized from him and passed around. Rachel had pulled out her handkerchief and was weeping into it but she kept a close eye on the three men. Concealed in her saddlebag was a pistol and, on Daniel's advice, she kept it loaded. She had an uneasy feeling that it might be needed.

The leader of the trio looked up at them.

'Where are you going?' he asked.

'Mons is our destination,' said Daniel. 'My sister and I are visiting our mother to console her. We had news of our father's death but were too far away to reach the town in time for the funeral. We need to pay our respects at his grave.'

'Then you can go on your way.' He stood aside. When the two of them nudged their horses forward, the man pointed his weapon at Rachel. 'Not you,' he said. 'We have need of some female company.'

The three soldiers looked at her and grinned lasciviously. What they had in mind was all too obvious. Having deserted the army, they'd been living rough in the woods. A prize had just fallen into their hands and they wanted to make the most of it.

'My sister is overcome with grief,' said Daniel, indignantly.

'Then we know the perfect way to cheer her up,' said the man with a coarse laugh. 'Be on your way or you'll join your father in the grave.' He cocked the pistol and aimed it at Daniel's head. 'This is no place for a priest. There's man's work to be done with your sister. Now – will you go or would you rather stay and be shot?'

Chapter Fifteen

Whenever he was outnumbered, Daniel followed the same rule. He always attacked the person who was strongest and most dangerous. In this case, it was the man with the pistol. The other two soldiers were apparently unarmed. Surprise was on Daniel's side. Nobody would expect a parish priest to be able to take care of himself in a fight. The soldier clearly thought that the threat of death would send him on his way so that they could take it in turns with his sister. Daniel pretended to concede defeat. After a gesture of helplessness to Rachel, he turned his horse as if to leave. The man lowered his weapon and switched his gaze to Rachel. She was plainly outraged at the thought of being raped by all three of them and braced herself to resist. Daniel came to her aid. Flinging himself suddenly from the saddle, he knocked the man beside him to the ground, forcing him to drop his weapon in the process. Face in the mud and with

Daniel on his back, he was quite unable to defend himself properly. Daniel grabbed his head, pulled it upwards and twisted it with great force so that the man's neck broke with an awesome crack.

The other soldiers gaped at what they saw, allowing Rachel time to pull the pistol from her saddlebag. As one of the men dashed to avenge the death of his friend by grappling with Daniel, she took aim and fired, hitting him between the shoulder blades. Though it didn't kill him outright, the shot sapped all his energy. He slumped against Daniel who dispatched him with a dagger he'd kept hidden in his boot. The third soldier reviewed the odds. He was up against a priest who could kill with his bare hands and a woman who obviously knew how to defend herself. His chance of sexual pleasure had vanished in less than a minute. Lust became panic. Without offering any fight, he raced off into the trees as if his breeches were on fire.

Daniel went after him. Mounting his horse, he used his heels to goad it into a canter and pursued the man through the undergrowth. His quarry didn't get very far. Before he'd gone fifty yards, he was panting for breath. When he heard the hoof beats behind him, he broke into a nervous sweat. There was no escape. Unable to outrun the rider, he turned to confront him, hoping to pull him from the saddle and somehow overpower him. But Daniel gave him no opportunity to do that. Instead, he used the bottom of his foot to stamp hard against the man's chest, sending him cartwheeling backwards. Bringing the horse to a halt, Daniel leapt off and dived on top of the soldier, pinning him to the ground and hitting him with a relay of punches until he was groggy. Arms up to protect his head, the man cowered and begged for mercy.

'Don't hurt me, Father,' he pleaded. 'We meant no harm.'

'You meant a great deal of harm,' said Daniel, vehemently.

'I swear that it was all in fun.'

'Don't lie to me. You're deserters with nothing to lose. You tried to take advantage of what you thought were two defenceless travellers. Your friends paid with their lives. You've been left to suffer a different fate.'

When Daniel stood up, the man knelt before him in supplication.

'Don't take me back to my regiment,' he wailed. 'Desertion means death.'

'It's no more than you deserve,' said Daniel, 'but I have work for you to do before I start thinking about your punishment. You can help to bury your friends in a shallow grave. Like you, they're despicable cowards but they still deserve a decent burial.'

'Yes, yes – I'll do that gladly.'

'Afterwards, I have a much more important task for you.'

'What's that, Father?'

Daniel yanked him to his feet. 'I want you to tell me everything you know about the disposition of the French army.'

The soldier became suspicious. His eyes narrowed as he appraised the curé. 'You're not a priest at all, are you?'

'No,' said Daniel with a grin. 'I'm the Bishop of Beauvais and I've come to take confession.'

Holding him by the collar, Daniel led him back in the direction of Rachel Rees, taking the horse's rein in the other. Being accosted by three deserters had been a testing experience for them but they might reap something of real value from it. The deserter would be a mine of information about the French army, telling them things they could never glean elsewhere. Such intelligence would be very welcome in the Allied camp.

The citadel was holding out but there were distinct signs that its resistance was slowly diminishing. Its artillery was less active, its musket fire more sporadic and its successes in the tunnels largely neutralised. Walls repeatedly pounded by cannon fire had been breached in several places. Viewing the stronghold through a telescope, Marlborough could see that the Allies were finally getting the upper hand. To do so, however, they'd suffered appreciable losses. As well as taking far longer than anticipated, the siege of Tournai had so far accounted for over five thousand casualties, many killed in horrific circumstances. Plague victims had to be added to the number of those who fell in combat. As the prospect of enemy surrender came nearer, there was no triumphalism in the Allied camp. What the captain-general and his men felt was an overwhelming sense of fatigue and disappointment. The siege had been debilitating.

On other fronts, the news was no more inspiring. Allied probes in the direction of Marchiennes had been effectively repulsed by the French and the word from Spain was that a virtual stalemate had been reached. But it was further east and south that the major setback came.

Marlborough had pinned faith in a double attack launched in Piedmont and on the Rhine. Its aim was to distract the French from Flanders and leave Villars substantially weakened. The plan was now in chaos. Reports filtered through that the Elector of Hanover had been soundly beaten at Rumersheim depriving the Allies of the advance on which they'd counted. None of Villars' troops would be diverted from Flanders now. Marlborough would face an army that was heartened by the news of a French victory in the field. While they still commanded the sea, the Allies had only shifting control on land. The frontiers of France remained inviolate.

It was no wonder that Marlborough was suffering from one of his migraines. When he returned to his quarters, he found something that turned a headache into a small explosion inside his cranium. A courier had brought letters from England. Marlborough read those from Godolphin and Walpole first. Written days earlier, they displayed an ignorance of recent developments at Tournai but they both contained useful information about political machinations back in England. The third letter was from Sarah, Duchess of Marlborough. Having recognised her characteristic hand, her husband had saved it to the end. He opened it with dread.

'God help us!' he gasped as he read the contents.

'What's the matter?' asked Cardonnel.

'The fat is truly in the fire now, Adam.'

'In what way?'

'I *implored* my dear wife to show tact and restraint with regard to Her Majesty but she's incapable of doing so. Sarah has continued to bully and blame her.'

256

'Yet she must realise what harm that can do to you.'

'When she loses her temper, she forgets the consequences.'

'What's provoked this latest outburst?'

'A rebuff from Her Majesty,' said Marlborough, worriedly. 'She is clearly exasperated at Sarah's incessant ranting and has told her that it is impossible for her to recover her former kindness.'

'It was more than kindness, Your Grace. They were like sisters.'

'The bond between them has been broken irreparably. Henceforth, Sarah will be treated solely as my wife and as the Groom of the Stole. Position and prerogative have been taken away. The Queen's coldness has an Arctic feel to it.'

'I can imagine how Her Grace reacted,' said Cardonnel with a slight grimace. 'That would only have made matters worse.'

'It will certainly not advantage us,' groaned Marlborough, both hands to his head in a vain attempt to still the agony within it. 'Blenheim Palace will never be finished if we antagonise the very person who holds the purse strings. No matter how many victories I deliver, Her Majesty will not be appeased. And the worst of it is that Sarah wishes me to intercede as if I can wave a magic wand and make this falling-out disappear. I lack the power to do so, Adam,' he went on. 'When I raised the issue with the Queen, she refused even to discuss it and she dismissed my request that I might be made captain-general for life as if I'd made an obscene suggestion. There was no precedent for it, she claimed, and my hopes were snuffed out like so many candles. Oh, why am I doing this?' he cried, wincing as a hammer struck the anvil of his brain.

'What do I stand to gain? Where is the profit from all this suffering?'

'The profit lies in the proof of your superiority as a commander.'

'Have I not provided evidence enough of that?'

'Undoubtedly – but France has not yet been forced into abject capitulation. There's work still to be done – more sieges, more battles and more victories.'

Marlborough brandished the letter. 'What use is victory when I have this to contend with at home?' he asked. 'When I look to the future, I shudder. If Sarah persists in abusing the Queen, she'll bring Blenheim Palace crashing down around our ears and we'll spend the rest of our lives as outcasts.'

'Why did you desert your regiment?' asked Daniel.

'The pay was poor and the food was dreadful.'

'A soldier should be used to that.'

'We were afraid we'd be killed.'

'Why?'

'The Duke of Marlborough always wins a battle.'

'If you fear death, why did you join the army?'

'We were drunk. The recruiting officer duped us.'

'When did you realise you'd made a mistake?'

'When we built our defences in the pouring rain,' said the man, bitterly, 'and stood guard in trenches with mud up to our knees. We were bored, famished and soaked to the skin. The water tasted like piss. There were rats everywhere. When we complained about the conditions, we were threatened with a flogging.'

'So you decided to make a run for it?'

'Anything was better than staying there.'

After the two soldiers had been buried, Daniel questioned the man closely. His name was Marc Goujon and he was pathetically eager to provide all the information sought. He talked about the structure of command in the French army and gave full details of his own regiment and its movements. From snatches of conversation he'd picked up from officers, he was able to give some indication of French intentions. He and his two companions had not been the only deserters. While Daniel sat on a log beside the man, Rachel was a short distance away, watching them carefully. Goujon might be cooperative but she didn't trust him for a moment. He was a greasy man in his late twenties with swarthy skin and a rough beard. The prospect of being assaulted by him made her stomach churn. Unnoticed by Goujon, she'd reloaded her pistol and kept it within easy reach.

'What will happen to me?' wondered Goujon.

'I know what ought to happen to you,' said Daniel. 'You should be lying beside those other two renegades under the ground.'

The man was frantic. 'Please don't kill me. I can be of use to you.'

'How?'

'I can enlist in *your* army instead. I can fight for you.'

'Our soldiers respect women. They don't try to rape them.'

'That wasn't in our minds,' claimed Goujon. 'We just wanted some sport. We'd not have harmed her at all.'

'You're a liar.'

'Let me make amends. I know from the interest you've

shown in the French army that you're in the pay of the Allies. Take me back with you. Give me a red coat and I'll fight as hard as the next man.'

Daniel was unmoved by the offer. 'You'd desert within a week.'

'I won't, I promise you. Give me a chance to atone for what I've done.'

'We don't want your kind polluting our army.'

'Then what do you want?'

Before he answered, Daniel had to ponder. They couldn't keep the man as a prisoner, nor could they let him go. There was always the chance that he might return to the French camp and buy favour by disclosing details of a spy posing as a curé and accompanied by a chubby female. Goujon knew that they were heading for Mons. Daniel didn't want to be caught there by a French patrol alerted by the deserter. As he turned over the possibilities in his mind, Daniel was momentarily distracted. Goujon was quick to take advantage. The cringing figure beside Daniel sprang into life, punching him hard in the face and knocking him backwards off the log. When he made a dash for it this time, Goujon headed for the horses, intending to take one and pull the other behind him. But he had to get past Rachel in order to reach the animals. Getting up, she tried to reach for the pistol but was far too slow. Goujon deliberately cannoned into her and knocked her flying. Seeing the weapon on a boulder nearby, he snatched it up.

Daniel had recovered swiftly. When he leapt to his feet to chase the deserter, however, he saw the pistol pointing directly at him and slowed to a halt.

'Come on,' beckoned Goujon, teeth bared. 'I'm going to blow your brains out then fuck your sister or whoever this fat cow really is.'

The insult was like a bee sting to Rachel's pride. Rolling over, she reached a hand between Goujon's open legs and squeezed his genitals so hard that he let out a yell of agony. After crouching for a moment with a hand to his groin, he turned on Rachel and levelled the weapon at her head. But the momentary delay was fatal because it gave Daniel time to hurtle towards him and tackle him around the waist. Both men hit the ground hard and the pistol went off, its bullet shooting upwards into a tree and evicting its tenants. As the birds squawked in protest, they looked down at a fierce struggle below. Goujon was strong and fighting desperately for his life. He tried everything to get the better of his adversary, punching, pulling, biting, spitting and using his knees to explore Daniel's ribs. With a surge of energy, he rolled Daniel onto his back and tried to get hands to his neck. He squeezed hard. Daniel broke the man's grip and bucked so violently that he dislodged his attacker. It was Goujon's turn to be trapped on the ground with a pair of hands at his throat. Daniel showed no mercy. Though Goujon continued to twist, turn and flail away with both arms, Daniel tightened his hold inexorably. Taking all the punishment that the deserter's fists could hand out, he exerted pressure until the Frenchmen's expletives became no more than a gurgle of despair. Goujon's resistance faded, his face changed colour and his eyes bulged. A minute later, he was dead.

Daniel dragged himself upright and swayed over the

man. Rachel was back on her feet now and had watched the fight with satisfaction.

'Thank you, Daniel,' she said. 'If *you* hadn't strangled that bastard, I'd have done it. Nobody calls me a fat cow and lives to boast about it.'

Panting from his efforts, Daniel tried to dust off some of the dirt he'd picked up. Angry with himself for being caught unawares, he was at the same time content. In making his bid for freedom, Goujon had solved a problem. They no longer had to wonder what they'd do with him. He'd join his friends in a shallow grave, leaving them to continue on their way unhindered by their prisoner. Daniel started to remove the dead man's uniform.

Though he'd never been a father, Henry Welbeck had a paternal streak that he took care to keep well hidden in case it was perceived as a sign of softness on his part. He hated to lose men under his charge, even the ones he detested. He felt a nagging responsibility towards them. Each fatality caused him pain. After a long acquaintance with the systematic butchery of war, he could still be shocked and upset. It made him fight on even harder and exhort the survivors in the 24th Foot to do the same. Welbeck and his men were part of an assault that was launched on the citadel. It was above ground this time so they didn't have to brave the hazards of the tunnels. Scrambling over rubble, they tried to get close enough to fire their muskets at the figures on the ramparts and they seemed to be having some initial success. Then a cannon gun roared and the shot landed in the midst of his men.

Over a dozen were killed instantly and others were badly wounded by the flying debris it stirred up. The one who caught Welbeck's attention was Ben Plummer, thrown several yards and stretched out on his back. His brains were draped across his forehead like a bunch of grapes. In spite of the trouble Plummer had caused him, the sergeant felt a twinge of sorrow and he crossed over to the fallen soldier. When he got close to him, however, he realised that Plummer had only been stunned. The brains had belonged to a soldier who'd been hit by the shot and whose head had been blown apart. As Welbeck slapped Plummer's face to try to revive him, he heard the drum call signalling a retreat. Musket fire was still peppering them and the occasional cannon were causing more havoc. After waving to his men to pull back, Welbeck heaved Plummer onto his shoulder and carried him away from danger. The further he went, the heavier the load became, but Welbeck was a powerful man and didn't once slow his pace.

When he was eventually able to put his burden down in the safety of the camp, Welbeck was joined by another sergeant. Leo Curry looked down at Plummer with undisguised contempt.

'I'd have left the bastard there to die,' he said, cruelly.

'We need every man we've got, Leo.'

'What use is a lily-livered coward?'

'I'll make a soldier of him yet,' said Welbeck, wiping the sweat from his brow. 'I don't think he's seriously hurt. He was knocked unconscious.'

Curry looked down at the body. 'Or is he just *pretending*?' he asked, unsympathetically. He kicked Plummer and produced a groan. 'Open your eyes, you rotten cheat. We know your little game.'

'It's no game, Leo. I saw him tossed into the air like a rag doll.'

'I'm not surprised. He's about as much bleeding use as a rag doll.'

'Plummer was worth saving,' argued Welbeck. 'I wasn't going to leave an able-bodied soldier where he was likely to be shot. You've rescued men in the past. I've seen you do it.'

'They *deserved* to be rescued, Henry – unlike this filthy pimp.'

Plummer opened an eye. 'Are you talking about me, Sergeant?'

'You're a menace to the British army,' accused Curry.

'What happened?'

'You were nearby when a shot killed your comrades,' said Welbeck.

'And your sergeant was fool enough to save your life and carry you back here,' added Curry. 'I'd have left you as target practice for the enemy.'

Plummer was touched. 'You *saved* me, Sergeant Welbeck?'

'I'd have done the same for any of my men,' said Welbeck, briskly.

'Thank you, thank you very much.'

'Show your gratitude by mending your ways. Become a proper soldier.'

'And keep away from my men,' warned Curry. 'Since the siege began, you haven't been able to sneak across to our part of the camp to stir up mischief. You've been too busy trying not to fight. Stay where you bleeding well belong. If

I see you within fifty yards of any of my soldiers, I'll kick you from here to Amsterdam.'

To reinforce his threat, he booted Plummer in the ribs before marching off. With a cry of pain, Plummer sat up and rubbed his side tenderly. He shook his head to bring himself fully awake.

'How are you?' asked Welbeck.

'I feel half dead.'

'You look it. Can you stand up?'

'I don't know.'

'Let me help you up.'

'I'd rather stay here, Sergeant.'

'Come on,' said Welbeck, 'we've got to see if there's any real damage.'

Putting his hands under Plummer's arms, he lifted him gingerly to his feet. Plummer moaned and rubbed an elbow. He was very unsteady but, when he was released, he didn't fall over. There were bruises on his face and a sticky mark on his forehead where someone else's brains had briefly lodged. Welbeck thought it best not to mention that to him. He ran his hands over Plummer's limbs then got the private to lift his knees in turn.

'Nothing seems to be broken,' he decided.

'I've got this pain in my elbow,' said Plummer, 'and I think that Sergeant Curry might have cracked my ribs.'

'That was only a tap he gave you. If the sergeant had really kicked you hard, you'd be rolling in agony. Best to be on the safe side,' Welbeck continued. 'If you can find a surgeon who's not patching up wounded soldiers, get him to look at that elbow of yours. It may need attention.'

Plummer brightened. 'Does that mean I'll be invalided out of action?'

'No, you're fit enough to walk and fire a musket.'

'I want to be nursed by a buxom woman. In fact, *any* woman would do. I miss the touch of a female hand. I might even be nursed by your lady love.'

Welbeck tensed. 'Who're you talking about?'

'Why – Rachel Rees, of course.'

'She is *not* my lady love.'

Plummer smirked. 'I see what I see.'

'You won't see a bloody thing if I hit you,' said Welbeck, holding a fist under Plummer's chin. 'I didn't rescue you so that you could taunt me. I've nothing to do with Rachel Rees, do you hear?'

'Yes, Sergeant – I'll tell her that when I see her.'

'You won't be able to do that because she's no longer in camp.'

'Oh – where is she?'

'Mind you own business and look for a surgeon. I want you ready to carry a musket in the next attack. Go on,' he said, shoving him. 'Off you go.'

Plummer gave him a sly grin then walked slowly away. Welbeck was annoyed by the mention of Rachel Rees. He had no wish to be reminded of her existence. He knew that she wasn't there because Daniel had told him that she'd agreed to help him. Unaware of what the two of them were actually doing, he hoped for the safe return of his friend and for the complete disappearance of Rachel Rees.

'What was his name?' asked Rachel.

'Henri Dupuy,' said Daniel, reading the inscription

chiselled into the headstone. 'He died almost a fortnight ago.'

'It's nice to know who our father was.'

'There's only one problem, Rachel.'

'Is there?'

'Yes – his wife is buried here as well. She passed away two years ago.'

She grinned. 'Perhaps we should find another grave.'

They'd arrived in Mons and told their tale to the guards at the gate. The surname on their forged papers was Terreau and it got them inside the town. Just in case they'd aroused enough suspicion to be followed, Daniel led the way to the nearest churchyard and looked for a recent burial. When he saw a mound of fresh earth, he paused beside it to read the epitaph relating to Henri and Emma Dupuy. If anyone was watching them, they'd see two dutiful children paying their respects beside a parental grave. In fact, when he looked around, Daniel saw that nobody had been keeping them under observation. Their story had been plausible enough to win genuine sympathy at the gate. Having overcome one obstacle, however, they were confronted by another one.

'Good day to you both,' said a soft and friendly voice.

They looked up to see an old man shuffling towards them with an almost toothless smile. He was the parish priest at the church and was interested to spot a fellow curé there. Blinking at them from beneath bushy, white eyebrows, he spread his bony arms in welcome.

'What brings you here to my church?' he asked.

Rachel brought the handkerchief to her face to escape the embarrassment of having to speak. She'd picked up enough French over the years to be able to hold a conversation but had nothing like Daniel's fluency. If she opened her mouth, she'd give the game away at once. Daniel spoke the language like a true-born Frenchman. Since they were caught beside a particular grave, he quickly converted them from children of the deceased to nephew and niece, extolling the virtues of their uncle and saying how distressed they were to hear of his demise. Because Henri Dupuy was a parishioner of his, the priest would know him and his family well. It was far safer to claim to be relatives who lived some distance away. Rachel was staggered at the ease with which Daniel talked about the need they felt to visit Mons. He seemed to be able to invent convincing details at will. The old man expressed his condolences and suggested that they might all enter the church to pray for the salvation of the dead man's soul. As they walked up the path, Daniel saw the opportunity to probe for information.

'Why are there so many soldiers about?' he wondered.

'You're mistaken,' said the priest. 'There are far too few of them. We fear that we may be besieged, yet a proportion of our garrison has been withdrawn by Marshal Villars. We're not able to defend ourselves properly and can only hope that the enemy spares us and marches elsewhere.'

'We came past their encampment at Tournai.'

'The town must be suffering dreadfully.'

'Sieges always bring misery, alas.'

'That's horribly true!' exclaimed the old man.

They went into the building and walked down the aisle before kneeling at the altar rail. It was the first time that Rachel had been inside a Roman Catholic church and she was struck by its ornate design and by the plenitude of candlesticks, gold plate and other valuables on display. There was a colour, richness and embellishment to the place that made the little church she'd once attended in Brecon look bare, dull and poverty-stricken. Kneeling beside her, Daniel offered up a silent prayer of thanks that he and Rachel had survived the perils of the journey then he listened to the words spoken by the priest in memory of Henri Dupuy. When the old man had finished, he invited them to join him for refreshment.

'That's a very kind offer,' said Daniel, 'and we thank you for it. But we are both tired after the long ride and need some rest.'

'Of course,' said the other with an understanding smile. 'Besides, you'll want to see your cousin while you're here. I presume that you know where he lives. If not, I can conduct you there.'

'No, no – that won't be necessary.'

'Then I'll insist on calling on you later to speak to you at length.'

'We look forward to that.'

As they took their leave, Rachel felt confident enough to bid the priest adieu. Once outside the church, however, she lapsed back into English. She was concerned.

'I didn't know that we had a cousin in Mons.'

'Neither did I until he mentioned it.'

'Why did you agree to see him later?'

'It was the only way to purchase some time,' said Daniel, looking around. 'We need to leave the town as soon as possible.'

'I thought that you wanted to take stock of its defences.'

'We can do that as we head for another gate. We can't leave by the one through which we entered or we'd be recognised. They'd wonder just how bereaved we really were if we quit Mons after so short a visit.'

Rachel raised quizzical shoulders. 'Why is there such a rush to leave?'

'Our ruse is going to be discovered.'

'Only if I open my mouth out of turn and I'll try not to do that.'

'We're members of the Dupuy family,' he reminded her, 'and we have a cousin living here. When the curé visits him later today, he'll soon realise that we're impostors. We don't want to be here when that happens, Rachel.'

'I agree,' she said.

They mounted their horses and trotted in a northerly direction. Daniel took note of the preparations being made for a siege. Soldiers from the garrison were up on the ramparts or marching through the streets to take up their positions. There was an air of urgency, as if an attack were imminent. People shopping in the market had a nervous look about them, glancing over their shoulders as they haggled with stallholders. Mons was patently anxious. Daniel and Rachel crossed the town from one side to another, committing everything they saw to memory. When they reached the gate, they became the brother and sister named in their papers, claiming that they'd been in the town for days with their mother and were now beginning the long ride home to Ypres. Daniel's plausibility and Rachel's performance as a sorrowful daughter once again convinced the guards. They were permitted to leave.

Once outside the gates, they quickened their pace and tried to put distance between themselves and the town in case there was pursuit. Bobbing up and down in the saddle, Rachel Rees was curious.

'Why did you choose to disguise yourself as a parish priest?' she asked.

'I thought it might earn me respect.'

'Perhaps you should go into the church when you retire from the army.'

Daniel chuckled. 'As a penance for my bad deeds, do you mean?'

'No – I think that you'd make a good curé.'

'There are two insurmountable obstacles, Rachel.'

'What are they?'

'First,' he said, 'I'm not and never could be a Roman Catholic. By birth and inclination, I'm a Protestant and proud to be so.'

'What's the second obstacle, Daniel?'

'It's rather too late for me to take a vow of celibacy.'

Rachel hooted with laughter. 'Amalia will be relieved to hear that.'

'She'll also be relieved to hear that we got safely away from Mons.'

'I never had any doubts that we would, you silver-tongued devil. When you talked to the old man about our uncle, I believed every single word of it.'

'Let's hope that he did.'

'You had him eating out of your hand, Daniel. Well,' she added, 'we bid farewell to Henri Dupuy and greetings to Henry Welbeck. I can be myself with him. I'm fed up with grieving over a dead man I never even met. I want real life.' She saw Daniel look behind him. 'And you can forget about the old man. I watched his eyes. He didn't suspect a thing.'

The priest had first been alerted by the fact that the woman had taken pains to say so little. Again, they had never entirely convinced him that they were a brother and sister. There was scant facial resemblance. Why, then, were they paying their respects to Henri Dupuy? The old man had known him well. He didn't recall that his former parishioner had had relatives in Ypres. It would surely have been mentioned at some stage. Who were the strangers and what did they really want?

Later that day, he took his suspicions to the captain of the guard at the gate through which the visitors had entered. He gave a good description of them and the man remembered them feeling sorry for them.

'I don't think pity is in order,' said the priest.

'Why not, Father?'

'It's because they were here under false pretences.'

'That's a bold claim to make.'

'I can substantiate it. The man was no curé and the woman was no sister. They had no connection at all with the person they said was their uncle.'

'How can you be sure of that?'

'I talked to Henri Dupuy's son. He has no cousins in Ypres or elsewhere, for that matter. He was as baffled as I am.' He leant forward. 'My eyesight may be fading, Captain, but my instincts are as sharp as ever. That fellow was a clever actor but I sense that he was too worldly to be a man of the cloth. There's one more thing to consider – why would a priest ask me about the soldiers in the town?'

The captain rubbed his chin with a thoughtful hand. 'What were they doing in Mons?' he asked.

'I suggest that you catch them and find out.'

CHAPTER SIXTEEN

Amalia Janssen had always wanted a brother or sister but it was not to be. As an only child, she enjoyed a monopoly of her parents' attention, yet felt that she was missing something. Gregarious and affable, she'd had plenty of childhood friends. There were even those who occasionally spent the night under her roof. She led a full and happy life. What she lacked, however, was a sibling with whom she could grow up and in whom she could confide her most secret thoughts. Everything changed when Kees Dopff came to the house. Notwithstanding his handicaps, he turned out to be a model apprentice and was virtually adopted by Emanuel Janssen. Dopff became the brother that Amalia had never had. She was able to communicate with him in ways that no other person could manage. She sensed his moods, anticipated his needs and loved their conversations mixing words and mime.

When Dopff began to feel unwell, therefore, Amalia was

the first to notice. She urged him to have an early night and he was glad to take her advice. Next morning, he was late for breakfast, an event so unusual as to arouse concern. He finally appeared with an apologetic smile but it was his pale cheeks that worried Amalia.

'Are you sure you're feeling well enough to get up, Kees?'

Nodding his head, he rubbed his stomach to show that he was hungry.

'That's a good sign, I suppose,' she said. 'Whenever I feel poorly, I can't eat a thing. What do you think, Father? Are you to blame for his fatigue? Have you been making Kees work too hard?'

'I can't stop him from doing that, Amalia,' said Janssen. 'I have to drag him away from his loom sometimes.'

'I think he should have a morning off.'

Dopff shook his head and looked alarmed. He was keen to work. To prove that there was nothing wrong with his appetite, he had a hearty breakfast and clearly enjoyed his food. It made Amalia feel less anxious about him. Dopff was not merely a skilled weaver, he was a talented artist who was always creating designs that he hoped might one day appear on a tapestry. Amalia loved to watch him making his sketches and tried her own hand at the exercise. While she could conjure up pretty designs, she had nothing like Dopff's natural artistic ability.

By the end of the meal, he seemed much better. There was even a touch of colour in his cheeks now. If he was feeling any discomfort, it was not showing in his face. Amalia decided that she was worrying unnecessarily. When Dopff went off to start work, she nevertheless asked her father to keep an eye on him.

'I'm sure there's *something* amiss, Father.'

'I can't remember him having a day's illness,' he said.

'There's always a first time.'

'He's probably the healthiest of all of us, Amalia. I'm too old, Aelbert has never been robust and Nick drinks too much. One of us will start to falter before Kees does. He has an iron constitution.'

'Well, *you* don't, Father,' she told him. 'Bear that in mind. There are limits to what you can do in a day. You must keep within them.'

He smiled fondly. 'You've been saying that to me for ages.'

'Then why don't you do what I ask you?'

They chatted away until a servant came to clear the table. Janssen was ready to start work and talked about the project in hand. Amalia walked with him to the workshop. Geel and Pienaar were already there but it was Dopff who was actually busy at his loom. Amalia glanced across at him. He seemed happily absorbed in what he was doing, yet she was instantly disturbed. There was something about the way that his shoulders stooped. Dopff had put his legs much further apart than usual as if to brace himself. Then he began to sway. Amalia moved forward involuntarily.

'Are you all right, Kees?' she asked.

When he turned to face her, she could see the perspiration on his face. He couldn't even answer her question with a gesture. He looked shaky and confused. After blinking in dismay, he wobbled for a second then collapsed on the floor.

'Heavens!' exclaimed Janssen. 'What's wrong with him?'

'He needs a doctor,' decided Amalia, bending over him.

'Poor fellow!' said Pienaar at her elbow. 'Shall I help him to his room?'

Geel was decisive. 'No,' he said, coming forward, 'I'll do that.' He bent down to pick up Dopff. 'Come on, Kees. The best place for you is in bed.'

'Can you manage on your own, Nick?' asked Amalia.

'Yes. He's as light as a feather.'

It was a downright lie but Geel was eager to impress her. Adjusting his hold, he carried Dopff out of the workshop and up the stairs. Amalia was at his heels. Her father, meanwhile, was sending one of the servants to fetch a doctor. Dopff had a room at the very top of the house. It was hard work climbing the steep staircase but Geel didn't utter a word of complaint. Though his arms were aching and shooting pains were attacking his legs, he soldiered on until he reached the upper landing. Amalia went past him to open the door and he carried Dopff the last few yards into the room. Between them, he and Amalia lowered the body on to the bed. Beads of sweat covered Dopff's face now but he was conscious again and even managed a brave smile.

Geel wasn't interested in the patient. He was relishing the rare treat of standing so close to Amalia. His prompt action had won her gratitude. Though she was preoccupied with Dopff, she hadn't forgotten who'd carried him to his bed.

'Thank you, Nick,' she said, turning to him. 'It's so kind of you.'

When she grasped his arm for a second, the pain in his limbs vanished.

*   *   *

They spent the night in the open. Both of them were used to sleeping under the stars. The weather was fine and a warm breeze helped to dry the grass somewhat. When they set off next morning, they didn't do so as a French curé and his sister. That disguise was no longer needed. After leaving Mons, Daniel had guided them back to the woods where they'd had the encounter with the three deserters. Rachel realised why he'd stripped two of the men of their uniforms and hidden them in a hollow trunk. They were there to be retrieved. One had belonged to Goujon who'd been as tall and well built as Daniel. The other had been worn by the man with the pistol, a stout individual of middle height. Daniel had discounted the third uniform because it was the wrong size for either of them and it had a bullet hole between the shoulder blades. Down the back of that blue uniform was a long, red bloodstain.

'Are you ready yet?' asked Daniel.

'I can't get into this coat.'

'You ought to – that deserter was more or less your size.'

'The breeches are too long and the coat is too tight,' she protested.

'Force yourself into them.'

Daniel was anxious to be on their way. Having collected the uniforms from their hiding place, they'd ridden on until darkness forced them to look for shelter. When they set out again next morning, he wanted them to look like French soldiers. Close up, Rachel would deceive nobody but she'd look far more convincing from a distance. Anyone searching for a parish priest and a plump woman would ride past without subjecting them to any scrutiny.

Rachel came out from behind the tree for an inspection.

The coat was tight and the breeches were ridiculously wrinkled. With her tricorn hat on, however, she did have a military air about her. She was by no means the first woman to pose as a soldier. Others had chosen to conceal their gender in the past so that they could don a uniform and fight alongside men. Daniel could recall an instance after the Battle of Ramillies when a wounded British soldier, examined by a surgeon, was found to be female. The woman had enlisted in the army to be close to her husband and had revelled in the life. Rachel wouldn't need to go to those extremes. She just needed to be able to fool a casual observer. As he adjusted her uniform for her, Daniel felt confident that she would. It was not only the uniforms, boots and hats that he'd borrowed from the deserters. He'd also taken the pistol with which he'd been threatened by one of the men. It was secreted beneath his coat and the ammunition was in his pocket. His dagger – a gift from Rachel for coming to her rescue – was concealed in his boot. She, too, was armed with a pistol, loaded and kept in her saddlebag.

'I'll need a hand to mount,' she warned him.

'Be my guest,' he said.

Daniel held the stirrup while she put her foot into it then heaved her upwards into the saddle. As she sat astride the horse, she flexed her muscles.

'It doesn't feel quite so tight now.'

'Let's go.'

'Don't forget that you're a French soldier.'

'*Oui, oui, monsieur.*'

Hauling himself into the saddle, he rode off beside her, making sure that the road was clear before emerging from the cover of the trees. Sunshine was at last trying to make a belated appearance. The track was still muddy but at least they didn't have to ride with rain in their faces. They skirted the small fortress of St-Ghislain which sat squarely on the line of march from Tournai to Mons and collected friendly waves from soldiers who were heading for the town. With benign weather and with a breeze at their backs, they made good progress.

Rachel was uncomfortable and became increasingly restless.

'How much longer will I have to be in the French army?' she asked.

'Keep the uniform on until I'm certain that we're not being followed.'

'If there was a posse after us, we'd have seen them by now.'

'It's too early to make that assumption, Rachel.'

'This coat is pinching me all over.'

'It's served its purpose so far,' Daniel pointed out. 'Those soldiers thought you were one of their own.'

'I don't think we need this disguise at all,' she argued. 'Even if that priest did learn that we'd lied to him, he wouldn't do anything about it. He'd probably think we were a pair of harmless lunatics and pray for us to be cured. It's time to stop being so furtive, Daniel. Nobody is on our tail.'

When the parish priest reported his suspicions, his warning was not ignored. If strangers had come to Mons and made false claims about a recently deceased man, then the likelihood was that their visit had more sinister intentions.

Soldiers had been sent to scour the streets for a curé in his thirties with a female companion of similar age. In the course of their search, they also checked the other gates in case the mysterious pair had already left the town. By the time that they established that the wanted couple had already left, it was too dark to go after them. At dawn on the following day, however, five soldiers left under the command of a sergeant. They took the road used by Daniel and Rachel after their departure. It wasn't long before they picked up the trail. A shepherd remembered seeing a priest ride past on the previous evening with a woman beside him. A mile further on, the posse spoke to a farmer who'd also seen the fugitives.

The sergeant led the troop off at a steady canter, wondering how far ahead his quarry might be. Riding beside him was a jaded corporal.

'This could all be a terrible waste of time, Sergeant,' he said.

'We have our orders.'

'If you ask me, they're stupid orders.'

'I *didn't* ask you,' said the sergeant, pointedly.

'If they ride all night, they'll be miles away by now.'

'Then we press on until we catch up with them.'

'They could be entirely innocent,' said the corporal, batting away a fly with the flat of his hand. 'We have no proof that they've done anything wrong.'

'Yes, we do. We have proof that they're impostors and the fact that they stayed such a short time in Mons shows that they realised they'd aroused suspicion. That's why they fled after less than an hour.'

'What do you think they were doing in the town?'

'I mean to ask them that very question.'

'You'd have to catch them first and we don't even know that we're on the right road. Supposing that they turned off somewhere?'

The sergeant glowered at him. 'Supposing that you shut your mouth, Corporal?'

'I'm only saying what the others are saying. It's a wild goose chase.'

'I *like* chasing wild geese because I always catch one in the end. Shall I tell you why I'm certain they're directly ahead of us? That,' said the sergeant, using an arm to indicate, 'is the road to Tournai. My guess is that they're heading there to deliver their report. They've been on a reconnaissance, Corporal.'

'Oh – have they?'

'That's why we need to track them down – they're enemy spies.'

The problem with wearing the uniforms was that it made it impossible for both of them to stop at a wayside inn or to seek refreshment at a farmstead. Rachel would be seen for what she really was – an attractive, vigorous, full-bodied woman. When they were in need of a meal, therefore, Daniel left her in hiding nearby while he went off to buy food and drink. The first thing she did in the privacy of a copse was to take off her coat so that she could breathe properly again. Breeches and boots were left on but the coat was hung from a low branch. Sitting on the grass with her back against a tree, Rachel was able to relax for the first time that day. Weary from spending so many hours in the saddle, she consoled herself with the thought that she was far safer there than she would have been if still burrowing through the tunnels at

Tournai. It had been dangerous, filthy, back-breaking work. Instead of risking her life at the siege, she was riding through open countryside with a handsome man she adored. Rachel was so glad that she'd decided to leave Wales and return to army life. It gave her an exhilaration that couldn't be found anywhere else. All she needed to complete her happiness was a husband in the 24th Foot and she'd already picked him out.

Lost in her reverie, she didn't hear the sound of a twig breaking close by. When something thudded against the trunk of a tree, however, Rachel tensed. The noise was too clear to be ignored. She chided herself for leaving her weapon in the saddlebag. Her horse was over ten yards away. Could she reach it in time? She levered herself up off the ground and looked around the little clearing. Nobody was visible but she knew that she wasn't alone. She began to creep slowly towards the horses, intending to snatch her pistol from the saddlebag in order to defend herself. But she never reached her target. Yards short of the animals, she heard stealthy footsteps behind her then a hand was clasped over her mouth. Rachel tried to struggle but a strong arm enveloped her and held her tight.

Hand and arm were then released by Daniel. He was laughing now. Face reddened with indignation, Rachel turned on him.

'You scared me, Daniel!' she complained.

'That was the intention.'

'I nearly jumped out of my skin.'

'You were off guard,' he said, 'so I decided to teach you a lesson. I threw a stone against that tree to startle you. When you're alone, you should always have a weapon to hand. And you must keep your eyes open and your ears pricked.'

'I was miles away,' she confessed.

'I gathered that.'

'It won't happen again.'

'Good – we have to stay alert at all times.'

Annoyed that she'd let herself down, Rachel was nevertheless angry with him. Instead of embarrassing her the way that he had, Daniel could simply have warned her not to get distracted. Seeing her disapproval, he apologised for frightening her and, by way of reconciliation, he slipped off into the trees and returned with his horse. Out of the saddlebag, he extracted a large pie and a flask of wine. Rachel let out a whoop of joy and forgave him instantly. They shared a delicious meal together.

'I bought enough food to see us through tomorrow as well,' he said.

Rachel was wary. 'Will we have to spend another night sleeping in the open? What if it rains, Daniel? We'll be drenched.'

'There is one alternative.'

'I know,' she said. 'I can take off this uniform and put on my own attire again. Then we can hire two rooms at an inn and enjoy some comfort.'

'I was thinking of something else, Rachel.'

Her eyes ignited. 'Do you mean that we'd *share* the same room?'

'I'm afraid not,' he replied. 'The alternative is to forget about sleep altogether and ride on through the night. If we pace the horses, we should reach Tournai by late afternoon. The sooner I deliver my report, the better. Also, of course, it would keep us well ahead of any pursuit.'

'Nobody is pursuing us,' she insisted.

'I think that they may be.'

'Well – if you want my honest opinion – I'd much rather return to being a woman and to sleep under a roof again. What difference will one more night make, Daniel? We can be off at sunrise.' She cackled. 'If the sun actually rises again, that is. By the look of the sky, we're in for another long period of rain. Do you really want to ride through the dark in a downpour?'

'Perhaps not,' he conceded.

'Stop thinking like a soldier – put yourself in my position for once.'

'You're a soldier as well,' he teased, 'even though you're in the wrong army. But I take your point. I think we've earned better accommodation than Mother Nature can provide. And we did have a head start on any pursuit,' he added. 'We should be safe by now.'

The corporal was still convinced that they'd never find the two people they were after. It was several miles since anyone had remembered seeing a curé and a woman on the road to Tournai. That suggested that they were heading elsewhere. The sergeant disagreed. He sensed that they were still on the right track. When they entered the wood, he had an opportunity to persuade the others that their journey was not in vain.

'How much further must we go, Sergeant?' complained the corporal as they rode along together. 'They've disappeared into thin air.'

'We'll go on until we find them,' said the other.

'But this is the wrong road.'

'No, it isn't. I've told you before. Tournai is their destination.'

'Then why has nobody seen them passing?' asked the corporal. 'We talked to the best part of a dozen people along the way yet none of them saw the fugitives you described. In fact, not one of them had even seen a woman go by.' The sergeant raised a hand and brought the troop to a halt. 'What's wrong now?'

They were in a clearing and the sergeant's eye had fallen on three mounds of earth topped by branches snapped off trees and bushes. He dismounted and walked across to the first mound, lifting off the branches then using his foot to move the soil. Less than eighteen inches below ground, his toe struck something solid. Signalling to his men, he snapped an order. Two of them dismounted and rushed across to him. Getting down on their hands and knees, they scooped away the earth until they uncovered a blue uniform. The corpse then came into view, its head twisted at an unnatural angle.

The sergeant ordered the other men to help. Having brought one dead soldier to the surface, they began to dig into the remaining graves. It was not long before three bodies were on display. The men were shocked by their discovery. It was the sergeant who first saw its significance.

'What do you see, Corporal?' he asked.

The man shrugged. 'I see three men in shallow graves.'

'Is that *all* you see?'

'What else should I be looking at, Sergeant?'

'All three of them are French soldiers?'

'How can you tell?' said the corporal. 'Two of them are almost naked.'

'Someone took their uniforms. They'd only do that if they needed them.'

The corporal was baffled. 'I don't understand.'

'Cover them up again,' said the sergeant. As the men looked bemused, he put more force into the command. 'Cover them up. Bury them where they are. There's nothing else we can do for them.'

The men did as they were told, using branches to sweep the earth back over the bodies then tossing them on top of the mounds. While they worked, the sergeant was cogitating. He snapped his fingers and gave a cold smile.

'*That's* why nobody has seen them,' he said. 'They killed these men and stole their uniforms.'

'But that's impossible,' claimed the corporal.

'Is it?'

'How could a curé and a fat woman kill three trained soldiers?'

'It's something that I'd like to know as well,' said the sergeant. 'But I'm certain that that's what they did. And I'm equally certain that we're on their tail. But remember this, all of you,' he went on, raising his voice. 'We're not looking for a priest and a woman anymore. They're disguised as French soldiers now.'

Rachel was much happier now that she'd shed her uniform and returned to civilian life. Daniel had discarded one disguise and assumed another, looking and sounding like a parish priest escorting his sister. Rain was threatening but they managed to find an inn before the clouds broke and the torrents fell. After a meal, they retired to their respective rooms, agreeing to rise early next day to be on their way. Small, bare and without pretension they might be, but their rooms were a welcome alternative to a wet night outdoors.

Before she dropped off to sleep, Rachel made sure that her pistol was within reach. Daniel also had his weapons nearby. As he lay in bed, he could hear the rain beating on the roof tiles and rapping at the shutters. It was past midnight when he finally closed his eyes.

Almost immediately, it seemed, he was awake again, roused by the sound of horses below in the courtyard. Out of his bed in a flash, he opened the shutters far enough to be able to look out. Six riders could be seen in murky silhouette. When he heard an order being barked, Daniel knew that they were soldiers. While five of them dismounted and walked around to the main entrance, the remaining man stood guard at the rear door. Daniel didn't need to alert Rachel this time. She'd heard the clatter of hooves and identified the newcomers as a threat. After tapping on Daniel's door, she let herself in. Like him, she'd slept in her clothing so it was only a matter of seconds before she was ready to leave. Daniel put on his hat and pulled his cloak around his shoulders then they went quickly down the backstairs.

The man on guard had stepped under the eaves to get some protection from the rain. His back was to the wall of the inn. Inching open the rear door, Daniel saw where the soldier was standing. He whispered to Rachel, then eased the door gently open so that she could creep out and scurry across to the stables. When the man saw a figure dashing past in the gloom, he tried to go in pursuit but Daniel intercepted him. Grabbing him by the collar, he swung him so hard against the wall that he opened a gash in the soldier's head. Too dazed to know what was happening, the man put up no resistance when Daniel thrust a dagger through his heart. Letting him fall to the ground, he swiftly undid the girth on each of the six horses so that he could remove their saddles. He then untethered the animals.

Rachel, meanwhile, had collected their horses from the stable. They'd been left saddled and ready for a hasty departure. Mounting one, she led the other into the courtyard by the rein. Daniel was quickly in the saddle. Inside the inn, five soldiers were engaged in a frantic search. He reasoned that they had to have been sent from Mons to capture them. The old priest had clearly reported their deception and set retribution in motion. The only way to outrun the soldiers was to slow them down. Taking out his pistol, he fired it into the air, stampeding the other six horses and sending them galloping off into the night. Shutters were flung open in the upstairs rooms and angry faces peered out. The sergeant yelled to the man he'd left below in the courtyard but got no reply. He and the other soldiers ran down the backstairs and emerged into the rain. Six saddles and a corpse lay on the ground. By the time that the soldiers realised what had happened, Daniel and Rachel were riding hell for leather along the road to Tournai and sending up clods of mud in their wake.

Thanks to good medical attention, Kees Dopff was slowly recovering from his fever but had to convalesce for some time. His illness had two benefits for Nicholaes Geel. Since it was he who'd carried Dopff up to his room, he'd earned Amalia's warmest thanks and received some of the routine praise that had earlier been monopolised by Aelbert Pienaar. It gave Geel a surge of pride. The second benefit was that he had an excuse to visit the invalid. Arriving early for work that morning, he asked his employer if he might go and see Dopff. He was duly given permission and went trotting off. As Geel was going up the staircase, Amalia came out of her room and began to descend the steps. She gave him a cheery greeting.

'Are you going up to Kees?' she asked.

'Yes, Miss Amalia. I just want to see how he's getting on.'

'That's very kind of you, Nick.'

'He's much more than someone I work beside. He's a good friend.'

'I think you'll find that he's over the worst.'

'I'm glad to hear it,' said Geel.

He stood aside so that she could walk past him, savouring the brush of her shoulder as he did so. Walking along the landing, he went up the second flight of stairs. When he got to the room on the top floor, however, he was less interested in Dopff's condition than in the brief exchange he'd had with Amalia. Dopff was clearly grateful for the visit and explained, by means of an elaborate mime, that he felt much better and expected to return to work very soon. Wanting further excuses to visit him, Geel tried to persuade him that he needed a longer time to recover. Though the fever had broken, it had left Dopff weakened. As he left the room, Geel was still thinking about Amalia's kind words to him. A dangerous idea stirred at the back of his mind. In order to get back down to the ground floor, he would go right past her bedchamber. Nobody else was about. There was nothing to stop him peeping inside it. The idea took root and grew. What began as a faint temptation soon flowered into an irresistible urge. It was too good an opportunity to miss.

When he got back down to the landing, he looked around to make sure that nobody could see him then he opened the door and stepped inside the room. Simply being in the privacy of her bedchamber was a thrill for him and he stood there in silent ecstasy as his eyes took in every wonderful detail. He could sense her presence and inhale her fragrance. There was something at once sacred and exciting about the place. It was a holy of holies that encouraged libidinous thoughts, a reverence tinged with arousal. On impulse he walked across to the bed and picked up a pillow, holding it against his face to feel its softness. It was minutes before he remembered where he was. Giving the pillow a farewell kiss, he replaced it and hurried to the door, opening it enough to be able to peep out and see that the coast was clear. A minute later he was back at his loom again. His secret smile lasted the whole day.

When Daniel finally arrived back to deliver his report, he discovered that Tournai was on the verge of surrender. Conditions inside the citadel had deteriorated and Allied assaults were becoming more intense as they pressed home their advantage. The siege had lasted over two months and spilt large quantities of blood on both sides. Now that the end was in sight, Marlborough called a council of war to discuss the next move. Daniel was there to report his findings and to display the rough sketches of Mons that he'd drawn. He gave an estimate of the time it would take to move the bulk of the army there and warned that it might be held up by the well-defended outpost of St-Ghislain on the River Haine. He also passed on information about French troop movements forced out of one of the deserters. Daniel was congratulated on the detail of his report then the debate began. Marlborough outlined his plan of action.

'I believe that we should move swiftly to invest Mons,' he declared, looking around the table at each man in turn. 'We should also heed Captain Rawson's warning about the resistance we may meet at St-Ghislain. I therefore propose that I immediately dispatch a strong force of horse and foot under the command of Lord Orkney.' He indicated the map. 'They can march past Mortagne to mask the fortress of St-Ghislain in order to clear the way to Mons. At the same time, of course, they will provide protection on the flanks for our main army as it moves forward.'

'What is the French expectation?' asked Prince Eugene.

'Villars will fear an attack on Ypres much more than one on Mons. His attention will be fixed on the north-west whereas our target is in the south-east.'

'Can we surprise him?'

'We can if we move quickly enough.'

'That will mean setting off on a night march.'

'It's a tactic we've used before to great effect,' said Marlborough.

Most of those present agreed with the captain-general's plan but there were those who felt that Ypres should be invested first. One bold Dutch commander even advocated a frontal assault on the French lines. They examined the alternatives at length before coming back to the original plan. Mons would be their next objective.

Daniel always felt privileged to be there when major decisions were taken. It allowed him to see Marlborough at his most imposing. During the debate, the captain-general had cogently presented his own case, yet listened with respect to those who argued for other targets to be selected. Now that the assembled generals had departed, he was left alone with Daniel and Cardonnel. In front of them, he was able to show his weariness, removing his periwig and putting a hand to his aching head.

After all the effort he'd made to reach Mons, Daniel was grateful that the information he'd gathered would be put to good use. Even though his visit to the town had necessarily been brief, he'd seen enough to estimate its degree of readiness against a siege. And his comments on St-Ghislain had been valued. It meant that he'd be able to tell Rachel that their escapades had not been in vain. They would soon be travelling on a road that held unforgettable memories for them.

If only to have some relief from the onus of command, Marlborough asked for more detail of Daniel's journey to and from the town, chuckling at some of the adventures described and highly amused at the notion of Rachel Rees in the uniform of the French army.

'I've had the pleasure of meeting the lady,' he said, smiling, 'and I wouldn't have thought she was an entirely appropriate companion for a Catholic priest. She's altogether too feminine and worldly.'

'You underestimate her skill as an actress, Your Grace,' said Daniel.

'Evidently, I do. But I admire her courage in assisting you.'

'Now that the danger is past, I rather think that Rachel enjoyed the trip.'

'She's obviously an asset to us,' noted Cardonnel. 'At

your side, she's got inside the enemy fortresses of Lille and Mons. Where will the pair of you go next?'

'That remains to be seen,' said Daniel. He turned to Marlborough. 'I gather that much has happened during our absence.'

'Indeed it has,' replied Marlborough. 'We've been battering Tournai until it shook at its very foundations. Deserters tell us of intolerable privations within the citadel. They can't keep us out for long.'

'So I'll be on my way back to Mons within a matter of days.'

'That would be a reasonable assumption.'

'Let's hope that a second siege will not drag on as long as this one, Your Grace,' said Daniel. 'When he's made aware of your movements, Marshal Villars might even be provoked to battle.'

'He needs no provocation,' said Cardonnel. 'He's already chafing at the bit.'

'Yes,' added Marlborough, 'and, according to the latest report, he's been joined by no less a person than Marshal Boufflers, the man who held us at bay at Lille for almost five months. Boufflers will be a wise counsellor to have at his shoulder. I have the utmost respect for him. It will be good to lock horns with Boufflers again.'

Though he spoke with confidence, he didn't look as if he was physically capable of leading an army into action. His eyes were lifeless, his cheeks hollowed and his normally upright frame now formed an arch. Once again, Daniel was worried about the captain-general's health and state of mind. The continuous pressures of command were leaving deep footprints. He was about to withdraw from the quarters so that Marlborough could rest when a messenger arrived. Opening the note he was handed, the captain-general needed only a second to read it. He immediately reached for his periwig and placed it back on his head. Breathing in deeply, he drew himself up and straightened his shoulders. He exuded power and authority.

'The *chamade* has just been beaten,' he announced, grandly. 'Come with me, gentlemen. I am about to accept the surrender of the citadel. Tournai is ours.'

Chapter Seventeen

The siege of Tournai was over. While their captain-general was presenting the articles of capitulation for the governor's signature, the Allied army enjoyed a temporary lull in activity. They were able to rest, lick their wounds, trade their woes, remember fallen comrades and take some comfort from the fact that the town was finally in their hands. Henry Welbeck celebrated the victory by having his hair cut. He sat on a stool outside his tent while the one-legged Joel Drew clicked away with his scissors.

'This siege almost ruined me,' complained Drew.

'Why is that, Joel?'

'Nobody wants a haircut when they're fighting every day. The only customer whose hair I trimmed in the past month was my dog – and he didn't pay a penny.'

'We were too busy being barbered by the French,' said

Welbeck, sourly. 'That shot of theirs could take off your head as well as your hair.'

'I'm glad it's all over.'

'There'll be more to come. As one siege ends, another begins.'

Drew gave a philosophical shrug. 'It was ever thus.'

'It's not like you to be downhearted, Joel. Even when our soldiers are being killed at your feet, you usually keep your spirits up somehow.'

'I do,' said the other with a grin. 'It's because I know that we'll always win in the end. I'm proud to be part of this army, if only as a regimental barber. I help to keep you all looking well groomed and appearance is important when you wear a British uniform. Ah,' he went on, looking up, 'we seem to have company.'

Rachel Rees was walking towards them. Welbeck ducked behind Drew.

'For heaven's sake, hide me,' he pleaded. 'Don't let her see me.'

'It's too late, I'm afraid.'

'Stay in front of me.'

Drew did as he was told but to no avail. Rachel had picked the sergeant out from a distance of fifty yards. She was not going to be baulked. When the barber tried to conceal his customer, she simply shoved Drew aside with a firm hand.

'Hello, Henry,' she said, jovially. 'I hope that this haircut is for my benefit. It takes years off you.'

'That's what I told him,' said Drew, pleased with the compliment.

'He looks like a stripling.'

'Well, I feel like an old man after that siege,' said Welbeck, mordantly. 'So I'll be grateful if you'll give me some time to recover. I can only do that alone. I don't need visitors.'

'I think that's *exactly* what you need,' she argued. 'You need your friends to remind you that you're a flesh-and-blood human being and not just a soldier. You're a real man.'

'I can't contradict that,' said Drew, chortling. 'I've seen him with his shirt off. The sergeant is about as manly as you can be.'

Rachel moved in closer. 'Have you spoken with Daniel yet?'

'Yes,' admitted Welbeck. 'He told me about your antics on the way to Mons.'

'Weren't you impressed?'

'No – I'm used to daring deeds from Captain Rawson.'

'I'm not talking about *him*,' she said, prodding him playfully. 'I'm talking about myself. What did you think when you heard what I went through?'

Welbeck scowled. 'I was just grateful that you were far away from here.'

'That's not a kind thing to say to a lady,' chided Drew.

'Keep out of this, Joel.'

'And what was that about Captain Rawson?'

'My haircut is finished,' said Welbeck irritably, rising from his stool and pressing some coins into Drew's hand. 'Thank you and farewell.'

Drew winked at Rachel. 'I think I'm in the way,' he confided. 'I just wish that Henry would make up his mind. One minute, he wants to hide behind me. Next minute, he's sending me away.'

He hobbled off to find another customer, leaving Welbeck to glower at Rachel. She responded with a radiant smile. He felt slightly chastened. Though he'd never admit it to her, he'd been struck by her bravery in travelling with Daniel through territory bristling with enemy patrols. Welbeck had seen clear evidence of her pluck before but had been unable to acknowledge it on the grounds that it might encourage her. All that he wanted at that moment was to be alone. Before he could dive into his tent, however, he saw someone else striding towards him. Leo Curry was grinning from ear to ear.

'Who says that miracles never happen?' he asked with a guffaw. 'Henry Welbeck is seen with a beautiful woman at long last.'

'I'm not with anybody,' retorted Welbeck.

Rachel laughed. 'He always pretends to dislike me,' she said, 'but I know when I set a man's heart fluttering.'

'You're certainly doing that to me,' said Curry, ogling her. 'Aren't you going to introduce us, Henry?'

'Of course,' said Welbeck, seeing a chance to get rid of an unwanted visitor. 'This is Rachel Rees, one of the sutlers. And this,' he went on, indicating the sergeant, 'is Leo Curry, the ugliest man in Christendom.'

'Oh, my first husband was a lot uglier,' said Rachel, looking at Curry with approval. 'But Will Baggott was very handsome on the inside. He had so many good qualities, you see. Are you handsome on the inside, Sergeant Curry?'

Curry beamed. 'You'll find none more handsome, Rachel.'

'I judge a man by character and not by appearance.'

'Then why are you bothering with someone like Henry?

His character is a disgrace and his appearance frightens the horses.'

'Listen to *him*!' said Welbeck with indignation.

'I've always liked the sound of a Welsh lilt,' said Curry, sliding a brawny arm around her waist and easing her away. 'Tell me about yourself, Rachel. Why is it that I haven't seen you in camp before?'

Welbeck was livid. Though he'd wanted to get rid of Rachel, he'd been hurt by the readiness with which she'd gone off with Curry. The other sergeant had been too familiar with her but she was in no way offended. Indeed, she seemed to welcome his interest in her. As he looked after them, Welbeck could see that they were chatting amiably and that Curry's arm remained around her waist. While he felt anger and resentment at what had just happened, it was another emotion that was uppermost in his breast and its sheer novelty made him gasp.

Henry Welbeck had experienced the pangs of jealousy.

When a town was taken, it had to be held. Marlborough therefore had to leave a sizeable garrison there to secure Tournai and to rebuild its defences. The existing garrison in the citadel was allowed to go to France on parole to await the formal exchange with the Allied garrison of Warneton, captured earlier by the French. In releasing his prisoners, Marlborough was thus able to gain additional troops, though they'd take no part in hostilities in the immediate future. As agreed at the council of war, Lord Orkney led a substantial force of cavalry and infantry to the walls of St-Ghislain, where it met such stubborn resistance that it was held up longer than anticipated. As a result of the delay, the main army had to make a diversion and march instead through Sirault. Prince Frederick of Hesse-Cassel was charged with protecting them. Fearing an attack by French cavalry at any moment, his troops waded across the River Haine with their eyes peeled. Fortunately, intervention never came and they were able to press on to Mons to assist in the siege.

In the course of a skirmish, a number of French prisoners were taken. One of them was the Marquis de Cheldon, a man of great charm and remarkable openness. Like so many others in the higher ranks of the French army, he was an admirer of Marlborough and of his unrivalled military record. Daniel was in the captain-general's quarters when the prisoner was questioned and couldn't fail to notice his exquisite apparel and impeccable manners. After an exchange of pleasantries, Marlborough began his interrogation. Though he had a reasonable command of French, he was glad to have Daniel on hand to translate any words that he didn't understand. The marquis had such a rapid delivery that it needed Daniel's keener ear and more comprehensive knowledge of the language to pick up everything that was said. Reclining in a chair, the prisoner might have been talking to two old friends. There was no attempt to mislead and no refusal to answer a question.

'What may we expect from Mons?' asked Marlborough, politely.

'The garrison was heavily depleted when Marshal Villars withdrew soldiers to bolster his defences,' said the marquis, 'but it's now been reinforced by a regiment of dragoons and four battalions of Spanish infantry. That was all the support that could be rushed to the town before you closed in on it. The speed of your strike to the south-east took us all by surprise.'

'That was the intention.'

'I congratulate you on its success.'

'Our aim is to expel your army entirely from the Spanish Netherlands.'

'And thereby maintain pressure on us in the peace negotiations,' said the other with a knowing smile. 'It's a clever tactic, Your Grace.'

'Is it true that Marshall Boufflers has joined your commander?'

'Yes, it is, and he's most welcome. Old as he is, he's put on his cuirass and reached for his weapons once again.'

'I understood that he'd been ill.'

'We were blessed by the news of his recovery.'

'What role has been assigned to him?'

'None that I know of, Your Grace,' said the marquis with an expressive gesture. 'He has simply offered his services in a cause to which he's dedicated his whole life. Marshall Villars retains the command and will not yield it to anyone.'

'What frame of mind is he in?'

'Villars is always sanguine.'

'Have you been apprised of his immediate plans?'

'Naturally – he keeps me well informed.'

Daniel could not believe the candour with which the prisoner revealed details of the French intentions. In another person, it might be viewed as a betrayal but the Marquis de Cheldon was no turncoat. He was a flamboyant French aristocrat with a firm belief in the superiority of his national army. Once started on his account, he couldn't be stopped. Words gushed out of him like a miniature waterfall and Daniel was called upon to translate those that put a furrow into Marlborough's brow. They learnt precise numbers of the French forces and their approximate disposition. More importantly, they were told of Villars' prime objective.

'Royal permission has finally arrived,' explained the marquis. 'Marshal Boufflers brought it with him from Versailles. The King is rightly alarmed that Mons might fall and leave our frontiers unprotected. He's instructed Marshal Villars that – if conditions are propitious – he is to have *carte blanche*.'

Marlborough was pleased. 'He means to risk all and venture a battle?'

'Oh, yes,' replied the prisoner with a disarming smile. 'Battle will soon be joined. Given what I know, I'd go so far as to guarantee it.'

When he first heard of the movements of the Allied army, Villars had crossed the headwaters of the Scheldt and marched north-eastwards with the River Sambre away to his right. Having reached Bavay, he'd gone along one of the many Roman roads that branched out from it like the spokes of a wheel. After a careful study of the terrain, he chose his ground and camped about a mile north of the tiny village of Malplaquet. His swift response to the enemy actions had been endorsed by Boufflers, a veteran commander in his sixties with an enthusiasm undimmed by the passage of time. Ready to serve in any capacity, he'd been given a cordial welcome by Villars and his senior officers. The arrival of such a famous soldier had given an immediate boost to the morale of the French army.

Boufflers used a telescope to survey the landscape. His nod was affirmative.

'You've done exactly what I'd have done,' he said.

'I wanted to limit Marlborough's room for manoeuvre.'

'That's always a wise thing to do.'

'At Blenheim and at Ramillies, he had the enticing prospect of a large plain on which he could marshal his army. He'll have no such freedom here,' said Villars. 'He'll have thick woods to contend with, not to mention ditches, streams, ponds, hollows and muddy lanes. That should slow his army down.'

'The woodland also gives you a good supply of timber for your defences.'

'It's been felled from the moment we arrived. Some of the trunks have already been chained together to form abattis. Redoubts have also been built.'

'You've made a difference,' said Boufflers, gazing round with satisfaction. 'In the relatively short time you've been in command, you've made a profound difference and I'll write to His Majesty to tell him so. It will be an honour to fight under you.'

Applying an eye to the telescope, he took a second look at the battlefield that would confront the Allied army. Thanks to Villars, everything seemed to favour the French. The whole area was defined by water. The River Haine ran along the north while its tributary, the Hogneau, flowed to the south-east. The Sambre went south, past the town of Maubeuge. To the east, emanating from the vicinity of Mons, was a network of streams. The most important was the Trouille, which, like all the other waterways, had been swollen by the almost constant summer rain. Within the area enclosed by the rivers were four expanses of dense woodland. The Bois de Boussu was in the north, then came the Bois de Sars, the largest of them, the small Bois de Thiery was next in line followed by the much bigger Bois de la Lanière which arced southwards until it faced the plain of Maubeuge. In total the broad-leaved woods extended over a distance of some twelve miles.

Putting the telescope away, Boufflers emitted a low chuckle.

'The woods will screen any movement you make,' he observed.

'It will also be a perfect place in which to hide some battalions,' said Villars, smugly. 'Marlborough will be forced to attack through the narrow gap in the woods. He can be ambushed by soldiers tucked away in readiness among the trees.'

'First, however, you have to lure him away from Mons before he does any real damage to the town. Not that he'll be able to make much impact without the support of his heavy artillery.'

'Our intelligence is that he sent his siege train by river to Brussels and will bring it south to Mons. That will move slowly,' noted Villars. 'It might not get here until the end of the month.'

'Then it will be far too late,' said Boufflers, smiling. 'By that time, you'll have defeated the Allied army and saved Mons into the bargain. It will be wonderful news for me to take back to Versailles.'

Scanning the potential battlefield, Villars was brimming with confidence.

'It's a victory that will echo around the whole of Europe,'

he said, striking a pose. 'In offering him battle, I'm giving the illustrious captain-general what he most ardently seeks. In the three previous encounters, he's put a French army to flight. That won't be the case here,' he stressed. 'With our fortifications improving by the hour, we have advantages here at Malplaquet. I can't wait to reap the benefits from them.'

With a battle in the offing, Daniel dashed off a letter to Amalia. It was not simply a means of sending his love and giving her a succinct account of the fall of Tournai, it was a possible last bequest. In case anything tragic befell him in combat, he wanted her to have a memento of him. Daniel didn't fear the encounter. If anything, he was too eager for it to take place. But he knew how much Amalia worried about him and he wanted her to know how much he missed and thought about her. Having handed over the letter to be taken to Amsterdam with other correspondence, he rode to the area of the camp reserved for the 24th Foot and looked for Henry Welbeck. He located the sergeant in a familiar situation, exchanging verbal blows with Leo Curry. When he saw Daniel coming to interrupt them, Curry laughed derisively at Welbeck before strutting away like a turkey cock.

'What was all that about?' asked Daniel, dismounting.

'It was nothing, Dan.'

'Sergeant Curry looked as if he'd just won an argument.'

'He's always trying to crow over me,' said Welbeck, 'but it's meaningless. Leo has the brain of a simpleton and the stupidity to match.' He appraised his friend. 'I hear that we may actually face the Frenchies in battle.'

'Marshal Villars has thrown down the gauntlet.'

Welbeck groaned. 'We haven't fully recovered from the siege of Tournai yet, let alone the long march to get here. We're close to exhaustion.'

'The sound of the drums will put fresh energy into you.'

'It will just make me want to puke.'

'You're usually ready to stand your ground in a fight.'

'I lost too many good men in the siege,' said Welbeck. 'There are times when a battle should be avoided. This is one of them.'

'I'll pass your opinion on to His Grace,' joked Daniel.

'He doesn't care what *I* think.'

'He cares for what you represent, Henry, and that's the rank and file. Nobody shows as much concern for his troops.'

'Then why did he let so many of us get killed and maimed at Tournai?'

'It wasn't in his power to prevent the slaughter,' said Daniel, sadly. 'Sieges always produce a large butcher's bill.' His tone lightened. 'By the way, have you seen Rachel yet?'

'I had that misfortune.'

'Don't be so hostile to her. Rachel Rees is an extraordinary woman.'

'You know my view,' said Welbeck. 'I abhor women, extraordinary or not.'

'She told me that she left some rum for you as a gift.'

'I threw it away.'

'Come now,' said Daniel, jocularly, 'even you would never do that. You drank it, didn't you? Be honest about it, Henry.'

'I may have had a sip,' conceded the sergeant.

'And did you remember to thank her for the gift?'

'How could I know that it came from her?'

Daniel laughed. 'How many other women shower you with flasks of rum?'

Welbeck was embarrassed. He'd both drunk and enjoyed the gift from Rachel but hadn't been able to offer her any thanks. After his last encounter with her, he was having regrets. The very least that she deserved was an expression of gratitude, if only coupled with the request to refrain from giving him anything else in the future. It was simple courtesy. When – as he perceived it – he was Rachel's sole target, he defended himself by falling back on rudeness. Now that she'd sparked off interest in another man, however, Welbeck's mind was in turmoil. Had it been anybody other than Leo Curry, it might not have mattered, but he couldn't tolerate the thought of having Rachel whipped away from under his nose by a man with whom he was routinely at odds. Before he could stop himself, he heard an apology tumble from his lips.

'I'm sorry, Dan,' he said, shuffling his feet. 'I ought to have thanked her. Perhaps you could do so on my behalf.'

Daniel was firm. 'No, Henry,' he insisted. 'If you've something to tell her, then you must tell it to her yourself. I'm not your intercessor.'

'I don't know how to talk to women.'

'Then it's an art you must learn.'

'It's much easier to keep them out of my life.'

'You didn't keep Beatrix at bay,' Daniel reminded him. 'When we stayed in Amsterdam, you got to like her. I often saw the pair of you talking together.'

'She doesn't frighten me like Rachel Rees.'

'Behind all that bluster, I fancy that you're quite fond of her.'

'No, I'm not,' said Welbeck with sudden force. He became apologetic once more. 'But I will try to thank her for the rum, if the occasion arises.'

'Make sure that you do, Henry. It won't cost you anything.'

Welbeck sensed that it would cost him a great deal but he wasn't prepared to discuss his innermost feelings. Since Daniel was part of the captain-general's staff, the sergeant wanted to know when and where the battle would take place and what sort of odds they'd be facing. He was also interested to hear about the appearance of Marshal Boufflers, a commander whose stout defence of Lille had earned him Welbeck's respect. Daniel told him what they'd gleaned from the captive Marquis de Cheldon and what their scouts had reported about French movements. He explained that a battle was now inevitable. It made Welbeck resolve to speak to Rachel before he marched off to take on the enemy. He didn't want to perish in combat with her kindness unacknowledged.

After taking his leave, Daniel mounted his horse and rode off. Before he could duck into his tent, Welbeck saw Ben Plummer approaching with long strides. His first instinct was to turn away. Ever since he'd rescued Plummer during an assault on the citadel in Tournai, he'd been the unwilling recipient of the man's gratitude. The private thanked him day after day and it became tiresome. There was a benefit. As a result of his experience at Tournai, Plummer had turned from being an insolent mischief-maker into a competent soldier. Welbeck was in no mood for another salvo of thanks but curiosity made him wait for his visitor. Plummer's appearance was eye-catching. Most of the troops had torn and sullied their uniforms during the siege and Plummer had done the same. When rescued by Welbeck, he'd been filthy and bedraggled. Yet here he was now, smartly attired in a new uniform and marching along as if he was on parade.

'What do you want?' asked Welbeck. 'If it's to go on about what happened at the siege, you can save your breath to cool your porridge. I want no more thanks.'

'I wasn't about to give you any, Sergeant,' said Plummer.

'Praise the Lord!'

'I came on an errand.'

Welbeck studied him. 'Where did you get this new uniform from?'

'I bought it.'

'How could you afford something like that?'

Plummer smirked. 'I told you. I had an inheritance.'

'The only thing you ever inherited was the pox from those whores of yours.'

'Those days are behind me, Sergeant. I'm a reformed character now.'

'So where did your money come from?' pressed Welbeck. 'Did you find it under a tree or did it drop out of heaven right in front of you?'

'My uncle died. I was his favourite nephew.' Welbeck gave a mirthless laugh. 'But I didn't come to discuss my good fortune. I brought something for you.'

Welbeck was cautious. 'Is this some kind of jest?'

'Not at all,' said Plummer, taking something from his pocket. 'Rachel Rees asked me to give this to you.' He handed over a flask of rum. 'She left a similar one for you weeks ago but is afraid that someone stole it from your tent. You obviously didn't get it or you'd have said something to her.'

'Yes, yes, I would . . .'

The sergeant felt more than a twinge of guilt. He was also mortified that Plummer had been used as the messenger. Yet the private didn't ridicule him as he'd done on previous occasions when Rachel's name had come into the conversation. Having run his errand, he was about to go. Something made Plummer hesitate.

'Is there any message?' he asked.

'Yes,' said Welbeck, astonished at the affection with which he spoke. 'Please give the lady my thanks. Her gift is appreciated.'

Ever since she and Daniel Rawson had been so close, Amalia had never shown the slightest interest in another man. Her mind was filled with pleasant memories of the time they'd spent together and fervent hopes for their future together. She fell asleep musing about Daniel and woke up wondering where he was at that precise moment and whether or not he was thinking about her. If Amalia was largely unaware of anybody else who had feelings for her, Beatrix was not. Bustling around the Janssen household, she saw everything that was going on and took note of it. Little escaped her shrewd gaze. As she and Amalia were enjoying a walk that morning, she broached a subject that she felt needed airing.

'When will Kees return to work?' she asked.

'Oh, I think he'll be well enough in a day or two.'

'Nick has been to see him several times.'

'Yes,' said Amalia. 'I didn't realise he was so considerate.'

'He and Kees have never been particular friends.'

'That's why it's so admirable of him, Beatrix. He was the person who picked Kees up when he collapsed and he carried him all the way up to his room. It was a real effort.'

'He'd willingly make it for you.'

Amalia laughed. 'It was Kees he was carrying, not me.'

'You were the one he wanted to impress,' said Beatrix. 'And while he likes Kees enough to be sorry about his illness, he really enjoys coming into the house because it gives him a chance to see you.'

'Oh, I don't think that's true,' said Amalia, dismissively.

'I've watched him.'

'Nick is one of Father's employees. We speak from time to time and he's never been anything but polite and attentive.'

Beatrix was upset. 'Forget that I mentioned his name.'

'You're making a wrong assumption, that's all.'

'Then let's talk about something else.'

'No,' said Amalia, placating her with a smile, 'this obviously means something to you or you wouldn't have raised it with me. I know that you're aware of things that pass me by completely and I can't help it. My head is in the clouds.'

'Mine would be if Captain Rawson was dancing attendance on *me*.'

Amalia giggled. 'I wouldn't say that he danced attendance, Beatrix. He does that to His Grace, perhaps, but I see far too little of him. Coming back to Nick Geel,' she went on, 'I'd like to hear your opinion of him.'

'He's friendly, hard-working and very loyal.'

'That would be my estimate of him as well.'

'He's very ambitious.'

'I regard that as a good thing.'

Beatrix took a deep breath then blurted out her claim. 'I think he's in love with you, Miss Amalia.'

'That's nonsense,' said Amalia. 'He likes me, of course. I've never given him cause to *dislike* me, but that's as far as it goes, Beatrix. He knows quite well that I'm spoken for and he's met Daniel a number of times. No,' she added, meditatively, 'I really can't see Nick as an admirer. He's more like a brother to me. And he probably looks upon me as a kind of sister.'

'I disagree. I've heard the way his voice changes when he talks about you.'

'You're mistaken. I'm no more than a friend to him.'

'Be warned,' said Beatrix. 'He adores you.'

'I don't believe that for a second. I'm usually impressed by the way you can judge people but you've made a mistake this time. Weeks go by when I don't even catch a glimpse of Nick.'

'But when you do see him, it's because he's contrived it.'

Amalia came to a halt and turned to face her. 'You make him sound as if he's stalking me,' she said, 'and that's ridiculous. It would never cross Nick's mind to do that. He values his position here and rightly so. He knows what a privilege it is to work for my father and he'd never do anything to jeopardise that.'

'I still think I'm right,' muttered Beatrix.

'It's a silly idea.'

'You don't know him as well as I do.'

'I know him well enough to be certain about his feelings

for me,' said Amalia with a trace of petulance. 'There's
nothing improper in them.'

'Then I'm sorry I spoke.'

'Nick is simply someone who happens to work for
Father.'

'That doesn't stop him nursing hopes.'

'Enough of this,' rebuked Amalia. 'I don't want to hear
any more. You get above yourself sometimes, Beatrix.
There's no reason why you should take any notice of Nick
– or of Aelbert, for that matter. Kees is different. He lives
with us. The others come and go. So please don't make any
more of these absurd suggestions about Nick. It's upsetting.'

Beatrix was cowed. 'I'm sorry, Miss Amalia.'

'So you should be.'

'I won't venture an opinion again.'

'Let's walk on,' said Amalia, setting the pace.

The servant fell in beside her and they walked on
in silence. Though she was still smarting from a rare
reprimand, Beatrix didn't modify her view of Geel in any
way. She sensed that there might well be problems ahead.

When Emanuel Janssen was away on business, Aelbert
Pienaar took charge of the workshop. He liked to make
the others aware of his position, giving orders, making
comments on their work and quietly asserting his authority.
With Dopff still confined to his bed, only two of them were
there. When they came to the end of their day, Pienaar
strolled across to Geel's loom to see what he'd been doing. In
order to remind Geel who was in charge, he made some mild
criticism. All that the younger man could do was to accept
it, apologise and promise to follow his advice. Knowing that

he'd one day have to work under him permanently, Geel was forcing himself to appear amenable to a man with whom he had no real affinity. It meant that he had to swallow his pride and bite his tongue. Life in the workshop was so much more enjoyable when Janssen was there but Geel had to face reality. His new master would be Aelbert Pienaar.

'Time to go home,' announced Pienaar, reaching for his coat and hat.

'I want to call on Kees first.'

'I thought you saw him this morning.'

'Only for a few minutes,' said Geel. 'I promised that I'd look in on him again before I left. Why don't *you* pay him a visit, Aelbert?'

'Oh, he doesn't want me there.'

'Kees will be glad to see anybody. He's so bored.'

'Perhaps I'll go tomorrow,' said Pienaar, evasively. 'I've got too much to do this evening. Goodbye, Nick – and remember what I said.'

'Yes, I will. Goodbye.'

Geel knew the reason that Pienaar would never climb the stairs to see Dopff. It wasn't because he didn't care about his colleague. He was fond of Dopff. What held him back was the fear of seeing someone lying in a sickbed. Memories of his wife's long and harrowing illness were still too painful to contemplate. Pienaar didn't want them revived by the sight of another patient. He'd wait until Dopff had recovered and returned to the workshop.

Geel, by contrast, was very keen to see how Dopff was faring. He was unlikely to meet Amalia on the stairs again but he'd pass her bedchamber and be able to luxuriate in warm thoughts of his brief time inside the room. It had been a magical experience and he intended to repeat it. On this occasion, he wanted more than simply to stand there and absorb the atmosphere. However, Dopff came first. Reaching the room on the upper landing, he tapped on the door and let himself in. He was both shocked and disappointed. Instead of being in bed, Dopff was sitting in a chair in his dressing gown. He looked altogether healthier than he had done earlier in the day. Geel was annoyed. He needed Dopff to remain as an invalid.

'You ought to be in bed, Kees,' he urged.

Dopff shook his head then stood up to show that he felt much better. He spread his arms then turned around. He pointed downstairs to indicate that he might return to work the next day.

'That's wonderful news,' said Geel, masking his true feelings, 'but the doctor told you not to rush things. You need a couple more days of complete rest.'

With his deft hands describing shapes in the air, Dopff thanked him for being so kind as to visit him again. Though it was untrue, Geel told him that Pienaar had sent his best wishes and was looking forward to working beside him again. After ten minutes of conversation, Geel began to get restless. He had something more important to do than soothe a patient.

'Well,' he said, shaking hands with his friend, 'I must be off. I have a lot to do this evening. But it's wonderful to see you looking so much better.'

Collecting a farewell wave from Dopff, he opened the door and descended the stairs to the other landing. Nobody saw him sidle up to Amalia's bedchamber and let himself in. It was as enchanting as it had been on his first visit.

He felt emboldened to take more liberties this time, sitting on the bed to feel the mattress on which she slept then stretching full length so that his head rested on her pillow. A warm glow suffused his whole body. Filled with excitement, he gave his imagination full rein. He longed to have Amalia beside him on the bed to love and caress. He yearned to possess her. Since that was impossible at the moment, Geel wanted a keepsake, something private and personal that he could take away with him. He needed a trophy from his visit.

His preference was for an item of clothing but, after consideration, he decided that its disappearance was certain to be noticed. He searched the room for minutes, opening drawers and looking in cupboards, touching everything he found simply because it belonged to her. In the final drawer, he discovered exactly what he wanted. It was a collection of ribbons and he slipped one of them into his pocket, vowing to place it on his own pillow that night. With his prize tucked safely away, he left the room furtively, went down the stairs and departed quietly from the house. On the walk back home, he was sustained by a sense of triumph.

Chapter Eighteen

Marlborough always liked to reconnoitre a potential battlefield in person. Early on 9th September, therefore, he rode out with some of his senior officers to survey the terrain. Daniel was among those at his side. They were surprised and not a little dismayed to see Villars' army coming up in four large columns in the distance. It seemed as if they might try to push through one of the gaps beside the Bois de Thiery and the Allies were simply not ready to withstand a frontal assault. The absent Prince Eugene was covering the gap in the Bois de Boussu and other commanders were spread out across a wide area to watch various gaps in the woodland. Marlborough felt that he lacked the strength to launch an attack of his own and was relieved when he saw the French entrenching a position that included the Bois de Sars on its left and the Bois de la Lanière on its right. Swirling rain didn't help the reconnaissance. Men and horses were thoroughly soaked and they found it difficult to see properly through the downpour.

As the party was returning to camp, Daniel was close enough to the captain-general to initiate a conversation. He was always keen to discuss tactics.

'The French are digging in, Your Grace,' he observed. 'When will we begin a bombardment?'

'Not until this afternoon when we have sufficient guns.'

'We could certainly use the men who are still besieging St-Ghislain. When Rachel Rees and I rode past the town, I had a feeling that it might prove to be an awkward proposition.'

'According to General Withers, it's almost on the point of surrender,' said Marlborough, 'and not before time. That will liberate a sizeable number to join us.'

'What about Mons? You've committed appreciable forces there.'

'They'll need to be thinned slightly. I've ordered four battalions of Germans to leave the town in order to swell our ranks. In whatever conflict lies ahead, we're going to rely heavily on our German and Austrian forces.'

'By the same token,' noted Daniel, 'the French will rely heavily on their Bavarian contingents. It will be a truly international battle.'

His comment was appropriate. A large proportion of the Allied army was made up of Dutch and Austrian troops with a substantial number of British and Prussian regiments in support. Daniel's beloved 24th Foot was only one of a number of British infantry regiments. He had friends in the 16th, 19th and the 26th, the Cameronians, but there were several others at the disposal of the captain-general. Hanoverians and Danes served in the Allied army while regiments of Scots, Irish and Swiss had been recruited by both sides. Soldiers were impelled by different motives. Idealists were there in pursuit of their perceived cause, patriots fought for their respective countries and mercenaries simply killed for money. Victory would offer huge political gains, a sense of national pride or a hefty profit. When they finally clashed, something of the order of two hundred thousand soldiers would be engaged.

'We'll have to hold another council of war,' said Marlborough.

Daniel's eyebrow lifted meaningfully. 'Then a further delay is likely.'

'It's the Dutch who are always overcautious, Daniel. Is there some way that you could prod your fellow countrymen into action?'

'When I see them fighting, I'm glad to be Dutch. During a council of war, however, I'm relieved that my father was English. There are times,' admitted Daniel, 'when having a foot in both camps, so to speak, puts a real strain on me.'

'You seem to cope remarkably well with it.'

'I've had to, Your Grace.'

'What would happen if ever the British and Dutch governments fell out?'

'I can't see that happening somehow.'

'Nothing should be ruled out,' said Marlborough, sagely. 'You're a British soldier with Dutch sympathies. Which side would you support?'

'Neither and both,' said Daniel.

'That's the answer of a born diplomat.'

'I'd find it difficult to bear arms against the country I serve.'

'Difficult but not impossible,' said Marlborough. 'The British army is your paymaster but I fancy that its claims would be outweighed by your very beautiful paymistress. Am I right?'

Cantering along in the rain was not the best time to discuss his private life. As it happened, Daniel was spared the problem of making a reply by the arrival of the Dutch general, who eased his mount beside Marlborough so that he could ply him with questions. Daniel was free to ponder the response he would have given. Which would he choose – England or Holland? Would the home of his father count for more than the birthplace of his mother? Or would the issue be decided by Amalia Janssen? It seemed more than likely. Daniel couldn't conceive of fighting against the country in which she lived and whose language she spoke. Unknown to her, Amalia had settled the argument in a flash. In the event of conflict between the two countries, Daniel would resign his commission in the British army to fight under the Dutch flag. He just hoped that such a circumstance would never arise.

Having viewed the French army and seen its controlled movements, he knew that any battle would be a ferocious one. Death was bound to garner a rich harvest and it would not do it slowly over a period of time, as in a siege. Widespread slaughter might take only a matter of hours. No matter what role would be assigned to Daniel, there would be a strong element of danger. Reports of the conflict would inevitably be published in the Dutch newspapers and help to stoke Amalia's concern. Should he be killed in action, all that she would have to remember him by was a sequence of letters that chartered their relationship from its early warm friendship to the full-blooded romance it had now become. Amalia deserved more. Commitment in words did not hold the same power and reassurance as a legal and spiritual partnership. When he thought about it, he believed that Amalia might have drawn comfort from the fact that she was sending a husband off to war and not merely the man she loved.

Though he was surrounded by over a dozen people in a very public place, Daniel nevertheless reached a crucial private decision. If – God willing – he came through the forthcoming battle intact, he would offer Amalia Janssen a proposal of marriage. Nobody around him could understand why he let out a whoop of joy.

'Hurry up, Father,' said Amalia, impatiently. 'I want to read it.'

'I've told you. There's nothing about the latest developments. The article is about the surrender of Tournai and that was several days ago.'

'Daniel was *there* at the time. Every detail is important to me.'

'It's important to me as well,' said Janssen, mildly, 'but I can see that I'll get no peace to read the report until you've seen it first. Here you are,' he went on, yielding it up, 'but I want it back as soon as you've finished with it.'

'Thank you.'

Amalia buried her head in the newspaper and read every word pertaining to the Allied army in Flanders. It didn't matter that it was all out of date. Anything that had involved

Daniel was significant to her. She recoiled when she saw the scale of Allied losses at Tournai and prayed that Daniel was not among them. If he'd survived one siege, he might now be taking part in another one at Mons. There would be more carnage on both sides. It was frightening. After poring over every word, she finally handed the newspaper back to her father.

'I wish I knew what was going on,' she said in exasperation.

'From what I can see in this report,' remarked her father, 'I'm not sure that anyone knows exactly what's happening. It must be so confusing for His Grace, the Duke of Marlborough. Trying to wage war in foul weather is almost impossible. It slows everything down. The roads are rivers of mud and the rivers themselves must be swollen by this terrible rain. We're fighting the elements as much as the French.'

'I'm only thinking about Daniel.'

'Then you're being rather selfish.'

'I know but I can't help it.'

'A lot of Dutch soldiers will be taking part in any battle,' he scolded, gently, 'and they all have families who are worried sick about them. Spare a thought for *them* as well, Amalia.'

'I will,' she said, shamefacedly. 'There are so many people in Amsterdam already in mourning for lost sons and fathers. The list of casualties gets longer and longer each week.' She made an effort to shake off her anxieties. 'From now on, I'll try to concentrate on good things instead of dwelling on bad ones that may never happen. For instance, Kees came back to work today. That really pleased me.'

'It pleased me even more, Amalia. We missed him in the workshop.'

'Aelbert was saying that the place seemed empty without him.'

'We're delighted to have him back,' said Janssen. 'Or at least, Aelbert and I are. I'm not so sure about Nick.'

She was puzzled. 'But he's very fond of Kees. He visited him every day when Kees was off work. That's more than Aelbert did.'

'He had his own reasons for staying away but he wasn't ignoring Kees. In fact, Aelbert bought him a number of gifts to cheer him up. And when Kees turned up this morning, Aelbert embraced him warmly.'

'How did Nick react?'

'Well,' said Janssen, 'he *appeared* to welcome Kees but I thought I sensed a whisper of disappointment. It was almost as if he'd wanted Kees to have a longer convalescence so that he could go on visiting him. Heaven knows why.'

While her father began to read the newspaper again, Amalia was troubled. She recalled what Beatrix had said to her about Geel. Having dismissed the servant's warning out of hand, she now felt slightly guilty for doing so. Beatrix's judgement was to some extent supported by what her father had told her. Could it really be true that Geel was less interested in the health of a sick friend and colleag͡ne than he was in Amalia herself? Were his regular visits with patient undertaken in the hope of a chance meeel had her? It was unlikely yet not impossible. Nich other than started to unsettle her. Amalia now had s͡ Daniel to worry about.

* * *

Everyone knew that a major battle was close at hand. By mid-afternoon on 9th September, the French had already started to cannonade Allied lines. British regiments were relieved when their own artillery returned fire, albeit in a rather desultory fashion. Their confidence was tinged with apprehension. Everything they'd heard about the opposing army suggested that Villars had instilled a new vigour and pride into it. Some soldiers – Joel Drew, the barber, was one of them – were old enough to remember a time when French armies held sway over the whole of Europe. Fighting was in their blood. That tradition had not wholly disappeared. Led by the right commander, they were a formidable enemy, especially when, as now, they'd been able to choose the ground for the battle.

British regiments of horse and foot watched and prayed. Some cleaned their weapons, others wrote letters to their loved ones and others again sat in groups and reminisced about past victories in order to banish present fears. At such a time, the one thing guaranteed to bolster their spirits was the sight of their captain-general, strolling through the camp with an air of buoyancy. Seeing that the rain had largely eased off, Marlborough perambulated through the British ranks, speaking or waving to all and sundry as he did so. It was his approachability that had earned him the nickname of Corporal John. Unlike so many commanders, that was neither aloof nor indifferent. By showing his men their understood and sympathised with them, he gained him. t and gratitude. They rushed to get a glimpse of

Since seized the c part of Marlborough's entourage, Daniel slip away in search of the 24th Foot.

He discovered Welbeck outside the sergeant's tent, calmly smoking a pipe.

'Don't you want to see His Grace?' asked Daniel.

'I've seen him before.'

'He's trying to put some cheer into the men.'

'Cheer is useless,' said Welbeck. 'They need steel inside them.'

Daniel sniffed. 'That smells like a different tobacco. It's got a much nicer aroma than the one you usually smoke. Why did you change?'

'It was a gift.'

'Ah, I see . . .'

'And before you reproach me again, Dan, I *did* thank her this time.'

'Did you do so in person?'

'Yes,' said Welbeck, 'though Rachel was only here for a minute.'

'I wish I had someone to supply me with rum and tobacco.'

'You don't bleeding well smoke a pipe.'

'I was speaking figuratively, Henry.'

Distant explosions seemed to be getting nearer as each army bombarded the other with increasing force. Welbeck glanced in the direction of the French lines.

'When do we attack, Dan?'

'The final decision hasn't yet been made.'

'It has to be tomorrow, surely.'

'That's up to the council of war,' said Daniel. 'Let's just say that a battle is imminent and that it promises to be a fierce one. Villars and Boufflers are fine commanders. They'll make their men fight to the death.'

A flicker of alarm appeared in Welbeck's eyes. Daniel was surprised. His friend was one of the most fearless men he'd ever met. Welbeck always marched bravely into battle without any concern for his own safety. He relied on his skills as a soldier to survive and they'd never let him down. Though he still had unquestioning faith in his abilities, Welbeck was no longer immune to dread. Daniel guessed what lay behind the transformation. Welbeck now had a much stronger reason to stay alive. Rum and tobacco had induced a change of heart.

The thunder of the artillery was louder than ever. They could hear the cries of wounded soldiers and the sound of drums giving commands to the infantry in the line of fire. In the early exchanges, the French were more than holding their own. Daniel could not stay long. Because of their close friendship, he and Welbeck embraced each other warmly. Rachel Rees caught them stepping apart and she clapped her hands together in delight.

'How wonderful!' she exclaimed. 'I meet my two favourite men at once.'

Daniel greeted her cordially but Welbeck was more reserved.

'I thought that someone else was your favourite,' he said, moodily.

'Now why should you think that?' she asked.

'Leo Curry has been boasting that you belong to him.'

'Then he must be *twp*,' she said. 'That's a Welsh word for "stupid", by the way. How could I prefer a shaggy old bear like Sergeant Curry to you and Daniel?'

Daniel grinned. 'You're a woman of discernment, Rachel.'

'There aren't many of us about.'

'Tell that to Henry – I have to take my leave, I'm afraid.'

After an exchange of farewells, Daniel went back to join Marlborough, who was still touring the camp. Rachel gazed fondly at Welbeck. He took a final pull on his pipe then tapped it on the bottom of his boot to dislodge the ash.

'I still prefer my old tobacco,' he said.

'Then I'll have to give you some of that instead, won't I?'

'There won't be much time for enjoying a pipe from now on. The only smoke I'll see will be coming out of a musket.' He studied her shrewdly for a few seconds. 'Why did you send Ben Plummer with that flask of rum?'

'I didn't think that you'd take it from my hands.'

'But why pick on Plummer?'

'It was the other way round, Henry,' she explained. 'I know that he used to be the bane of your life but, since you carried him to safety at Tournai, Ben worships you now. He asked me if I had anything he could buy from me to give to you. I insisted that it would come as a gift from me.'

'It was a very welcome one,' he confessed.

'That's all I wanted to hear.'

'But you don't have to press anything else on me, Rachel. I can afford to pay for my drink and tobacco.'

'I wouldn't even consider it,' she said with a cackle. 'Everything I have is yours, Henry. I make a handsome profit out of everybody else so I'm entitled to spoil my special man.'

He was tentative. 'Is that what I am?'

'Why else would I say it?'

He regarded her with an amalgam of curiosity and affection. She smiled back at him. Welbeck searched for words that simply refused to come. Rachel seemed to understand his dilemma.

'Tell me afterwards,' she suggested. 'Tell me when the battle is over.'

'Can I ask you a favour?'

'It's granted before you even ask.'

'If you do have another gift for me,' he said, 'don't send Plummer with it.'

'I wouldn't dream of it.'

'Good – we don't need anyone else, do we?'

To block out their fear of the approaching battle, many soldiers in the 24th Foot turned to gambling and risked their pay on the turn of a card. Those gathered in a tent with Ben Plummer were seeking their reward through the roll of some dice. It was not the first session that Plummer had organised. It was his regular source of income. He'd been so successful among his comrades in the past that they refused to play with him. As a result, he'd inveigled his way into the detachment of men under the charge of Leo Curry. Since they didn't know his reputation, Plummer was able to operate freely. He was very cunning, ensuring that some of the others won from time to time. At the end of every session, however, he always managed to walk away with the bulk of the winnings. It astonished and annoyed the men playing with him that afternoon.

'You've got the luck of the devil,' said one of them as Plummer threw the winning numbers yet again. 'You almost never lose.'

Plummer smirked. 'It's all to do with the way you throw the dice.'

'Show us. Tell us your secret.'

'Yes,' urged the other four in the tent. 'What's the trick?'

'There is no trick,' said Plummer. 'I simply do this.'

Holding the dice tightly, he first kissed his fingers before twisting his wrist and opening his hand to scatter the dice. They were amazed at the result.

'It's yet another double six,' said one.

'The dice are loaded,' challenged another.

'No, they're not,' said Plummer, gathering them up again. 'I won fairly and squarely. You're just a bad loser, my friend. Here,' he went on, opening his hand. 'If you don't believe me, take a close look at them.'

His accuser took the dice, weighed them on his palm then examined them very closely. When he could find nothing wrong with them, he flung them on to the ground. His low score brought him howls of derision.

'Well,' said Plummer, picking up the dice again, 'I think the game is over. If I'm not trusted, there's no point in playing on.'

There were yells of protest and they all exhorted him to continue the game. Pretending to yield to their persuasion, he handed the dice over, taking care to lose the first few games. The soldier who'd accused him earlier actually won a substantial amount and apologised for his suspicions. Plummer placed his wager for the next game and the others followed suit. He was to throw the dice last. When it came to his turn, however, he didn't use the dice that the others all had. They were cleverly palmed and substituted by the loaded dice he kept hidden up a sleeve. He went through the same routine – a kiss, a twist of the wrist and a throw. When the winning numbers turned up yet again, there were groans of pain.

'Fortune favours the brave,' said Plummer, scooping up the money. 'One thing is certain, anyway. If I die in battle, at least they can buy me an expensive coffin with my winnings. My thanks to one and all,' he added, distributing a radiant smile among them. 'Do give my regards to Sergeant Curry, won't you?'

On 10th September there was still no sign that the Allied army was preparing for an immediate attack. The delay suited Villars and gave his men additional time to strengthen their defences. They worked with feverish energy to build five redoubts shaped like arrowheads and reinforced by parapets so thick that they could withstand direct hits from cannon. The redoubts were thrown up on open ground between the Bois de Sars and Blairon Farm. A gentle slope separated these fortifications from the Allies. The daunting solidity of the redoubts impressed Lieutenant-Colonel Morellon.

'They'd keep a siege train at bay,' he commented.

'Our defences need to be sound,' said Villars. 'Colonel de la Colonie has reported seeing the Allies arranging a battery of about thirty heavy guns.'

'Where will the colonel serve?'

'Right in our centre – I've put him in charge of a Bavarian brigade. It may help to assuage his hurt feelings,' added Villars with a faint smile. 'The colonel was unhappy when I ordered him to escort the baggage here. It's an important duty but he felt that it was beneath him.'

'Colonel de la Colonie longs to be in the thick of a battle.'

'His chance will come.'

'We have outstanding commanders, excellently deployed

by you. It was a brilliant move on your part to put Marshal Boufflers in command of the right wing. We are honoured by his presence. He brings a wealth of military wisdom.'

They were riding along the French lines, far enough behind them to be out of range of the Allied guns still booming away at intervals, yet close enough to carry out an inspection of their fortifications. Their voices were raised above the echoing clamour of artillery. Villars sat upright in the saddle, poised, debonair and inspirational. Morellon cut a poor figure beside him. He was too sycophantic to challenge any of the commander-in-chief's decisions but he was bound to wonder why Villars had detached his reserve cavalry, under the Chevalier de Luxembourg, and moved them south to protect a gap in the woods opposite Maubeuge, a town that was in no way threatened. It had also occurred to him that they might profitably have attacked the Allies on the previous day when many of their horses were out foraging and when their guns were still on the road. With their resources scattered over a wide area, the Allies had been vulnerable, yet the French held back. Holding Villars in such high esteem, Morellon accepted that the strategy was a sound one. He trusted the commander-in-chief implicitly. All that Morellon wanted was to take part in a great French victory and he was utterly convinced that Villars would deliver it.

'Why do they hesitate?' he asked.

'I blame Marlborough for that.'

'In the past, he's always been so purposeful.'

'Yes,' said Villars, watching a cannonball hit a French barricade and bounce harmlessly off. 'That was in the past.

As I told you before, he's not infallible. He's already made two bad mistakes.'

'You think that he should have invested Ypres, don't you?'

'That would have distressed me far more than the attack on Mons. We could not have moved in the direction of Ypres quickly enough to save it. As it is, the Allies came south-east instead. I concede that they caught us by surprise but it was not an unpleasant one. I'd much rather have them here. Our arrival has prevented the siege being prosecuted with full vigour. Because we represent such a potent menace to him, Marlborough dare not even begin his lines of circumvallation around Mons.'

'You said that Marlborough had made two mistakes.'

'I did, Charles. He should have attacked yesterday before we'd had time to extend and secure our defensive line. Peppering us with shot may cause some casualties,' Villars went on, 'but it will not decide the issue. Besides, our artillery is more accurate. We've cannonaded the British battalions with success. Some of their regiments of foot have suffered badly.'

'Will they make their move today?'

'I doubt it – they've left it too late.'

'Then they've given us another precious day to dig ourselves in.'

'When they do finally attack,' said Villars, who had mastered the geography of the area, 'they'll have to choose between three gaps in the wood. Every other route is impractical because of marshy ground. They'll come through the *trouée de Boussu* north of the Bois de Sars, the *trouée de la Louvière* north of the Bois de Thiery or the Aulnois

Gap to its south. We have all three well covered. From the way that he's drawn up his army, Marlborough has clearly chosen to concentrate his attention on the Aulnois Gap.'

'Then where is he?' asked Morellon. 'What's holding him back?'

'Some of his generals are probably dithering.'

'Why doesn't he show strong leadership and sweep their objections aside?'

'I don't know, Charles,' said Villars with disdain, 'but it's a glaring fault. His grasp is slipping. He's failed to impose himself on his allies. In the two days he's been here, Marlborough has weakened his chances of success and thereby strengthened our own. When he does finally offer us battle,' he continued, 'he'll live to regret it. Malplaquet will be the graveyard of Allied ambitions.'

When he attended the council of war that day as an interpreter, Daniel witnessed a familiar story. Everybody was anxious to express his views. Since their troops were likely to bear the brunt of French power, Dutch generals were particularly vocal. The Earl of Orkney, also given a vital role, was keen to make his opinions heard and Prince Eugene – recalled from the Bois de Boussu – stressed that any impulse towards bold action had to be held in check.

'Since we do not know the lie of the land,' he stressed, 'we dare take even less risks. The terrain is very uneven and cut up by many creeks, brooks and ponds, all of them filled up by recent rain.'

'Yes,' said Marlborough, attempting to introduce a touch of humour into the discussion, 'there's so much standing water that this is more like a maritime exercise than anything else. Perhaps we should summon naval support.'

There was polite laughter but it didn't dispel the solemnity of the occasion.

Daniel discharged his duties with his usual skill but he was troubled. He could not understand why Marlborough had been so inactive for another whole day. It might well be that the troops from Mons were still on the road and that those under the command of General Withers – St-Ghislain having now capitulated – had not yet arrived. The Allies nevertheless had a numerical advantage over the enemy and could have pressed it home while the French positions were still only half complete. Giving them an extra day seemed to Daniel to be foolhardy. When the council of war broke up and its members went their separate ways, he raised the matter with Marlborough.

'I think that your plan of action is correct, Your Grace,' he said, 'but it would have been equally correct today and – had you implemented it – been more effective. Delay plays into the hands of Marshal Villars.'

'It also gives us time to make a detailed reconnaissance of his army,' said Marlborough. 'I understand your impatience. To some extent, I share it, but the warning from Prince Eugene was timely. We're in unknown territory. To move too soon could have been a costly mistake.'

'We'll never know if that was the case.'

Marlborough chuckled. 'You're a true soldier, Daniel. When there's a sniff of action, every sinew of you tingles in anticipation. I know – I felt the same at your age. But we have to adapt our tactics to the conditions of the battlefield,' he said, bending over the map on the table. 'It's taking time to make full assessments. Whole areas of the terrain are bedevilled by quagmires. We need to know exactly where the enemy is entrenched and how we can best approach them over solid ground.'

'I accept that, Your Grace,' said Daniel.

'You'll not be denied any action,' remarked Cardonnel, patting his arm, 'but you'll have to wait until tomorrow before it comes.'

'It will be *early* tomorrow,' added Marlborough. 'I'm as eager to engage Villars as anybody. If I know him, he'll have had his men working through the night to improve their defences even more. However, I beg leave to doubt that they'll be strong enough to withstand the full fury of our attack. It's the Allied army that will be cheering at the end of the day. Talking of cheers,' he went on, looking at Daniel, 'I've not had a moment to ask you about that extraordinary outburst of joy we heard from you during our reconnaissance yesterday.'

'Yes,' said Cardonnel, 'I heard mention of that.'

'It was a private matter,' said Daniel.

'Yet you celebrated it in public, it seems.'

'May we know its source?' asked Marlborough.

'The truth of it is,' confessed Daniel, 'that I made an important decision and it filled me with elation. I decided to offer a proposal of marriage to Amalia Janssen.'

'I'd have thought you'd already done that by now.'

'We have an understanding, Your Grace, but no formal betrothal.'

'Congratulations!' said Cardonnel, pumping his hand.

'But Amalia hasn't accepted me yet.'

'Would the lady dare to refuse you after all this time?'

'I suppose not,' decided Daniel.

'Then congratulations are in order,' said Marlborough, beaming. 'The pair of you will make a handsome couple. Now that that's settled, I implore you to forget all about your beloved until more pressing business is over tomorrow. We need you addressing yourself solely to the defeat of the French army. Enchanting as she is, Miss Amalia Janssen will have to wait her turn.'

It was wrong. In hindsight, Geel could see that. It was wrong to steal something that belonged to Amalia as a souvenir. When he left the house with the ribbon concealed in his pocket, he had a sense of triumph but it failed to deliver what he'd expected of it. Though he slept with it beside his head on the pillow, it gave him none of the pleasure for which he'd hoped. Instead, it stirred up feelings of guilt and kept him awake. He was a thief. In a house where he'd been given the privilege of work and enjoyed the friendship of all who lived there, he'd abused the trust put in him. In some ways, he was as despicable as the men who stole the tapestry. The ribbon might have nothing like the same value but it was Amalia's, private property he had no right even to touch, let alone purloin. After writhing in self-disgust, Geel decided that the first thing he had to do was to return the ribbon to the drawer in her bedchamber. At least the sight of it would no longer fill him with remorse. It wouldn't make amends for the crime he'd committed, but it would ease his conscience.

The problem was that he had no legitimate reason to enter the house, still less the bedchamber. Dopff's return to work had robbed him of his excuse to visit his friend's room. He racked his brains to discover a means of contriving access, even thinking of bribing one of the servants. In the end, he decided that it was *his* responsibility to put the ribbon back exactly where he'd found it. It would be unfair and dangerous to involve anyone else. His chance came at the end of the working day. Pienaar had left, Dopff had gone up to his room and Janssen was going through his accounts. Geel knew that Amalia was out of the house, which meant that Beatrix was accompanying her. None of the other servants would be anywhere near the landing. If he was swift enough, Geel could return the ribbon to the appropriate drawer then quit the house in less than a minute.

Opening the door of the workshop, he peered into the house to make sure that nobody was about. His throat had gone dry and his heart was beating like the hooves of a runaway horse. The audacity he'd shown when stealing the ribbon had deserted him; he was furtive and anxious now. Geel took a deep breath as he tried to compose himself then he sprinted towards the stairs and crept up them at speed. Reaching the landing, he crossed to Amalia's bedchamber and took another precautionary look around him. He was safe. He opened the door, stepped into the room and closed the door silently behind him. Going to the drawer from which he'd taken the keepsake, he pulled it open and tossed the ribbon into it. A sense of relief flooded through him. He was about to close the drawer when he noticed something that had evaded his gaze the first time. Something was poking out from beneath the pile of ribbons. His curiosity got the better of his desperation.

As he grasped the object in his hand, he realised that he was holding a pile of letters held together by a ribbon. He guessed immediately that they must have come from Daniel

Rawson and were treasured mementos of their romance. He winced as he felt another stab of guilt. Daniel's letters had the right to be there. Geel did not. It was ignoble of him even to touch the private correspondence. Pulling his hand away as if it had just been bitten, he closed the drawer and turned to leave. But his exit was now blocked. Geel had not heard the door being opened behind him. Nor had he realised that he was no longer alone. In trying to atone for one crime of trespass, he'd committed another and this time he'd been caught. Standing in the open doorway with an expression of surprise and disapproval was Kees Dopff.

CHAPTER NINETEEN

Given the unexpected bonus of an extra day to reinforce their defensive line, the French exploited it to the full. They toiled until light began to fade then lit fires to illumine the area and enable them to work on in the dark. Across the Aulnois Gap there were now nine stout redoubts, built by French pioneers under the watchful gaze of Marshal Villars. Each of these outworks was equipped with artillery which could cover the narrow approaches that climbed the gentle, mud-covered gradient between the woods. Blairon Farm to the right had been commandeered, barricaded and loopholed for defence, turning it into a minor fortress. Its livestock had been driven away from danger. In the Bois de la Lanière on the French right, infantry under the command of the Comte d'Artagnan had laboured manfully to create a series of breastworks and abattis that would be formidable obstacles. Between the wood and Blairon Farm was a large battery, carefully concealed and capable of firing along a dip in the ground across the front of the trees. Wherever possible, the French had made good use of the contours of the terrain.

Over to the left of the French position, the infantry was under the command of the Comte d'Albergotti and the Marquis de Goesbriand. They had constructed three lines of breastworks reaching deep into the Bois de Sars and jutting out into the Aulnois Gap to form a shape that resembled a triangle. Villars had ordered a fourth line of entrenchments to be dug in the open ground to the south of the woods but, in spite of the heroic efforts of his men, it was clear that it would not be completed by morning. Disappointed by the failure, he nevertheless felt sufficiently confident to be able to manage without a continuous trench running close to La Folie Farm.

Not every member of the French army was engaged in building work. In the course of the evening, a rumour spread that peace negotiations had been reopened and might actually make a battle unnecessary. A whiff of euphoria wafted through the ranks and an informal truce was arranged, allowing officers and soldiers on both sides to approach each other without fear of attack. Many called out in friendly terms and struck up conversations. Some even shook hands with members of the enemy and wished them well. There was a mutual respect between two armies who had now been fighting each other for several years. The truce, however, didn't last. When the French saw that the Allies were taking more than a casual interest in the enemy defences, the camaraderie vanished abruptly. Harsh words and vile taunts were now exchanged and the soldiers returned quickly to their respective camps, knowing that a battle was unavoidable. The rumour was false. There were no overtures of peace on the anvil.

Captain Daniel Rawson had never believed in the rumour. Having seen it built up steadily over the preceding weeks, he knew that the momentum was too great to be halted. Villars was ready to commit his whole army to a battle and had royal authority to do so. For his part, Marlborough was more than willing to oblige the French commander. Daniel recalled that, at the council of war, the one option never even considered was to give priority to the siege of Mons, protecting it with the main army in a purely defensive position. Marlborough had waited so long to draw the French out into the open that he wouldn't spurn the rare chance to meet them face to face. Both armies were vast, well armed, fuelled by self-belief, primed for action and led by experienced commanders. Everything pointed to a titanic confrontation.

As a member of the captain-general's staff, Daniel knew that he'd be given special duties that would keep him well away from his own regiment during the battle. He was anxious to make contact with old friends beforehand, accepting that some of them would inevitably perish on the next day. With darkness enshrouding the Allied army, therefore, he rode to the section where the 24th Foot were encamped. On the eve of every battle, the soldiers were restless but they seemed even more agitated than usual. The mood of edginess was exemplified by Henry Welbeck.

'I don't like it, Dan,' he grumbled. 'I can't put my finger on it but something is seriously amiss.'

'If you have any doubts,' advised Daniel, 'don't let your men see them.'

Welbeck was scornful. 'I'm not that stupid.'

'What's the problem exactly?'

'I wish I knew.'

'This will be our fourth major battle against the French. Perhaps you should remind yourself that we won the other three decisively.'

'Yes,' said the sergeant, 'and on each occasion I was confident of victory before we clashed. It's different here. I don't have that feeling inside me.'

'Once the firing starts, you soon will.'

'Are *you* certain that we'll trounce the Frenchies again?'

'Of course,' said Daniel, clapping him on the shoulder.

They were inside Welbeck's tent, talking by the light of a candle. The sergeant was smoking his pipe, filling the air with the smell of tobacco. On the table was a flask of rum. Daniel suspected that he knew what lay behind his friend's feeling of insecurity. In all previous battles, Welbeck had had only himself to care about. There was no family to consider, nobody pining away at home for him. That situation had changed. Rachel Rees had finally broken through his granite exterior and discovered a softness that nobody knew was there. For the first time, Welbeck had an emotional commitment, albeit one that he didn't yet fully understand. After the horrors of the following day, someone would be waiting for him and he was unsettled by the thought that he might not live to see her again.

'Try to think about something else, Henry,' suggested Daniel.

'Is that what *you're* doing?'

'As a matter of fact, it is.'

'Then you're not the Dan Rawson I know,' said Welbeck, disparagingly. 'In the past, your mind would be filled with the possibilities of what might lay ahead on the battlefield. Nothing would distract you.'

'Well, it has this time.'

'Be careful, Dan. Distraction can be fatal.'

'My mind will be fully concentrated tomorrow,' said Daniel. 'It's just that I'll go into battle with even more determination to survive. I've made a decision, Henry. When I next have the pleasure of seeing her, I'll ask for Amalia's hand in marriage.'

Welbeck exploded. 'This is no time to talk about a woman!'

'I can't think of any topic more satisfying.'

'Amalia doesn't even exist until the battle is over.'

'Yes, she does – and so does Rachel.'

'Why drag that demented Welsh harridan into this?'

'Fie on you, Henry!' exclaimed Daniel. 'You're smoking her tobacco and you have a flask of her rum on the table there. How can you be so ungrateful? I've never met any woman less like a harridan. She's a good, decent, warm-hearted woman with amazing courage.'

'That's true,' mumbled Welbeck, apologetically. 'I spoke too harshly.'

'You should be ashamed.'

'I stand corrected.'

'Rachel might be better off with Sergeant Curry, after all.'

The comment was intended to be a gentle prod but Welbeck reacted as if he'd just been impaled on a stake.

Letting out a roar of protest, he listed ten reasons why no woman was safe near Leo Curry then insisted that he had first claim on Rachel Rees. In his wrath, he was able to say things to Daniel that he'd never even admitted to himself. Rachel was his and she was committed to him. Since she'd rejoined the army, he explained, his horizons had suddenly widened because he'd let a woman into his life at last. Daniel heard him out then smiled in approval.

'Have you told all this to Rachel herself?'

Welbeck was suddenly uneasy. 'No, Dan.'

'I think she'd like to hear it.'

'The battle comes first.'

'You've already won a skirmish against Sergeant Curry, it seems.'

'Leo doesn't get any rum and tobacco.'

'While you're enjoying them,' said Daniel, 'spare a thought for the woman who gave them to you. And when the order for attack is given tomorrow, take her with you in your heart. That's what I'll be doing with Amalia.'

Ever since she'd befriended him, Daniel had been a regular visitor to Amalia's dreams. He usually appeared in a romantic glow, loving, attentive and gallant. Even when she was most anxious about him, she was not distressed by any terrifying nightmares. The nocturnal visions she had of him on a battlefield were always somehow reassuring. By a combination of expertise and daring, Daniel would invariably survive any action and be rewarded with new honours. Amalia liked to think that he was given invisible protection by the strength of her love but she knew that such an idea was fanciful. He was an outstanding soldier. It was as simple as that. Others might fall or suffer crippling injuries but Daniel led a charmed life. Whatever happened, he would always come safely back to her.

It didn't stop Amalia worrying about him during the day. Judging by the information she'd gathered from reports in the newspaper, a battle of some sort seemed inescapable and she knew that Daniel would be facing a severe test of his abilities. He was the victim of his own success. Because he'd been able to complete perilous assignments time and again, he was always among the first people to whom Marlborough turned in a crisis. In the forthcoming battle, she believed, Daniel would once again be called upon to risk his life in some hazardous exercise. What it would be Amalia didn't know and that made it more unnerving. While she was still deeply concerned about him when she went to bed that night, Amalia felt that sleep would restore her peace of mind. Warm and comforting dreams of Daniel would take away the gnawing apprehension and she'd awake refreshed.

Her confidence was misplaced. When she eventually dozed off, her slumber was soon interrupted by a dream so vivid and frightening that it sent tremors through her body. Battle was joined. The opposing armies bombarded each other until smoke covered the whole battlefield like a swirling fog. There were cavalry charges from both sides then surges of Allied and French infantry. The noise was deafening and the scene chaotic. It was impossible to work out which army was in the ascendant. What was unmistakable, however, was the constant, stomach-churning wail of the wounded and the dying. Amalia saw limbs hacked viciously off, heads removed by sabres and bodies shattered by cannon fire. She watched horse after horse being cut down then writhing madly on the ground. Blood was everywhere, gushing into the streams and turning them red. The stink of death invaded her nostrils and made her retch.

Then a man came galloping into her nightmare in the uniform of a British captain. His face was smeared with blood but she knew that it was Daniel, riding into the very heart of the enemy infantry and slashing away with his sword as if he intended to slay the entire French army on his own. Amalia tried to shout a warning to him but her voice was drowned out by the pandemonium. All that she could do was to watch in horror as the valiant Captain Rawson was hit by a musket ball, stabbed by the upward thrust of a bayonet, then hauled from his horse to be clubbed to death by the unforgiving butts of a dozen French muskets. His head was smashed to a pulp and his body needlessly mutilated. The uniform he'd worn with such pride was sodden with blood. As he lay sprawled helplessly on the ground, a troop of French cavalry charged over him and pummelled him into a misshapen heap of flesh and bone.

Amalia could take no more. She came out of the nightmare with a scream of agony, sitting up in her bed with perspiration dripping from every pore. Daniel had been killed. All her hopes for their future together had been snuffed out. Her grief was unbearable. She was still sobbing uncontrollably when a worried Beatrix came into the room with a candle to see what had happened. The servant put an arm around her.

'What's the trouble?' she asked.

'He's dead,' said Amalia, mournfully. 'Daniel was killed in battle.'

* * *

The plan on which the Allies had agreed had been finalised by Marlborough and Prince Eugene. Late adjustments had had to be made as fresh intelligence came in regarding the disposition of French forces. In essence, however, the battle plan resembled those that had been so successful at Blenheim and Ramillies. Sustained attacks were to be launched at the enemy flanks so that Villars would be compelled to weaken his centre in order to reinforce them. Massed cavalry would then descend on the French centre to administer the *coup de grâce*. Marlborough did not underestimate the enemy. Reports confirmed that they could deploy almost one hundred and thirty battalions of foot, two hundred and sixty squadrons of horse and a total of eighty guns. Against this mighty army, the Allies could muster an equivalent number of battalions, two hundred and fifty-two squadrons and just over one hundred guns. Paper strength seemed to balance the two forces fairly evenly but some of the French battalions were somewhat smaller than they should have been and, on the Allied side, the battalions and squadrons under the command of General Withers had yet to arrive.

Marlborough could wait no longer for them. The decision to attack on the morning of 11th September had been taken. As always, the captain-general placed great emphasis on combined tactical support, insisting that horse, foot and artillery worked as a unified team that was able to adapt swiftly to individual conditions in different parts of the battlefield. The Allies were split into three sections. Prince Eugene was given overall command of the right flank where General Schulenburg was to lead several battalions and supporting guns into the Bois de Sars. A welcome contingent from Mons reinforced him. To Schulenburg's left, occupying the inner flank, was a substantial force of foot, horse and guns under General Lottum. While some British battalions were occupied on the right flank, many more were kept in reserve. German and Austrian forces therefore dominated.

In the centre, entrusted to General Lord Orkney, the fifteen battalions included eleven British formations, backed by the reserve strength of the Allied horse, numbering almost one hundred and eighty squadrons. When the time was ripe, a massive strike force could thus be unleashed in a cavalry charge to penetrate and overwhelm the French centre. Its success depended on Allied advances on both flanks. They had to pierce the French wings in order to threaten a pincer movement that was in reality a feint. The left flank was under the command of the youthful Prince of Orange, supported by Generals Tilly and Oxenstiern. In the original plan, Marlborough had placed General Withers in a supporting role on the left flank but he was too tardy. When he did finally appear, Withers was switched to the extreme right instead.

Early that morning, Daniel was in the Allied headquarters in Blaregnies when Marlborough explained the last-minute change of plan to a concerned Dutch general.

'General Withers will be of more use on the right flank,' he declared. 'He'll be concealed from the French in the Bois de Sars and, when the opportunity arises, will be able to loop around the furthest extremity of the enemy's left and cause confusion by rolling behind their lines from east to west.'

'That's a clever strategy,' said the Dutchman, 'but you strengthen one flank at the expense of another. The Prince of Orange needs every battalion and squadron that can be spared.'

'I judge the force at his disposal to be sufficient.'

'But we don't know what resistance they'll find in the Bois de la Lanière.'

'Whatever it is,' said Marlborough, 'they'll be able to overcome it.'

'You know best, Your Grace,' conceded the other, 'but I'm bound to have qualms when intelligence reports say that the French right flank is under Marshal Boufflers. I have the greatest respect for the Prince of Orange. He's a man of great courage. Pitted against him, however, is one of the most astute commanders in Europe. After we humbled him at Lille, he'll want his revenge.'

Marlborough was adamant. 'Our left flank will deny it to him.'

'You say that with supreme confidence.'

'I have every right to do so, General,' said Marlborough, stoutly. 'We have the best commanders in the correct positions and our line of battle is well balanced. I wouldn't even entertain the notion of a defeat. Victory is there for the taking.'

Daniel was heartened by the captain-general's tone. Like the Dutchman, he'd been disturbed by the apparent imbalance of forces on the Allied flanks. He'd also been worried by the state of Marlborough's health. The Duke had been dogged by fatigue and prone to migraines. Letters from England had lowered his morale with their tales of political machinations and loss of royal support. Now that the day of the battle had dawned, however, he looked spry and eager. It was the Marlborough of old and everyone around him was inspired by his example. The omens were good.

* * *

'Kept in reserve?' cried Curry, indignantly.

'That's the decision, Leo,' said Welbeck.

'One British regiment is worth two Dutch or German regiments.'

'I know.'

'So why are they in the front line while we twiddle our thumbs here?'

'We'll be called upon in due course.'

'Why didn't you use your influence with Captain Rawson?' demanded Curry. 'You should have got him to persuade His Grace to give us preference.'

'Dan wasn't able to do that.'

'It's an insult, Henry – a bleeding insult.'

Along with the rest of the army, the soldiers of the 24th Foot had been roused early and given a nip of rum or gin to steady them. Battalions were formed and orders given. Sergeant Curry objected to what he saw as an unfair restraint on him and his men. He was desperate to be part of the initial onslaught so that he could impress Rachel Rees with his heroic conduct. Welbeck harboured the same ambition. He wanted to win her admiration by his performance in battle. As he glanced along the ranks of his men, he noticed that one stood out from the others. Private Ben Plummer not only had the smartest uniform, he was sporting a black eye and a swollen lip. Curry nudged his fellow sergeant.

'I caught the bastard at last,' he boasted. 'He'd been leading my men astray in a dice game. He's lucky I didn't black his other eye as well and split his nose open.'

'You should have reported him to me. I'd have dealt with Plummer.'

'It's because you *didn't* deal with him that he came

pestering my lads. At least we know where his money comes from now – gambling.'

'Is he lucky or just crooked?'

'Plummer would cheat his own grandmother.'

Welbeck was upset. He'd seen such an improvement in the man's behaviour that he believed him to have turned over a new leaf. Plummer was obedient, willing and soldierly. Now, it transpired, he hadn't abandoned all of his former waywardness. His punishment had been deserved. Welbeck just wished that he'd been the one to administer it. As it was, someone else had done so and made much of the fact. Curry was soon given a second opportunity to crow over Welbeck. Catching a glimpse of Rachel Rees in the middle distance, he gave a proprietary chuckle.

'There she is,' said Curry, 'the love of my life.'

'How many times have I heard you say that about a woman?' asked Welbeck, cynically. 'They come and go in their dozens.'

'I can't help it if I'm popular.'

'You chase anything in a dress with your prick hanging out.'

'Rachel is different.'

'Yes,' said Welbeck, pointedly, 'she's already spoken for, so you can keep your groping hands to yourself or you'll have two black eyes to match the one you gave Ben Plummer.'

Curry grinned. 'You're just jealous, Henry.'

'I believe in a woman's right to choose and Rachel has chosen.'

'It's no surprise that she chose the better man – me.'

Though it was difficult to pick out two people in the massed ranks, Rachel did so with ease. As she waited to follow the first battalions so that she could scour the battlefield for booty in their wake, she gave them a cheery wave. Curry waved back in acknowledgement but it was Welbeck who had more cause for satisfaction. Rachel was looking directly at him. The signal was unambiguous. She was his.

When he arrived before the others for work that morning, Geel fully expected to be dismissed. He'd been caught in Amalia's bedchamber and had no defence to offer. Dopff had stared at him with a mixture of accusation and disillusion, blaming him for an outrageous act of trespass while realising that Geel's earlier visits upstairs had not been motivated by concern for a sick man's well-being, after all. He'd simply used his colleague's illness as a means of gaining freedom to move around the house. Dopff clearly felt shocked and betrayed. Geel was certain that he'd be reported for his audacity. Even such a mild-mannered employer as Emanuel Janssen would not tolerate such behaviour. Yet when he came into the workshop, Janssen gave Geel his usual friendly greeting. At his master's shoulder, Kees Dopff limited himself to a polite nod, shooting Geel a warning glance that was easy to interpret. Dopff had so far told nobody about the incident the previous day but – if there was the slightest trouble from Geel in the future – the truth would come out. Amalia would be duly horrified and her father would promptly dispatch the errant weaver. With such a threat hanging over him, Geel felt a sense of shame that burnt inside him like a flame.

Aelbert Pienaar joined them and moved swiftly to his loom. The four of them started work. They were disturbed within minutes by the sudden arrival of Beatrix who whispered something to Janssen. Face darkening with consternation, he muttered an apology and rushed off into the house.

'What's the matter?' asked Geel.

'It's Miss Amalia,' she replied. 'She had a terrible nightmare last night and it's haunting her still. She's taken to her bed again.'

'Is she unwell?' said Pienaar.

'No, Aelbert, she's healthier than I am. But her mind is troubled. Miss Amalia is a bag of nerves and nothing I can say seems to calm her down.'

Geel was inquisitive. 'What was this terrible nightmare, Beatrix?'

'She thinks it was a premonition.'

'Go on.'

'When I got to her in the middle of the night, she was shaking all over.'

'Why – what was the dream about?'

Beatrix gave a wan smile. 'Do you really need to ask that, Nick? It was about Captain Rawson, of course. She watched him die a hideous death in battle. Miss Amalia is convinced that he's either been killed or is about to be.'

Geel was even more grateful that his venture into her bedchamber hadn't been reported. Distressed over a nightmare, Amalia would be at her most vulnerable. To learn that someone had been caught trespassing in her room would be an unbearable torment. Fearing that she'd lost Daniel, she'd also find that she was being stalked by someone who worked under the same roof. Geel could imagine the hysteria it might provoke.

He had to help. The only way that he could redeem

himself was to relieve her anguish in some way. News from
the front took days to trickle back to Amsterdam. Until she
knew that Daniel was safe, Amalia would be on tenterhooks.
A wild idea came into Geel's head and he blurted out his
offer.

'There's no need for Miss Amalia to suffer,' he said,
impetuously. 'I'll go to Flanders and find out the truth for
her.'

As the Allied army advanced towards the enemy, they were
half hidden by mists that arose from the sodden fields.
Sunlight slowly pierced the murk and burnt it away to reveal
the beautiful undulating landscape. Allied cannon opened
fire and the battle of Malplaquet had begun. In command
of the centre, Orkney was elated at the sight of his battalions
marching in formation in their differing uniforms. It was a
scene that had colour, nobility and deadly purpose. Before
they could reach the plain on which they could confront
the French, however, they had to go through a dense wood.
Obeying the steady beat of the drums, they surged on into
the trees with no idea that forty battalions of enemy infantry
had been deployed in depth to greet them. It was only when
they were hit by the first volley of musket fire that they
realised they'd walked into an ambush. To get anywhere near
the French, they had to cope with lines of trenches and thick
entanglements of branches sharpened to a point.

In the early exchanges of fire, the Allies were cut down
remorselessly. When they reached the gap in the woods at
the centre of the French position, they discovered that it
was blocked by earthen ramparts strengthened with chained
logs, angled to permit flanking fire and with strategic

gaps through which counter-attacking cavalry could pour. Defending the ramparts, Villars had posted the vast majority of his guns and they were wreaking devastation. All of thirty-seven battalions of foot were firing at the Allies from behind their concealed positions. Orkney had no time to admire the sight of his men on the march now. He'd just led them into a death trap.

The situation was no more encouraging for the Allies on their right flank. General Schulenburg marched his battalions, three lines deep, across the best part of half a mile towards the Bois de Sars. Before they reached the trees, a shot rang out then an invisible enemy discharged a volley. On a command from the general, the Allied infantry stormed forward to tackle the first of the French parapets, meeting with concerted and accurate fire. Musket balls fell in a hailstorm and the Allies were embroiled in a hellish fight. Schulenburg's first line was halted by the searing volleys of French brigades drawn up in four rows and firing by alternating lines at fairly close range. Casualties among the Allied officers were particularly high, with some Austrian units having barely a few survivors to issue orders to their men.

Supporting Schulenburg on the inner right flank, General Lottum's forces had severe problems of their own. They marched across a plain striped with ravines and dappled with ponds and bogs. Skirting the wood in which their compatriots had come to grief, they were met by a fierce bombardment from the various redoubts ahead of them. Additional guns were rushed to the front by the French and Lottum's men started to fall in droves. Changing their angle of attack, they plunged into the wood on their right and fought hand-to-hand among the abattis cleverly prepared by the enemy. It was violent, ferocious, uninhibited warfare with no quarter given. Marlborough's faith in the efficacy of his right flank was beginning to look unfounded. The only battalions and squadrons unopposed were those led by General Withers in a wide arc intended to take them beyond the western end of the French defences.

While the Allied centre and right flank were being repulsed, an even worse fate awaited those of the left flank. The Prince of Orange led his Dutch and Scottish battalions against the defences of the Comte d'Artagnan that fringed the Bois de la Lanière. Advancing bravely in five columns, they were wholly unprepared for what happened next. When they got close enough to the French ramparts, a gun battery suddenly burst into life, firing salvoes of enfilading shot through the Dutch lines with disastrous effect. General Oxenstiern was among the hundreds who were killed in the first lethal explosion of cannon fire. Blown out of alignment, the five columns immediately reformed, closed their ranks and marched on over the bodies of their dead comrades. Urged on by their commander, they gave a display of suicidal courage, making small territorial gains at the expense of enormous casualties. Within half an hour, the best part of five thousand Dutch soldiers had fallen. After incurring more losses in a tempestuous fight, they eventually captured Blairon Farm but it could not be held. Outnumbered and outmanoeuvred, the Dutch attack fell back in good order, leaving the ground carpeted with their dead and dying.

Stirred by their success, the French regiments on the right flank sallied forth and formed up for a bayonet charge.

The retreating Dutch infantry were only saved from further destruction by the intervention of the Prince of Hesse-Cassel. Seeing the predicament they were in, he spurred his squadrons towards the left flank and sent the French scrambling back behind their barricades. Four Hanoverian battalions were also rushed forward from Marlborough's reserve to the south-western corner of the Bois de Thiery and their musket volleys discouraged the French from surging out from behind their defences a second time. All in all, however, it was an unpropitious start for the Allies. In a matter of a couple of hours, their attacks had been repulsed or put under brutal pressure on all fronts. Marlborough's battle plan was not as yet working.

Daniel was all too aware of the initial failures and setbacks. He was employed in the way he'd been used at Ramillies, taking orders from the captain-general to various parts of the battlefield and bringing back reports of how Allied troops were faring. Such information was vital. At Ramillies, Marlborough had been able to watch the whole conflict from a vantage point on raised ground, moving his battalions and squadrons about like pieces on a gigantic chessboard. He had no such luxury here. Much of the action was screened from him by woodland and he could only guess at what was happening among the trees. Daredevil riders like Daniel kept him up to date with the latest developments in every section. The fact that Daniel was fluent in Dutch and German meant that he could converse easily with any of the Allied generals.

After delivering orders to General Lottum on the inner right flank, Daniel raced back to headquarters, dodging the enemy shot that came hurtling out of the air until he was out of its range. When he reached the point where Marlborough and his staff were seated astride their horses, Daniel reined in his own steed and gave his account of the situation he'd found.

'General Lottum sends his regards and reports that his attack has been brought to a standstill. To renew the assault,' Daniel continued, 'he's committed the Duke of Argyll's brigade supported by two battalions sent over by General Lord Orkney.'

'I commend the strategy,' said Marlborough, 'but I have a lurking fear. When they enter the woods to their right, Orkney's men will present a target for the artillery in the redoubts. That will refresh the enemy's ambitions.'

'They appear to be preparing a counter-attack, Your Grace.'

'I observed that through my telescope and I plan to stem it before it even begins. I'll bring up the Prince of Auvergne's cavalry to meet the threat. The sight of thirty squadrons of Dutch horse should be enough to dissuade Villars from risking his infantry in a counter-attack.'

'What orders am I to deliver?' asked Daniel.

'Acquaint General Lottum with my decision and urge him to press on.'

'Yes, Your Grace.'

'Command of the Bois de Sars is crucial. Whatever resistance we meet there must somehow be crushed. Expel the French from their positions among the trees and we've struck a telling blow.'

Daniel wanted to ask about the state of the battle on the Allied left flank but it was not the time to do so. As he galloped off, he could hear uproar in the woods to his left. Enemy cannon thundered away and there was an interminable popping of musket volleys. Evidently, the Dutch battalions were involved in an increasingly desperate struggle. Daniel's task was to return to General Lottum on the inner right flank. To do that, he had to ride through enemy fire, swerving past runaway horses and jumping over the corpses of those who'd fallen in the first assaults. Camp followers were already busy, running at the heels of the Allied battalions in the hope of plunder from French casualties. Rachel Rees was among them, checking to see if any of the fallen from the Allied ranks was still alive and giving survivors a swig of rum to dull their pain or restore their spirits. When she encountered a French casualty, she searched him expertly for anything of value and slipped it into the large bag slung over her shoulder. Rachel made light of the turmoil all around her. She had a job to do.

As he plunged into the Bois de Sars on his right, Daniel first came upon the reinforcements sent from the Allied centre by Orkney. A glance at their uniforms and facings told him that he was looking at a battalion of the Second Guards and one of the Royal Scots. They were being pounded by the guns in the French redoubts but fought back gallantly. To their right, at last starting to make a significant advance, were General Lottum's battalions. Beyond them were Schulenburg's forces, also making some headway. The wood was a deafening echo chamber, trees crashing to the ground as they were struck by stray cannon shot, musket balls whizzing in all directions and sparks flying as bayonets met each other over the parapets. Daniel rode as hard as he could in such hazardous conditions but his mission was doomed. Before he got anywhere near Lottum, Daniel's horse was shot from under him and went down with its body riddled with musket balls and its legs splayed helplessly. Daniel was thrown violently to the ground, rolling over until his head struck the trunk of a tree with an awesome thud and sent blood cascading down his face.

CHAPTER TWENTY

'It would be madness,' argued Janssen. 'There's no point in it, Nick.'

'There's every point,' insisted Geel. 'I hate to see Miss Amalia suffering.'

'It was a bad dream, that's all. My daughter will get over it.'

'I want to go. It will soothe her mind.'

'It's more likely to trouble it,' said Pienaar. 'She's already worried enough about Captain Rawson. If you go haring off to Flanders, Miss Amalia will have your safety to fret over as well.'

'Besides,' Janssen pointed out, 'you're no horseman. How can you expect to ride all that way on your own? It's lunacy. If there *is* bad news about Captain Rawson, it would already be on its way to us. His Grace would surely inform us of the details in his own hand.'

'I *must* go,' said Geel, smarting with frustration. 'Don't you see?'

'Frankly, I don't.'

'And neither do I,' added Pienaar.

They were in the workshop and Geel's offer was being flatly rejected. Dopff was the only person who understood why he'd made it. While he approved of the gesture, however, Dopff saw how unrealistic it was. Geel could never ride alone through hostile countryside. Last reports placed the Allied army near Mons. Even if he survived the journey, it might take Geel weeks to get there and back again. Dopff foresaw another potential problem. If, by chance, Daniel's death was confirmed by Geel, it would hardly bring any solace to Amalia. In trying to alleviate her pain, he'd only be making it more intense.

Yet Geel felt impelled to do something on her behalf in order to fend off the stabbing guilt. The prospect of staying in Amsterdam while Amalia was suffering so much upset him. His relationship with her had altered. Having done everything he could to contrive a meeting with her, he'd now be terrified to cross Amalia's path. After his gross intrusion into her privacy, he felt unworthy of her. His redemption lay in courting danger on the road to Flanders. Geel needed to be seen by Amalia to be making a huge sacrifice for her. His firm belief was that Daniel was still alive. Since he could never claim her for himself, Geel could at least take satisfaction from being instrumental in securing her happiness. By acting as her go-between, he hoped to find Daniel, tell him of Amalia's distress and bear a letter from her beloved back to the Janssen household to reassure her. Geel wanted no thanks for his efforts. What he would be doing was in expiation of his crime. His behaviour had been dishonourable.

'Why don't we all get back to work?' suggested Janssen.

'Yes,' agreed Pienaar. 'Forget this idea of yours, Nick.'

Geel gritted his teeth. 'I can't do that, Aelbert.'

'It's too reckless.'

'Perhaps it's high time I showed a bit of recklessness.'

'Not when you're at your loom,' said Janssen with a smile. 'Reckless weavers are no use to me. It's an occupation that requires concentration and precision.'

'Let's talk it over later,' said Pienaar, 'when you've calmed down a little.'

Geel bridled. 'I'm perfectly calm.'

'Then why are you behaving in this headstrong manner?'

'It's because I want to do something to help.'

'You're taking this far too seriously,' said Janssen. 'My daughter had a nightmare. It happens to all of us occasionally. Amalia will recover from the shock. Meanwhile,' he went on, staring at Geel, 'I think that you should carry on doing the work for which you're paid.'

'I endorse that,' said Pienaar.

'I didn't ask for *your* opinion, Aelbert,' snapped Geel.

'You're a weaver, not a soldier.'

'Unlike you, I happen to *care*.'

The intensity of his declaration brought the discussion to an end. There was an awkward pause. Dopff and Pienaar eventually turned away and resumed their work. Janssen studied Geel with mild alarm. He'd never seen him so animated. Geel was squirming with embarrassment. His plan to help Amalia had been dismissed and he'd lost his temper with Pienaar. He'd also given himself away. Life in the workshop was going to be very uncomfortable from now on.

'Nobody cares as much about Amalia as I do,' said Janssen, firmly. 'I'm her father and understand her best. There's no reason at all for you to interfere in family matters, Nick. I hope that I make myself clear.'

Geel was mortified. He moved to his loom with his mind aflame.

Stunned by the blow to his head, Daniel took time to recover consciousness. When he tried to open his eyes, he was horrified to discover that he could only see out of one of them. The fear that he'd been partially blinded was the stimulus that brought him fully awake. He sat up, put a hand to the sightless eye and realised that it was simply covered in blood from his scalp wound. He'd not suffered any permanent blindness. The throbbing pain in his head helped him to locate the gash. Blood was still oozing from it. Hauling himself to his feet, he staggered slightly and needed a moment to regain his balance. Then he walked across to one of the many puddles and knelt down beside it. After washing his face and cleansing his wound, he went in search of some bandaging. It was donated by an Austrian soldier who'd been shot dead and who lay motionless in the mud. Daniel opened the man's uniform, pulled it off then tore the shirt from his back. He put a strip of it over the top of his head to stop the bleeding, tying it tightly under his chin before putting on his hat again.

Having dealt with his wound, Daniel was at last able to take his bearings. He was on the western edge of the Bois de Sars beside his dead horse. The battle was raging. Cannonballs from French batteries were still claiming victims or crashing into the trees. Musket volleys rattled continuously. Forlorn howls of dying soldiers were punctuated by the despairing neighs of wounded horses as they threshed about on the ground. Drums dictated the movements of battalions. Daniel had a message to deliver but could hardly do that on foot. He needed a mount. Now that he was back on his feet, he was able to defend himself. Armed with his sword and pistol, he was fit for action. All that the fall had done was to give him an aching head and an assortment of bruises. It didn't take long to find a riderless horse. He only had to wait in a clearing for a few minutes before one came cantering towards him. It had belonged to a German officer who'd been shot from his saddle. Daniel spread his arms wide to slow the animal down then grabbed the reins as it reared up on its hind legs. After some soothing pats on its neck, the horse became more amenable and allowed Daniel to put his foot in the stirrup.

The battle for control of the woods seemed even more intense than on his first visit. With additional troops in support, General Lottum's battalions were pushing forward. He was difficult to find at first but Daniel eventually tracked him down. Sweating profusely and barking orders, Lottum was glad to hear that Marlborough had staved off the possibility of a counter-attack in the centre. Undaunted by the scale of their losses, he and Schulenburg would press on until they were masters of the wood. He looked at Daniel's makeshift bandaging.

'That wound needs proper treatment from a surgeon.'

'I've no time for that, General,' said Daniel.

'Brave man!'

'It's just a scratch. Others have real injuries.'

'What news of our left flank?' asked Lottum.

'The last thing I heard was that the Prince of Orange had been driven back. The French defences are stout and Marshal Boufflers is deploying his men well.'

'It's the same here, Captain. The enemy gave us a hiding at first. It's taken us hours to make any real advance. But you can tell His Grace that we are in good heart.'

'Thank you, General.'

'The enemy is finally starting to buckle.'

Yet it didn't sound as if they were anywhere near defeat. The resistance that Daniel could hear was robust and positive. They might be slowly buckling but they would kill or wound scores of Allied soldiers before they cracked. As he rode through the woods on his way back to the captain-general, Daniel was already convinced of one thing. Malplaquet was the bloodiest battle in which he'd ever taken part. There was a sobering footnote to add – the result was still very much in doubt.

Though they'd been held back in reserve, the 24th Foot was not excluded from the fray. Henry Welbeck was glad when the order was given for them to move forward to the beat of the drum. Listening to the colossal struggle that was taking place made him yearn to be involved and it was a feeling shared by the whole regiment. They marched in formation with a collective urgency, muskets loaded, bayonets fixed, eyes locked on the battle ahead. Welbeck knew that his men would acquit themselves well. He'd drilled them hard and instructed them repeatedly in the technique of platoon firing. When some were cut down by enemy fire, the others would close ranks and move on, discharging their muskets in rehearsed sequence. Somewhere ahead of him was Rachel Rees, one of the fearless scavengers who'd scorned danger in their pursuit of rich prizes. In hoping that she came to no harm, Welbeck realised just how much he cared for her. Then an enemy musket ball whistled past his ear and he forgot all about Rachel. It was time to kill French soldiers.

His voice rose above the cacophony, exhorting his men to fire. As their muskets popped, there was an answering volley from the marksmen behind the daunting triangular breastwork and dozens of British soldiers fell to their knees. One of them was Ben Plummer, grasping his neck before going limp and collapsing to the ground. When Welbeck rushed across to him, he saw that the private was beyond help. Plummer had been shot in the throat and the head. Barely able to recognise Welbeck through the haze closing over his eyes, he reached into his pocket, took something out and thrust it into Welbeck's hand. The sergeant was holding four dice in his palm. It was Plummer's last bequest.

When Daniel came galloping up to him, Marlborough was disturbed by the sight of the bandage around his head and urged him to have the wound properly dressed. Dismissing the suggestion, Daniel apologised for the

delay in returning and told him about developments in
the western side of the Bois de Sars. Lottum was about
to take command of it but it had taken thirty thousand
troops to win what was a comparatively small stretch of
woodland and almost a quarter of them had been killed
or wounded. Carnage was also occurring on the left
flank.

'Take this message to the Prince of Orange,' said
Marlborough, handing over written orders. 'He's to hold his
position without moving forward.'

'Yes, Your Grace.'

'He's already led two attacks on the French entrenchments
and his men have been cut to pieces. The Prince must not
expose them again until ordered to do so.'

'I'll see this delivered,' said Daniel.

'Make all haste.'

It was unnecessary encouragement. Digging his heels
into the horse's flanks, Daniel set off at a fierce gallop. He
was not simply determined to hand over the orders as soon
as possible. He knew that a moving target was far more
difficult to hit. To get to the left flank, he had to race across
open ground that was well within range of the enemy. Shot
was falling everywhere and musket balls were still raining.
As he glanced back towards the right, he was pleased to see
that his own regiment had been called up in reserve. With
other British regiments, they were firing at the triangular
redoubt jutting out from the Bois de Sars. If and when
victory was achieved, the 24th would therefore have its share
of glory.

When he finally reached the Bois de la Lanière, it
was as perilous and full of clamour as the rest of the

woodland. Artillery and musket fire seemed to come from every side. Daniel was stunned to learn the full details of Dutch losses. After two failed charges, the casualties were horrendous. Yet the sheer bravery of the survivors was inspiring. They were eager to attack again and hoped that the fresh orders would help them to do so. The Prince of Orange opened the letter and read it with obvious dismay.

'We are to hold our position?' he asked, balefully.

'That's what His Grace has decided.'

'But we have a score to settle with the French.'

'Our information is that they're too well defended,' said Daniel.

The prince was annoyed. 'His Grace should have more confidence in our ability to judge the circumstances,' he said, huffily. 'It's true that we've twice been repulsed but the French have sustained losses as well. And if Marshal Boufflers really thinks that he has the beating of us, why hasn't he come out from behind his barricades and launched an attack?'

It was not Daniel's place to argue with him. He had neither the rank nor the authority to do so. As for the exact situation in the Bois de la Lanière, the Prince had a far more detailed knowledge of what was going on. All that Daniel could do was to deliver the orders. Whether or not they'd be obeyed was a different matter.

Marshal Villars had been perfectly satisfied with the early stages of the battle. In the centre and on both flanks, the French had either driven the attackers back or kept them comfortably at bay. As the reserve forces of foot and horse were brought into the arena of battle by Marlborough, however, the odds tilted slightly in favour of the Allies. When his men were in a dominant position, Villars had sanctioned a bold counter-attack by twelve battalions under General Chemerault. The strategy had been seen and neutralised by Marlborough. The French battalions therefore remained behind the fortifications in the centre. With Morellon mounted on a horse beside him, Villars reviewed the situation in the light of reports coming from each sector.

'The Bois de Sars may soon be lost,' he said darkly. 'They've taken all that we can throw at them, yet they still come on. Our left flank is in severe danger.'

'Yet our centre holds and our right flank prospers. Marshal Boufflers has not so much ruffled Dutch feathers as plucked them out wholesale.'

'His entrenchments are almost impregnable and I admire him for the way he has put the enemy to flight. But I do wonder at his lack of ambition.'

'How so, Your Grace?' asked Morellon, surprised at the criticism.

'He had the opportunity to sally forth and harry them before reinforcements arrived,' said Villars. 'By that means, Boufflers might have secured the right flank completely.'

'It will not be pierced while he holds command.'

'But the chance to counter-attack has been lost.'

'He's done what was asked of him,' said Morellon, reasonably, 'and that was to frustrate the attack. As you so rightly predicted, Marlborough has used his stale tactics once again, concentrating his assault on the flanks in order to draw our men out of the centre. Marshal Boufflers has driven them back heroically.'

'I wish that the same could be said of our left flank,' said Villars, sadly, 'but Marlborough has committed too many troops to the area. Lottum and Schulenburg are shrewd generals and they have Prince Eugene at their heels to bring out the best in them. More worrying,' he admitted, 'is the news of a secondary force of foot and horse, moving in a wide arc to loop around the western edge of our defences.'

Morellon blenched. 'If they get behind our lines, we are in dire trouble.'

'Our first task is to hold our left flank and that can only be done with fresh soldiers. I propose to move the dozen battalions poised for the counter-attack to a position close to the Bois de Sars.'

'But you'd be doing exactly what Marlborough intends you to do.'

'I have no choice,' said Villars, brusquely. 'When Schulenburg fights his way out of the wood, he'll find that I've posted a substantial force to receive him.'

Daniel arrived back at headquarters to find Marlborough in a state of controlled excitement. He'd been summoned by Schulenburg to view the advance made on the right flank. Daniel joined the party as they cantered off together. Entering the Bois de Sars for the third time, he found it even more littered with Allied corpses but the losses had not been in vain. Schulenburg's men had forced their way out of the wood, held off the French reinforcements and somehow managed to get seven large cannon behind enemy lines.

This enabled them to batter the French cavalry stationed on a ridge behind their foot and guns. Hit by a merciless salvo of shot, they were forced to pull back out of range. Schulenburg's artillery could now turn its fury on the French entrenchments, distracting them before Orkney's imminent attack on the enemy centre.

After all the tribulations, it was a rewarding sight for the Allied high command but it was not without danger. They were surveying the scene from just beyond the wood and within range of enemy fire. Daniel had already ducked under some musket balls and his companions also took evasive action from time to time. Prince Eugene was unlucky. As he turned his horse, he was grazed behind the ear by a musket ball that drew blood and left a stinging wound.

'You must be attended by a surgeon at once,' said Marlborough.

'I wouldn't hear of it, Your Grace.'

'It may be more serious than you think.'

'There's a battle to win first,' said the other, determined not to quit the field. 'Besides, I'm only following the example of Captain Rawson. His injury looks worse than mine, yet he still remains in the saddle.'

'And I intend to stay in it this time,' said Daniel with a grin.

'Let's withdraw,' advised Marlborough, as another spattering of musket balls came in their direction. 'We offer too tempting a target.'

They pulled back into the woods now cleared of French positions. As they picked their way through the trees, a rider came hurtling towards them along a twisting track. From his uniform, Daniel identified him as belonging to one of the regiments under the Prince of Orange. The man tugged on the reins and his horse came to a skidding halt.

'The Prince of Orange requests urgent reinforcements, Your Grace,' he said, panting. 'Our latest attack had fatal results and we lack the numbers to offer the French right flank sufficient threat.'

Marlborough stiffened. 'There should have *been* no attack,' he said. 'I sent Captain Rawson with orders to the contrary and I know he delivered them.'

'I did indeed, Your Grace,' confirmed Daniel.

'Then why was another suicidal charge made?'

'I can't answer that, Your Grace,' said the messenger, 'but I know how desperate we are for additional reserves.'

Daniel could see how angry Marlborough was. The thought that his orders had been ignored was a blow to his pride. Daniel sought to provide an explanation that might placate him slightly.

'I cannot believe that your orders were disobeyed,' he said. 'The Prince of Orange was probably confused by the smoke of battle. I've been there, Your Grace, and know how treacherous the fog of war can be. It's likely that he lost his way and found himself by accident at the French barricades.'

It was not impossible. Blinded by the smoke and deafened by the din, it was easy to go astray in unfamiliar territory. But Marlborough did not accept that that was the excuse here. The Prince of Orange was hot-headed. A more likely explanation was that he'd been piqued at the orders to hold back. Marlborough concealed his feelings from the messenger but Daniel could read his face. Excellent news on the right flank had been counterbalanced by bad news on the left. There was a long way to go yet.

Henry Welbeck was still involved in the battle to take the triangular redoubt constructed with such skill and solidarity. Impervious to all but the heaviest artillery, it was equipped with punitive guns and a small garrison of well-drilled soldiers whose accurate fire from behind the logs had killed or crippled wave after wave of the Allied attack. The Duke of Argyll's brigade was under the command of Sir Richard Temple and comprised the 8th, 18th and 21st alongside the 24th Foot. Weight of numbers eventually told. Aware that they'd lost control of the Bois de Sars to their immediate left, the men in the redoubt felt their confidence being sapped. Some talked of retreat while others insisted on fighting to the last man. In the event, the decision was taken for them by a sudden charge from the Allied foot. Bayonets glinting in the sun, they ran towards the tiny stronghold.

Defying sporadic enemy fire, Leo Curry lumbered along with Welbeck.

'This is why I joined the army,' yelled Curry. 'I love to kill.'

'Save your breath, Leo. You'll need it.'

'I'm a fitter man than you, Henry, and a lustier one as well. Rachel prefers me because I can give her what a woman craves.'

'No woman craves a man with as big a mouth as yours,' snarled Welbeck.

Curry sniggered. 'It's not my big mouth she wants,' he

said, one hand to his crutch. 'Farewell, Henry.'

With an unexpected burst of speed, Curry sprinted forward and was in the front line that scrambled onto some of the thick logs surrounding the redoubt on three sides. When he climbed to the top, he held his musket aloft in a gesture of triumph then fell backwards as he was shot between the eyes. He landed on his back at Welbeck's feet. Feeling an odd sense of loss, Welbeck stepped over the dead body of his friend and clambered over the logs. In the desperate hand-to-hand encounter, he was able to shoot one man and kill two more with his bayonet. All around him French soldiers were being summarily slaughtered. When the redoubt was finally taken, he climbed back over the logs and looked down at Curry. Welbeck afforded him a sigh of regret. The other sergeant had been a foul-mouthed braggart but his bravery was beyond question. Dying in action, Curry had unwittingly done Welbeck a favour. There would only be one suitor for Rachel Rees now.

By mid-afternoon, the outcome had been decided. On the Allied right flank, Prince Eugene's forces renewed their attack and forced the French left to retire in disarray towards Quiévrain. On the French right, the Dutch attack had been rebuffed but not before it had crossed three lines of entrenchments. Seeing that reinforcements were massing for another attack, d'Artagnan ordered a retreat in the direction of Bavay and Maubeuge. With his compatriots turning tail, all that Boufflers could do was to follow suit, ordering his squadrons to fall back beyond the Hogneau river. As their flanks gave way, the French centre also collapsed, unable to hold out on its own against a rampant enemy with the smell of victory in its nostrils. To compound his miseries, Marshal Villars was shot in the knee and carried from the field in agony.

The battle of Malplaquet was over but it was essentially a pyrrhic victory. The Allies had suffered some twenty-five thousand killed or wounded, over a third of them coming from the Dutch battalions under the Prince of Orange. The French sustained only thirteen thousand casualties and the fact that they left barely five hundred able-bodied men to be taken as prisoners showed how disciplined their retreat had been. Marlborough summed up the bloodbath in an evocative phrase. When he later wrote to Godolphin, he described it as 'a very murdering battle'.

Welbeck knew that she was there somewhere. Various figures were moving across the battlefield and searching the corpses of French soldiers. Rachel should have been among them but he could see her nowhere. Welbeck plodded on, scanning the landscape as he did so. His hopes were faint. If she was not burrowing for loot among the enemy, there was only one explanation. She was dead. Her luck had finally run out. Rachel always took more chances than the others, scuttling along the lines of the dead and sniffing out the spoils of war. Welbeck admired her for her tenacity but wished she'd been more circumspect. Her ample frame offered too big a target. It had been a day of terrible losses for him. He'd lost Curry, Plummer and dozens of other men from his regiment. Now, it seemed, he'd lost Rachel as well and it was her death that brought a tear to his eye. It was ironic. For so many years, he'd spurned the company of women and denigrated the whole sex. Now that he'd changed his mind and found someone who'd actually aroused feelings of love in him, she'd been snatched away. It was cruel. When he and Rachel had gradually become close, there was the promise of a happiness he'd never dared to believe existed. That dizzying promise had perished on a battlefield.

With the vestigial flickers of hope slowly fading, Welbeck trudged on over broken bodies and past dead horses. A pall of silence hung over the scene now. It was like a vision of hell and it appalled him. He was still forcing his weary legs on when he heard a cry from some distance to his right.

'Sergeant!' yelled a man. 'Come over here!'

'What is it?' called Welbeck in response.

'I've found a woman – I think she's still alive.'

Welbeck summoned up a burst of energy and broke into a trot, zigzagging past the corpses as he did so and praying that he'd found Rachel at last. There were not many women scouring the battlefield and few who'd ventured so close to the enemy. The man who'd alerted him was a scavenger himself, bending over the body and trying to revive the woman with a nip of rum. As it dribbled over her lips, Welbeck arrived. He was tense and breathless. Curled up on the ground as if she was sleeping was Rachel Rees. Welbeck was overjoyed. There was an ugly bruise on her temple and blood trickled from a flesh wound in her shoulder but she seemed otherwise unhurt. Grabbing the flask from the man, Welbeck put his other arm under her shoulder and raised her up. When he offered her the rum, her lips parted to accept it and it gurgled down her throat. After a few seconds, her eyelids blinked. Still dazed, she managed a weary smile.

'Hello, Henry,' she said, 'I knew that you'd come for me.'

* * *

Pacing his horse, Daniel rode north-east through open countryside. He was acting as a courier, bearing details of the battle to Grand Pensionary Heinsius in The Hague. The report would not make comfortable reading for a Dutchman, recording, as it did, the monumental scale of Dutch losses. Having delivered the report, Daniel had expected to be recalled to take part in the continuing siege of Mons but Marlborough had shown compassion. He'd remembered Daniel's vow to propose to Amalia after the battle and he ensured that there was minimum delay. After his visit to the nation's capital, therefore, Daniel had been given permission to ride on to Amsterdam.

'On an occasion like this,' Marlborough had said with a gracious smile, 'a lady should not be kept waiting.'

Daniel cherished those words and was overwhelmed with a feeling of gratitude towards the captain-general. It was couched in sympathy for him. Daniel knew that there'd be repercussions. The Allies had achieved a victory that was shot through with elements of defeat. The losses were staggering and blame for them would be heaped onto Marlborough. The harshest recriminations would take place back in England, where his enemies would seize the excuse to attack, malign and undermine him. Whatever else it might have done, the Battle of Malplaquet had not made peace on Allied terms inevitable. If anything, French morale had been lifted by the way their army had performed in the field. The war would go on.

It was a salutary reminder to Daniel that there would be other occasions when he'd gather intelligence behind enemy lines, bear arms once more against the French and have his horse shot from under him as at Malplaquet. Danger was ever present. For that reason, he had to make Amalia his wife so that they could enjoy some happiness together before it was too late. Settling into the long ride, he started to rehearse his proposal of marriage and found it extremely difficult to choose the right words. Amalia wouldn't wish to be rushed. How long should he wait before he spoke to her father? Should he make his proposal in the house, the garden or at a more romantic venue? When could he expect the wedding to take place? Who would be invited? Where would they set up house? What about children?

Rocked by a startling new thought, Daniel slowed his horse to a trot.

Was it conceivable that Amalia might actually reject his proposal?

Ever since the first rumours of a battle filtered through to Amsterdam, Amalia spent most of the daylight hours standing in the front window in the hope that Daniel would eventually arrive to quell her fears. As she stood there that morning, she looked anxiously up and down the street but there was no sign of him. Instead of seeing someone coming to the house, however, she spotted someone leaving. Nicholaes Geel had left the workshop for the last time and walked to the front of the building so that he could take a valedictory look at it. When he caught sight of Amalia, he backed away with a look of profound apology on his face. Amalia was surprised. It was still early. Geel had not long arrived for work. Why was he leaving so suddenly and what was the cause of his embarrassment? When Beatrix came into the room, Amalia put the first question to her.

'Nick doesn't work here anymore,' said Beatrix, bluntly.

Amalia was taken aback. 'Has Father dismissed him?'

'No, he went of his own accord.'

'For what possible reason?'

'I think that he felt that he couldn't stay here, Miss Amalia. He's been acting strangely for well over a week now. In the past, he always liked to stop and talk but he turned away whenever I met him.'

'That doesn't sound like Nick Geel.'

'He seemed to be on edge.'

'Does he have another position to go to?' asked Amalia.

'Not as a weaver,' said Beatrix. 'He's going to enlist in the army.'

Amalia was astonished. The idea that Geel would give up a well-paid job in order to put himself in jeopardy in the Dutch army was incomprehensible. What had possessed him to take such precipitate action? Why had he felt unable to stay? She watched him disappear down the street with a sadness laced with relief, upset to lose him yet bolstered by the thought that a problem had just walked out of her life. Almost immediately, Amalia saw something that wiped away all memory of Geel. She blinked to make sure that it was not a mirage. Bolt upright in the saddle, Daniel was riding up the street towards the house in his uniform. It was a miracle. He was alive and well, after all. Her involuntary cry of joy was matched by Beatrix's uninhibited yell of delight.

The two of them rushed to open the front door but Daniel only saw Amalia. When he dismounted, Beatrix stepped forward to take charge of the horse, allowing him to move forward and hug Amalia.

'I thought you were dead,' she gasped, pulling back to appraise him.

He grinned. 'That's one theory I can easily disprove.'

'I had the most awful nightmare about you.'

'Put it out of your mind.'

She peered at him. 'You look tired, Daniel.'

'I've ridden a very long way,' he said, glancing over his shoulder at the busy street. 'Is there somewhere a little more private than your threshold?'

'Of course – follow me.'

'That's exactly why I came.'

Closing the door behind him, he went into the parlour after her and removed his hat, glad that his scalp wound had now healed and grateful that Amalia had not seen him when his head was swathed in a bloodstained bandage. She was excited, nervous and full of questions about the terrible battle that everyone was talking about. Amalia was also more beautiful than he'd remembered. Her cheeks were glowing, her eyes were dancing and her hair was burnished by the light flooding through the window. Daniel had rehearsed his proposal a hundred times and resolved to wait patiently until the right moment arose for him to make it. Seeing her before him at last, however, and sharing her exhilaration, he instantly abandoned his plan, sweeping her into his arms and holding her in a passionate embrace.

'I love you, Amalia,' he said. 'Will you marry me?'

'Oh, Daniel!' she exclaimed.

'Well – what's your answer?'

'My answer is yes – yes, *please*.'

He pulled her close and they kissed away the long, fraught absence apart. No more words were necessary. The bond was sealed. Out of the horrors of war, they had plucked true happiness.

In the wake of the battle, the siege of Mons continued and the town was eventually forced to surrender on 20th October 1709.